The
Hound
of the
Baskervilles
AND
The Valley
of Fear

The Hound of the Baskervilles

AND

The Valley of Fear

SIR ARTHUR CONAN DOYLE

ARCTURUS

ARCTURUS

This edition published in 2022 by Arcturus Publishing Limited
26/27 Bickels Yard, 151–153 Bermondsey Street,
London SE1 3HA

ISBN: 978-1-78428-821-1
AD005725UK

Printed in China

Contents

Introduction 7

The Hound of the Baskervilles 11

The Valley of Fear 215

Introduction

Arthur Conan Doyle was born on 22 May 1859 in Edinburgh. He studied medicine at Edinburgh University and encountered a professor who became his model for the character of Sherlock Holmes; Joseph Bell taught his students the importance of close observation and displayed amazing powers of deduction on very little evidence.

After two voyages as a ship's doctor, Conan Doyle set up a medical practice in Southsea, Hampshire. The practice struggled for five or six years and so did Conan Doyle's finances. As his writing career progressed, Conan Doyle increasingly turned towards short stories. Many of these first appeared in *The Strand* magazine, one of the most popular British literary magazines of the age that saw contributions from writers as varied as H. G. Wells, Agatha Christie and P. G. Wodehouse. The first two series of stories featuring Sherlock Holmes published in *The Strand* between 1891 and 1893 and subsequently collected into two volumes entitled *The Adventures of Sherlock Holmes* and *The Memoirs of Sherlock Holmes*.

As fascinating as Holmes was, almost as important a character was his faithful companion Dr John Watson. Watson is both participant and narrator in these stories and his relationship with the solitary detective humanises the brilliant detective. Watson is an intelligent gentleman, with a keen eye and a sharp intelligence, yet even he is often bemused by Holmes' deductions. The interplay between these two characters, as much as the joy of uncovering the mystery, is what makes Conan Doyle's stories so entertaining.

The Hound of the Baskervilles is the most popular of the Sherlock Holmes stories. It appeared eight years after Conan Doyle had apparently killed off his detective in the 'Final Problem'. Conan Doyle had grown tired of the character and turned his hand to a range of popular fiction, but eventually the lure of writing another Holmes story became too great to resist. The inspiration for the story came while holidaying in Norfolk with his friend Bertram Fletcher Robinson. Robinson told him of the legend of a giant hound terrorising Dartmoor, but initially it was not intended as a Sherlock Holmes novel at all. Only when he struggled to create an enticing enough central character did Conan Doyle decide on Holmes as the protagonist. *The Strand* paid what was at the time an extraordinary rate for the book - £100 per 1,000 words.

The Valley of Fear is the final Sherlock Holmes novel. Like most of Conan Doyle's Holmes stories, it began life in *The Strand* magazine, being published between September 1914 and May 1915. The plot of the novel is loosely based on the activities of the Pinkerton agent James McParland and the Irish secret society known as the Molly Maguires. Sherlock's nemesis Professor James Moriarty makes an appearance as Holmes and Watson investigate an unusual murder.

The unwavering popularity of the Sherlock Holmes stories lured Conan Doyle back to writing. Eventually, he returned to medicine in a field hospital during the Boer War (1899–1902) and received a knighthood in 1902. He died in Crowborough, Sussex on 7 July 1930.

The Sherlock Holmes stories had a lasting influence. Several authors, including Anthony Burgess, Stephen King, and P. G. Wodehouse have all written Sherlock Holmes stories of their own. Conan Doyle's stories have been adapted several times for film, television, and even in video games. His classic detective stories set the stage for the golden age of detective fiction that began in the 1930s. While detective novels had begun to emerge in the 19th century, it took the success of Sherlock Holmes to encourage publishers to take a chance on new authors in the genre. Renowned authors such as Agatha Christie owed a great debt to Conan Doyle. In Sherlock Holmes, he created the world's most popular detective.

The
Hound
of the
Baskervilles

CONTENTS

Chapter 1 – Mr Sherlock Holmes 15

Chapter 2 – The Curse of the Baskervilles 23

Chapter 3 – The Problem.. 36

Chapter 4 – Sir Henry Baskerville 47

Chapter 5 – Three Broken Threads 61

Chapter 6 – Baskerville Hall 73

Chapter 7 – The Stapletons of Merripit House 85

Chapter 8 – First Report of Dr Watson 101

Chapter 9 – The Light upon the Moor

   [Second Report of Dr Watson] 110

Chapter 10 – Extract from the Diary of Dr Watson 131

Chapter 11 – The Man on the Tor 143

Chapter 12 – Death on the Moor 158

Chapter 13 – Fixing the Nets 173

Chapter 14 – The Hound of the Baskervilles 187

Chapter 15 – A Retrospection 200

CHAPTER 1

MR SHERLOCK HOLMES

Mr Sherlock Holmes, who was usually very late in the mornings, save upon those not infrequent occasions when he was up all night, was seated at the breakfast table. I stood upon the hearth-rug and picked up the stick which our visitor had left behind him the night before. It was a fine, thick piece of wood, bulbous-headed, of the sort which is known as a 'Penang lawyer.' Just under the head was a broad silver band nearly an inch across. 'To James Mortimer, M.R.C.S., from his friends of the C.C.H.,' was engraved upon it, with the date '1884.' It was just such a stick as the old-fashioned family practitioner used to carry – dignified, solid, and reassuring.

'Well, Watson, what do you make of it?'

Holmes was sitting with his back to me, and I had given him no sign of my occupation.

'How did you know what I was doing? I believe you have eyes in the back of your head.'

'I have, at least, a well-polished, silver-plated coffee-pot in front of me,' said he. 'But, tell me, Watson, what do you make of our visitor's stick? Since we have been so unfortunate as to miss him and have no notion of his errand, this accidental souvenir becomes of importance. Let me hear you reconstruct the man by an examination of it.'

'I think,' said I, following as far as I could the methods of my companion, 'that Dr Mortimer is a successful, elderly medical man, well-esteemed since those who know him give him this mark of their appreciation.'

'Good!' said Holmes. 'Excellent!'

'I think also that the probability is in favour of his being a country practitioner who does a great deal of his visiting on foot.'

'Why so?'

'Because this stick, though originally a very handsome one has been so knocked about that I can hardly imagine a town practitioner carrying it. The thick-iron ferrule is worn down, so it is evident that he has done a great amount of walking with it.'

'Perfectly sound!' said Holmes.

'And then again, there is the "friends of the C.C.H." I should guess that to be the Something Hunt, the local hunt to whose members he has possibly given some surgical assistance, and which has made him a small presentation in return.'

'Really, Watson, you excel yourself,' said Holmes, pushing back his chair and lighting a cigarette. 'I am bound to say that in all the accounts which you have been so good as to give of my own small achievements you have habitually underrated your own abilities. It may be that you are not yourself luminous, but you are a conductor of light. Some people without possessing genius have a remarkable power of stimulating it. I confess, my dear fellow, that I am very much in your debt.'

He had never said as much before, and I must admit that his words gave me keen pleasure, for I had often been piqued by his indifference to my admiration and to the attempts which I had made to give publicity to his methods. I was proud, too, to think that I had so far mastered his system as to apply it in a way which earned his approval. He now took the stick from my hands and examined it for a few minutes with his naked eyes. Then with an expression of interest he laid down his cigarette, and carrying the cane to the window, he looked over it again with a convex lens.

'Interesting, though elementary,' said he as he returned to his favourite corner of the settee. 'There are certainly one or two indications upon the stick. It gives us the basis for several deductions.'

'Has anything escaped me?' I asked with some self-importance. 'I trust that there is nothing of consequence which I have overlooked?'

'I am afraid, my dear Watson, that most of your conclusions were erroneous. When I said that you stimulated me I meant, to be frank, that in noting your fallacies I was occasionally guided towards the truth. Not that you are entirely wrong in this instance. The man is certainly a country practitioner. And he walks a good deal.'

'Then I was right.'

'To that extent.'

'But that was all.'

'No, no, my dear Watson, not all – by no means all. I would suggest, for example, that a presentation to a doctor is more likely to come from a hospital than from a hunt, and that when the initials "C.C." are placed before that hospital the words "Charing Cross" very naturally suggest themselves.'

'You may be right.'

'The probability lies in that direction. And if we take this as a working hypothesis we have a fresh basis from which to start our construction of this unknown visitor.'

'Well, then, supposing that "C.C.H." does stand for "Charing Cross Hospital," what further inferences may we draw?'

'Do none suggest themselves? You know my methods. Apply them!'

'I can only think of the obvious conclusion that the man has practised in town before going to the country.'

'I think that we might venture a little farther than this. Look at it in this light. On what occasion would it be most probable that such a presentation would be made? When would his friends unite to give him a pledge of their good will? Obviously at the moment when Dr Mortimer withdrew from the service of the hospital in order to start a practice for himself. We know there has been a presentation. We believe there has been a change from a town hospital to a country practice. Is it, then, stretching our inference too far to say that the presentation was on the occasion of the change?'

'It certainly seems probable.'

'Now, you will observe that he could not have been on the staff of the hospital, since only a man well-established in a London practice could hold such a position, and such a one would not drift into the country. What was he, then? If he was in the hospital and yet not on the staff he could only have been a house-surgeon or a house-physician – little more than a senior student. And he left five years ago – the date is on the stick. So your grave, middle-aged family practitioner vanishes into thin air, my dear Watson, and there emerges a young fellow under thirty, amiable, unambitious, absent-minded, and the possessor of a favourite dog, which I should describe roughly as being larger than a terrier and smaller than a mastiff.'

I laughed incredulously as Sherlock Holmes leaned back in his settee and blew little wavering rings of smoke up to the ceiling.

'As to the latter part, I have no means of checking you,' said I, 'but at least it is not difficult to find out a few particulars about the man's age and professional career.' From my small medical shelf I took down the Medical Directory and turned up the name. There were several Mortimers, but only one who could be our visitor. I read his record aloud.

"Mortimer, James, M.R.C.S., 1882, Grimpen, Dartmoor, Devon. House-surgeon, from 1882 to 1884, at Charing Cross Hospital. Winner of the Jackson prize for Comparative Pathology, with essay entitled "Is Disease a Reversion?" Corresponding member of the Swedish Pathological Society. Author of "Some Freaks of Atavism" (Lancet 1882). "Do We Progress?" (Journal of Psychology, March, 1883). Medical Officer for the parishes of Grimpen, Thorsley, and High Barrow."

'No mention of that local hunt, Watson,' said Holmes with a mischievous smile, 'but a country doctor, as you very astutely observed. I think that I am fairly justified in my inferences. As to the adjectives, I said, if I remember right, amiable, unambitious, and absent-minded. It is my experience that it is only an amiable man in this world who receives testimonials, only an unambitious one who abandons a London career for the country, and only an absent-minded one who leaves his stick and not his visiting-card after waiting an hour in your room.'

'And the dog?'

'Has been in the habit of carrying this stick behind his master. Being a heavy stick the dog has held it tightly by the middle, and the marks of his teeth are very plainly visible. The dog's jaw, as shown in the space between these marks, is too broad in my opinion for a terrier and not broad enough for a mastiff. It may have been – yes, by Jove, it is a curly-haired spaniel.'

He had risen and paced the room as he spoke. Now he halted in the recess of the window. There was such a ring of conviction in his voice that I glanced up in surprise.

'My dear fellow, how can you possibly be so sure of that?'

'For the very simple reason that I see the dog himself on our very door-step, and there is the ring of its owner. Don't move, I beg you, Watson. He is a professional brother of yours, and your presence may be of assistance to me. Now is the dramatic moment of fate, Watson, when you hear a step upon the stair which is walking into your life, and you know not whether for good or ill. What does Dr James Mortimer, the man of science, ask of Sherlock Holmes, the specialist in crime? Come in!'

The appearance of our visitor was a surprise to me, since I had expected a typical country practitioner. He was a very tall, thin man, with a long nose like a beak, which jutted out between two keen, grey eyes, set closely together and sparkling brightly from behind a pair of gold-rimmed glasses. He was clad in a professional but rather slovenly fashion, for his frock-coat was dingy and his trousers frayed. Though young, his long back was already bowed, and he walked with a forward thrust of his head and a general air of peering benevolence. As he entered his eyes fell upon the stick in Holmes's hand, and he ran towards it with an exclamation of joy. 'I am so very glad,' said he. 'I was not sure whether I had left it here or in the Shipping Office. I would not lose that stick for the world.'

'A presentation, I see,' said Holmes.

'Yes, sir.'

'From Charing Cross Hospital?'

'From one or two friends there on the occasion of my marriage.'

'Dear, dear, that's bad!' said Holmes, shaking his head.

Dr Mortimer blinked through his glasses in mild astonishment. 'Why was it bad?'

'Only that you have disarranged our little deductions. Your marriage, you say?'

'Yes, sir. I married, and so left the hospital, and with it all hopes of a consulting practice. It was necessary to make a home of my own.'

'Come, come, we are not so far wrong, after all,' said Holmes. 'And now, Dr James Mortimer—'

'Mister, sir, Mister – a humble M.R.C.S.'

'And a man of precise mind, evidently.'

'A dabbler in science, Mr Holmes, a picker up of shells on the shores of the great unknown ocean. I presume that it is Mr Sherlock Holmes whom I am addressing and not—'

'No, this is my friend Dr Watson.'

'Glad to meet you, sir. I have heard your name mentioned in connection with that of your friend. You interest me very much, Mr Holmes. I had hardly expected so dolichocephalic a skull or such well-marked supra-orbital development. Would you have any objection to my running my finger along your parietal fissure? A cast of your skull, sir, until the original is available, would be an ornament to any anthropological museum. It is not my intention to be fulsome, but I confess that I covet your skull.'

Sherlock Holmes waved our strange visitor into a chair. 'You are an enthusiast in your line of thought, I perceive, sir, as I am in mine,' said he. 'I observe from your forefinger that you make your own cigarettes. Have no hesitation in lighting one.'

The man drew out paper and tobacco and twirled the one up in the other with surprising dexterity. He had long, quivering fingers as agile and restless as the antennae of an insect.

Holmes was silent, but his little darting glances showed me the interest which he took in our curious companion. 'I presume, sir,' said he at last, 'that it was not merely for the purpose of examining my skull that you have done me the honour to call here last night and again today?'

'No, sir, no; though I am happy to have had the opportunity of doing that as well. I came to you, Mr Holmes, because I recognised that I am myself an unpractical man and because I am suddenly confronted with a most serious and extraordinary problem. Recognising, as I do, that you are the second highest expert in Europe—'

'Indeed, sir! May I inquire who has the honour to be the first?' asked Holmes with some asperity.

'To the man of precisely scientific mind the work of Monsieur Bertillon must always appeal strongly.'

'Then had you not better consult him?'

'I said, sir, to the precisely scientific mind. But as a practical man of affairs it is acknowledged that you stand alone. I trust, sir, that I have not inadvertently—'

'Just a little,' said Holmes. 'I think, Dr Mortimer, you would do wisely if without more ado you would kindly tell me plainly what the exact nature of the problem is in which you demand my assistance.'

CHAPTER 2

THE CURSE OF THE BASKERVILLES

'I have in my pocket a manuscript,' said Dr James Mortimer.

'I observed it as you entered the room,' said Holmes.

'It is an old manuscript.'

'Early eighteenth century, unless it is a forgery.'

'How can you say that, sir?'

'You have presented an inch or two of it to my examination all the time that you have been talking. It would be a poor expert who could not give the date of a document within a decade or so. You may possibly have read my little monograph upon the subject. I put that at 1730.'

'The exact date is 1742.' Dr Mortimer drew it from his breast-pocket. 'This family paper was committed to my care by Sir Charles Baskerville, whose sudden and tragic death some three months ago created so much excitement in Devonshire. I may say that I was his personal friend as well as his medical attendant. He was a strong-minded man, sir, shrewd, practical, and as unimaginative as I am myself. Yet he took this document very seriously, and his mind was prepared for just such an end as did eventually overtake him.'

Holmes stretched out his hand for the manuscript and flattened it upon his knee.

'You will observe, Watson, the alternative use of the long s and the short. It is one of several indications which enabled me to fix the date.'

I looked over his shoulder at the yellow paper and the faded script. At the head was written: "Baskerville Hall," and below in large, scrawling figures: "1742."

'It appears to be a statement of some sort.'

'Yes, it is a statement of a certain legend which runs in the Baskerville family.'

'But I understand that it is something more modern and practical upon which you wish to consult me?'

'Most modern. A most practical, pressing matter, which must be decided within twenty-four hours. But the manuscript is short and is intimately connected with the affair. With your permission I will read it to you.'

Holmes leaned back in his chair, placed his finger-tips together, and closed his eyes, with an air of resignation. Dr Mortimer turned the manuscript to the light and read in a high, cracking voice the following curious, old-world narrative:

"Of the origin of the Hound of the Baskervilles there have been many statements, yet as I come in a direct line from Hugo Baskerville, and as I had the story from my father, who also had it from his, I have set it down with all belief that it occurred even as is here set forth. And I would have you believe, my sons, that the same Justice which punishes sin may also most graciously forgive it, and that no ban is so heavy but that by prayer and repentance it may be removed. Learn then from this story not to fear the fruits of the past, but rather to be circumspect in the future, that those foul passions whereby our family has suffered so grievously may not again be loosed to our undoing.

"Know then that in the time of the Great Rebellion (the history of which by the learned Lord Clarendon I most earnestly commend to your attention) this Manor of Baskerville was held by Hugo of that name, nor can it be gainsaid that he was a most wild, profane, and godless man. This, in truth, his neighbours might have pardoned, seeing that saints have never flourished in those parts, but there was in him a certain wanton and cruel humour which made his name a by-word through the West. It chanced that this Hugo came to love (if, indeed, so dark a passion may be known under so bright a name) the daughter of a yeoman who held lands near the Baskerville estate. But the young maiden, being discreet and of good repute would ever avoid him, for she feared his evil name. So it came to pass that one Michaelmas this Hugo, with five or six of his idle and wicked companions, stole down upon the farm and carried off the maiden, her father and brothers being from home, as he well knew. When they had brought her to the Hall the maiden was placed in an upper chamber, while Hugo and his friends sat down to a long carouse, as was their nightly custom. Now, the poor lass upstairs was like to have her wits turned at the singing and shouting and terrible oaths which came up to her from below, for they say that the words used by Hugo Baskerville, when he was in wine, were such as might blast the man who said them. At last in the stress of her fear she did that which might have daunted the bravest or most active man, for by the aid of the growth of ivy which covered (and still covers) the south wall she came down from under the eaves, and so homeward across the moor, there being three leagues betwixt the Hall and her father's farm.

"It chanced that some little time later Hugo left his guests to carry food and drink – with other worse things, perchance – to his captive, and so found the cage empty and the bird escaped. Then, as it would seem, he became as one that hath a devil, for, rushing down the stairs into the dining-hall, he sprang upon the great table, flagons and trenchers flying before him, and he cried aloud before all the company that he would that very night render his body and soul to the Powers of Evil if he might but overtake the wench. And while the revellers stood aghast at the fury of the man, one more wicked or, it may be, more drunken than the rest, cried out that they should put the hounds upon her. Whereat Hugo ran from the house, crying to his grooms that they should saddle his mare and unkennel the pack, and giving the hounds a kerchief of the maid's, he swung them to the line, and so off full cry in the moonlight over the moor.

"Now, for some space the revellers stood agape, unable to understand all that had been done in such haste. But anon their bemused wits awoke to the nature of the deed which was like to be done upon the moorlands. Everything was now in an uproar, some calling for their pistols, some for their horses, and some for another flask of wine. But at length some sense came back to their crazed minds, and the whole of them, thirteen in number, took horse and started in pursuit. The moon shone clear above them, and they rode swiftly abreast, taking that course which the maid must needs have taken if she were to reach her own home.

"They had gone a mile or two when they passed one of the night shepherds upon the moorlands, and they cried to him to know if he had seen the hunt. And the man, as the story goes, was so crazed with fear that he could scarce speak, but at last he said that he had indeed seen the unhappy maiden, with the hounds upon her track. 'But I have seen more than that,' said he, 'for Hugo Baskerville passed me upon his black mare, and there ran mute behind him such a hound of hell as God forbid should ever be at my heels.'

"So the drunken squires cursed the shepherd and rode onward. But soon their skins turned cold, for there came a galloping across the moor, and the black mare, dabbled with white froth, went past with trailing bridle and empty saddle. Then the revellers rode close together, for a great fear was on them, but they still followed over the moor, though each, had he been alone, would have been right glad to have turned his horse's head. Riding slowly in this fashion they came at last upon the hounds. These, though known for their valour and their breed, were whimpering in a cluster at the head of a deep dip or goyal, as we call it, upon the moor, some slinking away and some, with starting hackles and staring eyes, gazing down the narrow valley before them.

"The company had come to a halt, more sober men, as you may guess, than when they started. The most of them would by no means advance, but three of them, the boldest, or it may be the most drunken, rode forward down the goyal. Now, it opened into a broad space in which stood two of those great stones, still to be seen there, which were set by certain forgotten peoples in the days of old. The moon was shining bright upon the clearing, and there in the centre lay the unhappy maid where she had fallen, dead of fear and of fatigue. But it was not the sight of her body, nor yet was it that of the body of Hugo Baskerville lying near her, which raised the hair upon the heads of these three dare-devil roysterers, but it was that, standing over Hugo, and plucking at his throat, there stood a foul thing, a great, black beast, shaped like a hound, yet larger than any hound that ever mortal eye has rested upon. And even as they looked the thing tore the throat out of Hugo Baskerville, on which, as it turned its blazing eyes and dripping jaws upon them, the three shrieked with fear and rode for dear life, still screaming, across the moor. One, it is said, died that very night of what he had seen, and the other twain were but broken men for the rest of their days.

"Such is the tale, my sons, of the coming of the hound which is said to have plagued the family so sorely ever since. If I have set it down it is because that which is clearly known hath less terror than that which is but hinted at and guessed. Nor can it be denied that many of the family have been unhappy in their deaths, which have been sudden, bloody, and mysterious. Yet may we shelter ourselves in the infinite goodness of Providence, which would not forever punish the innocent beyond that third or fourth generation which is threatened in Holy Writ. To that Providence, my sons, I hereby commend you, and I counsel you by way of caution to forbear from crossing the moor in those dark hours when the powers of evil are exalted.

"[This from Hugo Baskerville to his sons Rodger and John, with instructions that they say nothing thereof to their sister Elizabeth.]"

When Dr Mortimer had finished reading this singular narrative he pushed his spectacles up on his forehead and stared across at Mr Sherlock Holmes. The latter yawned and tossed the end of his cigarette into the fire.

'Well?' said he.

'Do you not find it interesting?'

'To a collector of fairy tales.'

Dr Mortimer drew a folded newspaper out of his pocket.

'Now, Mr Holmes, we will give you something a little more recent. This is the *Devon County Chronicle* of May 14th of this year. It is a short account of the facts elicited at the death of Sir Charles Baskerville which occurred a few days before that date.'

My friend leaned a little forward and his expression became intent. Our visitor readjusted his glasses and began:

"The recent sudden death of Sir Charles Baskerville, whose name has been mentioned as the probable Liberal candidate for Mid-Devon at the next election, has cast a gloom over the county. Though Sir Charles had resided at Baskerville Hall for a comparatively short period his amiability of character and extreme generosity had won the affection and respect of all who had been brought into contact with him. In these days of *nouveaux riches* it is refreshing to find a case where the scion of an old county family which has fallen upon evil days is able to make his own fortune and to bring it back with him to restore the fallen grandeur of his line. Sir Charles, as is well known, made large sums of money in South African speculation. More wise than those who go on until the wheel turns against them, he realized his gains and returned to England with them. It is only two years since he took up his residence at Baskerville Hall, and it is common talk how large were those schemes of reconstruction and improvement which have been interrupted by his death. Being himself childless, it was his openly expressed desire that the whole countryside should, within his own lifetime, profit by his good fortune, and many will have personal reasons for bewailing his untimely end. His generous donations to local and county charities have been frequently chronicled in these columns.

"The circumstances connected with the death of Sir Charles cannot be said to have been entirely cleared up by the inquest, but at least enough has been done to dispose of those rumours to which local superstition has given rise. There is no reason whatever to suspect foul play, or to imagine that death could be from any but natural causes. Sir Charles was a widower, and a man who may be said to have been in some ways of an eccentric habit of mind. In spite of his considerable wealth he was simple in his personal tastes, and his indoor servants at Baskerville Hall consisted of a married couple named Barrymore, the husband acting as butler and the wife as housekeeper. Their evidence, corroborated by that of several friends, tends to show that Sir Charles's health has for some time been impaired, and points especially to some affection of the heart, manifesting itself in changes of colour, breathlessness, and acute attacks of nervous depression. Dr James Mortimer, the friend and medical attendant of the deceased, has given evidence to the same effect.

"The facts of the case are simple. Sir Charles Baskerville was in the habit every night before going to bed of walking down the famous yew alley of Baskerville Hall. The evidence of the Barrymores shows that this had been his custom. On the fourth of May Sir Charles had declared his intention of starting next day for London, and had ordered Barrymore to prepare his luggage. That night he went out as usual for his nocturnal walk, in the course of which he was in the habit of smoking a cigar. He never returned. At twelve o'clock Barrymore, finding the hall door still open, became alarmed, and, lighting a lantern, went in search of his master. The day had been wet, and Sir Charles's footmarks were easily traced down the alley. Halfway down this walk there is a gate which leads out on to the moor. There were indications that Sir Charles had stood for some little time here. He then proceeded down the alley, and it was at the far end of it that his body was discovered. One fact which has not been explained is the statement of Barrymore that his master's footprints altered their character from the time that he passed the moor-gate, and that he appeared from thence onward to have been walking upon his toes. One Murphy, a gipsy horse-dealer, was on the moor at no great distance at the time, but he appears by his own confession to have been the worse for drink. He declares that he heard cries but is unable to state from what direction they came. No signs of violence were to be discovered upon Sir Charles's person, and though the doctor's evidence pointed to an almost incredible facial distortion – so great that Dr Mortimer refused at first to believe that it was indeed his friend and patient who lay before him – it was explained that that is a symptom which is not unusual in cases of dyspnoea and death from cardiac exhaustion. This explanation was borne out by the post-mortem examination, which showed long-standing organic disease, and the coroner's jury returned a verdict in accordance with the medical evidence. It is well that this is so, for it is obviously of the utmost importance that Sir Charles's heir should settle at the Hall and continue the good work which has been so sadly inter-rupted. Had the prosaic finding of the coroner not finally put an end to the romantic stories which have been whispered in connection with the affair, it might have been difficult to find a tenant for Baskerville Hall. It is understood that the next of kin is Mr Henry Baskerville, if he be still alive, the son of Sir Charles Baskerville's younger brother. The young man when last heard of was in America, and inquiries are being instituted with a view to informing him of his good fortune."

Dr Mortimer refolded his paper and replaced it in his pocket. 'Those are the public facts, Mr Holmes, in connec-tion with the death of Sir Charles Baskerville.'

'I must thank you,' said Sherlock Holmes, 'for calling my attention to a case which certainly presents some features of interest. I had observed some newspaper comment at the time, but I was exceedingly preoccupied by that little affair of the Vatican cameos, and in my anxiety to oblige the Pope I lost touch with several interesting English cases. This article, you say, contains all the public facts?'

'It does.'

'Then let me have the private ones.' He leaned back, put his finger-tips together, and assumed his most impassive and judicial expression.

'In doing so,' said Dr Mortimer, who had begun to show signs of some strong emotion, 'I am telling that which I have not confided to anyone. My motive for withholding it from the coroner's inquiry is that a man of science shrinks from placing himself in the public position of seeming to indorse a popular superstition. I had the further motive that Baskerville Hall, as the paper says, would certainly remain untenanted if anything were done to increase its already rather grim reputation. For both these reasons I thought that I was justified in telling rather less than I knew, since no practical good could result from it, but with you there is no reason why I should not be perfectly frank.

'The moor is very sparsely inhabited, and those who live near each other are thrown very much together. For this reason I saw a good deal of Sir Charles Baskerville. With the exception of Mr Frankland, of Lafter Hall, and Mr Stapleton, the naturalist, there are no other men of education within many miles. Sir Charles was a retiring man, but the chance of his illness brought us together, and a community of interests in science kept us so. He had brought back much scientific information from South Africa, and many a charming evening we have spent together discussing the comparative anatomy of the Bushman and the Hottentot.

'Within the last few months it became increasingly plain to me that Sir Charles's nervous system was strained to the breaking point. He had taken this legend which I have read you exceedingly to heart – so much so that, although he would walk in his own grounds, nothing would induce him to go out upon the moor at night. Incredible as it may appear to you, Mr Holmes, he was honestly convinced that a dreadful fate overhung his family, and certainly the records which he was able to give of his ancestors were not encouraging. The idea of some ghastly presence constantly haunted him, and on more than one occasion he has asked me whether I had on my medical journeys at night ever seen any strange creature or heard the baying of a hound. The latter question he put to me several times, and always with a voice which vibrated with excitement.

'I can well remember driving up to his house in the evening some three weeks before the fatal event. He chanced to be at his hall door. I had descended from my gig and was standing in front of him, when I saw his eyes fix themselves over my shoulder and stare past me with an expression of the most dreadful horror. I whisked round and had just time to catch a glimpse of something which I took to be a large black calf passing at the head of the drive. So excited and alarmed was he that I was compelled to go down to the spot where the animal had been and look around for it. It was gone, however, and the incident appeared to make the worst impression upon his mind. I stayed with him all the evening, and it was on that occasion, to explain the emotion which he had shown, that he confided to my keeping that narrative which I read to you when first I came. I mention this small episode because it assumes some importance in view of the tragedy which followed, but I was convinced at the time that the matter was entirely trivial and that his excitement had no justification.

'It was at my advice that Sir Charles was about to go to London. His heart was, I knew, affected, and the constant anxiety in which he lived, however chimerical the cause of it might be, was evidently having a serious effect upon his health. I thought that a few months among the distractions of town would send him back a new man. Mr Stapleton, a mutual friend who was much concerned at his state of health, was of the same opinion. At the last instant came this terrible catastrophe.

'On the night of Sir Charles's death Barrymore the butler, who made the discovery, sent Perkins the groom on horseback to me, and as I was sitting up late I was able to reach Baskerville Hall within an hour of the event. I checked and corroborated all the facts which were mentioned at the inquest. I followed the footsteps down the yew alley, I saw the spot at the moor-gate where he seemed to have waited, I remarked the change in the shape of the prints after that point, I noted that there were no other footsteps save those of Barrymore on the soft gravel, and finally I carefully examined the body, which had not been touched until my arrival. Sir Charles lay on his face, his arms out, his fingers dug into the ground, and his features convulsed with some strong emotion to such an extent that I could hardly have sworn to his identity. There was certainly no physical injury of any kind. But one false statement was made by Barrymore at the inquest. He said that there were no traces upon the ground round the body. He did not observe any. But I did – some little distance off, but fresh and clear.'

'Footprints?'

'Footprints.'

'A man's or a woman's?'

Dr Mortimer looked strangely at us for an instant, and his voice sank almost to a whisper as he answered.

'Mr Holmes, they were the footprints of a gigantic hound!'

CHAPTER 3

THE PROBLEM

I confess at these words a shudder passed through me. There was a thrill in the doctor's voice which showed that he was himself deeply moved by that which he told us. Holmes leaned forward in his excitement and his eyes had the hard, dry glitter which shot from them when he was keenly interested.

'You saw this?'

'As clearly as I see you.'

'And you said nothing?'

'What was the use?'

'How was it that no one else saw it?'

'The marks were some twenty yards from the body and no one gave them a thought. I don't suppose I should have done so had I not known this legend.'

'There are many sheep-dogs on the moor?'

'No doubt, but this was no sheep-dog.'

'You say it was large?'

'Enormous.'

'But it had not approached the body?'

'No.'

'What sort of night was it?'

'Damp and raw.'

'But not actually raining?'

'No.'

'What is the alley like?'

'There are two lines of old yew hedge, twelve feet high and impenetrable. The walk in the centre is about eight feet across.'

'Is there anything between the hedges and the walk?'

'Yes, there is a strip of grass about six feet broad on either side.'

'I understand that the yew hedge is penetrated at one point by a gate?'

'Yes, the wicket-gate which leads on to the moor.'

'Is there any other opening?'

'None.'

'So that to reach the yew alley one either has to come down it from the house or else to enter it by the moor-gate?'

'There is an exit through a summer-house at the far end.'

'Had Sir Charles reached this?'

'No; he lay about fifty yards from it.'

'Now, tell me, Dr Mortimer – and this is important – the marks which you saw were on the path and not on the grass?'

'No marks could show on the grass.'

'Were they on the same side of the path as the moor-gate?'

'Yes; they were on the edge of the path on the same side as the moor-gate.'

'You interest me exceedingly. Another point. Was the wicket-gate closed?'

'Closed and padlocked.'

'How high was it?'

'About four feet high.'

'Then anyone could have got over it?'

'Yes.'

'And what marks did you see by the wicket-gate?'

'None in particular.'

'Good heaven! Did no one examine?'

'Yes, I examined, myself.'

'And found nothing?'

'It was all very confused. Sir Charles had evidently stood there for five or ten minutes.'

'How do you know that?'

'Because the ash had twice dropped from his cigar.'

'Excellent! This is a colleague, Watson, after our own heart. But the marks?'

'He had left his own marks all over that small patch of gravel. I could discern no others.'

Sherlock Holmes struck his hand against his knee with an impatient gesture.

'If I had only been there!' he cried. 'It is evidently a case of extraordinary interest, and one which presented immense opportunities to the scientific expert. That gravel page upon which I might have read so much has been long ere this smudged by the rain and defaced by the clogs of curious peasants. Oh, Dr Mortimer, Dr Mortimer, to think that you should not have called me in! You have indeed much to answer for.'

'I could not call you in, Mr Holmes, without disclosing these facts to the world, and I have already given my reasons for not wishing to do so. Besides, besides—'

'Why do you hesitate?'

'There is a realm in which the most acute and most experienced of detectives is helpless.'

'You mean that the thing is supernatural?'

'I did not positively say so.'

'No, but you evidently think it.'

'Since the tragedy, Mr Holmes, there have come to my ears several incidents which are hard to reconcile with the settled order of Nature.'

'For example?'

'I find that before the terrible event occurred several people had seen a creature upon the moor which corresponds with this Baskerville demon, and which could not possibly be any animal known to science. They all agreed that it was a huge creature, luminous, ghastly, and spectral. I have cross-examined these men, one of them a hard-headed countryman, one a farrier, and one a moorland farmer, who all tell the same story of this dreadful apparition, exactly corresponding to the hell-hound of the legend. I assure you that there is a reign of terror in the district, and that it is a hardy man who will cross the moor at night.'

'And you, a trained man of science, believe it to be supernatural?'

'I do not know what to believe.'

Holmes shrugged his shoulders. 'I have hitherto confined my investigations to this world,' said he. 'In a modest way I have combated evil, but to take on the Father of Evil himself would, perhaps, be too ambitious a task. Yet you must admit that the footmark is material.'

'The original hound was material enough to tug a man's throat out, and yet he was diabolical as well.'

'I see that you have quite gone over to the supernaturalists. But now, Dr Mortimer, tell me this. If you hold these views, why have you come to consult me at all? You tell me in the same breath that it is useless to investigate Sir Charles's death, and that you desire me to do it.'

'I did not say that I desired you to do it.'

'Then, how can I assist you?'

'By advising me as to what I should do with Sir Henry Baskerville, who arrives at Waterloo Station' – Dr

Mortimer looked at his watch – 'in exactly one hour and a quarter.'

'He being the heir?'

'Yes. On the death of Sir Charles we inquired for this young gentleman and found that he had been farming in Canada. From the accounts which have reached us he is an excellent fellow in every way. I speak now not as a medical man but as a trustee and executor of Sir Charles's will.'

'There is no other claimant, I presume?'

'None. The only other kinsman whom we have been able to trace was Rodger Baskerville, the youngest of three brothers of whom poor Sir Charles was the elder. The second brother, who died young, is the father of this lad Henry. The third, Rodger, was the black sheep of the family. He came of the old masterful Baskerville strain and was the very image, they tell me, of the family picture of old Hugo. He made England too hot to hold him, fled to Central America, and died there in 1876 of yellow fever. Henry is the last of the Baskervilles. In one hour and five minutes I meet him at Waterloo Station. I have had a wire that he arrived at Southampton this morning. Now, Mr Holmes, what would you advise me to do with him?'

'Why should he not go to the home of his fathers?'

'It seems natural, does it not? And yet, consider that every Baskerville who goes there meets with an evil fate. I feel sure that if Sir Charles could have spoken with me before his death he would have warned me against bringing this, the last of the old race, and the heir to great wealth, to that deadly place. And yet it cannot be denied that the prosperity of the whole poor, bleak countryside depends upon his presence. All the good work which has been done by Sir Charles will crash to the ground if there is no tenant of the Hall. I fear lest I should be swayed too much by my own obvious interest in the matter, and that is why I bring the case before you and ask for your advice.'

Holmes considered for a little time.

'Put into plain words, the matter is this,' said he. 'In your opinion there is a diabolical agency which makes Dartmoor an unsafe abode for a Baskerville – that is your opinion?'

'At least I might go the length of saying that there is some evidence that this may be so.'

'Exactly. But surely, if your supernatural theory be correct, it could work the young man evil in London as easily as in Devonshire. A devil with merely local powers like a parish vestry would be too inconceivable a thing.'

'You put the matter more flippantly, Mr Holmes, than you would probably do if you were brought into personal contact with these things. Your advice, then, as I understand it, is that the young man will be as safe in Devonshire as in London. He comes in fifty minutes. What would you recommend?'

'I recommend, sir, that you take a cab, call off your spaniel who is scratching at my front door, and proceed to Waterloo to meet Sir Henry Baskerville.'

'And then?'

'And then you will say nothing to him at all until I have made up my mind about the matter.'

'How long will it take you to make up your mind?'

'Twenty-four hours. At ten o'clock tomorrow, Dr Mortimer, I will be much obliged to you if you will call upon me here, and it will be of help to me in my plans for the future if you will bring Sir Henry Baskerville with you.'

'I will do so, Mr Holmes.' He scribbled the appointment on his shirt-cuff and hurried off in his strange, peering, absent-minded fashion. Holmes stopped him at the head of the stair.

'Only one more question, Dr Mortimer. You say that before Sir Charles Baskerville's death several people saw this apparition upon the moor?'

'Three people did.'

'Did any see it after?'

'I have not heard of any.'

'Thank you. Good-morning.'

Holmes returned to his seat with that quiet look of inward satisfaction which meant that he had a congenial task before him.

'Going out, Watson?'

'Unless I can help you.'

'No, my dear fellow, it is at the hour of action that I turn to you for aid. But this is splendid, really unique from some points of view. When you pass Bradley's, would you ask him to send up a pound of the strongest shag tobacco? Thank you. It would be as well if you could make it convenient not to return before evening. Then I should be very glad to compare impressions as to this most interesting problem which has been submitted to us this morning.'

I knew that seclusion and solitude were very necessary for my friend in those hours of intense mental concentration during which he weighed every particle of evidence, constructed alternative theories, balanced one against the other, and made up his mind as to which points were essential and which immaterial. I therefore spent the day at my club and did not return to Baker Street until evening. It was nearly nine o'clock when I found myself in the sitting-room once more.

My first impression as I opened the door was that a fire had broken out, for the room was so filled with smoke that the light of the lamp upon the table was blurred by it. As I entered, however, my fears were set at rest, for it was the acrid fumes of strong coarse tobacco which took me by the throat and set me coughing. Through the haze I had a vague vision of Holmes in his dressing-gown coiled up in an armchair with his black clay pipe between his lips. Several rolls of paper lay around him.

'Caught cold, Watson?' said he.

'No, it's this poisonous atmosphere.'

'I suppose it is pretty thick, now that you mention it.'

'Thick! It is intolerable.'

'Open the window, then! You have been at your club all day, I perceive.'

'My dear Holmes!'

'Am I right?'

'Certainly, but how?'

He laughed at my bewildered expression. 'There is a delightful freshness about you, Watson, which makes it a pleasure to exercise any small powers which I possess at your expense. A gentleman goes forth on a showery and miry day. He returns immaculate in the evening with the gloss still on his hat and his boots. He has been a fixture therefore all day. He is not a man with intimate friends. Where, then, could he have been? Is it not obvious?'

'Well, it is rather obvious.'

'The world is full of obvious things which nobody by any chance ever observes. Where do you think that I have been?'

'A fixture also.'

'On the contrary, I have been to Devonshire.'

'In spirit?'

'Exactly. My body has remained in this armchair and has, I regret to observe, consumed in my absence two large pots of coffee and an incredible amount of tobacco. After you left I sent down to Stamford's for the Ordnance map of this portion of the moor, and my spirit has hovered over it all day. I flatter myself that I could find my way about.'

'A large-scale map, I presume?'

'Very large.'

He unrolled one section and held it over his knee. 'Here you have the particular district which concerns us. That is Baskerville Hall in the middle.'

'With a wood round it?'

'Exactly. I fancy the yew alley, though not marked under that name, must stretch along this line, with the moor, as you perceive, upon the right of it. This small clump of buildings here is the hamlet of Grimpen, where our friend Dr Mortimer has his headquarters. Within a radius of five miles there are, as you see, only a very few scattered dwellings. Here is Lafter Hall, which was mentioned in the narrative. There is a house indicated here which may be the residence of the naturalist – Stapleton, if I remember right, was his name. Here are two moorland farmhouses, High Tor and Foulmire. Then fourteen miles away the great convict prison of Princetown. Between and around these scattered points extends the desolate, lifeless moor. This, then, is the stage upon which tragedy has been played, and upon which we may help to play it again.'

'It must be a wild place.'

'Yes, the setting is a worthy one. If the devil did desire to have a hand in the affairs of men—'

'Then you are yourself inclining to the supernatural explanation.'

'The devil's agents may be of flesh and blood, may they not? There are two questions waiting for us at the outset. The one is whether any crime has been committed at all; the second is, what is the crime and how was it committed? Of course, if Dr Mortimer's surmise should be correct, and we are dealing with forces outside the ordinary laws of Nature, there is an end of our investigation. But we are bound to exhaust all other hypotheses before falling back upon this one. I think we'll shut that window again, if you don't mind. It is a singular thing, but I find that a concentrated atmosphere helps a concentration of thought. I have not pushed it to the length of getting into a box to think, but that is the logical outcome of my convictions. Have you turned the case over in your mind?'

'Yes, I have thought a good deal of it in the course of the day.'

'What do you make of it?'

'It is very bewildering.'

'It has certainly a character of its own. There are points of distinction about it. That change in the footprints, for example. What do you make of that?'

'Mortimer said that the man had walked on tiptoe down that portion of the alley.'

'He only repeated what some fool had said at the inquest. Why should a man walk on tiptoe down the alley?'

'What then?'

'He was running, Watson – running desperately, running for his life, running until he burst his heart – and fell dead upon his face.'

'Running from what?'

'There lies our problem. There are indications that the man was crazed with fear before ever he began to run.'

'How can you say that?'

'I am presuming that the cause of his fears came to him across the moor. If that were so, and it seems most probable, only a man who had lost his wits would have run from the house instead of towards it. If the gipsy's evidence may be taken as true, he ran with cries for help in the direction where help was least likely to be. Then, again, whom was he waiting for that night, and why was he waiting for him in the yew alley rather than in his own house?'

'You think that he was waiting for someone?'

'The man was elderly and infirm. We can understand his taking an evening stroll, but the ground was damp and the night inclement. Is it natural that he should stand for five or ten minutes, as Dr Mortimer, with more practical sense than I should have given him credit for, deduced from the cigar ash?'

'But he went out every evening.'

'I think it unlikely that he waited at the moor-gate every evening. On the contrary, the evidence is that he avoided the moor. That night he waited there. It was the night before he made his departure for London. The thing takes shape, Watson. It becomes coherent. Might I ask you to hand me my violin, and we will postpone all further thought upon this business until we have had the advantage of meeting Dr Mortimer and Sir Henry Baskerville in the morning.'

CHAPTER 4

SIR HENRY BASKERVILLE

Our breakfast table was cleared early, and Holmes waited in his dressing-gown for the promised interview. Our clients were punctual to their appointment, for the clock had just struck ten when Dr Mortimer was shown up, followed by the young baronet. The latter was a small, alert, dark-eyed man about thirty years of age, very sturdily built, with thick black eyebrows and a strong, pugnacious face. He wore a ruddy-tinted tweed suit and had the weather-beaten appearance of one who has spent most of his time in the open air, and yet there was something in his steady eye and the quiet assurance of his bearing which indicated the gentleman.

'This is Sir Henry Baskerville,' said Dr Mortimer.

'Why, yes,' said he, 'and the strange thing is, Mr Sherlock Holmes, that if my friend here had not proposed coming round to you this morning I should have come on my own account. I understand that you think out little puzzles, and I've had one this morning which wants more thinking out than I am able to give it.'

'Pray take a seat, Sir Henry. Do I understand you to say that you have yourself had some remarkable experience since you arrived in London?'

'Nothing of much importance, Mr Holmes. Only a joke, as like as not. It was this letter, if you can call it a letter, which reached me this morning.'

He laid an envelope upon the table, and we all bent over it. It was of common quality, greyish in colour. The address, "Sir Henry Baskerville, Northumberland Hotel," was printed in rough characters; the post-mark "Charing Cross", and the date of posting the preceding evening.

'Who knew that you were going to the Northumberland Hotel?' asked Holmes, glancing keenly across at our visitor.

'No one could have known. We only decided after I met Dr Mortimer.'

'But Dr Mortimer was no doubt already stopping there?'

'No, I had been staying with a friend,' said the doctor.

'There was no possible indication that we intended to go to this hotel.'

'Hum! Someone seems to be very deeply interested in your movements.' Out of the envelope he took a half-sheet of foolscap paper folded into four. This he opened and spread flat upon the table. Across the middle of it a single sentence had been formed by the expedient of pasting printed words upon it. It ran:

"As you value your life or your reason keep away from the moor."

The word "moor" only was printed in ink.

'Now,' said Sir Henry Baskerville, 'perhaps you will tell me, Mr Holmes, what in thunder is the meaning of that, and who it is that takes so much interest in my affairs?'

'What do you make of it, Dr Mortimer? You must allow that there is nothing supernatural about this, at any rate?'

'No, sir, but it might very well come from someone who was convinced that the business is supernatural.'

'What business?' asked Sir Henry sharply. 'It seems to me that all you gentlemen know a great deal more than I do about my own affairs.'

'You shall share our knowledge before you leave this room, Sir Henry. I promise you that,' said Sherlock Holmes. 'We will confine ourselves for the present with your permission to this very interesting document, which must have been put together and posted yesterday evening. Have you yesterday's *Times*, Watson?'

'It is here in the corner.'

'Might I trouble you for it – the inside page, please, with the leading articles?' He glanced swiftly over it, running his eyes up and down the columns. 'Capital article this on free trade. Permit me to give you an extract from it.

"You may be cajoled into imagining that your own special trade or your own industry will be encouraged by a protective tariff, but it stands to reason that such legislation must in the long run keep away wealth from the country, diminish the value of our imports, and lower the general conditions of life in this island."

'What do you think of that, Watson?' cried Holmes in high glee, rubbing his hands together with satisfaction. 'Don't you think that is an admirable sentiment?'

Dr Mortimer looked at Holmes with an air of professional interest, and Sir Henry Baskerville turned a pair of puzzled dark eyes upon me.

'I don't know much about the tariff and things of that kind,' said he, 'but it seems to me we've got a bit off the trail so far as that note is concerned.'

'On the contrary, I think we are particularly hot upon the trail, Sir Henry. Watson here knows more about my methods than you do, but I fear that even he has not quite grasped the significance of this sentence.'

'No, I confess that I see no connection.'

'And yet, my dear Watson, there is so very close a connection that the one is extracted out of the other. "You," "your," "your," "life," "reason," "value," "keep away," "from the." Don't you see now whence these words have been taken?'

'By thunder, you're right! Well, if that isn't smart!' cried Sir Henry.

'If any possible doubt remained it is settled by the fact that "keep away" and "from the" are cut out in one piece.'

'Well, now – so it is!'

'Really, Mr Holmes, this exceeds anything which I could have imagined,' said Dr Mortimer, gazing at my friend in amazement. 'I could understand anyone saying that the words were from a newspaper; but that you should name which, and add that it came from the leading article, is really one of the most remarkable things which I have ever known. How did you do it?'

'I presume, Doctor, that you could tell the skull of a negro from that of an Esquimau?'

'Most certainly.'

'But how?'

'Because that is my special hobby. The differences are obvious. The supra-orbital crest, the facial angle, the maxillary curve, the—'

'But this is my special hobby, and the differences are equally obvious. There is as much difference to my eyes between the leaded bourgeois type of a *Times* article and the slovenly print of an evening half-penny paper as there could be between your negro and your Esquimau. The detection of types is one of the most elementary branches of knowledge to the special expert in crime, though I confess that once when I was very young I confused the *Leeds Mercury* with the *Western Morning News*. But a Times leader is entirely distinctive, and these words could have been taken from nothing else. As it was done yesterday the strong probability was that we should find the words in yesterday's issue.'

'So far as I can follow you, then, Mr Holmes,' said Sir Henry Baskerville, 'someone cut out this message with a scissors—'

'Nail-scissors,' said Holmes. 'You can see that it was a very short-bladed scissors, since the cutter had to take two snips over "keep away."'

'That is so. Someone, then, cut out the message with a pair of short-bladed scissors, pasted it with paste –'

'Gum,' said Holmes.

'With gum on to the paper. But I want to know why the word "moor" should have been written?'

'Because he could not find it in print. The other words were all simple and might be found in any issue, but "moor" would be less common.'

'Why, of course, that would explain it. Have you read anything else in this message, Mr Holmes?'

'There are one or two indications, and yet the utmost pains have been taken to remove all clues. The address, you observe is printed in rough characters. But the Times is a paper which is seldom found in any hands but those of the highly educated. We may take it, therefore, that the letter was composed by an educated man who wished to pose as an uneducated one, and his effort to conceal his own writing suggests that that writing might be known, or come to be known, by you. Again, you will observe that the words are not gummed on in an accurate line, but that some are much higher than others. "Life," for example is quite out of its proper place. That may point to carelessness or it may point to agitation and hurry upon the part of the cutter. On the whole I incline to the latter view, since the matter was evidently important, and it is unlikely that the composer of such a letter would be careless. If he were in a hurry it opens up the interesting question why he should be in a hurry, since any letter posted up to early morning would reach Sir Henry before he would leave his hotel. Did the composer fear an interruption – and from whom?'

'We are coming now rather into the region of guesswork,' said Dr Mortimer.

'Say, rather, into the region where we balance probabilities and choose the most likely. It is the scientific use of the imagination, but we have always some material basis on which to start our speculation. Now, you would call it a guess, no doubt, but I am almost certain that this address has been written in a hotel.'

'How in the world can you say that?'

'If you examine it carefully you will see that both the pen and the ink have given the writer trouble. The pen has spluttered twice in a single word and has run dry three times in a short address, showing that there was very little ink in the bottle. Now, a private pen or ink-bottle is seldom allowed to be in such a state, and the combination of the two must be quite rare. But you know the hotel ink and the hotel pen, where it is rare to get anything else. Yes, I have very little hesitation in saying that could we examine the waste-paper baskets of the hotels around

Charing Cross until we found the remains of the mutilated *Times* leader we could lay our hands straight upon the person who sent this singular message. Halloa! Halloa! What's this?'

He was carefully examining the foolscap, upon which the words were pasted, holding it only an inch or two from his eyes.

'Well?'

'Nothing,' said he, throwing it down. 'It is a blank half-sheet of paper, without even a water-mark upon it. I think we have drawn as much as we can from this curious letter; and now, Sir Henry, has anything else of interest happened to you since you have been in London?'

'Why, no, Mr Holmes. I think not.'

'You have not observed anyone follow or watch you?'

'I seem to have walked right into the thick of a dime novel,' said our visitor. 'Why in thunder should anyone follow or watch me?'

'We are coming to that. You have nothing else to report to us before we go into this matter?'

'Well, it depends upon what you think worth reporting.'

'I think anything out of the ordinary routine of life well worth reporting.'

Sir Henry smiled. 'I don't know much of British life yet, for I have spent nearly all my time in the States and in Canada. But I hope that to lose one of your boots is not part of the ordinary routine of life over here.'

'You have lost one of your boots?'

'My dear sir,' cried Dr Mortimer, 'it is only mislaid. You will find it when you return to the hotel. What is the use of troubling Mr Holmes with trifles of this kind?'

'Well, he asked me for anything outside the ordinary routine.'

'Exactly,' said Holmes, 'however foolish the incident may seem. You have lost one of your boots, you say?'

'Well, mislaid it, anyhow. I put them both outside my door last night, and there was only one in the morning. I could get no sense out of the chap who cleans them. The worst of it is that I only bought the pair last night in the Strand, and I have never had them on.'

'If you have never worn them, why did you put them out to be cleaned?'

'They were tan boots and had never been varnished. That was why I put them out.'

'Then I understand that on your arrival in London yesterday you went out at once and bought a pair of boots?'

'I did a good deal of shopping. Dr Mortimer here went round with me. You see, if I am to be squire down there I must dress the part, and it may be that I have got a little careless in my ways out West. Among other things I bought these brown boots – gave six dollars for them – and had one stolen before ever I had them on my feet.'

'It seems a singularly useless thing to steal,' said Sherlock Holmes. 'I confess that I share Dr Mortimer's belief that it will not be long before the missing boot is found.'

'And, now, gentlemen,' said the baronet with decision, 'it seems to me that I have spoken quite enough about the little that I know. It is time that you kept your promise and gave me a full account of what we are all driving at.'

'Your request is a very reasonable one,' Holmes answered. 'Dr Mortimer, I think you could not do better than to tell your story as you told it to us.'

Thus encouraged, our scientific friend drew his papers from his pocket and presented the whole case as he had done upon the morning before. Sir Henry Baskerville listened with the deepest attention and with an occasional exclamation of surprise.

'Well, I seem to have come into an inheritance with a vengeance,' said he when the long narrative was finished. 'Of course, I've heard of the hound ever since I was in the nursery. It's the pet story of the family, though I never thought of taking it seriously before. But as to my uncle's death – well, it all seems boiling up in my head, and I can't get it clear yet. You don't seem quite to have made up your mind whether it's a case for a policeman or a clergyman.'

'Precisely.'

'And now there's this affair of the letter to me at the hotel. I suppose that fits into its place.'

'It seems to show that someone knows more than we do about what goes on upon the moor,' said Dr Mortimer.

'And also,' said Holmes, 'that someone is not ill-disposed towards you, since they warn you of danger.'

'Or it may be that they wish, for their own purposes, to scare me away.'

'Well, of course, that is possible also. I am very much indebted to you, Dr Mortimer, for introducing me to a problem which presents several interesting alternatives. But the practical point which we now have to decide, Sir Henry, is whether it is or is not advisable for you to go to Baskerville Hall.'

'Why should I not go?'

'There seems to be danger.'

'Do you mean danger from this family fiend or do you mean danger from human beings?'

'Well, that is what we have to find out.'

'Whichever it is, my answer is fixed. There is no devil in

hell, Mr Holmes, and there is no man upon earth who can prevent me from going to the home of my own people, and you may take that to be my final answer.' His dark brows knitted and his face flushed to a dusky red as he spoke. It was evident that the fiery temper of the Baskervilles was not extinct in this their last representative. 'Meanwhile,' said he, 'I have hardly had time to think over all that you have told me. It's a big thing for a man to have to understand and to decide at one sitting. I should like to have a quiet hour by myself to make up my mind. Now, look here, Mr Holmes, it's half-past eleven now and I am going back right away to my hotel. Suppose you and your friend, Dr Watson, come round and lunch with us at two. I'll be able to tell you more clearly then how this thing strikes me.'

'Is that convenient to you, Watson?'

'Perfectly.'

'Then you may expect us. Shall I have a cab called?'

'I'd prefer to walk, for this affair has flurried me rather.'

'I'll join you in a walk, with pleasure,' said his companion.

'Then we meet again at two o'clock. Au revoir, and good-morning!'

We heard the steps of our visitors descend the stair and the bang of the front door. In an instant Holmes had changed from the languid dreamer to the man of action.

'Your hat and boots, Watson, quick! Not a moment to lose!' He rushed into his room in his dressing-gown and was back again in a few seconds in a frock-coat. We hurried together down the stairs and into the street. Dr Mortimer and Baskerville were still visible about two hundred yards ahead of us in the direction of Oxford Street.

'Shall I run on and stop them?'

'Not for the world, my dear Watson. I am perfectly satisfied with your company if you will tolerate mine. Our friends are wise, for it is certainly a very fine morning for a walk.'

He quickened his pace until we had decreased the distance which divided us by about half. Then, still keeping a hundred yards behind, we followed into Oxford Street and so down Regent Street. Once our friends stopped and stared into a shop window, upon which Holmes did the same. An instant afterwards he gave a little cry of satisfaction, and, following the direction of his eager eyes, I saw that a hansom cab with a man inside which had halted on the other side of the street was now proceeding slowly onward again.

'There's our man, Watson! Come along! We'll have a good look at him, if we can do no more.'

At that instant I was aware of a bushy black beard and a pair of piercing eyes turned upon us through the side window of the cab. Instantly the trapdoor at the top flew up, something was screamed to the driver, and the cab flew madly off down Regent Street. Holmes looked eagerly round for another, but no empty one was in sight. Then he dashed in wild pursuit amid the stream of the traffic, but the start was too great, and already the cab was out of sight.

'There now!' said Holmes bitterly as he emerged panting and white with vexation from the tide of vehicles. 'Was ever such bad luck and such bad management, too? Watson, Watson, if you are an honest man you will record this also and set it against my successes!'

'Who was the man?'

'I have not an idea.'

'A spy?'

'Well, it was evident from what we have heard that Baskerville has been very closely shadowed by someone since he has been in town. How else could it be known so quickly that it was the Northumberland Hotel which he had chosen? If they had followed him the first day I argued that they would follow him also the second. You may have observed that I twice strolled over to the window while Dr Mortimer was reading his legend.'

'Yes, I remember.'

'I was looking out for loiterers in the street, but I saw none. We are dealing with a clever man, Watson. This matter cuts very deep, and though I have not finally made up my mind whether it is a benevolent or a malevolent agency which is in touch with us, I am conscious always of power and design. When our friends left I at once followed them in the hopes of marking down their invisible attendant. So wily was he that he had not trusted himself upon foot, but he had availed himself of a cab so that he could loiter behind or dash past them and so escape their notice. His method had the additional advantage that if they were to take a cab he was all ready to follow them. It has, however, one obvious disadvantage.'

'It puts him in the power of the cabman.'

'Exactly.'

'What a pity we did not get the number!'

'My dear Watson, clumsy as I have been, you surely do not seriously imagine that I neglected to get the number? No. 2704 is our man. But that is no use to us for the moment.'

'I fail to see how you could have done more.'

'On observing the cab I should have instantly turned and walked in the other direction. I should then at my leisure have hired a second cab and followed the first at a respectful distance, or, better still, have driven to the Northumberland Hotel and waited there. When our unknown had followed Baskerville home we should have had the opportunity of playing his own game upon himself and seeing where he made for. As it is, by an indiscreet eagerness, which was taken advantage of with extraordinary quickness and energy by our opponent, we have betrayed ourselves and lost our man.'

We had been sauntering slowly down Regent Street during this conversation, and Dr Mortimer, with his companion, had long vanished in front of us.

'There is no object in our following them,' said Holmes. 'The shadow has departed and will not return. We must see what further cards we have in our hands and play them with decision. Could you swear to that man's face within the cab?'

'I could swear only to the beard.'

'And so could I – from which I gather that in all probability it was a false one. A clever man upon so delicate an errand has no use for a beard save to conceal his features. Come in here, Watson!'

He turned into one of the district messenger offices, where he was warmly greeted by the manager.

'Ah, Wilson, I see you have not forgotten the little case in which I had the good fortune to help you?'

'No, sir, indeed I have not. You saved my good name, and perhaps my life.'

'My dear fellow, you exaggerate. I have some recollection, Wilson, that you had among your boys a lad named Cartwright, who showed some ability during the investigation.'

'Yes, sir, he is still with us.'

'Could you ring him up? – thank you! And I should be glad to have change of this five-pound note.'

A lad of fourteen, with a bright, keen face, had obeyed the summons of the manager. He stood now gazing with great reverence at the famous detective.

'Let me have the Hotel Directory,' said Holmes. 'Thank you! Now, Cartwright, there are the names of twenty-three hotels here, all in the immediate neighbourhood of Charing Cross. Do you see?'

'Yes, sir.'

'You will visit each of these in turn.'

'Yes, sir.'

'You will begin in each case by giving the outside porter one shilling. Here are twenty-three shillings.'

'Yes, sir.'

'You will tell him that you want to see the waste-paper of yesterday. You will say that an important telegram has miscarried and that you are looking for it. You understand?'

'Yes, sir.'

'But what you are really looking for is the centre page of the Times with some holes cut in it with scissors. Here is a copy of the Times. It is this page. You could easily recognise it, could you not?'

'Yes, sir.'

'In each case the outside porter will send for the hall porter, to whom also you will give a shilling. Here are twenty-three shillings. You will then learn in possibly twenty cases out of the twenty-three that the waste of the day before has been burned or removed. In the three other cases you will be shown a heap of paper and you will look for this page of the *Times* among it. The odds are enormously against your finding it. There are ten shillings over in case of emergencies. Let me have a report by wire at Baker Street before evening. And now, Watson, it only remains for us to find out by wire the identity of the cabman, No. 2704, and then we will drop into one of the Bond Street picture galleries and fill in the time until we are due at the hotel.'

CHAPTER 5

THREE BROKEN THREADS

Sherlock Holmes had, in a very remarkable degree, the power of detaching his mind at will. For two hours the strange business in which we had been involved appeared to be forgotten, and he was entirely absorbed in the pictures of the modern Belgian masters. He would talk of nothing but art, of which he had the crudest ideas, from our leaving the gallery until we found ourselves at the Northumberland Hotel.

'Sir Henry Baskerville is upstairs expecting you,' said the clerk. 'He asked me to show you up at once when you came.'

'Have you any objection to my looking at your register?' said Holmes.

'Not in the least.'

The book showed that two names had been added after that of Baskerville. One was Theophilus Johnson and family, of Newcastle; the other Mrs Oldmore and maid, of High Lodge, Alton.

'Surely that must be the same Johnson whom I used to know,' said Holmes to the porter. 'A lawyer, is he not, greyheaded, and walks with a limp?'

'No, sir, this is Mr Johnson, the coal-owner, a very active gentleman, not older than yourself.'

'Surely you are mistaken about his trade?'

'No, sir! he has used this hotel for many years, and he is very well known to us.'

'Ah, that settles it. Mrs Oldmore, too; I seem to remember the name. Excuse my curiosity, but often in calling upon one friend one finds another.'

'She is an invalid lady, sir. Her husband was once mayor of Gloucester. She always comes to us when she is in town.'

'Thank you; I am afraid I cannot claim her acquaintance. We have established a most important fact by these questions, Watson,' he continued in a low voice as we went upstairs together. 'We know now that the people who are so interested in our friend have not settled down in his own hotel. That means that while they are, as we have seen, very anxious to watch him, they are equally anxious that he should not see them. Now, this is a most suggestive fact.'

'What does it suggest?'

'It suggests – halloa, my dear fellow, what on earth is the matter?'

As we came round the top of the stairs we had run up against Sir Henry Baskerville himself. His face was flushed with anger, and he held an old and dusty boot in one of his hands. So furious was he that he was hardly articulate, and when he did speak it was in a much broader and more Western dialect than any which we had heard from him in the morning.

'Seems to me they are playing me for a sucker in this hotel,' he cried. 'They'll find they've started in to monkey with the wrong man unless they are careful. By thunder, if that chap can't find my missing boot there will be trouble. I can take a joke with the best, Mr Holmes, but they've got a bit over the mark this time.'

'Still looking for your boot?'

'Yes, sir, and mean to find it.'

'But, surely, you said that it was a new brown boot?'

'So it was, sir. And now it's an old black one.'

'What! you don't mean to say—?'

'That's just what I do mean to say. I only had three pairs in the world – the new brown, the old black, and the patent leathers, which I am wearing. Last night they took one of my brown ones, and today they have sneaked one of the black. Well, have you got it? Speak out, man, and don't stand staring!'

An agitated German waiter had appeared upon the scene.

'No, sir; I have made inquiry all over the hotel, but I can hear no word of it.'

'Well, either that boot comes back before sundown or I'll see the manager and tell him that I go right straight out of this hotel.'

'It shall be found, sir – I promise you that if you will have a little patience it will be found.'

'Mind it is, for it's the last thing of mine that I'll lose in this den of thieves. Well, well, Mr Holmes, you'll excuse my troubling you about such a trifle—'

'I think it's well worth troubling about.'

'Why, you look very serious over it.'

'How do you explain it?'

'I just don't attempt to explain it. It seems the very maddest, queerest thing that ever happened to me.'

'The queerest perhaps – ' said Holmes thoughtfully.

'What do you make of it yourself?'

'Well, I don't profess to understand it yet. This case of yours is very complex, Sir Henry. When taken in conjunction with your uncle's death I am not sure that of all the five hundred cases of capital importance which I have handled there is one which cuts so deep. But we hold several threads in our hands, and the odds are that one or other of them guides us to the truth. We may waste time in following the wrong one, but sooner or later we must come upon the right.'

We had a pleasant luncheon in which little was said of the business which had brought us together. It was in the private sitting-room to which we afterwards repaired that Holmes asked Baskerville what were his intentions.

'To go to Baskerville Hall.'

'And when?'

'At the end of the week.'

'On the whole,' said Holmes, 'I think that your decision is a wise one. I have ample evidence that you are being dogged in London, and amid the millions of this great city it is difficult to discover who these people are or what their object can be. If their intentions are evil they might do you a mischief, and we should be powerless to prevent it. You did not know, Dr Mortimer, that you were followed this morning from my house?'

Dr Mortimer started violently. 'Followed! By whom?'

'That, unfortunately, is what I cannot tell you. Have you among your neighbours or acquaintances on Dartmoor any man with a black, full beard?'

'No – or, let me see – why, yes. Barrymore, Sir Charles's butler, is a man with a full, black beard.'

'Ha! Where is Barrymore?'

'He is in charge of the Hall.'

'We had best ascertain if he is really there, or if by any possibility he might be in London.'

'How can you do that?'

'Give me a telegraph form. "Is all ready for Sir Henry?" That will do. Address to Mr Barrymore, Baskerville Hall. What is the nearest telegraph-office? Grimpen. Very good, we will send a second wire to the postmaster, Grimpen: "Telegram to Mr Barrymore to be delivered into his own hand. If absent, please return wire to Sir Henry Baskerville, Northumberland Hotel." That should let us know before evening whether Barrymore is at his post in Devonshire or not.'

'That's so,' said Baskerville. 'By the way, Dr Mortimer, who is this Barrymore, anyhow?'

'He is the son of the old caretaker, who is dead. They have looked after the Hall for four generations now. So far as I know, he and his wife are as respectable a couple as any in the county.'

'At the same time,' said Baskerville, 'it's clear enough that so long as there are none of the family at the Hall these people have a mighty fine home and nothing to do.'

'That is true.'

'Did Barrymore profit at all by Sir Charles's will?' asked Holmes.

'He and his wife had five hundred pounds each.'

'Ha! Did they know that they would receive this?'

'Yes; Sir Charles was very fond of talking about the provisions of his will.'

'That is very interesting.'

'I hope,' said Dr Mortimer, 'that you do not look with suspicious eyes upon everyone who received a legacy from

Sir Charles, for I also had a thousand pounds left to me.'

'Indeed! And anyone else?'

'There were many insignificant sums to individuals, and a large number of public charities. The residue all went to Sir Henry.'

'And how much was the residue?'

'Seven hundred and forty thousand pounds.'

Holmes raised his eyebrows in surprise. 'I had no idea that so gigantic a sum was involved,' said he.

'Sir Charles had the reputation of being rich, but we did not know how very rich he was until we came to examine his securities. The total value of the estate was close on to a million.'

'Dear me! It is a stake for which a man might well play a desperate game. And one more question, Dr Mortimer. Supposing that anything happened to our young friend here – you will forgive the unpleasant hypothesis! – who would inherit the estate?'

'Since Rodger Baskerville, Sir Charles's younger brother died unmarried, the estate would descend to the Desmonds, who are distant cousins. James Desmond is an elderly clergyman in Westmoreland.'

'Thank you. These details are all of great interest. Have you met Mr James Desmond?'

'Yes; he once came down to visit Sir Charles. He is a man of venerable appearance and of saintly life. I remember that he refused to accept any settlement from Sir Charles, though he pressed it upon him.'

'And this man of simple tastes would be the heir to Sir Charles's thousands.'

'He would be the heir to the estate because that is entailed.

He would also be the heir to the money unless it were willed otherwise by the present owner, who can, of course, do what he likes with it.'

'And have you made your will, Sir Henry?'

'No, Mr Holmes, I have not. I've had no time, for it was only yesterday that I learned how matters stood. But in any case I feel that the money should go with the title and estate. That was my poor uncle's idea. How is the owner going to restore the glories of the Baskervilles if he has not money enough to keep up the property? House, land, and dollars must go together.'

'Quite so. Well, Sir Henry, I am of one mind with you as to the advisability of your going down to Devonshire without delay. There is only one provision which I must make. You certainly must not go alone.'

'Dr Mortimer returns with me.'

'But Dr Mortimer has his practice to attend to, and his house is miles away from yours. With all the goodwill in the world he may be unable to help you. No, Sir Henry, you must take with you someone, a trusty man, who will be always by your side.'

'Is it possible that you could come yourself, Mr Holmes?'

'If matters came to a crisis I should endeavour to be present in person; but you can understand that, with my extensive consulting practice and with the constant appeals which reach me from many quarters, it is impossible for me to be absent from London for an indefinite time. At the present instant one of the most revered names in England is being besmirched by a blackmailer, and only I can stop a disastrous scandal. You will see how impossible it is for me to go to Dartmoor.'

'Whom would you recommend, then?'

Holmes laid his hand upon my arm. 'If my friend would undertake it there is no man who is better worth having at your side when you are in a tight place. No one can say so more confidently than I.'

The proposition took me completely by surprise, but before I had time to answer, Baskerville seized me by the hand and wrung it heartily.

'Well, now, that is real kind of you, Dr Watson,' said he. 'You see how it is with me, and you know just as much about the matter as I do. If you will come down to Baskerville Hall and see me through I'll never forget it.'

The promise of adventure had always a fascination for me, and I was complimented by the words of Holmes and by the eagerness with which the baronet hailed me as a companion.

'I will come, with pleasure,' said I. 'I do not know how I could employ my time better.'

'And you will report very carefully to me,' said Holmes. 'When a crisis comes, as it will do, I will direct how you shall act. I suppose that by Saturday all might be ready?'

'Would that suit Dr Watson?'

'Perfectly.'

'Then on Saturday, unless you hear to the contrary, we shall meet at the ten-thirty train from Paddington.'

We had risen to depart when Baskerville gave a cry, of triumph, and diving into one of the corners of the room he drew a brown boot from under a cabinet.

'My missing boot!' he cried.

'May all our difficulties vanish as easily!' said Sherlock Holmes.

'But it is a very singular thing,' Dr Mortimer remarked. 'I searched this room carefully before lunch.'

'And so did I,' said Baskerville. 'Every inch of it.'

'There was certainly no boot in it then.'

'In that case the waiter must have placed it there while we were lunching.'

The German was sent for but professed to know nothing of the matter, nor could any inquiry clear it up. Another item had been added to that constant and apparently purposeless series of small mysteries which had succeeded each other so rapidly. Setting aside the whole grim story of Sir Charles's death, we had a line of inexplicable incidents all within the limits of two days, which included the receipt of the printed letter, the black-bearded spy in the hansom, the loss of the new brown boot, the loss of the old black boot, and now the return of the new brown boot. Holmes sat in silence in the cab as we drove back to Baker Street, and I knew from his drawn brows and keen face that his mind, like my own, was busy in endeavouring to frame some scheme into which all these strange and apparently disconnected episodes could be fitted. All afternoon and late into the evening he sat lost in tobacco and thought.

Just before dinner two telegrams were handed in. The first ran:

"Have just heard that Barrymore is at the Hall. BASKERVILLE."

The second:

"Visited twenty-three hotels as directed, but sorry to report unable to trace cut sheet of *Times*. CARTWRIGHT."

'There go two of my threads, Watson. There is nothing

more stimulating than a case where everything goes against you. We must cast round for another scent.'

'We have still the cabman who drove the spy.'

'Exactly. I have wired to get his name and address from the Official Registry. I should not be surprised if this were an answer to my question.'

The ring at the bell proved to be something even more satisfactory than an answer, however, for the door opened and a rough-looking fellow entered who was evidently the man himself.

'I got a message from the head office that a gent at this address had been inquiring for No. 2704,' said he. 'I've driven my cab this seven years and never a word of complaint. I came here straight from the Yard to ask you to your face what you had against me.'

'I have nothing in the world against you, my good man,' said Holmes. 'On the contrary, I have half a sovereign for you if you will give me a clear answer to my questions.'

'Well, I've had a good day and no mistake,' said the cabman with a grin. 'What was it you wanted to ask, sir?'

'First of all your name and address, in case I want you again.'

'John Clayton, 3 Turpey Street, the Borough. My cab is out of Shipley's Yard, near Waterloo Station.'

Sherlock Holmes made a note of it.

'Now, Clayton, tell me all about the fare who came and watched this house at ten o'clock this morning and afterwards followed the two gentlemen down Regent Street.'

The man looked surprised and a little embarrassed. 'Why, there's no good my telling you things, for you seem to know as much as I do already,' said he. 'The truth is that the gentleman told me that he was a detective and that I was to say nothing about him to anyone.'

'My good fellow; this is a very serious business, and you may find yourself in a pretty bad position if you try to hide anything from me. You say that your fare told you that he was a detective?'

'Yes, he did.'

'When did he say this?'

'When he left me.'

'Did he say anything more?'

'He mentioned his name.'

Holmes cast a swift glance of triumph at me. 'Oh, he mentioned his name, did he? That was imprudent. What was the name that he mentioned?'

'His name,' said the cabman, 'was Mr Sherlock Holmes.'

Never have I seen my friend more completely taken aback than by the cabman's reply. For an instant he sat in silent amazement. Then he burst into a hearty laugh.

'A touch, Watson – an undeniable touch!' said he. 'I feel a foil as quick and supple as my own. He got home upon me very prettily that time. So his name was Sherlock Holmes, was it?'

'Yes, sir, that was the gentleman's name.'

'Excellent! Tell me where you picked him up and all that occurred.'

'He hailed me at half-past nine in Trafalgar Square. He said that he was a detective, and he offered me two guineas if I would do exactly what he wanted all day and ask no questions. I was glad enough to agree. First we drove down to the Northumberland Hotel and waited there until two gentlemen came out and took a cab from the rank. We followed their cab until it pulled up somewhere near here.'

'This very door,' said Holmes.

'Well, I couldn't be sure of that, but I dare say my fare knew all about it. We pulled up halfway down the street and waited an hour and a half. Then the two gentlemen passed us, walking, and we followed down Baker Street and along—'

'I know,' said Holmes.

'Until we got three-quarters down Regent Street. Then my gentleman threw up the trap, and he cried that I should drive right away to Waterloo Station as hard as I could go. I whipped up the mare and we were there under the ten minutes. Then he paid up his two guineas, like a good one, and away he went into the station. Only just as he was leaving he turned round and he said: "It might interest you to know that you have been driving Mr Sherlock Holmes." That's how I come to know the name.'

'I see. And you saw no more of him?'

'Not after he went into the station.'

'And how would you describe Mr Sherlock Holmes?'

The cabman scratched his head. 'Well, he wasn't altogether such an easy gentleman to describe. I'd put him at forty years of age, and he was of a middle height, two or three inches shorter than you, sir. He was dressed like a toff, and he had a black beard, cut square at the end, and a pale face. I don't know as I could say more than that.'

'Colour of his eyes?'

'No, I can't say that.'

'Nothing more that you can remember?'

'No, sir; nothing.'

'Well, then, here is your half-sovereign. There's another

one waiting for you if you can bring any more information. Good-night!'

'Good-night, sir, and thank you!'

John Clayton departed chuckling, and Holmes turned to me with a shrug of his shoulders and a rueful smile.

'Snap goes our third thread, and we end where we began,' said he. 'The cunning rascal! He knew our number, knew that Sir Henry Baskerville had consulted me, spotted who I was in Regent Street, conjectured that I had got the number of the cab and would lay my hands on the driver, and so sent back this audacious message. I tell you, Watson, this time we have got a foeman who is worthy of our steel. I've been checkmated in London. I can only wish you better luck in Devonshire. But I'm not easy in my mind about it.'

'About what?'

'About sending you. It's an ugly business, Watson, an ugly dangerous business, and the more I see of it the less I like it. Yes, my dear fellow, you may laugh, but I give you my word that I shall be very glad to have you back safe and sound in Baker Street once more.'

CHAPTER 6

BASKERVILLE HALL

Sir Henry Baskerville and Dr Mortimer were ready upon the appointed day, and we started as arranged for Devonshire. Mr Sherlock Holmes drove with me to the station and gave me his last parting injunctions and advice.

'I will not bias your mind by suggesting theories or suspicions, Watson,' said he; 'I wish you simply to report facts in the fullest possible manner to me, and you can leave me to do the theorising.'

'What sort of facts?' I asked.

'Anything which may seem to have a bearing however indirect upon the case, and especially the relations between young Baskerville and his neighbours or any fresh particulars concerning the death of Sir Charles. I have made some inquiries myself in the last few days, but the results have, I fear, been negative. One thing only appears to be certain, and that is that Mr James Desmond, who is the next heir, is an elderly gentleman of a very amiable disposition, so that this persecution does not arise from him. I really think that we may eliminate him entirely from our calculations. There remain the people who will actually surround Sir Henry Baskerville upon the moor.'

'Would it not be well in the first place to get rid of this Barrymore couple?'

'By no means. You could not make a greater mistake. If they are innocent it would be a cruel injustice, and if they are guilty we should be giving up all chance of bringing it home to them. No, no, we will preserve them upon our list of suspects. Then there is a groom at the Hall, if I remember right. There are two moorland farmers. There is our friend Dr Mortimer, whom I believe to be entirely honest, and there is his wife, of whom we know nothing. There is this naturalist, Stapleton, and there is his sister, who is said to be a young lady of attractions. There is Mr Frankland, of Lafter Hall, who is also an unknown factor, and there are one or two other neighbours. These are the folk who must be your very special study.'

'I will do my best.'

'You have arms, I suppose?'

'Yes, I thought it as well to take them.'

'Most certainly. Keep your revolver near you night and day, and never relax your precautions.'

Our friends had already secured a first-class carriage and were waiting for us upon the platform.

'No, we have no news of any kind,' said Dr Mortimer in answer to my friend's questions. 'I can swear to one thing, and that is that we have not been shadowed during the last two days. We have never gone out without keeping a sharp watch, and no one could have escaped our notice.'

'You have always kept together, I presume?'

'Except yesterday afternoon. I usually give up one day to pure amusement when I come to town, so I spent it at the Museum of the College of Surgeons.'

'And I went to look at the folk in the park,' said Baskerville.

'But we had no trouble of any kind.'

'It was imprudent, all the same,' said Holmes, shaking his head and looking very grave. 'I beg, Sir Henry, that you will not go about alone. Some great misfortune will befall you if you do. Did you get your other boot?'

'No, sir, it is gone forever.'

'Indeed. That is very interesting. Well, good-bye,' he added as the train began to glide down the platform. 'Bear in mind, Sir Henry, one of the phrases in that queer old legend which Dr Mortimer has read to us, and avoid the moor in those hours of darkness when the powers of evil are exalted.'

I looked back at the platform when we had left it far

behind and saw the tall, austere figure of Holmes standing motionless and gazing after us.

The journey was a swift and pleasant one, and I spent it in making the more intimate acquaintance of my two companions and in playing with Dr Mortimer's spaniel. In a very few hours the brown earth had become ruddy, the brick had changed to granite, and red cows grazed in well-hedged fields where the lush grasses and more luxuriant vegetation spoke of a richer, if a damper, climate. Young Baskerville stared eagerly out of the window and cried aloud with delight as he recognised the familiar features of the Devon scenery.

'I've been over a good part of the world since I left it, Dr Watson,' said he; 'but I have never seen a place to compare with it.'

'I never saw a Devonshire man who did not swear by his county,' I remarked.

'It depends upon the breed of men quite as much as on the county,' said Dr Mortimer. 'A glance at our friend here reveals the rounded head of the Celt, which carries inside it the Celtic enthusiasm and power of attachment. Poor Sir Charles's head was of a very rare type, half Gaelic, half Ivernian in its characteristics. But you were very young when you last saw Baskerville Hall, were you not?'

'I was a boy in my teens at the time of my father's death and had never seen the Hall, for he lived in a little cottage on the South Coast. Thence I went straight to a friend in America. I tell you it is all as new to me as it is to Dr Watson, and I'm as keen as possible to see the moor.'

'Are you? Then your wish is easily granted, for there is your first sight of the moor,' said Dr Mortimer, pointing out of the carriage window.

Over the green squares of the fields and the low curve of a wood there rose in the distance a grey, melancholy hill, with a strange jagged summit, dim and vague in the distance, like some fantastic landscape in a dream. Baskerville sat for a long time, his eyes fixed upon it, and I read upon his eager face how much it meant to him, this first sight of that strange spot where the men of his blood had held sway so long and left their mark so deep. There he sat, with his tweed suit and his American accent, in the corner of a prosaic railway-carriage, and yet as I looked at his dark and expressive face I felt more than ever how true a descendant he was of that long line of high-blooded, fiery, and masterful men. There were pride, valour, and strength in his thick brows, his sensitive nostrils, and his large hazel eyes. If on that forbidding moor a difficult and dangerous quest should lie before us, this was at least a comrade for whom one might venture to take a risk with the certainty that he would bravely share it.

The train pulled up at a small wayside station and we all descended. Outside, beyond the low, white fence, a wagonette with a pair of cobs was waiting. Our coming was evidently a great event, for station-master and porters clustered round us to carry out our luggage. It was a sweet, simple country spot, but I was surprised to observe that by the gate there stood two soldierly men in dark uniforms who leaned upon their short rifles and glanced keenly at us as we passed. The coachman, a hard-faced, gnarled little fellow, saluted Sir Henry Baskerville, and in a few minutes we were flying swiftly down the broad, white road. Rolling pasture lands curved upward on either side of us, and old gabled houses peeped out from amid the thick green foliage, but behind the peaceful and sunlit countryside there rose ever, dark against the evening sky, the long, gloomy curve of the moor, broken by the jagged and sinister hills.

The wagonette swung round into a side road, and we curved upward through deep lanes worn by centuries of wheels, high banks on either side, heavy with dripping moss and fleshy hart's-tongue ferns. Bronzing bracken and mottled bramble gleamed in the light of the sinking sun. Still steadily rising, we passed over a narrow granite bridge and skirted a noisy stream which gushed swiftly down, foaming and roaring amid the grey boulders. Both road and stream wound up through a valley dense with scrub oak and fir. At every turn Baskerville gave an exclamation of delight, looking eagerly about him and asking countless questions. To his eyes all seemed beautiful, but to me a tinge of melancholy lay upon the countryside, which bore so clearly the mark of the waning year. Yellow leaves carpeted the lanes and fluttered down upon us as we passed. The rattle of our wheels died away as we drove through drifts of rotting vegetation – sad gifts, as it seemed to me, for Nature to throw before the carriage of the returning heir of the Baskervilles.

'Halloa!' cried Dr Mortimer, 'what is this?'

A steep curve of heath-clad land, an outlying spur of the moor, lay in front of us. On the summit, hard and clear like an equestrian statue upon its pedestal, was a mounted soldier, dark and stern, his rifle poised ready over his forearm. He was watching the road along which we travelled.

'What is this, Perkins?' asked Dr Mortimer.

Our driver half turned in his seat. 'There's a convict escaped from Princetown, sir. He's been out three days now, and the warders watch every road and every station, but they've had no sight of him yet. The farmers about here don't like it, sir, and that's a fact.'

'Well, I understand that they get five pounds if they can give information.'

'Yes, sir, but the chance of five pounds is but a poor thing compared to the chance of having your throat cut. You see, it isn't like any ordinary convict. This is a man that would stick at nothing.'

'Who is he, then?'

'It is Selden, the Notting Hill murderer.'

I remembered the case well, for it was one in which Holmes had taken an interest on account of the peculiar ferocity of the crime and the wanton brutality which had marked all the actions of the assassin. The commutation of his death sentence had been due to some doubts as to his complete sanity, so atrocious was his conduct. Our wagonette had topped a rise and in front of us rose the huge expanse of the moor, mottled with gnarled and craggy cairns and tors. A cold wind swept down from it and set us shivering. Somewhere there, on that desolate plain, was lurking this fiendish man, hiding in a burrow like a wild beast, his heart full of malignancy against the whole race which had cast him out. It needed but this to complete the grim suggestiveness of the barren waste, the chilling wind, and the darkling sky. Even Baskerville fell silent and pulled his overcoat more closely around him.

We had left the fertile country behind and beneath us. We looked back on it now, the slanting rays of a low sun turning the streams to threads of gold and glowing on the red earth new turned by the plough and the broad tangle of the woodlands. The road in front of us grew bleaker and wilder over huge russet and olive slopes, sprinkled with giant boulders. Now and then we passed a moorland cottage, walled and roofed with stone, with no creeper to break its harsh outline. Suddenly we looked down into a cuplike depression, patched with stunted oaks and firs which had been twisted and bent by the fury of years of storm. Two high, narrow towers rose over the trees. The driver pointed with his whip.

'Baskerville Hall,' said he.

Its master had risen and was staring with flushed cheeks and shining eyes. A few minutes later we had reached the lodge-gates, a maze of fantastic tracery in wrought iron, with weather-bitten pillars on either side, blotched with lichens, and surmounted by the boars' heads of the Baskervilles. The lodge was a ruin of black granite and bared ribs of rafters, but facing it was a new building, half constructed, the first fruit of Sir Charles's South African gold.

Through the gateway we passed into the avenue, where the wheels were again hushed amid the leaves, and the old trees shot their branches in a sombre tunnel over our heads. Baskerville shuddered as he looked up the long, dark drive to where the house glimmered like a ghost at the farther end.

'Was it here?' he asked in a low voice.

'No, no, the yew alley is on the other side.'

The young heir glanced round with a gloomy face.

'It's no wonder my uncle felt as if trouble were coming on him in such a place as this,' said he. 'It's enough to scare any man. I'll have a row of electric lamps up here inside of six months, and you won't know it again, with a thousand candle-power Swan and Edison right here in front of the hall door.'

The avenue opened into a broad expanse of turf, and the house lay before us. In the fading light I could see that the centre was a heavy block of building from which a porch projected. The whole front was draped in ivy, with a patch clipped bare here and there where a window or a coat of arms broke through the dark veil. From this central block rose the twin towers, ancient, crenelated, and pierced with many loopholes. To right and left of the turrets were more modern wings of black granite. A dull light shone through heavy mullioned windows, and from the high chimneys which rose from the steep, high-angled roof there sprang a single black column of smoke.

'Welcome, Sir Henry! Welcome to Baskerville Hall!'

A tall man had stepped from the shadow of the porch to open the door of the wagonette. The figure of a woman was silhouetted against the yellow light of the hall. She came out and helped the man to hand down our bags.

'You don't mind my driving straight home, Sir Henry?' said Dr Mortimer. 'My wife is expecting me.'

'Surely you will stay and have some dinner?'

'No, I must go. I shall probably find some work awaiting me. I would stay to show you over the house, but Barrymore will be a better guide than I. Good-bye, and never hesitate night or day to send for me if I can be of service.'

The wheels died away down the drive while Sir Henry and I turned into the hall, and the door clanged heavily behind us. It was a fine apartment in which we found ourselves, large, lofty, and heavily raftered with huge baulks of age-blackened oak. In the great old-fashioned fireplace behind the high iron dogs a log-fire crackled and snapped. Sir Henry and I held out our hands to it, for we were numb from our long drive. Then we gazed round us at the high, thin window of old stained glass, the oak panelling, the stags' heads, the coats of arms upon the walls, all dim and sombre in the subdued light of the central lamp.

'It's just as I imagined it,' said Sir Henry. 'Is it not the very picture of an old family home? To think that this should be the same hall in which for five hundred years my people have lived. It strikes me solemn to think of it.'

I saw his dark face lit up with a boyish enthusiasm as he gazed about him. The light beat upon him where he stood, but long shadows trailed down the walls and hung like a black canopy above him. Barrymore had returned from taking our luggage to our rooms. He stood in front of us now with the subdued manner of a well-trained servant. He was a remarkable-looking man, tall, handsome, with a square black beard and pale, distinguished features.

'Would you wish dinner to be served at once, sir?'

'Is it ready?'

'In a very few minutes, sir. You will find hot water in your rooms. My wife and I will be happy, Sir Henry, to stay with you until you have made your fresh arrangements, but you will understand that under the new conditions this house will require a considerable staff.'

'What new conditions?'

'I only meant, sir, that Sir Charles led a very retired life, and we were able to look after his wants. You would, naturally, wish to have more company, and so you will need changes in your household.'

'Do you mean that your wife and you wish to leave?'

'Only when it is quite convenient to you, sir.'

'But your family have been with us for several generations, have they not? I should be sorry to begin my life here by breaking an old family connection.'

I seemed to discern some signs of emotion upon the butler's white face.

'I feel that also, sir, and so does my wife. But to tell the truth, sir, we were both very much attached to Sir Charles, and his death gave us a shock and made these surroundings very painful to us. I fear that we shall never again be easy in our minds at Baskerville Hall.'

'But what do you intend to do?'

'I have no doubt, sir, that we shall succeed in establishing ourselves in some business. Sir Charles's generosity has given us the means to do so. And now, sir, perhaps I had best show you to your rooms.'

A square balustraded gallery ran round the top of the old hall, approached by a double stair. From this central point two long corridors extended the whole length of the building, from which all the bedrooms opened. My own was in the same wing as Baskerville's and almost next door to it. These rooms appeared to be much more modern than the central part of the house, and the bright paper and numerous candles did something to remove the sombre impression which our arrival had left upon my mind.

But the dining-room which opened out of the hall was a place of shadow and gloom. It was a long chamber with a step separating the dais where the family sat from the lower portion reserved for their dependents. At one end a minstrel's gallery overlooked it. Black beams shot across above our heads, with a smoke-darkened ceiling beyond them. With rows of flaring torches to light it up, and the colour and rude hilarity of an old-time banquet, it might have softened; but now, when two black-clothed gentlemen sat in the little circle of light thrown by a shaded lamp, one's voice became hushed and one's spirit subdued. A dim line of ancestors, in every variety of dress, from the Elizabethan knight to the buck of the Regency, stared down upon us and daunted us by their silent company. We talked little, and I for one was glad when the meal was over and we were able to retire into the modern billiard-room and smoke a cigarette.

'My word, it isn't a very cheerful place,' said Sir Henry. 'I suppose one can tone down to it, but I feel a bit out of the picture at present. I don't wonder that my uncle got a little jumpy if he lived all alone in such a house as this. However, if it suits you, we will retire early tonight, and perhaps things may seem more cheerful in the morning.'

I drew aside my curtains before I went to bed and looked out from my window. It opened upon the grassy space which lay in front of the hall door. Beyond, two copses of trees moaned and swung in a rising wind. A half moon broke through the rifts of racing clouds. In its cold light I saw beyond the trees a broken fringe of rocks, and the long, low curve of the melancholy moor. I closed the curtain, feeling that my last impression was in keeping with the rest.

And yet it was not quite the last. I found myself weary and yet wakeful, tossing restlessly from side to side, seeking for the sleep which would not come. Far away a chiming clock struck out the quarters of the hours, but otherwise a deathly silence lay upon the old house. And then suddenly, in the very dead of the night, there came a sound to my ears, clear, resonant, and unmistakable. It was the sob of a woman, the muffled, strangling gasp of one who is torn by an uncontrollable sorrow. I sat up in bed and listened intently. The noise could not have been far away and was certainly in the house. For half an hour I waited with every nerve on the alert, but there came no other sound save the chiming clock and the rustle of the ivy on the wall.

CHAPTER 7

THE STAPLETONS OF MERRIPIT HOUSE

The fresh beauty of the following morning did something to efface from our minds the grim and grey impression which had been left upon both of us by our first experience of Baskerville Hall. As Sir Henry and I sat at breakfast the sunlight flooded in through the high mullioned windows, throwing watery patches of colour from the coats of arms which covered them. The dark panelling glowed like bronze in the golden rays, and it was hard to realise that this was indeed the chamber which had struck such a gloom into our souls upon the evening before.

'I guess it is ourselves and not the house that we have to blame!' said the baronet. 'We were tired with our journey and chilled by our drive, so we took a grey view of the place. Now we are fresh and well, so it is all cheerful once more.'

'And yet it was not entirely a question of imagination,' I answered. 'Did you, for example, happen to hear someone, a woman I think, sobbing in the night?'

'That is curious, for I did when I was half asleep fancy that I heard something of the sort. I waited quite a time, but there was no more of it, so I concluded that it was all a dream.'

'I heard it distinctly, and I am sure that it was really the sob of a woman.'

'We must ask about this right away.' He rang the bell and asked Barrymore whether he could account for our experience. It seemed to me that the pallid features of the butler turned a shade paler still as he listened to his master's question.

'There are only two women in the house, Sir Henry,' he answered. 'One is the scullery-maid, who sleeps in the other wing. The other is my wife, and I can answer for it that the sound could not have come from her.'

And yet he lied as he said it, for it chanced that after breakfast I met Mrs Barrymore in the long corridor with the sun full upon her face. She was a large, impassive, heavy-featured woman with a stern set expression of mouth. But her telltale eyes were red and glanced at me from between swollen lids. It was she, then, who wept in the night, and if she did so her husband must know it. Yet he had taken the obvious risk of discovery in declaring that it was not so. Why had he done this? And why did she weep so bitterly? Already round this pale-faced, handsome, black-bearded man there was gathering an atmosphere of mystery and of gloom. It was he who had been the first to discover the body of Sir Charles, and we had only his word for all the circumstances which led up to the old man's death. Was it possible that it was Barrymore, after all, whom we had seen in the cab in Regent Street? The beard might well have been the same. The cabman had described a somewhat shorter man, but such an impression might easily have been erroneous. How could I settle the point forever? Obviously the first thing to do was to see the Grimpen postmaster and find whether the test telegram had really been placed in Barrymore's own hands. Be the answer what it might, I should at least have something to report to Sherlock Holmes.

Sir Henry had numerous papers to examine after breakfast, so that the time was propitious for my excursion. It was a pleasant walk of four miles along the edge of the moor, leading me at last to a small grey hamlet, in which two larger buildings, which proved to be the inn and the house of Dr Mortimer, stood high above the rest. The postmaster, who was also the village grocer, had a clear recollection of the telegram.

'Certainly, sir,' said he, 'I had the telegram delivered to Mr Barrymore exactly as directed.'

'Who delivered it?'

'My boy here. James, you delivered that telegram to Mr Barrymore at the Hall last week, did you not?'

'Yes, father, I delivered it.'

'Into his own hands?' I asked.

'Well, he was up in the loft at the time, so that I could not put it into his own hands, but I gave it into Mrs Barrymore's hands, and she promised to deliver it at once.'

'Did you see Mr Barrymore?'

'No, sir; I tell you he was in the loft.'

'If you didn't see him, how do you know he was in the loft?'

'Well, surely his own wife ought to know where he is,' said the postmaster testily. 'Didn't he get the telegram? If there is any mistake it is for Mr Barrymore himself to complain.'

It seemed hopeless to pursue the inquiry any farther, but it was clear that in spite of Holmes's ruse we had no proof that Barrymore had not been in London all the time. Suppose that it were so – suppose that the same man had been the last who had seen Sir Charles alive, and the first to dog the new heir when he returned to England. What then? Was he the agent of others or had he some sinister design of his own? What interest could he have in persecuting the Baskerville family? I thought of the strange warning clipped out of the leading article of the *Times*. Was that his work or was it possibly the doing of someone who was bent upon counteracting his schemes? The only conceivable motive was that which had been suggested by Sir Henry, that if the family could be scared away a comfortable and permanent home would be secured for the Barrymores. But surely such an explanation as that would be quite inadequate to account for the deep and subtle scheming which seemed to be weaving an invisible net round the young baronet. Holmes himself had said that no more complex case had come to him in all the long series of his sensational investigations. I prayed, as I walked back along the grey, lonely road, that my friend might soon be freed from his preoccupations and able to come down to take this heavy burden of responsibility from my shoulders.

Suddenly my thoughts were interrupted by the sound of running feet behind me and by a voice which called me by name. I turned, expecting to see Dr Mortimer, but to my surprise it was a stranger who was pursuing me. He was a small, slim, clean-shaven, prim-faced man, flaxen-haired and lean-jawed, between thirty and forty years of age, dressed in a grey suit and wearing a straw hat. A tin box for botanical specimens hung over his shoulder and he carried a green butterfly-net in one of his hands.

'You will, I am sure, excuse my presumption, Dr Watson,' said he as he came panting up to where I stood. 'Here on the moor we are homely folk and do not wait for formal introductions. You may possibly have heard my name from our mutual friend, Mortimer. I am Stapleton, of Merripit House.'

'Your net and box would have told me as much,' said I, 'for I knew that Mr Stapleton was a naturalist. But how did you know me?'

'I have been calling on Mortimer, and he pointed you out to me from the window of his surgery as you passed. As our road lay the same way I thought that I would overtake you and introduce myself. I trust that Sir Henry is none the worse for his journey?'

'He is very well, thank you.'

'We were all rather afraid that after the sad death of Sir Charles the new baronet might refuse to live here. It is asking much of a wealthy man to come down and bury himself in a place of this kind, but I need not tell you that it means a very great deal to the countryside. Sir Henry has, I suppose, no superstitious fears in the matter?'

'I do not think that it is likely.'

'Of course you know the legend of the fiend dog which haunts the family?'

'I have heard it.'

'It is extraordinary how credulous the peasants are about here! Any number of them are ready to swear that they have seen such a creature upon the moor.' He spoke with a smile, but I seemed to read in his eyes that he took the matter more seriously. 'The story took a great hold upon the imagination of Sir Charles, and I have no doubt that it led to his tragic end.'

'But how?'

'His nerves were so worked up that the appearance of any dog might have had a fatal effect upon his diseased heart. I fancy that he really did see something of the kind upon that last night in the yew alley. I feared that some disaster might occur, for I was very fond of the old man, and I knew that his heart was weak.'

'How did you know that?'

'My friend Mortimer told me.'

'You think, then, that some dog pursued Sir Charles, and that he died of fright in consequence?'

'Have you any better explanation?'

'I have not come to any conclusion.'

'Has Mr Sherlock Holmes?'

The words took away my breath for an instant but a glance at the placid face and steadfast eyes of my companion showed that no surprise was intended.

'It is useless for us to pretend that we do not know you, Dr Watson,' said he. 'The records of your detective have reached us here, and you could not celebrate him without being known yourself. When Mortimer told me your name he could not deny your identity. If you are here, then it follows that Mr Sherlock Holmes is interesting himself in the matter, and I am naturally curious to know what view he may take.'

'I am afraid that I cannot answer that question.'

'May I ask if he is going to honour us with a visit himself?'

'He cannot leave town at present. He has other cases which engage his attention.'

'What a pity! He might throw some light on that which is so dark to us. But as to your own researches, if there is any possible way in which I can be of service to you I trust that you will command me. If I had any indication of the nature of your suspicions or how you propose to investigate the case, I might perhaps even now give you some aid or advice.'

'I assure you that I am simply here upon a visit to my friend, Sir Henry, and that I need no help of any kind.'

'Excellent!' said Stapleton. 'You are perfectly right to be wary and discreet. I am justly reproved for what I feel was an unjustifiable intrusion, and I promise you that I will not mention the matter again.'

We had come to a point where a narrow grassy path struck off from the road and wound away across the moor. A steep, boulder-sprinkled hill lay upon the right which had in bygone days been cut into a granite quarry. The face which was turned towards us formed a dark cliff, with ferns and brambles growing in its niches. From over a distant rise there floated a grey plume of smoke.

'A moderate walk along this moor-path brings us to Merripit House,' said he. 'Perhaps you will spare an hour that I may have the pleasure of introducing you to my sister.'

My first thought was that I should be by Sir Henry's side. But then I remembered the pile of papers and bills with which his study table was littered. It was certain that I could not help with those. And Holmes had expressly said that I should study the neighbours upon the moor. I accepted Stapleton's invitation, and we turned together down the path.

'It is a wonderful place, the moor,' said he, looking round over the undulating downs, long green rollers, with crests of

jagged granite foaming up into fantastic surges. 'You never
tire of the moor. You cannot think the wonderful secrets
which it contains. It is so vast, and so barren, and so
mysterious.'

'You know it well, then?'

'I have only been here two years. The residents would call
me a newcomer. We came shortly after Sir Charles settled.
But my tastes led me to explore every part of the country
round, and I should think that there are few men who know
it better than I do.'

'Is it hard to know?'

'Very hard. You see, for example, this great plain to the
north here with the queer hills breaking out of it. Do you
observe anything remarkable about that?'

'It would be a rare place for a gallop.'

'You would naturally think so and the thought has cost
several their lives before now. You notice those bright green
spots scattered thickly over it?'

'Yes, they seem more fertile than the rest.'

Stapleton laughed. 'That is the great Grimpen Mire,' said
he. 'A false step yonder means death to man or beast. Only
yesterday I saw one of the moor ponies wander into it. He
never came out. I saw his head for quite a long time craning
out of the bog-hole, but it sucked him down at last. Even in
dry seasons it is a danger to cross it, but after these autumn
rains it is an awful place. And yet I can find my way to the
very heart of it and return alive. By George, there is another
of those miserable ponies!'

Something brown was rolling and tossing among the green
sedges. Then a long, agonised, writhing neck shot upward
and a dreadful cry echoed over the moor. It turned me cold

with horror, but my companion's nerves seemed to be stronger than mine.

'It's gone!' said he. 'The mire has him. Two in two days, and many more, perhaps, for they get in the way of going there in the dry weather and never know the difference until the mire has them in its clutches. It's a bad place, the great Grimpen Mire.'

'And you say you can penetrate it?'

'Yes, there are one or two paths which a very active man can take. I have found them out.'

'But why should you wish to go into so horrible a place?'

'Well, you see the hills beyond? They are really islands cut off on all sides by the impassable mire, which has crawled round them in the course of years. That is where the rare plants and the butterflies are, if you have the wit to reach them.'

'I shall try my luck some day.'

He looked at me with a surprised face. 'For God's sake put such an idea out of your mind,' said he. 'Your blood would be upon my head. I assure you that there would not be the least chance of your coming back alive. It is only by remembering certain complex landmarks that I am able to do it.'

'Halloa!' I cried. 'What is that?'

A long, low moan, indescribably sad, swept over the moor. It filled the whole air, and yet it was impossible to say whence it came. From a dull murmur it swelled into a deep roar, and then sank back into a melancholy, throbbing murmur once again. Stapleton looked at me with a curious expression in his face.

'Queer place, the moor!' said he.

'But what is it?'

'The peasants say it is the Hound of the Baskervilles

calling for its prey. I've heard it once or twice before, but never quite so loud.'

I looked round, with a chill of fear in my heart, at the huge swelling plain, mottled with the green patches of rushes. Nothing stirred over the vast expanse save a pair of ravens, which croaked loudly from a tor behind us.

'You are an educated man. You don't believe such nonsense as that?' said I. 'What do you think is the cause of so strange a sound?'

'Bogs make queer noises sometimes. It's the mud settling, or the water rising, or something.'

'No, no, that was a living voice.'

'Well, perhaps it was. Did you ever hear a bittern booming?'

'No, I never did.'

'It's a very rare bird – practically extinct – in England now, but all things are possible upon the moor. Yes, I should not be surprised to learn that what we have heard is the cry of the last of the bitterns.'

'It's the weirdest, strangest thing that ever I heard in my life.'

'Yes, it's rather an uncanny place altogether. Look at the hillside yonder. What do you make of those?'

The whole steep slope was covered with grey circular rings of stone, a score of them at least.

'What are they? Sheep-pens?'

'No, they are the homes of our worthy ancestors. Prehistoric man lived thickly on the moor, and as no one in particular has lived there since, we find all his little arrangements exactly as he left them. These are his wigwams with the roofs off. You can even see his hearth and his couch if you have the curiosity to go inside.

'But it is quite a town. When was it inhabited?'

'Neolithic man – no date.'

'What did he do?'

'He grazed his cattle on these slopes, and he learned to dig for tin when the bronze sword began to supersede the stone axe. Look at the great trench in the opposite hill. That is his mark. Yes, you will find some very singular points about the moor, Dr Watson. Oh, excuse me an instant! It is surely Cyclopides.'

A small fly or moth had fluttered across our path, and in an instant Stapleton was rushing with extraordinary energy and speed in pursuit of it. To my dismay the creature flew straight for the great mire, and my acquaintance never paused for an instant, bounding from tuft to tuft behind it, his green net waving in the air. His grey clothes and jerky, zigzag, irregular progress made him not unlike some huge moth himself. I was standing watching his pursuit with a mixture of admiration for his extraordinary activity and fear lest he should lose his footing in the treacherous mire, when I heard the sound of steps and, turning round, found a woman near me upon the path. She had come from the direction in which the plume of smoke indicated the position of Merripit House, but the dip of the moor had hid her until she was quite close.

I could not doubt that this was the Miss Stapleton of whom I had been told, since ladies of any sort must be few upon the moor, and I remembered that I had heard someone describe her as being a beauty. The woman who approached me was certainly that, and of a most uncommon type. There could not have been a greater contrast between brother and sister, for Stapleton was neutral tinted, with light hair and grey eyes, while she was darker than any brunette whom I have seen in England – slim, elegant, and tall. She had a proud, finely cut face, so regular that it might have seemed impassive were it not for the sensitive mouth and the beautiful dark, eager eyes. With her perfect figure and elegant dress she was, indeed, a strange apparition upon a lonely moorland path. Her eyes were on her brother as I turned, and then she quickened her pace towards me. I had raised my hat and was about to make some explanatory remark when her own words turned all my thoughts into a new channel.

'Go back!' she said. 'Go straight back to London, instantly.'

I could only stare at her in stupid surprise. Her eyes blazed at me, and she tapped the ground impatiently with her foot.

'Why should I go back?' I asked.

'I cannot explain.' She spoke in a low, eager voice, with a curious lisp in her utterance. 'But for God's sake do what I ask you. Go back and never set foot upon the moor again.'

'But I have only just come.'

'Man, man!' she cried. 'Can you not tell when a warning is for your own good? Go back to London! Start tonight! Get away from this place at all costs! Hush, my brother is coming! Not a word of what I have said. Would you mind getting that orchid for me among the mare's-tails yonder? We are very rich in orchids on the moor, though, of course, you are rather late to see the beauties of the place.'

Stapleton had abandoned the chase and came back to us breathing hard and flushed with his exertions.

'Halloa, Beryl!' said he, and it seemed to me that the

tone of his greeting was not altogether a cordial one.

'Well, Jack, you are very hot.'

'Yes, I was chasing a Cyclopides. He is very rare and seldom found in the late autumn. What a pity that I should have missed him!' He spoke unconcernedly, but his small light eyes glanced incessantly from the girl to me.

'You have introduced yourselves, I can see.'

'Yes. I was telling Sir Henry that it was rather late for him to see the true beauties of the moor.'

'Why, who do you think this is?'

'I imagine that it must be Sir Henry Baskerville.'

'No, no,' said I. 'Only a humble commoner, but his friend. My name is Dr Watson.'

A flush of vexation passed over her expressive face. 'We have been talking at cross purposes,' said she.

'Why, you had not very much time for talk,' her brother remarked with the same questioning eyes.

'I talked as if Dr Watson were a resident instead of being merely a visitor,' said she. 'It cannot much matter to him whether it is early or late for the orchids. But you will come on, will you not, and see Merripit House?'

A short walk brought us to it, a bleak moorland house, once the farm of some grazier in the old prosperous days, but now put into repair and turned into a modern dwelling. An orchard surrounded it, but the trees, as is usual upon the moor, were stunted and nipped, and the effect of the whole place was mean and melancholy. We were admitted by a strange, wizened, rusty-coated old manservant, who seemed in keeping with the house. Inside, however, there were large rooms furnished with an elegance in which I seemed to recognise the taste of the lady. As I looked from their windows at the interminable granite-flecked moor rolling unbroken to the farthest horizon I could not but marvel at what could have brought this highly educated man and this beautiful woman to live in such a place.

'Queer spot to choose, is it not?' said he as if in answer to my thought. 'And yet we manage to make ourselves fairly happy, do we not, Beryl?'

'Quite happy,' said she, but there was no ring of conviction in her words.

'I had a school,' said Stapleton. 'It was in the north country. The work to a man of my temperament was mechanical and uninteresting, but the privilege of living with youth, of helping to mould those young minds, and of impressing them with one's own character and ideals was very dear to me. However, the fates were against us. A serious epidemic broke out in the school and three of the boys died. It never recovered from the blow, and much of my capital was irretrievably swallowed up. And yet, if it were not for the loss of the charming companionship of the boys, I could rejoice over my own misfortune, for, with my strong tastes for botany and zoology, I find an unlimited field of work here, and my sister is as devoted to Nature as I am. All this, Dr Watson, has been brought upon your head by your expression as you surveyed the moor out of our window.'

'It certainly did cross my mind that it might be a little dull – less for you, perhaps, than for your sister.'

'No, no, I am never dull,' said she quickly.

'We have books, we have our studies, and we have inter-esting neighbours. Dr Mortimer is a most learned man in his own line. Poor Sir Charles was also an admirable companion.

We knew him well and miss him more than I can tell. Do you think that I should intrude if I were to call this afternoon and make the acquaintance of Sir Henry?'

'I am sure that he would be delighted.'

'Then perhaps you would mention that I propose to do so. We may in our humble way do something to make things more easy for him until he becomes accustomed to his new surroundings. Will you come upstairs, Dr Watson, and inspect my collection of Lepidoptera? I think it is the most complete one in the south-west of England. By the time that you have looked through them lunch will be almost ready.'

But I was eager to get back to my charge. The melancholy of the moor, the death of the unfortunate pony, the weird sound which had been associated with the grim legend of the Baskervilles, all these things tinged my thoughts with sadness. Then on the top of these more or less vague impressions there had come the definite and distinct warning of Miss Stapleton, delivered with such intense earnestness that I could not doubt that some grave and deep reason lay behind it. I resisted all pressure to stay for lunch, and I set off at once upon my return journey, taking the grass-grown path by which we had come.

It seems, however, that there must have been some short cut for those who knew it, for before I had reached the road I was astounded to see Miss Stapleton sitting upon a rock by the side of the track. Her face was beautifully flushed with her exertions and she held her hand to her side.

'I have run all the way in order to cut you off, Dr Watson,' said she. 'I had not even time to put on my hat. I must not stop, or my brother may miss me. I wanted to say to you how sorry I am about the stupid mistake I made in thinking that you were Sir Henry. Please forget the words I said, which have no application whatever to you.'

'But I can't forget them, Miss Stapleton,' said I. 'I am Sir Henry's friend, and his welfare is a very close concern of mine. Tell me why it was that you were so eager that Sir Henry should return to London.'

'A woman's whim, Dr Watson. When you know me better you will understand that I cannot always give reasons for what I say or do.'

'No, no. I remember the thrill in your voice. I remember the look in your eyes. Please, please, be frank with me, Miss Stapleton, for ever since I have been here I have been conscious of shadows all round me. Life has become like that great Grimpen Mire, with little green patches everywhere into which one may sink and with no guide to point the track. Tell me then what it was that you meant, and I will promise to convey your warning to Sir Henry.'

An expression of irresolution passed for an instant over her face, but her eyes had hardened again when she answered me.

'You make too much of it, Dr Watson,' said she. 'My brother and I were very much shocked by the death of Sir Charles. We knew him very intimately, for his favourite walk was over the moor to our house. He was deeply impressed with the curse which hung over the family, and when this tragedy came I naturally felt that there must be some grounds for the fears which he had expressed. I was distressed therefore when another member of the family came down to live here, and I felt that he should be warned of the danger which he will run.

That was all which I intended to convey.

'But what is the danger?'

'You know the story of the hound?'

'I do not believe in such nonsense.'

'But I do. If you have any influence with Sir Henry, take him away from a place which has always been fatal to his family. The world is wide. Why should he wish to live at the place of danger?'

'Because it is the place of danger. That is Sir Henry's nature. I fear that unless you can give me some more definite information than this it would be impossible to get him to move.'

'I cannot say anything definite, for I do not know anything definite.'

'I would ask you one more question, Miss Stapleton. If you meant no more than this when you first spoke to me, why should you not wish your brother to overhear what you said? There is nothing to which he, or anyone else, could object.'

'My brother is very anxious to have the Hall inhabited, for he thinks it is for the good of the poor folk upon the moor. He would be very angry if he knew that I have said anything which might induce Sir Henry to go away. But I have done my duty now and I will say no more. I must go back, or he will miss me and suspect that I have seen you. Good-bye!' She turned and had disappeared in a few minutes among the scattered boulders, while I, with my soul full of vague fears, pursued my way to Baskerville Hall.

CHAPTER 8

FIRST REPORT OF DR WATSON

From this point onward I will follow the course of events by transcribing my own letters to Mr Sherlock Holmes which lie before me on the table. One page is missing, but otherwise they are exactly as written and show my feelings and suspicions of the moment more accurately than my memory, clear as it is upon these tragic events, can possibly do.

Baskerville Hall, October 13th. MY DEAR HOLMES: My previous letters and telegrams have kept you pretty well up to date as to all that has occurred in this most God-forsaken corner of the world. The longer one stays here the more does the spirit of the moor sink into one's soul, its vastness, and also its grim charm. When you are once out upon its bosom you have left all traces of modern England behind you, but, on the other hand, you are conscious everywhere of the homes and the work of the prehistoric people. On all sides of you as you walk are the houses of these forgotten folk, with their graves and the huge monoliths which are supposed to have marked their temples. As you look at their grey stone huts against the scarred hillsides you leave your own age behind you, and if you were to see a skin-clad, hairy man crawl out from the low door fitting a flint-tipped arrow on to the string of his bow, you would feel that his presence there was more natural than your own. The strange thing is that they should have lived so thickly on what must always have been most unfruitful soil. I am no antiquarian, but I could imagine that they were some unwarlike and harried race who were forced to accept that which none other would occupy.

All this, however, is foreign to the mission on which you sent me and will probably be very uninteresting to your severely practical mind. I can still remember your complete indifference as to whether the sun moved round the earth or the earth round the sun. Let me, therefore, return to the facts concerning Sir Henry Baskerville.

If you have not had any report within the last few days it is because up to today there was nothing of importance to relate. Then a very surprising circumstance occurred, which I shall tell you in due course. But, first of all, I must keep you in touch with some of the other factors in the situation.

One of these, concerning which I have said little, is the escaped convict upon the moor. There is strong reason now to believe that he has got right away, which is a considerable relief to the lonely householders of this district. A fortnight has passed since his flight, during which he has not been seen and nothing has been heard of him. It is surely inconceivable that he could have held out upon the moor during all that time. Of course, so far as his concealment goes there is no difficulty at all. Any one of these stone huts would give him a hiding-place. But there is nothing to eat unless he were to catch and slaughter one of the moor sheep. We think, therefore, that he has gone, and the outlying farmers sleep the better in consequence.

We are four able-bodied men in this household, so that we could take good care of ourselves, but I confess that I have had uneasy moments when I have thought of the Stapletons. They live miles from any help. There are one maid, an old manservant, the sister, and the brother, the latter not a very strong man. They would be helpless in the hands of a desperate fellow like this Notting Hill criminal if he could once effect an entrance. Both Sir Henry and I were concerned at their situation, and it was suggested that Perkins the groom should go over to sleep there, but Stapleton would not hear of it.

The fact is that our friend, the baronet, begins to display a considerable interest in our fair neighbour. It is not to be wondered at, for time hangs heavily in this lonely spot to an active man like him, and she is a very fascinating and beautiful woman. There is something tropical and exotic about her which forms a singular contrast to her cool and unemotional brother. Yet he also gives the idea of hidden fires. He has certainly a very marked influence over her, for I have seen her continually glance at him as she talked as if seeking approbation for what she said. I trust that he is kind to her. There is a dry glitter in his eyes and a firm set of his thin lips, which goes with a positive and possibly a harsh nature. You would find him an interesting study.

He came over to call upon Baskerville on that first day, and the very next morning he took us both to show us the spot where the legend of the wicked Hugo is supposed to have had its origin. It was an excursion of some miles across the moor to a place which is so dismal that it might have suggested the story. We found a short valley between rugged tors which led to an open, grassy space flecked over with the white cotton grass. In the middle of it rose two great stones, worn and sharpened at the upper end until they looked like the huge corroding fangs of some monstrous beast. In every way it corresponded with the scene of the old tragedy. Sir Henry was much interested and asked Stapleton more than once whether he did really believe in the possibility of the interference of the supernatural in the affairs of men. He spoke lightly, but it was evident that he was very much in earnest. Stapleton was guarded in his replies, but it was easy to see that he said less than he might, and that he would not express his whole opinion out of consideration for the feelings of the baronet. He told us of similar cases, where families had suffered from some evil influence, and he left us with the impression that he shared the popular view upon the matter.

On our way back we stayed for lunch at Merripit House, and it was there that Sir Henry made the acquaintance of Miss Stapleton. From the first moment that he saw her he appeared to be strongly attracted by her, and I am much mistaken if the feeling was not mutual. He referred to her again and again on our walk home, and since then hardly a day has passed that we have not seen something of the brother and sister. They dine here tonight, and there is some talk of our going to them next week. One would imagine that such a match would be very welcome to Stapleton, and yet I have more than once caught a look of the strongest disapprobation in his face when Sir Henry has been paying some attention to his sister. He is much attached to her, no doubt, and would lead a lonely life without her, but it would seem the height of selfishness if he were to stand in the way of her making so brilliant a marriage. Yet I am certain that he does not wish their intimacy to ripen into love, and I have several times observed that he has taken pains to prevent them from being tete-a-tete. By the way, your instructions to me never to allow Sir Henry to go out alone will become very much more onerous if a love affair were to be added to our other difficulties. My popularity would soon suffer if I were to carry out your orders to the letter.

The other day – Thursday, to be more exact – Dr Mortimer lunched with us. He has been excavating a barrow at Long Down and has got a prehistoric skull which fills him with great joy. Never was there such a single-minded enthusiast as he! The Stapletons came in afterwards, and the good doctor took us all to the yew alley at Sir Henry's request to show us exactly how everything occurred upon that fatal night. It is a long, dismal walk, the yew alley, between two high walls of clipped hedge, with a narrow band of grass upon either side. At the far end is an old tumble-down summer-house. Halfway down is the moor-gate, where the old gentleman left his cigar-ash. It is a white wooden gate with a latch. Beyond it lies the wide moor. I remembered your theory of the affair and tried to picture all that had occurred. As the old man stood there he saw something coming across the moor, something which terrified him so that he lost his wits and ran and ran until he died of sheer horror and exhaustion. There was the long, gloomy tunnel down which he fled. And from what? A sheep-dog of the moor? Or a spectral hound, black, silent, and monstrous? Was there a human agency in the matter? Did the pale, watchful Barrymore know more than he cared to say? It was all dim and vague, but always there is the dark shadow of crime behind it.

One other neighbour I have met since I wrote last. This is Mr Frankland, of Lafter Hall, who lives some four miles to the south of us. He is an elderly man, red-faced, white-haired, and choleric. His passion is for the British law, and he has spent a large fortune in litigation. He fights for the mere pleasure of fighting and is equally ready to take up either side of a question, so that it is no wonder that he has found it a costly amusement. Sometimes he will shut up a right of way and defy the parish to make him open it. At others he will with his own hands tear down some other man's gate and declare that a path has existed there from time immemorial, defying the owner to prosecute him for trespass. He is learned in old manorial and communal rights, and he applies his knowledge sometimes in favour of the villagers of Fernworthy and sometimes against them, so that he is periodically either carried in triumph down the village street or else burned in effigy, according to his latest exploit. He is said to have about seven lawsuits upon his hands at present, which will probably swallow up the remainder of his fortune and so draw his sting and leave him harmless for the future. Apart from the law he seems a kindly, good-natured person, and I only mention him because you were particular that I should send some description of the people who surround us. He is curiously employed at present, for, being an amateur astronomer, he has an excellent telescope, with which he lies upon the roof of his own house and sweeps the moor all day in the hope of catching a glimpse of the escaped convict. If he would confine his energies to this all would be well, but there are rumours that he intends to prosecute Dr Mortimer for opening a grave without the consent of the next of kin because he dug up the Neolithic skull in the barrow on Long Down. He helps to keep our lives from being monotonous and gives a little comic relief where it is badly needed.

And now, having brought you up to date in the escaped convict, the Stapletons, Dr Mortimer, and Frankland, of Lafter Hall, let me end on that which is most important and tell you more about the Barrymores, and especially about the surprising development of last night.

First of all about the test telegram, which you sent from London in order to make sure that Barrymore was really here. I have already explained that the testimony of the postmaster shows that the test was worthless and that we have no proof one way or the other. I told Sir Henry how the matter stood, and he at once, in his downright fashion, had Barrymore up and asked him whether he had received the telegram himself. Barrymore said that he had.

'Did the boy deliver it into your own hands?' asked Sir Henry.

Barrymore looked surprised, and considered for a little time.

'No,' said he, 'I was in the box-room at the time, and my wife brought it up to me.'

'Did you answer it yourself?'

'No; I told my wife what to answer and she went down to write it.'

In the evening he recurred to the subject of his own accord.

'I could not quite understand the object of your questions this morning, Sir Henry,' said he. 'I trust that they do not mean that I have done anything to forfeit your confidence?'

Sir Henry had to assure him that it was not so and pacify him by giving him a considerable part of his old wardrobe, the London outfit having now all arrived.

Mrs Barrymore is of interest to me. She is a heavy, solid person, very limited, intensely respectable, and inclined to be puritanical. You could hardly conceive a less emotional subject. Yet I have told you how, on the first night here, I heard her sobbing bitterly, and since then I have more than once observed traces of tears upon her face. Some deep sorrow gnaws ever at her heart. Sometimes I wonder if she has a guilty memory which haunts her, and sometimes I suspect Barrymore of being a domestic tyrant. I have always felt that there was something singular and questionable in this man's character, but the adventure of last night brings all my suspicions to a head.

And yet it may seem a small matter in itself. You are aware that I am not a very sound sleeper, and since I have been on guard in this house my slumbers have been lighter than ever. Last night, about two in the morning, I was aroused by a stealthy step passing my room. I rose, opened my door, and peeped out. A long black shadow was trailing down the corridor. It was thrown by a man who walked softly down the passage with a candle held in his hand. He was in shirt and trousers, with no covering to his feet. I could merely see the outline, but his height told me that it was Barrymore. He walked very slowly and circumspectly, and there was something indescribably guilty and furtive in his whole appearance.

I have told you that the corridor is broken by the balcony which runs round the hall, but that it is resumed upon the farther side. I waited until he had passed out of sight and then I followed him. When I came round the balcony he had reached the end of the farther corridor, and I could see from the glimmer of light through an open door that he had entered one of the rooms. Now, all these rooms are unfurnished and unoccupied so that his expedition became more mysterious than ever. The light shone steadily as if he were standing motionless. I crept down the passage as noiselessly as I could and peeped round the corner of the door.

Barrymore was crouching at the window with the candle held against the glass. His profile was half turned towards me, and his face seemed to be rigid with expectation as he stared out into the blackness of the moor. For some minutes he stood watching intently. Then he gave a deep groan and with an impatient gesture he put out the light. Instantly I made my way back to my room, and very shortly came the stealthy steps passing once more upon their return journey. Long afterwards when I had fallen into a light sleep I heard a key turn somewhere in a lock, but I could not tell whence the sound came. What it all means I cannot guess, but there is some secret business going on in this house of gloom which sooner or later we shall get to the bottom of. I do not trouble you with my theories, for you asked me to furnish you only with facts. I have had a long talk with Sir Henry this morning, and we have made a plan of campaign founded upon my observations of last night. I will not speak about it just now, but it should make my next report interesting reading.

CHAPTER 9

THE LIGHT UPON THE MOOR
[SECOND REPORT OF DR WATSON]

Baskerville Hall, Oct. 15th. MY DEAR HOLMES: If I was compelled to leave you without much news during the early days of my mission you must acknowledge that I am making up for lost time, and that events are now crowding thick and fast upon us. In my last report I ended upon my top note with Barrymore at the window, and now I have quite a budget already which will, unless I am much mistaken, considerably surprise you. Things have taken a turn which I could not have anticipated. In some ways they have within the last forty-eight hours become much clearer and in some ways they have become more complicated. But I will tell you all and you shall judge for yourself.

Before breakfast on the morning following my adventure I went down the corridor and examined the room in which Barrymore had been on the night before. The western window through which he had stared so intently has, I noticed, one peculiarity above all other windows in the house – it commands the nearest outlook on to the moor. There is an opening between two trees which enables one from this point of view to look right down upon it, while from all the other windows it is only a distant glimpse which can be obtained. It follows, therefore, that Barrymore, since only this window would serve the purpose, must have been looking out for something or somebody upon the moor. The night was very dark, so that I can hardly imagine how he could have hoped to see anyone. It had struck me that it was possible that some love intrigue was on foot. That would have accounted for his stealthy movements and also for the uneasiness of his wife. The man is a striking-looking fellow, very well equipped to steal the heart of a country girl, so that this theory seemed to have something to support it. That opening of the door which I had heard after I had returned to my room might mean that he had gone out to keep some clandestine appointment. So I reasoned with myself in the morning, and I tell you the direction of my suspicions, however much the result may have shown that they were unfounded.

But whatever the true explanation of Barrymore's movements might be, I felt that the responsibility of keeping them to myself until I could explain them was more than I could bear. I had an interview with the baronet in his study after breakfast, and I told him all that I had seen. He was less surprised than I had expected.

'I knew that Barrymore walked about nights, and I had a mind to speak to him about it,' said he. 'Two or three times I have heard his steps in the passage, coming and going, just about the hour you name.'

'Perhaps then he pays a visit every night to that particular window,' I suggested.

'Perhaps he does. If so, we should be able to shadow him and see what it is that he is after. I wonder what your friend Holmes would do if he were here.'

'I believe that he would do exactly what you now suggest,' said I. 'He would follow Barrymore and see what he did.'

'Then we shall do it together.'

'But surely he would hear us.'

'The man is rather deaf, and in any case we must take our chance of that. We'll sit up in my room tonight and wait until he passes.' Sir Henry rubbed his hands with pleasure, and it was evident that he hailed the adventure as a relief to his somewhat quiet life upon the moor.

The baronet has been in communication with the architect who prepared the plans for Sir Charles, and with a contractor from London, so that we may expect great changes to begin here soon. There have been decorators and furnishers up from Plymouth, and it is evident that our friend has large ideas and means to spare no pains or expense to restore the grandeur of his family. When the house is renovated and refurnished, all that he will need will be a wife to make it complete. Between ourselves there are pretty clear signs that this will not be wanting if the lady is willing, for I have seldom seen a man more infatuated with a woman than he is with our beautiful neighbour, Miss Stapleton. And yet the course of true love does not run quite as smoothly as one would under the circumstances expect. Today, for example, its surface was broken by a very unexpected ripple, which has caused our friend considerable perplexity and annoyance.

After the conversation which I have quoted about Barrymore, Sir Henry put on his hat and prepared to go out. As a matter of course I did the same.

'What, are you coming, Watson?' he asked, looking at me in a curious way.

'That depends on whether you are going on the moor,' said I.

'Yes, I am.'

'Well, you know what my instructions are. I am sorry to intrude, but you heard how earnestly Holmes insisted that I should not leave you, and especially that you should not go alone upon the moor.'

Sir Henry put his hand upon my shoulder with a pleasant smile.

'My dear fellow,' said he, 'Holmes, with all his wisdom, did not foresee some things which have happened since I have been on the moor. You understand me? I am sure that you are the last man in the world who would wish to be a spoil-sport. I must go out alone.'

It put me in a most awkward position. I was at a loss what to say or what to do, and before I had made up my mind he picked up his cane and was gone.

But when I came to think the matter over my conscience reproached me bitterly for having on any pretext allowed him to go out of my sight. I imagined what my feelings would be if I had to return to you and to confess that some misfortune had occurred through my disregard for your instructions. I assure you my cheeks flushed at the very thought. It might not even now be too late to overtake him, so I set off at once in the direction of Merripit House.

I hurried along the road at the top of my speed without seeing anything of Sir Henry, until I came to the point where the moor path branches off. There, fearing that perhaps I had come in the wrong direction after all, I mounted a hill from which I could command a view – the same hill which is cut into the dark quarry. Thence I saw him at once. He was on the moor path about a quarter of a mile off, and a lady was by his side who could only be Miss Stapleton. It was clear that there was already an understanding between them and that they had met by appointment. They were walking slowly along in deep conversation, and I saw her making quick little movements of her hands as if she were very earnest in what she was saying, while he listened intently, and once or twice shook his head in strong dissent. I stood among the rocks watching them, very much puzzled as to what I should do next. To follow them and break into their intimate conversation seemed to be an outrage, and yet my clear duty was never for an instant to let him out of my sight. To act the spy upon a friend was a hateful task. Still, I could see no better course than to observe him from the hill, and to clear my conscience by confessing to him afterwards what I had done. It is true that if any sudden danger had threatened him I was too far away to be of use, and yet I am sure that you will agree with me that the position was very difficult, and that there was nothing more which I could do.

Our friend, Sir Henry, and the lady had halted on the path and were standing deeply absorbed in their conversation, when I was suddenly aware that I was not the only witness of their interview. A wisp of green floating in the air caught my eye, and another glance showed me that it was carried on a stick by a man who was moving among the broken ground. It was Stapleton with his butterfly-net. He was very much closer to the pair than I was, and he appeared to be moving in their direction. At this instant Sir Henry suddenly drew Miss Stapleton to his side. His arm was round her, but it seemed to me that she was straining away from him with her face averted. He stooped his head to hers, and she raised one hand as if in protest. Next moment I saw them spring apart and turn hurriedly round. Stapleton was the cause of the interruption. He was running wildly towards them, his absurd net dangling behind him. He gesticulated and almost danced with excitement in front of the lovers. What the scene meant I could not imagine, but it seemed to me that Stapleton was abusing Sir Henry, who offered explanations, which became more angry as the other refused to accept them. The lady stood by in haughty silence. Finally Stapleton turned upon his heel and beckoned in a peremptory way to his sister, who, after an irresolute glance at Sir Henry, walked off by the side of her brother. The naturalist's angry gestures showed that the lady was included in his displeasure. The baronet stood for a minute looking after them, and then he walked slowly back the way that he had come, his head hanging, the very picture of dejection.

What all this meant I could not imagine, but I was deeply ashamed to have witnessed so intimate a scene without my friend's knowledge. I ran down the hill therefore and met the baronet at the bottom. His face was flushed with anger and his brows were wrinkled, like one who is at his wit's ends what to do.

'Halloa, Watson! Where have you dropped from?' said he. 'You don't mean to say that you came after me in spite of all?'

I explained everything to him: how I had found it impossible to remain behind, how I had followed him, and how I had witnessed all that had occurred. For an instant his eyes blazed at me, but my frankness disarmed his anger, and he broke at last into a rather rueful laugh.

'You would have thought the middle of that prairie a fairly safe place for a man to be private,' said he, 'but, by thunder, the whole countryside seems to have been out to see me do my wooing – and a mighty poor wooing at that! Where had you engaged a seat?'

'I was on that hill.'

'Quite in the back row, eh? But her brother was well up to the front. Did you see him come out on us?'

'Yes, I did.'

'Did he ever strike you as being crazy – this brother of hers?'

'I can't say that he ever did.'

'I dare say not. I always thought him sane enough until today, but you can take it from me that either he or I ought to be in a straitjacket. What's the matter with me, anyhow? You've lived near me for some weeks, Watson. Tell me straight, now! Is there anything that would prevent me from making a good husband to a woman that I loved?'

'I should say not.'

'He can't object to my worldly position, so it must be myself that he has this down on. What has he against me? I

never hurt man or woman in my life that I know of. And yet
he would not so much as let me touch the tips of her fingers.'

'Did he say so?'

'That, and a deal more. I tell you, Watson, I've only
known her these few weeks, but from the first I just felt that
she was made for me, and she, too – she was happy when
she was with me, and that I'll swear. There's a light in a
woman's eyes that speaks louder than words. But he has
never let us get together and it was only today for the first
time that I saw a chance of having a few words with her
alone. She was glad to meet me, but when she did it was
not love that she would talk about, and she wouldn't have
let me talk about it either if she could have stopped it. She
kept coming back to it that this was a place of danger, and
that she would never be happy until I had left it. I told her
that since I had seen her I was in no hurry to leave it, and
that if she really wanted me to go, the only way to work it
was for her to arrange to go with me. With that I offered in
as many words to marry her, but before she could answer,
down came this brother of hers, running at us with a face
on him like a madman. He was just white with rage, and
those light eyes of his were blazing with fury. What was I
doing with the lady? How dared I offer her attentions which
were distasteful to her? Did I think that because I was a
baronet I could do what I liked? If he had not been her
brother I should have known better how to answer him. As
it was I told him that my feelings towards his sister were
such as I was not ashamed of, and that I hoped that she
might honour me by becoming my wife. That seemed to
make the matter no better, so then I lost my temper too, and
I answered him rather more hotly than I should perhaps,

considering that she was standing by. So it ended by his going off with her, as you saw, and here am I as badly puzzled a man as any in this county. Just tell me what it all means, Watson, and I'll owe you more than ever I can hope to pay.'

I tried one or two explanations, but, indeed, I was completely puzzled myself. Our friend's title, his fortune, his age, his character, and his appearance are all in his favour, and I know nothing against him unless it be this dark fate which runs in his family. That his advances should be rejected so brusquely without any reference to the lady's own wishes and that the lady should accept the situation without protest is very amazing. However, our conjectures were set at rest by a visit from Stapleton himself that very afternoon. He had come to offer apologies for his rudeness of the morning, and after a long private interview with Sir Henry in his study the upshot of their conversation was that the breach is quite healed, and that we are to dine at Merripit House next Friday as a sign of it.

'I don't say now that he isn't a crazy man,' said Sir Henry; 'I can't forget the look in his eyes when he ran at me this morning, but I must allow that no man could make a more handsome apology than he has done.'

'Did he give any explanation of his conduct?'

'His sister is everything in his life, he says. That is natural enough, and I am glad that he should understand her value. They have always been together, and according to his account he has been a very lonely man with only her as a companion, so that the thought of losing her was really terrible to him. He had not understood, he said, that I was becoming attached to her, but when he saw with his own eyes that it was really so, and that she might be taken away from him, it gave him such a shock that for a time he was not responsible for what he said or did. He was very sorry for all that had passed, and he recognised how foolish and how selfish it was that he should imagine that he could hold a beautiful woman like his sister to himself for her whole life. If she had to leave him he had rather it was to a neighbour like myself than to anyone else. But in any case it was a blow to him and it would take him some time before he could prepare himself to meet it. He would withdraw all opposition upon his part if I would promise for three months to let the matter rest and to be content with cultivating the lady's friendship during that time without claiming her love. This I promised, and so the matter rests.'

So there is one of our small mysteries cleared up. It is something to have touched bottom anywhere in this bog in which we are floundering. We know now why Stapleton looked with disfavour upon his sister's suitor – even when that suitor was so eligible a one as Sir Henry. And now I pass on to another thread which I have extricated out of the tangled skein, the mystery of the sobs in the night, of the tear-stained face of Mrs Barrymore, of the secret journey of the butler to the western lattice window. Congratulate me, my dear Holmes, and tell me that I have not disappointed you as an agent – that you do not regret the confidence which you showed in me when you sent me down. All these things have by one night's work been thoroughly cleared.

I have said "by one night's work," but, in truth, it was by two nights' work, for on the first we drew entirely blank. I sat up with Sir Henry in his rooms until nearly three o'clock in the morning, but no sound of any sort did we hear except the chiming clock upon the stairs. It was a most melancholy vigil and ended by each of us falling asleep in our chairs. Fortunately we were not discouraged, and we determined to try again. The next night we lowered the lamp and sat smoking cigarettes without making the least sound. It was incredible how slowly the hours crawled by, and yet we were helped through it by the same sort of patient interest which the hunter must feel as he watches the trap into which he hopes the game may wander. One struck, and two, and we had almost for the second time given it up in despair when in an instant we both sat bolt upright in our chairs with all our weary senses keenly on the alert once more. We had heard the creak of a step in the passage.

Very stealthily we heard it pass along until it died away in the distance. Then the baronet gently opened his door and we set out in pursuit. Already our man had gone round the gallery and the corridor was all in darkness. Softly we stole along until we had come into the other wing. We were just in time to catch a glimpse of the tall, black-bearded figure, his shoulders rounded as he tiptoed down the passage. Then he passed through the same door as before, and the light of the candle framed it in the darkness and shot one single yellow beam across the gloom of the corridor. We shuffled cautiously towards it, trying every plank before we dared to put our whole weight upon it. We had taken the precaution of leaving our boots behind us, but, even so, the old boards snapped and creaked beneath our tread. Sometimes it seemed impossible that he should fail to hear our approach. However, the man is fortunately rather deaf, and he was entirely preoccupied in that which he was doing. When at last we reached the door and peeped through we found him crouching at the window, candle in hand, his white, intent face pressed against the pane, exactly as I had seen him two nights before.

We had arranged no plan of campaign, but the baronet is a man to whom the most direct way is always the most natural. He walked into the room, and as he did so Barrymore sprang up from the window with a sharp hiss of his breath and stood, livid and trembling, before us. His dark eyes, glaring out of the white mask of his face, were full of horror and astonishment as he gazed from Sir Henry to me.

'What are you doing here, Barrymore?'

'Nothing, sir.' His agitation was so great that he could hardly speak, and the shadows sprang up and down from the shaking of his candle. 'It was the window, sir. I go round at night to see that they are fastened.'

'On the second floor?'

'Yes, sir, all the windows.'

'Look here, Barrymore,' said Sir Henry sternly, 'we have made up our minds to have the truth out of you, so it will save you trouble to tell it sooner rather than later. Come, now! No lies! What were you doing at that window?'

The fellow looked at us in a helpless way, and he wrung his hands together like one who is in the last extremity of doubt and misery.

'I was doing no harm, sir. I was holding a candle to the window.'

'And why were you holding a candle to the window?'

'Don't ask me, Sir Henry – don't ask me! I give you my word, sir, that it is not my secret, and that I cannot tell it. If it concerned no one but myself I would not try to keep it from you.'

A sudden idea occurred to me, and I took the candle from the trembling hand of the butler.

'He must have been holding it as a signal,' said I. 'Let us see if there is any answer.' I held it as he had done, and stared out into the darkness of the night. Vaguely I could discern the black bank of the trees and the lighter expanse of the moor, for the moon was behind the clouds. And then I gave a cry of exultation, for a tiny pinpoint of yellow light had suddenly transfixed the dark veil, and glowed steadily in the centre of the black square framed by the window.

'There it is!' I cried.

'No, no, sir, it is nothing – nothing at all!' the butler broke in; 'I assure you, sir—'

'Move your light across the window, Watson!' cried the baronet. 'See, the other moves also! Now, you rascal, do you deny that it is a signal? Come, speak up! Who is your confederate out yonder, and what is this conspiracy that is going on?'

The man's face became openly defiant. 'It is my business, and not yours. I will not tell.'

'Then you leave my employment right away.'

'Very good, sir. If I must I must.'

'And you go in disgrace. By thunder, you may well be ashamed of yourself. Your family has lived with mine for over a hundred years under this roof, and here I find you deep in some dark plot against me.'

'No, no, sir; no, not against you!' It was a woman's voice, and Mrs Barrymore, paler and more horror-struck than her husband, was standing at the door. Her bulky figure in a shawl and skirt might have been comic were it not for the intensity of feeling upon her face.

'We have to go, Eliza. This is the end of it. You can pack our things,' said the butler.

'Oh, John, John, have I brought you to this? It is my doing, Sir Henry – all mine. He has done nothing except for my sake and because I asked him.'

'Speak out, then! What does it mean?'

'My unhappy brother is starving on the moor. We cannot let him perish at our very gates. The light is a signal to him that food is ready for him, and his light out yonder is to show the spot to which to bring it.'

'Then your brother is—'

'The escaped convict, sir – Selden, the criminal.'

'That's the truth, sir,' said Barrymore. 'I said that it was not my secret and that I could not tell it to you. But now you have heard it, and you will see that if there was a plot it was not against you.'

This, then, was the explanation of the stealthy expeditions at night and the light at the window. Sir Henry and I both stared at the woman in amazement. Was it possible that this stolidly respectable person was of the same blood as one of the most notorious criminals in the country?

'Yes, sir, my name was Selden, and he is my younger brother. We humoured him too much when he was a lad and gave him his own way in everything until he came to think that the world was made for his pleasure, and that he could do what he liked in it. Then as he grew older he met wicked companions, and the devil entered into him until he broke my mother's heart and dragged our name in the dirt. From crime to crime he sank lower and lower until it is only the mercy of God which has snatched him from the scaffold; but to me, sir, he was always the little curly-headed boy that I had nursed and played with as an elder sister would. That was why he broke prison, sir. He knew that I was here and that we could not refuse to help him. When he dragged himself here one night, weary and starving, with the warders hard at his heels, what could we do? We took him in and fed him and cared for him. Then you returned, sir, and my brother thought he would be safer on the moor than anywhere else until the hue and cry was over, so he lay in hiding there. But every second night we made sure if he was still there by putting a light in the window, and if there was an answer my husband took out some bread and meat to him. Every day we hoped that he was gone, but as long as he was there we could not desert him. That is the whole truth, as I am an honest Christian woman and you will see that if there is blame in the matter it does not lie with my husband but with me, for whose sake he has done all that he has.'

The woman's words came with an intense earnestness which carried conviction with them.

'Is this true, Barrymore?'

'Yes, Sir Henry. Every word of it.'

'Well, I cannot blame you for standing by your own wife. Forget what I have said. Go to your room, you two, and we shall talk further about this matter in the morning.'

When they were gone we looked out of the window again. Sir Henry had flung it open, and the cold night wind beat in upon our faces. Far away in the black distance there still glowed that one tiny point of yellow light.

'I wonder he dares,' said Sir Henry.

'It may be so placed as to be only visible from here.'

'Very likely. How far do you think it is?'

'Out by the Cleft Tor, I think.'

'Not more than a mile or two off.'

'Hardly that.'

'Well, it cannot be far if Barrymore had to carry out the food to it. And he is waiting, this villain, beside that candle. By thunder, Watson, I am going out to take that man!'

The same thought had crossed my own mind. It was not as if the Barrymores had taken us into their confidence. Their secret had been forced from them. The man was a danger to the community, an unmitigated scoundrel for whom there was neither pity nor excuse. We were only doing our duty in taking this chance of putting him back where he could do no harm. With his brutal and violent nature, others would have to pay the price if we held our hands. Any night, for example, our neighbours the Stapletons might be attacked by him, and it may have been the thought of this which made Sir Henry so keen upon the adventure.

'I will come,' said I.

'Then get your revolver and put on your boots. The sooner we start the better, as the fellow may put out his light and be off.'

In five minutes we were outside the door, starting upon our expedition. We hurried through the dark shrubbery, amid the dull moaning of the autumn wind and the rustle of the falling leaves. The night air was heavy with the smell of damp and decay. Now and again the moon peeped out for an instant, but clouds were driving over the face of the sky, and just as we came out on the moor a thin rain began to fall. The light still burned steadily in front.

'Are you armed?' I asked.

'I have a hunting-crop.'

'We must close in on him rapidly, for he is said to be a desperate fellow. We shall take him by surprise and have him at our mercy before he can resist.'

'I say, Watson,' said the baronet, 'what would Holmes say to this? How about that hour of darkness in which the power of evil is exalted?'

As if in answer to his words there rose suddenly out of the vast gloom of the moor that strange cry which I had already heard upon the borders of the great Grimpen Mire. It came with the wind through the silence of the night, a long, deep mutter, then a rising howl, and then the sad moan in which it died away. Again and again it sounded, the whole air throbbing with it, strident, wild, and menacing. The baronet caught my sleeve and his face glimmered white through the darkness.

'My God, what's that, Watson?'

'I don't know. It's a sound they have on the moor. I heard it once before.'

It died away, and an absolute silence closed in upon us. We stood straining our ears, but nothing came.

'Watson,' said the baronet, 'it was the cry of a hound.'

My blood ran cold in my veins, for there was a break in his voice which told of the sudden horror which had seized him.

'What do they call this sound?' he asked.

'Who?'

'The folk on the countryside.'

'Oh, they are ignorant people. Why should you mind what they call it?'

'Tell me, Watson. What do they say of it?'

I hesitated but could not escape the question.

'They say it is the cry of the Hound of the Baskervilles.'

He groaned and was silent for a few moments.

'A hound it was,' he said at last, 'but it seemed to come from miles away, over yonder, I think.'

'It was hard to say whence it came.'

'It rose and fell with the wind. Isn't that the direction of the great Grimpen Mire?'

'Yes, it is.'

'Well, it was up there. Come now, Watson, didn't you think yourself that it was the cry of a hound? I am not a child. You need not fear to speak the truth.'

'Stapleton was with me when I heard it last. He said that it might be the calling of a strange bird.'

'No, no, it was a hound. My God, can there be some truth in all these stories? Is it possible that I am really in danger from so dark a cause? You don't believe it, do you, Watson?'

'No, no.'

'And yet it was one thing to laugh about it in London, and it is another to stand out here in the darkness of the moor and to hear such a cry as that. And my uncle! There was the footprint of the hound beside him as he lay. It all fits together. I don't think that I am a coward, Watson, but that sound seemed to freeze my very blood. Feel my hand!'

It was as cold as a block of marble.

'You'll be all right tomorrow.'

'I don't think I'll get that cry out of my head. What do you advise that we do now?'

'Shall we turn back?'

'No, by thunder; we have come out to get our man, and we will do it. We after the convict, and a hell-hound, as likely as not, after us. Come on! We'll see it through if all the fiends of the pit were loose upon the moor.'

We stumbled slowly along in the darkness, with the black loom of the craggy hills around us, and the yellow speck of light burning steadily in front. There is nothing so deceptive as the distance of a light upon a pitch-dark night, and sometimes the glimmer seemed to be far away upon the horizon and sometimes it might have been within a few yards of us. But at last we could see whence it came, and then we knew that we were indeed very close. A guttering candle was stuck in a crevice of the rocks which flanked it on each side so as to keep the wind from it and also to prevent it from being visible, save in the direction of Baskerville Hall. A boulder of granite concealed our approach, and crouching behind it we gazed over it at the signal light. It was strange to see this single candle burning there in the middle of the moor, with no sign of life near it – just the one straight yellow flame and the gleam of the rock on each side of it.

'What shall we do now?' whispered Sir Henry.

'Wait here. He must be near his light. Let us see if we can get a glimpse of him.'

The words were hardly out of my mouth when we both saw him. Over the rocks, in the crevice of which the candle burned, there was thrust out an evil yellow face, a terrible animal face, all seamed and scored with vile passions. Foul with mire, with a bristling beard, and hung with matted hair, it might well have belonged to one of those old savages who dwelt in the burrows on the hillsides. The light beneath him was reflected in his small, cunning eyes which peered fiercely to right and left through the darkness like a crafty and savage animal who has heard the steps of the hunters.

Something had evidently aroused his suspicions. It may have been that Barrymore had some private signal which we had neglected to give, or the fellow may have had some other reason for thinking that all was not well, but I could read his fears upon his wicked face. Any instant he might dash out the light and vanish in the darkness. I sprang forward therefore, and Sir Henry did the same. At the same moment the convict screamed out a curse at us and hurled a rock which splintered up against the boulder which had sheltered us. I caught one glimpse of his short, squat, strongly built figure as he sprang to his feet and turned to run. At the same moment by a lucky chance the moon broke through the clouds. We rushed over the brow of the hill, and there was our man running with great speed down the other side, springing over the stones in his way with the activity of a mountain goat. A lucky long shot of my revolver might have crippled him, but I had brought it only to defend myself if attacked and not to shoot an unarmed man who was running away.

We were both swift runners and in fairly good training, but we soon found that we had no chance of overtaking him. We saw him for a long time in the moonlight until he was only a small speck moving swiftly among the boulders upon the side of a distant hill. We ran and ran until we were completely blown, but the space between us grew ever wider. Finally we stopped and sat panting on two rocks, while we watched him disappearing in the distance.

And it was at this moment that there occurred a most strange and unexpected thing. We had risen from our rocks and were turning to go home, having abandoned the hopeless chase. The moon was low upon the right, and the jagged pinnacle of a granite tor stood up against the lower curve of its silver disc. There, outlined as black as an ebony statue on that shining background, I saw the figure of a man upon the tor. Do not think that it was a delusion, Holmes. I assure you that I have never in my life seen anything more clearly. As far as I could judge, the figure was that of a tall, thin man. He stood with his legs a little separated, his arms folded, his head bowed, as if he were brooding over that enormous wilderness of peat and granite which lay before him. He might have been the very spirit of that terrible place. It was not the convict. This man was far from the place where the latter had disappeared. Besides, he was a much taller man. With a cry of surprise I pointed him out to the baronet, but in the instant during which I had turned to grasp his arm the man was gone. There was the sharp pinnacle of granite still cutting the lower edge of the moon, but its peak bore no trace of that silent and motionless figure. I wished to go in that direction and to search the tor, but it was some distance away. The baronet's nerves were still quivering from that cry, which recalled the dark story of his family, and he was not in the mood for fresh adventures. He had not seen this lonely man upon the tor and could not feel the thrill which his strange presence and his commanding attitude had given to me. 'A warder, no doubt,' said he. 'The moor has been thick with them since this fellow escaped.' Well, perhaps his explanation may be the right one, but I should like to have some further proof of it. Today we mean to communicate to the Princetown people where they should look for their missing man, but it is hard lines that we have not actually had the triumph of bringing him back as our own prisoner. Such are the adventures of last night, and you must acknowledge, my dear Holmes, that I have done you very well in the matter of a report. Much of what I tell you is no doubt quite irrelevant, but still I feel that it is best that I should let you have all the facts and leave you to select for yourself those which will be of most service to you in helping you to your conclusions. We are certainly making some progress. So far as the Barrymores go we have found the motive of their actions, and that has cleared up the situation very much. But the moor with its mysteries and its strange inhabitants remains as inscrutable as ever. Perhaps in my next I may be able to throw some light upon this also. Best of all would it be if you could come down to us. In any case you will hear from me again in the course of the next few days.

CHAPTER 10

EXTRACT FROM THE DIARY OF DR WATSON

So far I have been able to quote from the reports which I have forwarded during these early days to Sherlock Holmes. Now, however, I have arrived at a point in my narrative where I am compelled to abandon this method and to trust once more to my recollections, aided by the diary which I kept at the time. A few extracts from the latter will carry me on to those scenes which are indelibly fixed in every detail upon my memory. I proceed, then, from the morning which followed our abortive chase of the convict and our other strange experiences upon the moor.

October 16th. A dull and foggy day with a drizzle of rain. The house is banked in with rolling clouds, which rise now and then to show the dreary curves of the moor, with thin, silver veins upon the sides of the hills, and the distant boulders gleaming where the light strikes upon their wet faces. It is melancholy outside and in. The baronet is in a black reaction after the excitements of the night. I am conscious myself of a weight at my heart and a feeling of impending danger – ever present danger, which is the more terrible because I am unable to define it.

And have I not cause for such a feeling? Consider the long sequence of incidents which have all pointed to some sinister influence which is at work around us. There is the death of the last occupant of the Hall, fulfilling so exactly the conditions of the family legend, and there are the repeated reports from peasants of the appearance of a strange creature upon the moor. Twice I have with my own ears heard the sound which resembled the distant baying of a hound. It is incredible, impossible, that it should really be outside the ordinary laws of nature. A spectral hound which leaves material footmarks and fills the air with its howling is surely not to be thought of. Stapleton may fall in with such a superstition, and Mortimer also, but if I have one quality upon earth it is common sense, and nothing will persuade me to believe in such a thing. To do so would be to descend to the level of these poor peasants, who are not content with a mere fiend dog but must needs describe him with hell-fire shooting from his mouth and eyes. Holmes would not listen to such fancies, and I am his agent. But facts are facts, and I have twice heard this crying upon the moor. Suppose that there were really some huge hound loose upon it; that would go far to explain everything. But where could such a hound lie concealed, where did it get its food, where did it come from, how was it that no one saw it by day? It must be confessed that the natural explanation offers almost as many difficulties as the other. And always, apart from the hound, there is the fact of the human agency in London, the man in the cab, and the letter which warned Sir Henry against the moor. This at least was real, but it might have been the work of a protecting friend as easily as of an enemy. Where is that friend or enemy now? Has he remained in London, or has he followed us down here? Could he – could he be the stranger whom I saw upon the tor?

It is true that I have had only the one glance at him, and yet there are some things to which I am ready to swear. He is no one whom I have seen down here, and I have now met all the neighbours. The figure was far taller than that of Stapleton, far thinner than that of Frankland. Barrymore it might possibly have been, but we had left him behind us, and I am certain that he could not have followed us. A stranger then is still dogging us, just as a stranger dogged us in London. We have never shaken him off. If I could lay my hands upon that man, then at last we might find ourselves at the end of all our difficulties. To this one purpose I must now devote all my energies.

My first impulse was to tell Sir Henry all my plans. My second and wisest one is to play my own game and speak as little as possible to anyone. He is silent and distrait. His nerves have been strangely shaken by that sound upon the moor. I will say nothing to add to his anxieties, but I will take my own steps to attain my own end.

We had a small scene this morning after breakfast. Barrymore asked leave to speak with Sir Henry, and they were closeted in his study some little time. Sitting in the billiard-room I more than once heard the sound of voices raised, and I had a pretty good idea what the point was which was under discussion. After a time the baronet opened his door and called for me. 'Barrymore considers that he has a grievance,' he said. 'He thinks that it was unfair on our part to hunt his brother-in-law down when he, of his own free will, had told us the secret.'

The butler was standing very pale but very collected before us.

'I may have spoken too warmly, sir,' said he, 'and if I have, I am sure that I beg your pardon. At the same time, I was very much surprised when I heard you two gentlemen come back this morning and learned that you had been chasing Selden. The poor fellow has enough to fight against without my putting more upon his track.'

'If you had told us of your own free will it would have been a different thing,' said the baronet, 'you only told us, or rather your wife only told us, when it was forced from you and you could not help yourself.'

'I didn't think you would have taken advantage of it, Sir Henry – indeed I didn't.'

'The man is a public danger. There are lonely houses scattered over the moor, and he is a fellow who would stick at nothing. You only want to get a glimpse of his face to see that. Look at Mr Stapleton's house, for example, with no one but himself to defend it. There's no safety for anyone until he is under lock and key.'

'He'll break into no house, sir. I give you my solemn word upon that. But he will never trouble anyone in this country again. I assure you, Sir Henry, that in a very few days the necessary arrangements will have been made and he will be on his way to South America. For God's sake, sir, I beg of you not to let the police know that he is still on the moor. They have given up the chase there, and he can lie quiet until the ship is ready for him. You can't tell on him without getting my wife and me into trouble. I beg you, sir, to say nothing to the police.'

'What do you say, Watson?'

I shrugged my shoulders. 'If he were safely out of the country it would relieve the tax-payer of a burden.'

'But how about the chance of his holding someone up before he goes?'

'He would not do anything so mad, sir. We have provided him with all that he can want. To commit a crime would be to show where he was hiding.'

'That is true,' said Sir Henry. 'Well, Barrymore—'

'God bless you, sir, and thank you from my heart! It would have killed my poor wife had he been taken again.'

'I guess we are aiding and abetting a felony, Watson? But, after what we have heard I don't feel as if I could give the man up, so there is an end of it. All right, Barrymore, you can go.'

With a few broken words of gratitude the man turned, but he hesitated and then came back.

'You've been so kind to us, sir, that I should like to do the best I can for you in return. I know something, Sir Henry, and perhaps I should have said it before, but it was long after the inquest that I found it out. I've never breathed a word about it yet to mortal man. It's about poor Sir Charles's death.'

The baronet and I were both upon our feet. 'Do you know how he died?'

'No, sir, I don't know that.'

'What then?'

'I know why he was at the gate at that hour. It was to meet a woman.'

'To meet a woman! He?'

'Yes, sir.'

'And the woman's name?'

'I can't give you the name, sir, but I can give you the initials. Her initials were L. L.'

'How do you know this, Barrymore?'

'Well, Sir Henry, your uncle had a letter that morning. He had usually a great many letters, for he was a public man and well known for his kind heart, so that everyone who was in trouble was glad to turn to him. But that morning, as it chanced, there was only this one letter, so I took the more notice of it. It was from Coombe Tracey, and it was addressed in a woman's hand.'

'Well?'

'Well, sir, I thought no more of the matter, and never would have done had it not been for my wife. Only a few weeks ago she was cleaning out Sir Charles's study – it had never been touched since his death – and she found the ashes of a burned letter in the back of the grate. The greater part of it was charred to pieces, but one little slip, the end of a page, hung together, and the writing could still be read, though it was grey on a black ground. It seemed to us to be a postscript at the end of the letter and it said: "Please, please, as you are a gentleman, burn this letter, and be at the gate by ten o clock." Beneath it were signed the initials "L. L."

'Have you got that slip?'

'No, sir, it crumbled all to bits after we moved it.'

'Had Sir Charles received any other letters in the same writing?'

'Well, sir, I took no particular notice of his letters. I should not have noticed this one, only it happened to come alone.'

'And you have no idea who L. L. is?'

'No, sir. No more than you have. But I expect if we could lay our hands upon that lady we should know more about Sir Charles's death.'

'I cannot understand, Barrymore, how you came to conceal this important information.'

'Well, sir, it was immediately after that our own trouble came to us. And then again, sir, we were both of us very fond of Sir Charles, as we well might be considering all that he has done for us. To rake this up couldn't help our poor master, and it's well to go carefully when there's a lady in the case. Even the best of us—'

'You thought it might injure his reputation?'

'Well, sir, I thought no good could come of it. But now you have been kind to us, and I feel as if it would be treating you unfairly not to tell you all that I know about the matter.'

'Very good, Barrymore; you can go.' When the butler had left us Sir Henry turned to me. 'Well, Watson, what do you think of this new light?'

'It seems to leave the darkness rather blacker than before.'

'So I think. But if we can only trace L. L. it should clear up the whole business. We have gained that much. We know that there is someone who has the facts if we can only find her. What do you think we should do?'

'Let Holmes know all about it at once. It will give him the clue for which he has been seeking. I am much mistaken if it does not bring him down.'

I went at once to my room and drew up my report of the morning's conversation for Holmes. It was evident to me that he had been very busy of late, for the notes which I had from Baker Street were few and short, with no comments upon the information which I had supplied and hardly any reference to my mission. No doubt his black-mailing case is absorbing all his faculties. And yet this new factor must surely arrest his attention and renew his interest. I wish that he were here.

October 17th. All day today the rain poured down, rustling on the ivy and dripping from the eaves. I thought of the convict out upon the bleak, cold, shelterless moor. Poor devil! Whatever his crimes, he has suffered something to atone for them. And then I thought of that other one – the face in the cab, the figure against the moon. Was he also out in that deluge – the unseen watcher, the man of darkness? In the evening I put on my waterproof and I walked far upon the sodden moor, full of dark imaginings, the rain beating upon my face and the wind whistling about my ears. God help those who wander into the great mire now, for even the firm uplands are becoming a morass. I found the black tor upon which I had seen the solitary watcher, and from its craggy summit I looked out myself across the melancholy downs. Rain squalls drifted across their russet face, and the heavy, slate-coloured clouds hung low over the landscape, trailing in grey wreaths down the sides of the fantastic hills. In the distant hollow on the left, half hidden by the mist, the two thin towers of Baskerville Hall rose above the trees. They were the only signs of human life which I could see, save only those prehistoric huts which lay thickly upon the slopes of the hills. Nowhere was there any trace of that lonely man whom I had seen on the same spot two nights before.

As I walked back I was overtaken by Dr Mortimer driving in his dog-cart over a rough moorland track which led from the outlying farmhouse of Foulmire. He has been very attentive to us, and hardly a day has passed that he has not called at the Hall to see how we were getting on. He insisted upon my climbing into his dog-cart, and he gave me a lift homeward. I found him much troubled over the disappearance of his little spaniel. It had wandered on to the moor and had never come back. I gave him such consolation as I might, but I thought of the pony on the Grimpen Mire, and I do not fancy that he will see his little dog again.

'By the way, Mortimer,' said I as we jolted along the rough road, 'I suppose there are few people living within driving distance of this whom you do not know?'

'Hardly any, I think.'

'Can you, then, tell me the name of any woman whose initials are L. L.?'

He thought for a few minutes.

'No,' said he. 'There are a few gipsies and labouring folk for whom I can't answer, but among the farmers or gentry there is no one whose initials are those. Wait a bit though,' he added after a pause. 'There is Laura Lyons – her initials are L. L. – but she lives in Coombe Tracey.'

'Who is she?' I asked.

'She is Frankland's daughter.'

'What! Old Frankland the crank?'

'Exactly. She married an artist named Lyons, who came sketching on the moor. He proved to be a blackguard and deserted her. The fault from what I hear may not have been entirely on one side. Her father refused to have anything to do with her because she had married without his consent and perhaps for one or two other reasons as well. So, between the old sinner and the young one, the girl has had a pretty bad time.'

'How does she live?'

'I fancy old Frankland allows her a pittance, but it cannot be more, for his own affairs are considerably involved. Whatever she may have deserved, one could not allow her to go hopelessly to the bad. Her story got about, and several of the people here did something to enable her to earn an honest living. Stapleton did for one, and Sir Charles for another. I gave a trifle myself. It was to set her up in a type-writing business.'

He wanted to know the object of my inquiries, but I managed to satisfy his curiosity without telling him too much, for there is no reason why we should take anyone into our confidence. Tomorrow morning I shall find my way to Coombe Tracey, and if I can see this Mrs Laura Lyons, of equivocal reputation, a long step will have been made towards clearing one incident in this chain of mysteries. I am certainly developing the wisdom of the serpent, for when Mortimer pressed his questions to an inconvenient extent I asked him casually to what type Frankland's skull belonged, and so heard nothing but craniology for the rest of our drive. I have not lived for years with Sherlock Holmes for nothing.

I have only one other incident to record upon this tempestuous and melancholy day. This was my conversation with Barrymore just now, which gives me one more strong card which I can play in due time.

Mortimer had stayed to dinner, and he and the baronet played ecarte afterwards. The butler brought me my coffee into the library, and I took the chance to ask him a few questions.

'Well,' said I, 'has this precious relation of yours departed, or is he still lurking out yonder?'

'I don't know, sir. I hope to heaven that he has gone, for he has brought nothing but trouble here! I've not heard of him since I left out food for him last, and that was three days ago.'

'Did you see him then?'

'No, sir, but the food was gone when next I went that way.'

'Then he was certainly there?'

'So you would think, sir, unless it was the other man who took it.'

I sat with my coffee-cup halfway to my lips and stared at Barrymore.

'You know that there is another man then?'

'Yes, sir; there is another man upon the moor.'

'Have you seen him?'

'No, sir.'

'How do you know of him then?'

'Selden told me of him, sir, a week ago or more. He's in hiding, too, but he's not a convict as far as I can make out. I don't like it, Dr Watson – I tell you straight, sir, that I don't like it.' He spoke with a sudden passion of earnestness.

'Now, listen to me, Barrymore! I have no interest in this matter but that of your master. I have come here with no object except to help him. Tell me, frankly, what it is that you don't like.'

Barrymore hesitated for a moment, as if he regretted his outburst or found it difficult to express his own feelings in words.

'It's all these goings-on, sir,' he cried at last, waving his hand towards the rain-lashed window which faced the moor. 'There's foul play somewhere, and there's black villainy brewing, to that I'll swear! Very glad I should be, sir, to see Sir Henry on his way back to London again!'

'But what is it that alarms you?'

'Look at Sir Charles's death! That was bad enough, for all that the coroner said. Look at the noises on the moor at night. There's not a man would cross it after sundown if he was paid for it. Look at this stranger hiding out yonder, and watching and waiting! What's he waiting for? What does it mean? It means no good to anyone of the name of Baskerville, and very glad I shall be to be quit of it all on the day that Sir Henry's new servants are ready to take over the Hall.'

'But about this stranger,' said I. 'Can you tell me anything about him? What did Selden say? Did he find out where he hid, or what he was doing?'

'He saw him once or twice, but he is a deep one and gives nothing away. At first he thought that he was the police, but soon he found that he had some lay of his own. A kind of gentleman he was, as far as he could see, but what he was doing he could not make out.'

'And where did he say that he lived?'

'Among the old houses on the hillside – the stone huts where the old folk used to live.'

'But how about his food?'

'Selden found out that he has got a lad who works for

him and brings all he needs. I dare say he goes to Coombe
Tracey for what he wants.'

'Very good, Barrymore. We may talk further of this some
other time.' When the butler had gone I walked over to the
black window, and I looked through a blurred pane at the
driving clouds and at the tossing outline of the wind-swept
trees. It is a wild night indoors, and what must it be in a
stone hut upon the moor. What passion of hatred can it be
which leads a man to lurk in such a place at such a time!
And what deep and earnest purpose can he have which calls
for such a trial! There, in that hut upon the moor, seems to
lie the very centre of that problem which has vexed me so
sorely. I swear that another day shall not have passed before
I have done all that man can do to reach the heart of the
mystery.

CHAPTER 11

THE MAN ON THE TOR

The extract from my private diary which forms the last
chapter has brought my narrative up to the eighteenth of
October, a time when these strange events began to move
swiftly towards their terrible conclusion. The incidents of
the next few days are indelibly graven upon my recollection,
and I can tell them without reference to the notes made at
the time. I start them from the day which succeeded that
upon which I had established two facts of great importance,
the one that Mrs Laura Lyons of Coombe Tracey had written
to Sir Charles Baskerville and made an appointment with
him at the very place and hour that he met his death, the

other that the lurking man upon the moor was to be found among the stone huts upon the hillside. With these two facts in my possession I felt that either my intelligence or my courage must be deficient if I could not throw some further light upon these dark places.

I had no opportunity to tell the baronet what I had learned about Mrs Lyons upon the evening before, for Dr Mortimer remained with him at cards until it was very late. At breakfast, however, I informed him about my discovery and asked him whether he would care to accompany me to Coombe Tracey. At first he was very eager to come, but on second thoughts it seemed to both of us that if I went alone the results might be better. The more formal we made the visit the less information we might obtain. I left Sir Henry behind, therefore, not without some prickings of conscience, and drove off upon my new quest.

When I reached Coombe Tracey I told Perkins to put up the horses, and I made inquiries for the lady whom I had come to interrogate. I had no difficulty in finding her rooms, which were central and well appointed. A maid showed me in without ceremony, and as I entered the sitting-room a lady, who was sitting before a Remington typewriter, sprang up with a pleasant smile of welcome. Her face fell, however, when she saw that I was a stranger, and she sat down again and asked me the object of my visit.

The first impression left by Mrs Lyons was one of extreme beauty. Her eyes and hair were of the same rich hazel colour, and her cheeks, though considerably freckled, were flushed with the exquisite bloom of the brunette, the dainty pink which lurks at the heart of the sulphur rose. Admiration was,

I repeat, the first impression. But the second was criticism. There was something subtly wrong with the face, some coarseness of expression, some hardness, perhaps, of eye, some looseness of lip which marred its perfect beauty. But these, of course, are afterthoughts. At the moment I was simply conscious that I was in the presence of a very hand-some woman, and that she was asking me the reasons for my visit. I had not quite understood until that instant how delicate my mission was.

'I have the pleasure,' said I, 'of knowing your father.'

It was a clumsy introduction, and the lady made me feel it. 'There is nothing in common between my father and me,' she said. 'I owe him nothing, and his friends are not mine. If it were not for the late Sir Charles Baskerville and some other kind hearts I might have starved for all that my father cared.'

'It was about the late Sir Charles Baskerville that I have come here to see you.'

The freckles started out on the lady's face.

'What can I tell you about him?' she asked, and her fingers played nervously over the stops of her typewriter.

'You knew him, did you not?'

'I have already said that I owe a great deal to his kind-ness. If I am able to support myself it is largely due to the interest which he took in my unhappy situation.'

'Did you correspond with him?'

The lady looked quickly up with an angry gleam in her hazel eyes.

'What is the object of these questions?' she asked sharply.

'The object is to avoid a public scandal. It is better that I should ask them here than that the matter should pass outside our control.'

She was silent and her face was still very pale. At last she looked up with something reckless and defiant in her manner.

'Well, I'll answer,' she said. 'What are your questions?'

'Did you correspond with Sir Charles?'

'I certainly wrote to him once or twice to acknowledge his delicacy and his generosity.'

'Have you the dates of those letters?'

'No.'

'Have you ever met him?'

'Yes, once or twice, when he came into Coombe Tracey. He was a very retiring man, and he preferred to do good by stealth.'

'But if you saw him so seldom and wrote so seldom, how did he know enough about your affairs to be able to help you, as you say that he has done?'

She met my difficulty with the utmost readiness.

'There were several gentlemen who knew my sad history and united to help me. One was Mr Stapleton, a neighbour and intimate friend of Sir Charles's. He was exceedingly kind, and it was through him that Sir Charles learned about my affairs.'

I knew already that Sir Charles Baskerville had made Stapleton his almoner upon several occasions, so the lady's statement bore the impress of truth upon it.

'Did you ever write to Sir Charles asking him to meet you?' I continued.

Mrs Lyons flushed with anger again. 'Really, sir, this is a very extraordinary question.'

'I am sorry, madam, but I must repeat it.'

'Then I answer, certainly not.'

'Not on the very day of Sir Charles's death?'

The flush had faded in an instant, and a deathly face was before me. Her dry lips could not speak the 'No' which I saw rather than heard.

'Surely your memory deceives you,' said I. 'I could even quote a passage of your letter. It ran "Please, please, as you are a gentleman, burn this letter, and be at the gate by ten o'clock."

I thought that she had fainted, but she recovered herself by a supreme effort.

'Is there no such thing as a gentleman?' she gasped.

'You do Sir Charles an injustice. He did burn the letter. But sometimes a letter may be legible even when burned. You acknowledge now that you wrote it?'

'Yes, I did write it,' she cried, pouring out her soul in a torrent of words. 'I did write it. Why should I deny it? I have no reason to be ashamed of it. I wished him to help me. I believed that if I had an interview I could gain his help, so I asked him to meet me.'

'But why at such an hour?'

'Because I had only just learned that he was going to London next day and might be away for months. There were reasons why I could not get there earlier.'

'But why a rendezvous in the garden instead of a visit to the house?'

'Do you think a woman could go alone at that hour to a bachelor's house?'

'Well, what happened when you did get there?'

'I never went.'

'Mrs Lyons!'

'No, I swear it to you on all I hold sacred. I never went. Something intervened to prevent my going.'

'What was that?'

'That is a private matter. I cannot tell it.'

'You acknowledge then that you made an appointment with Sir Charles at the very hour and place at which he met his death, but you deny that you kept the appointment.'

'That is the truth.'

Again and again I cross-questioned her, but I could never get past that point.

'Mrs Lyons,' said I as I rose from this long and inconclusive interview, 'you are taking a very great responsibility and putting yourself in a very false position by not making an absolutely clean breast of all that you know. If I have to call in the aid of the police you will find how seriously you are compromised. If your position is innocent, why did you in the first instance deny having written to Sir Charles upon that date?'

'Because I feared that some false conclusion might be drawn from it and that I might find myself involved in a scandal.'

'And why were you so pressing that Sir Charles should destroy your letter?'

'If you have read the letter you will know.'

'I did not say that I had read all the letter.'

'You quoted some of it.'

'I quoted the postscript. The letter had, as I said, been burned and it was not all legible. I ask you once again why it was that you were so pressing that Sir Charles should destroy this letter which he received on the day of his death.'

'The matter is a very private one.'

'The more reason why you should avoid a public investigation.'

'I will tell you, then. If you have heard anything of my

unhappy history you will know that I made a rash marriage and had reason to regret it.'

'I have heard so much.'

'My life has been one incessant persecution from a husband whom I abhor. The law is upon his side, and every day I am faced by the possibility that he may force me to live with him. At the time that I wrote this letter to Sir Charles I had learned that there was a prospect of my regaining my freedom if certain expenses could be met. It meant everything to me – peace of mind, happiness, self-respect – everything. I knew Sir Charles's generosity, and I thought that if he heard the story from my own lips he would help me.'

'Then how is it that you did not go?'

'Because I received help in the interval from another source.'

'Why then, did you not write to Sir Charles and explain this?'

'So I should have done had I not seen his death in the paper next morning.'

The woman's story hung coherently together, and all my questions were unable to shake it. I could only check it by finding if she had, indeed, instituted divorce proceedings against her husband at or about the time of the tragedy.

It was unlikely that she would dare to say that she had not been to Baskerville Hall if she really had been, for a trap would be necessary to take her there, and could not have returned to Coombe Tracey until the early hours of the morning. Such an excursion could not be kept secret. The probability was, therefore, that she was telling the truth, or, at least, a part of the truth. I came away baffled and disheartened. Once again I had reached that dead wall which seemed to be built across every path by which I tried to get at the object of my mission. And yet the more I thought of the lady's face and of her manner the more I felt that something was being held back from me. Why should she turn so pale? Why should she fight against every admission until it was forced from her? Why should she have been so reticent at the time of the tragedy? Surely the explanation of all this could not be as innocent as she would have me believe. For the moment I could proceed no farther in that direction, but must turn back to that other clue which was to be sought for among the stone huts upon the moor.

And that was a most vague direction. I realised it as I drove back and noted how hill after hill showed traces of the ancient people. Barrymore's only indication had been that the stranger lived in one of these abandoned huts, and many hundreds of them are scattered throughout the length and breadth of the moor. But I had my own experience for a guide since it had shown me the man himself standing upon the summit of the Black Tor. That, then, should be the centre of my search. From there I should explore every hut upon the moor until I lighted upon the right one. If this man were inside it I should find out from his own lips, at the point of my revolver if necessary, who he was and why he had dogged us so long. He might slip away from us in the crowd of Regent Street, but it would puzzle him to do so upon the lonely moor. On the other hand, if I should find the hut and its tenant should not be within it I must remain there, however long the vigil, until he returned. Holmes had missed him in London. It would indeed be a triumph for me if I could run him to earth where my master had failed.

Luck had been against us again and again in this inquiry, but now at last it came to my aid. And the messenger of good fortune was none other than Mr Frankland, who was standing, grey-whiskered and red-faced, outside the gate of his garden, which opened on to the highroad along which I travelled.

'Good-day, Dr Watson,' cried he with unwonted good humour, 'you must really give your horses a rest and come in to have a glass of wine and to congratulate me.'

My feelings towards him were very far from being friendly after what I had heard of his treatment of his daughter, but I was anxious to send Perkins and the wagonette home, and the opportunity was a good one. I alighted and sent a message to Sir Henry that I should walk over in time for dinner. Then I followed Frankland into his dining-room.

'It is a great day for me, sir – one of the red-letter days of my life,' he cried with many chuckles. 'I have brought off a double event. I mean to teach them in these parts that law is law, and that there is a man here who does not fear to invoke it. I have established a right of way through the centre of old Middleton's park, slap across it, sir, within a hundred yards of his own front door. What do you think of that? We'll teach these magnates that they cannot ride rough-shod over the rights of the commoners, confound them! And I've closed the wood where the Fernworthy folk used to picnic. These infernal people seem to think that there are no rights of property, and that they can swarm where they like with their papers and their bottles. Both cases decided, Dr Watson, and both in my favour. I haven't had such a day since I had Sir John Morland for trespass because he shot in his own warren.'

'How on earth did you do that?'

'Look it up in the books, sir. It will repay reading – Frankland v. Morland, Court of Queen's Bench. It cost me 200 pounds, but I got my verdict.'

'Did it do you any good?'

'None, sir, none. I am proud to say that I had no interest in the matter. I act entirely from a sense of public duty. I have no doubt, for example, that the Fernworthy people will burn me in effigy tonight. I told the police last time they did it that they should stop these disgraceful exhibitions. The County Constabulary is in a scandalous state, sir, and it has not afforded me the protection to which I am entitled. The case of Frankland v. Regina will bring the matter before the attention of the public. I told them that they would have occasion to regret their treatment of me, and already my words have come true.'

'How so?' I asked.

The old man put on a very knowing expression. 'Because I could tell them what they are dying to know; but nothing would induce me to help the rascals in any way.'

I had been casting round for some excuse by which I could get away from his gossip, but now I began to wish to hear more of it. I had seen enough of the contrary nature of the old sinner to understand that any strong sign of interest would be the surest way to stop his confidences.

'Some poaching case, no doubt?' said I with an indifferent manner.

'Ha, ha, my boy, a very much more important matter than that! What about the convict on the moor?'

I stared. 'You don't mean that you know where he is?' said I.

'I may not know exactly where he is, but I am quite sure

that I could help the police to lay their hands on him. Has it never struck you that the way to catch that man was to find out where he got his food and so trace it to him?'

He certainly seemed to be getting uncomfortably near the truth. 'No doubt,' said I; 'but how do you know that he is anywhere upon the moor?'

'I know it because I have seen with my own eyes the messenger who takes him his food.'

My heart sank for Barrymore. It was a serious thing to be in the power of this spiteful old busybody. But his next remark took a weight from my mind.

'You'll be surprised to hear that his food is taken to him by a child. I see him every day through my telescope upon the roof. He passes along the same path at the same hour, and to whom should he be going except to the convict?'

Here was luck indeed! And yet I suppressed all appearance of interest. A child! Barrymore had said that our unknown was supplied by a boy. It was on his track, and not upon the convict's, that Frankland had stumbled. If I could get his knowledge it might save me a long and weary hunt. But incredulity and indifference were evidently my strongest cards.

'I should say that it was much more likely that it was the son of one of the moorland shepherds taking out his father's dinner.'

The least appearance of opposition struck fire out of the old autocrat. His eyes looked malignantly at me, and his grey whiskers bristled like those of an angry cat.

'Indeed, sir!' said he, pointing out over the wide-stretching moor. 'Do you see that Black Tor over yonder? Well, do you see the low hill beyond with the thornbush upon it? It is the stoniest part of the whole moor. Is that a place where a shepherd would be likely to take his station? Your suggestion, sir, is a most absurd one.'

I meekly answered that I had spoken without knowing all the facts. My submission pleased him and led him to further confidences.

'You may be sure, sir, that I have very good grounds before I come to an opinion. I have seen the boy again and again with his bundle. Every day, and sometimes twice a day, I have been able – but wait a moment, Dr Watson. Do my eyes deceive me, or is there at the present moment something moving upon that hillside?'

It was several miles off, but I could distinctly see a small dark dot against the dull green and grey.

'Come, sir, come!' cried Frankland, rushing upstairs. 'You will see with your own eyes and judge for yourself.'

The telescope, a formidable instrument mounted upon a tripod, stood upon the flat leads of the house. Frankland clapped his eye to it and gave a cry of satisfaction.

'Quick, Dr Watson, quick, before he passes over the hill!'

There he was, sure enough, a small urchin with a little bundle upon his shoulder, toiling slowly up the hill. When he reached the crest I saw the ragged uncouth figure outlined for an instant against the cold blue sky. He looked round him with a furtive and stealthy air, as one who dreads pursuit. Then he vanished over the hill.

'Well! Am I right?'

'Certainly, there is a boy who seems to have some secret errand.'

'And what the errand is even a county constable could guess. But not one word shall they have from me, and I bind you to secrecy also, Dr Watson. Not a word! You understand!'

'Just as you wish.'

'They have treated me shamefully – shamefully. When the facts come out in Frankland v. Regina I venture to think that a thrill of indignation will run through the country. Nothing would induce me to help the police in any way. For all they cared it might have been me, instead of my effigy, which these rascals burned at the stake. Surely you are not going! You will help me to empty the decanter in honour of this great occasion!'

But I resisted all his solicitations and succeeded in dissuading him from his announced intention of walking home with me. I kept the road as long as his eye was on me, and then I struck off across the moor and made for the stony hill over which the boy had disappeared. Everything was working in my favour, and I swore that it should not be through lack of energy or perseverance that I should miss the chance which fortune had thrown in my way.

The sun was already sinking when I reached the summit of the hill, and the long slopes beneath me were all golden-green on one side and grey shadow on the other. A haze lay low upon the farthest sky-line, out of which jutted the fantastic shapes of Belliver and Vixen Tor. Over the wide expanse there was no sound and no movement. One great grey bird, a gull or curlew, soared aloft in the blue heaven. He and I seemed to be the only living things between the huge arch of the sky and the desert beneath it. The barren scene, the sense of loneliness, and the mystery and urgency of my task all struck a chill into my heart. The boy was nowhere to be seen. But down beneath me in a cleft of the hills there was a circle of the old stone huts, and in the middle of them there was one which retained sufficient roof to act as a screen against the weather. My heart leaped within me as I saw it. This must be the burrow where the stranger lurked. At last my foot was on the threshold of his hiding place – his secret was within my grasp.

As I approached the hut, walking as warily as Stapleton would do when with poised net he drew near the settled butterfly, I satisfied myself that the place had indeed been used as a habitation. A vague pathway among the boulders led to the dilapidated opening which served as a door. All was silent within. The unknown might be lurking there, or he might be prowling on the moor. My nerves tingled with the sense of adventure. Throwing aside my cigarette, I closed my hand upon the butt of my revolver and, walking swiftly up to the door, I looked in. The place was empty.

But there were ample signs that I had not come upon a false scent. This was certainly where the man lived. Some blankets rolled in a waterproof lay upon that very stone slab upon which Neolithic man had once slumbered. The ashes of a fire were heaped in a rude grate. Beside it lay some cooking utensils and a bucket half-full of water. A litter of empty tins showed that the place had been occupied for some time, and I saw, as my eyes became accustomed to the checkered light, a pannikin and a half-full bottle of spirits standing in the corner. In the middle of the hut a flat stone served the purpose of a table, and upon this stood a small cloth bundle – the same, no doubt, which I had seen through the telescope upon the shoulder of the boy. It contained a loaf of bread, a tinned tongue, and two tins of preserved peaches. As I set it down again, after having examined it, my heart leaped to see that beneath it there lay a sheet of paper with writing upon it. I raised it, and this was what I read, roughly scrawled in pencil: 'Dr Watson has gone to Coombe Tracey.'

For a minute I stood there with the paper in my hands thinking out the meaning of this curt message. It was I, then, and not Sir Henry, who was being dogged by this secret man. He had not followed me himself, but he had set an agent – the boy, perhaps – upon my track, and this was his report. Possibly I had taken no step since I had been upon the moor which had not been observed and reported. Always there was this feeling of an unseen force, a fine net drawn round us with infinite skill and delicacy, holding us so lightly that it was only at some supreme moment that one realised that one was indeed entangled in its meshes.

If there was one report there might be others, so I looked round the hut in search of them. There was no trace, however, of anything of the kind, nor could I discover any sign which might indicate the character or intentions of the man who lived in this singular place, save that he must be of Spartan habits and cared little for the comforts of life. When I thought of the heavy rains and looked at the gaping roof I understood how strong and immutable must be the purpose which had kept him in that inhospitable abode. Was he our malignant enemy, or was he by chance our guardian angel? I swore that I would not leave the hut until I knew.

Outside the sun was sinking low and the west was blazing with scarlet and gold. Its reflection was shot back in ruddy patches by the distant pools which lay amid the great Grimpen Mire. There were the two towers of Baskerville Hall, and there a distant blur of smoke which marked the village of Grimpen. Between the two, behind the hill, was the house of the Stapletons. All was sweet and mellow and peaceful in the golden evening light, and yet as I looked at them my soul shared none of the peace of Nature but quivered at the vagueness and the terror of that interview which every instant was bringing nearer. With tingling nerves but a fixed purpose, I sat in the dark recess of the hut and waited with sombre patience for the coming of its tenant.

And then at last I heard him. Far away came the sharp clink of a boot striking upon a stone. Then another and yet another, coming nearer and nearer. I shrank back into the darkest corner and cocked the pistol in my pocket, determined not to discover myself until I had an opportunity of seeing something of the stranger. There was a long pause which showed that he had stopped. Then once more the footsteps approached and a shadow fell across the opening of the hut.

'It is a lovely evening, my dear Watson,' said a well-known voice. 'I really think that you will be more comfortable outside than in.'

CHAPTER 12

DEATH ON THE MOOR

For a moment or two I sat breathless, hardly able to believe my ears. Then my senses and my voice came back to me, while a crushing weight of responsibility seemed in an instant to be lifted from my soul. That cold, incisive, ironical voice could belong to but one man in all the world.

'Holmes!' I cried—'Holmes!'

'Come out,' said he, 'and please be careful with the revolver.'

I stooped under the rude lintel, and there he sat upon a stone outside, his grey eyes dancing with amusement as they fell upon my astonished features. He was thin and worn, but clear and alert, his keen face bronzed by the sun and roughened by the wind. In his tweed suit and cloth cap he looked like any other tourist upon the moor, and he had contrived, with that catlike love of personal cleanliness which was one of his characteristics, that his chin should be as smooth and his linen as perfect as if he were in Baker Street.

'I never was more glad to see anyone in my life,' said I as I wrung him by the hand.

'Or more astonished, eh?'

'Well, I must confess to it.'

'The surprise was not all on one side, I assure you. I had no idea that you had found my occasional retreat, still less that you were inside it, until I was within twenty paces of the door.'

'My footprint, I presume?'

'No, Watson, I fear that I could not undertake to recognise your footprint amid all the footprints of the world. If you seriously desire to deceive me you must change your tobacconist; for when I see the stub of a cigarette marked Bradley, Oxford Street, I know that my friend Watson is in the neighbourhood. You will see it there beside the path. You threw it down, no doubt, at that supreme moment when you charged into the empty hut.'

'Exactly.'

'I thought as much – and knowing your admirable tenacity I was convinced that you were sitting in ambush, a weapon within reach, waiting for the tenant to return. So you actually thought that I was the criminal?'

'I did not know who you were, but I was determined to find out.'

'Excellent, Watson! And how did you localise me? You saw me, perhaps, on the night of the convict hunt, when I was so imprudent as to allow the moon to rise behind me?'

'Yes, I saw you then.'

'And have no doubt searched all the huts until you came to this one?'

'No, your boy had been observed, and that gave me a guide where to look.'

'The old gentleman with the telescope, no doubt. I could not make it out when first I saw the light flashing upon the lens.' He rose and peeped into the hut. 'Ha, I see that Cartwright has brought up some supplies. What's this paper? So you have been to Coombe Tracey, have you?'

'Yes.'

'To see Mrs Laura Lyons?'

'Exactly.'

'Well done! Our researches have evidently been running on parallel lines, and when we unite our results I expect we shall have a fairly full knowledge of the case.'

'Well, I am glad from my heart that you are here, for indeed the responsibility and the mystery were both becoming too much for my nerves. But how in the name of wonder did you come here, and what have you been doing? I thought that you were in Baker Street working out that case of black-mailing.'

'That was what I wished you to think.'

'Then you use me, and yet do not trust me!' I cried with some bitterness. 'I think that I have deserved better at your hands, Holmes.'

'My dear fellow, you have been invaluable to me in this as in many other cases, and I beg that you will forgive me if I have seemed to play a trick upon you. In truth, it was partly for your own sake that I did it, and it was my appreciation of the danger which you ran which led me to come down and examine the matter for myself. Had I been with Sir Henry and you it is confident that my point of view would have been the same as yours, and my presence would have warned our very formidable opponents to be on their guard. As it is, I have been able to get about as I could not possibly have done had I been living in the Hall, and I remain an unknown factor in the business, ready to throw in all my weight at a critical moment.'

'But why keep me in the dark?'

'For you to know could not have helped us and might possibly have led to my discovery. You would have wished to tell me something, or in your kindness you would have brought me out some comfort or other, and so an unnecessary risk would be run. I brought Cartwright down with me – you remember the little chap at the express office – and he has seen after my simple wants: a loaf of bread and a clean collar. What does man want more? He has given me an extra pair of eyes upon a very active pair of feet, and both have been invaluable.'

'Then my reports have all been wasted!' – My voice trembled as I recalled the pains and the pride with which I had composed them.

Holmes took a bundle of papers from his pocket.

'Here are your reports, my dear fellow, and very well thumbed, I assure you. I made excellent arrangements, and they are only delayed one day upon their way. I must compliment you exceedingly upon the zeal and the intelligence which you have shown over an extraordinarily difficult case.'

I was still rather raw over the deception which had been practised upon me, but the warmth of Holmes's praise drove my anger from my mind. I felt also in my heart that he was right in what he said and that it was really best for our purpose that I should not have known that he was upon the moor.

'That's better,' said he, seeing the shadow rise from my face. 'And now tell me the result of your visit to Mrs Laura Lyons – it was not difficult for me to guess that it was to see her that you had gone, for I am already aware that she is the one person in Coombe Tracey who might be of service to us in the matter. In fact, if you had not gone today it is exceedingly probable that I should have gone tomorrow.'

The sun had set and dusk was settling over the moor. The air had turned chill and we withdrew into the hut for warmth. There, sitting together in the twilight, I told Holmes of my conversation with the lady. So interested was he that I had to repeat some of it twice before he was satisfied.

'This is most important,' said he when I had concluded. 'It fills up a gap which I had been unable to bridge in this most complex affair. You are aware, perhaps, that a close intimacy exists between this lady and the man Stapleton?'

'I did not know of a close intimacy.'

'There can be no doubt about the matter. They meet, they write, there is a complete understanding between them. Now, this puts a very powerful weapon into our hands. If I could only use it to detach his wife—'

'His wife?'

'I am giving you some information now, in return for all

that you have given me. The lady who has passed here as Miss Stapleton is in reality his wife.'

'Good heavens, Holmes! Are you sure of what you say? How could he have permitted Sir Henry to fall in love with her?'

'Sir Henry's falling in love could do no harm to anyone except Sir Henry. He took particular care that Sir Henry did not make love to her, as you have yourself observed. I repeat that the lady is his wife and not his sister.'

'But why this elaborate deception?'

'Because he foresaw that she would be very much more useful to him in the character of a free woman.'

All my unspoken instincts, my vague suspicions, suddenly took shape and centred upon the naturalist. In that impassive colourless man, with his straw hat and his butterfly-net, I seemed to see something terrible – a creature of infinite patience and craft, with a smiling face and a murderous heart.

'It is he, then, who is our enemy – it is he who dogged us in London?'

'So I read the riddle.'

'And the warning – it must have come from her!'

'Exactly.'

The shape of some monstrous villainy, half seen, half guessed, loomed through the darkness which had girt me so long.

'But are you sure of this, Holmes? How do you know that the woman is his wife?'

'Because he so far forgot himself as to tell you a true piece of autobiography upon the occasion when he first met you, and I dare say he has many a time regretted it since. He was once a schoolmaster in the north of England.

Now, there is no one more easy to trace than a schoolmaster. There are scholastic agencies by which one may identify any man who has been in the profession. A little investigation showed me that a school had come to grief under atrocious circumstances, and that the man who had owned it – the name was different – had disappeared with his wife. The descriptions agreed. When I learned that the missing man was devoted to entomology the identification was complete.'

The darkness was rising, but much was still hidden by the shadows.

'If this woman is in truth his wife, where does Mrs Laura Lyons come in?' I asked.

'That is one of the points upon which your own researches have shed a light. Your interview with the lady has cleared the situation very much. I did not know about a projected divorce between herself and her husband. In that case, regarding Stapleton as an unmarried man, she counted no doubt upon becoming his wife.'

'And when she is undeceived?'

'Why, then we may find the lady of service. It must be our first duty to see her – both of us – tomorrow. Don't you think, Watson, that you are away from your charge rather long? Your place should be at Baskerville Hall.'

The last red streaks had faded away in the west and night had settled upon the moor. A few faint stars were gleaming in a violet sky.

'One last question, Holmes,' I said as I rose. 'Surely there is no need of secrecy between you and me. What is the meaning of it all? What is he after?'

Holmes's voice sank as he answered:

'It is murder, Watson – refined, cold-blooded, deliberate murder. Do not ask me for particulars. My nets are closing upon him, even as his are upon Sir Henry, and with your help he is already almost at my mercy. There is but one danger which can threaten us. It is that he should strike before we are ready to do so. Another day – two at the most – and I have my case complete, but until then guard your charge as closely as ever a fond mother watched her ailing child. Your mission today has justified itself, and yet I could almost wish that you had not left his side. Hark!'

A terrible scream – a prolonged yell of horror and anguish – burst out of the silence of the moor. That frightful cry turned the blood to ice in my veins.

'Oh, my God!' I gasped. 'What is it? What does it mean?'

Holmes had sprung to his feet, and I saw his dark, athletic outline at the door of the hut, his shoulders stooping, his head thrust forward, his face peering into the darkness.

'Hush!' he whispered. 'Hush!'

The cry had been loud on account of its vehemence, but it had pealed out from somewhere far off on the shadowy plain. Now it burst upon our ears, nearer, louder, more urgent than before.

'Where is it?' Holmes whispered; and I knew from the thrill of his voice that he, the man of iron, was shaken to the soul. 'Where is it, Watson?'

'There, I think.' I pointed into the darkness.

'No, there!'

Again the agonised cry swept through the silent night, louder and much nearer than ever. And a new sound mingled with it, a deep, muttered rumble, musical and yet menacing, rising and falling like the low, constant murmur of the sea.

'The hound!' cried Holmes. 'Come, Watson, come! Great heavens, if we are too late!'

He had started running swiftly over the moor, and I had followed at his heels. But now from somewhere among the broken ground immediately in front of us there came one last despairing yell, and then a dull, heavy thud. We halted and listened. Not another sound broke the heavy silence of the windless night.

I saw Holmes put his hand to his forehead like a man distracted. He stamped his feet upon the ground.

'He has beaten us, Watson. We are too late.'

'No, no, surely not!'

'Fool that I was to hold my hand. And you, Watson, see what comes of abandoning your charge! But, by Heaven, if the worst has happened we'll avenge him!'

Blindly we ran through the gloom, blundering against boulders, forcing our way through gorse bushes, panting up hills and rushing down slopes, heading always in the direction whence those dreadful sounds had come. At every rise Holmes looked eagerly round him, but the shadows were thick upon the moor, and nothing moved upon its dreary face.

'Can you see anything?'

'Nothing.'

'But, hark, what is that?'

A low moan had fallen upon our ears. There it was again upon our left! On that side a ridge of rocks ended in a sheer cliff which overlooked a stone-strewn slope. On its jagged face was spread-eagled some dark, irregular object. As we ran towards it the vague outline hardened into a definite shape. It was a prostrate man face downward upon the ground, the head doubled under him at a horrible angle, the shoulders rounded and the body hunched together as if in the act of throwing a somersault. So grotesque was the attitude that I could not for the instant realize that that moan had been the passing of his soul. Not a whisper, not a rustle, rose now from the dark figure over which we stooped. Holmes laid his hand upon him and held it up again with an exclamation of horror. The gleam of the match which he struck shone upon his clotted fingers and upon the ghastly pool which widened slowly from the crushed skull of the victim. And it shone upon something else which turned our hearts sick and faint within us – the body of Sir Henry Baskerville!

There was no chance of either of us forgetting that peculiar ruddy tweed suit – the very one which he had worn on the first morning that we had seen him in Baker Street. We caught the one clear glimpse of it, and then the match flickered and went out, even as the hope had gone out of our souls. Holmes groaned, and his face glimmered white through the darkness.

'The brute! The brute!' I cried with clenched hands. 'Oh Holmes, I shall never forgive myself for having left him to his fate.'

'I am more to blame than you, Watson. In order to have my case well rounded and complete, I have thrown away the life of my client. It is the greatest blow which has befallen me in my career. But how could I know – how could I know – that he would risk his life alone upon the moor in the face of all my warnings?'

'That we should have heard his screams – my God, those screams! – and yet have been unable to save him! Where is this brute of a hound which drove him to his death? It may be lurking among these rocks at this instant. And Stapleton, where is he? He shall answer for this deed.'

'He shall. I will see to that. Uncle and nephew have been murdered – the one frightened to death by the very sight of a beast which he thought to be supernatural, the other driven to his end in his wild flight to escape from it. But now we have to prove the connection between the man and the beast. Save from what we heard, we cannot even swear to the existence of the latter, since Sir Henry has evidently died from the fall. But, by heavens, cunning as he is, the fellow shall be in my power before another day is past!'

We stood with bitter hearts on either side of the mangled body, overwhelmed by this sudden and irrevocable disaster which had brought all our long and weary labours to so piteous an end. Then as the moon rose we climbed to the top of the rocks over which our poor friend had fallen, and from the summit we gazed out over the shadowy moor, half silver and half gloom. Far away, miles off, in the direction of Grimpen, a single steady yellow light was shining. It could only come from the lonely abode of the Stapletons. With a bitter curse I shook my fist at it as I gazed.

'Why should we not seize him at once?'

'Our case is not complete. The fellow is wary and cunning to the last degree. It is not what we know, but what we can prove. If we make one false move the villain may escape us yet.'

'What can we do?'

'There will be plenty for us to do tomorrow. Tonight we can only perform the last offices to our poor friend.'

Together we made our way down the precipitous slope and approached the body, black and clear against the silvered stones. The agony of those contorted limbs struck me with a spasm of pain and blurred my eyes with tears.

'We must send for help, Holmes! We cannot carry him all the way to the Hall. Good heavens, are you mad?'

He had uttered a cry and bent over the body. Now he was dancing and laughing and wringing my hand. Could this be my stern, self-contained friend? These were hidden fires, indeed!

'A beard! A beard! The man has a beard!'

'A beard?'

'It is not the baronet – it is – why, it is my neighbour, the convict!'

With feverish haste we had turned the body over, and that dripping beard was pointing up to the cold, clear moon. There could be no doubt about the beetling forehead, the sunken animal eyes. It was indeed the same face which had glared upon me in the light of the candle from over the rock – the face of Selden, the criminal.

Then in an instant it was all clear to me. I remembered how the baronet had told me that he had handed his old wardrobe to Barrymore. Barrymore had passed it on in order to help Selden in his escape. Boots, shirt, cap – it was all Sir Henry's. The tragedy was still black enough, but this man had at least deserved death by the laws of his country. I told Holmes how the matter stood, my heart bubbling over with thankfulness and joy.

'Then the clothes have been the poor devil's death,' said he. 'It is clear enough that the hound has been laid on from some article of Sir Henry's – the boot which was abstracted in the hotel, in all probability – and so ran this man down. There is one very singular thing, however: How came

Selden, in the darkness, to know that the hound was on his trail?'

'He heard him.'

'To hear a hound upon the moor would not work a hard man like this convict into such a paroxysm of terror that he would risk recapture by screaming wildly for help. By his cries he must have run a long way after he knew the animal was on his track. How did he know?'

'A greater mystery to me is why this hound, presuming that all our conjectures are correct—'

'I presume nothing.'

'Well, then, why this hound should be loose tonight. I suppose that it does not always run loose upon the moor. Stapleton would not let it go unless he had reason to think that Sir Henry would be there.'

'My difficulty is the more formidable of the two, for I think that we shall very shortly get an explanation of yours, while mine may remain forever a mystery. The question now is, what shall we do with this poor wretch's body? We cannot leave it here to the foxes and the ravens.'

'I suggest that we put it in one of the huts until we can communicate with the police.'

'Exactly. I have no doubt that you and I could carry it so far. Halloa, Watson, what's this? It's the man himself, by all that's wonderful and audacious! Not a word to show your suspicions – not a word, or my plans crumble to the ground.'

A figure was approaching us over the moor, and I saw the dull red glow of a cigar. The moon shone upon him, and I could distinguish the dapper shape and jaunty walk of the naturalist. He stopped when he saw us, and then came on again.

'Why, Dr Watson, that's not you, is it? You are the last man that I should have expected to see out on the moor at this time of night. But, dear me, what's this? Somebody hurt? Not – don't tell me that it is our friend Sir Henry!' He hurried past me and stooped over the dead man. I heard a sharp intake of his breath and the cigar fell from his fingers.

'Who – who's this?' he stammered.

'It is Selden, the man who escaped from Princetown.'

Stapleton turned a ghastly face upon us, but by a supreme effort he had overcome his amazement and his disappointment. He looked sharply from Holmes to me. 'Dear me! What a very shocking affair! How did he die?'

'He appears to have broken his neck by falling over these rocks. My friend and I were strolling on the moor when we heard a cry.'

'I heard a cry also. That was what brought me out. I was uneasy about Sir Henry.'

'Why about Sir Henry in particular?' I could not help asking.

'Because I had suggested that he should come over. When he did not come I was surprised, and I naturally became alarmed for his safety when I heard cries upon the moor. By the way' – his eyes darted again from my face to Holmes's—'did you hear anything else besides a cry?'

'No,' said Holmes; 'did you?'

'No.'

'What do you mean, then?'

'Oh, you know the stories that the peasants tell about a phantom hound, and so on. It is said to be heard at night upon the moor. I was wondering if there were any evidence of such a sound tonight.'

'We heard nothing of the kind,' said I.

'And what is your theory of this poor fellow's death?'

'I have no doubt that anxiety and exposure have driven him off his head. He has rushed about the moor in a crazy state and eventually fallen over here and broken his neck.'

'That seems the most reasonable theory,' said Stapleton, and he gave a sigh which I took to indicate his relief. 'What do you think about it, Mr Sherlock Holmes?'

My friend bowed his compliments. 'You are quick at identification,' said he.

'We have been expecting you in these parts since Dr Watson came down. You are in time to see a tragedy.'

'Yes, indeed. I have no doubt that my friend's explanation will cover the facts. I will take an unpleasant remembrance back to London with me tomorrow.'

'Oh, you return tomorrow?'

'That is my intention.'

'I hope your visit has cast some light upon those occurrences which have puzzled us?'

Holmes shrugged his shoulders.

'One cannot always have the success for which one hopes. An investigator needs facts and not legends or rumours. It has not been a satisfactory case.'

My friend spoke in his frankest and most unconcerned manner. Stapleton still looked hard at him. Then he turned to me.

'I would suggest carrying this poor fellow to my house, but it would give my sister such a fright that I do not feel justified in doing it. I think that if we put something over his face he will be safe until morning.'

And so it was arranged. Resisting Stapleton's offer of hospitality, Holmes and I set off to Baskerville Hall, leaving the naturalist to return alone. Looking back we saw the figure moving slowly away over the broad moor, and behind him that one black smudge on the silvered slope which showed where the man was lying who had come so horribly to his end.

CHAPTER 13

FIXING THE NETS

'We're at close grips at last,' said Holmes as we walked together across the moor. 'What a nerve the fellow has! How he pulled himself together in the face of what must have been a paralysing shock when he found that the wrong man had fallen a victim to his plot. I told you in London, Watson, and I tell you now again, that we have never had a foeman more worthy of our steel.'

'I am sorry that he has seen you.'

'And so was I at first. But there was no getting out of it.'

'What effect do you think it will have upon his plans now that he knows you are here?'

'It may cause him to be more cautious, or it may drive him to desperate measures at once. Like most clever criminals, he may be too confident in his own cleverness and imagine that he has completely deceived us.'

'Why should we not arrest him at once?'

'My dear Watson, you were born to be a man of action. Your instinct is always to do something energetic. But supposing, for argument's sake, that we had him arrested tonight, what on earth the better off should we be for that? We could prove nothing against him. There's the devilish cunning of it! If he were acting through a human agent we could get some evidence, but if we were to drag this great dog to the light of day it would not help us in putting a rope round the neck of its master.'

'Surely we have a case.'

'Not a shadow of one – only surmise and conjecture. We should be laughed out of court if we came with such a story and such evidence.'

'There is Sir Charles's death.'

'Found dead without a mark upon him. You and I know that he died of sheer fright, and we know also what frightened him, but how are we to get twelve stolid jurymen to know it? What signs are there of a hound? Where are the marks of its fangs? Of course we know that a hound does not bite a dead body and that Sir Charles was dead before ever the brute overtook him. But we have to prove all this, and we are not in a position to do it.'

'Well, then, tonight?'

'We are not much better off tonight. Again, there was no direct connection between the hound and the man's death. We never saw the hound. We heard it, but we could not prove that it was running upon this man's trail. There is a complete absence of motive. No, my dear fellow; we must reconcile ourselves to the fact that we have no case at present, and that it is worth our while to run any risk in order to establish one.'

'And how do you propose to do so?'

'I have great hopes of what Mrs Laura Lyons may do for us when the position of affairs is made clear to her. And I have my own plan as well. Sufficient for tomorrow is the evil thereof; but I hope before the day is past to have the upper hand at last.'

I could draw nothing further from him, and he walked, lost in thought, as far as the Baskerville gates.

'Are you coming up?'

'Yes; I see no reason for further concealment. But one last word, Watson. Say nothing of the hound to Sir Henry. Let him think that Selden's death was as Stapleton would have us believe. He will have a better nerve for the ordeal which he will have to undergo tomorrow, when he is engaged, if I remember your report aright, to dine with these people.'

'And so am I.'

'Then you must excuse yourself and he must go alone. That will be easily arranged. And now, if we are too late for dinner, I think that we are both ready for our suppers.'

Sir Henry was more pleased than surprised to see Sherlock Holmes, for he had for some days been expecting that recent events would bring him down from London. He did raise his eyebrows, however, when he found that my friend had neither any luggage nor any explanations for its absence. Between us we soon supplied his wants, and then over a belated supper we explained to the baronet as much of our experience as it seemed desirable that he should know. But first I had the unpleasant duty of breaking the news to Barrymore and his wife. To him it may have been an unmitigated relief, but she wept bitterly in her apron. To all the world he was the man of violence, half animal and half demon; but to her he always remained the little wilful boy of her own girlhood, the child who had clung to her hand. Evil indeed is the man who has not one woman to mourn him.

'I've been moping in the house all day since Watson went off in the morning,' said the baronet. 'I guess I should have some credit, for I have kept my promise. If I hadn't sworn not to go about alone I might have had a more lively evening, for I had a message from Stapleton asking me over there.'

'I have no doubt that you would have had a more lively evening,' said Holmes drily. 'By the way, I don't suppose you appreciate that we have been mourning over you as having broken your neck?'

Sir Henry opened his eyes. 'How was that?'

'This poor wretch was dressed in your clothes. I fear your servant who gave them to him may get into trouble with the police.'

'That is unlikely. There was no mark on any of them, as far as I know.'

'That's lucky for him – in fact, it's lucky for all of you, since you are all on the wrong side of the law in this matter. I am not sure that as a conscientious detective my first duty is not to arrest the whole household. Watson's reports are most incriminating documents.'

'But how about the case?' asked the baronet. 'Have you made anything out of the tangle? I don't know that Watson and I are much the wiser since we came down.'

'I think that I shall be in a position to make the situation rather more clear to you before long. It has been an exceedingly difficult and most complicated business. There are several points upon which we still want light – but it is coming all the same.'

'We've had one experience, as Watson has no doubt told you. We heard the hound on the moor, so I can swear that it is not all empty superstition. I had something to do with dogs when I was out West, and I know one when I hear one. If you can muzzle that one and put him on a chain I'll be ready to swear you are the greatest detective of all time.'

'I think I will muzzle him and chain him all right if you will give me your help.'

'Whatever you tell me to do I will do.'

'Very good; and I will ask you also to do it blindly, without always asking the reason.'

'Just as you like.'

'If you will do this I think the chances are that our little problem will soon be solved. I have no doubt—'

He stopped suddenly and stared fixedly up over my head into the air. The lamp beat upon his face, and so intent was it and so still that it might have been that of a clear-cut classical statue, a personification of alertness and expectation.

'What is it?' we both cried.

I could see as he looked down that he was repressing some internal emotion. His features were still composed, but his eyes shone with amused exultation.

'Excuse the admiration of a connoisseur,' said he as he waved his hand towards the line of portraits which covered the opposite wall. 'Watson won't allow that I know anything of art but that is mere jealousy because our views upon the subject differ. Now, these are a really very fine series of portraits.'

'Well, I'm glad to hear you say so,' said Sir Henry, glancing with some surprise at my friend. 'I don't pretend to know much about these things, and I'd be a better judge of a horse or a steer than of a picture. I didn't know that you found time for such things.'

'I know what is good when I see it, and I see it now. That's a Kneller, I'll swear, that lady in the blue silk over yonder, and the stout gentleman with the wig ought to be a Reynolds. They are all family portraits, I presume?'

'Every one.'

'Do you know the names?'

'Barrymore has been coaching me in them, and I think I can say my lessons fairly well.'

'Who is the gentleman with the telescope?'

'That is Rear-Admiral Baskerville, who served under Rodney in the West Indies. The man with the blue coat and the roll of paper is Sir William Baskerville, who was Chairman of Committees of the House of Commons under Pitt.'

'And this Cavalier opposite to me – the one with the black velvet and the lace?'

'Ah, you have a right to know about him. That is the cause of all the mischief, the wicked Hugo, who started the Hound of the Baskervilles. We're not likely to forget him.'

I gazed with interest and some surprise upon the portrait.

'Dear me!' said Holmes, 'he seems a quiet, meek-mannered man enough, but I dare say that there was a lurking devil in his eyes. I had pictured him as a more robust and ruffianly person.'

'There's no doubt about the authenticity, for the name and the date, 1647, are on the back of the canvas.'

Holmes said little more, but the picture of the old roysterer seemed to have a fascination for him, and his eyes were continually fixed upon it during supper. It was not until later, when Sir Henry had gone to his room, that I was able to follow the trend of his thoughts. He led me back into the banqueting-hall, his bedroom candle in his hand, and he held it up against the time-stained portrait on the wall.

'Do you see anything there?'

I looked at the broad plumed hat, the curling love-locks, the white lace collar, and the straight, severe face which was framed between them. It was not a brutal countenance, but it was prim, hard, and stern, with a firm-set, thin-lipped mouth, and a coldly intolerant eye.

'Is it like anyone you know?'

'There is something of Sir Henry about the jaw.'

'Just a suggestion, perhaps. But wait an instant!' He stood upon a chair, and, holding up the light in his left hand, he curved his right arm over the broad hat and round the long ringlets.

'Good heavens!' I cried in amazement.

The face of Stapleton had sprung out of the canvas.

'Ha, you see it now. My eyes have been trained to examine faces and not their trimmings. It is the first quality of a criminal investigator that he should see through a disguise.'

'But this is marvellous. It might be his portrait.'

'Yes, it is an interesting instance of a throwback, which appears to be both physical and spiritual. A study of family portraits is enough to convert a man to the doctrine of rein-carnation. The fellow is a Baskerville – that is evident.'

'With designs upon the succession.'

'Exactly. This chance of the picture has supplied us with

one of our most obvious missing links. We have him, Watson, we have him, and I dare swear that before tomorrow night he will be fluttering in our net as helpless as one of his own butterflies. A pin, a cork, and a card, and we add him to the Baker Street collection!' He burst into one of his rare fits of laughter as he turned away from the picture. I have not heard him laugh often, and it has always boded ill to somebody.

I was up betimes in the morning, but Holmes was afoot earlier still, for I saw him as I dressed, coming up the drive.

'Yes, we should have a full day today,' he remarked, and he rubbed his hands with the joy of action. 'The nets are all in place, and the drag is about to begin. We'll know before the day is out whether we have caught our big, lean-jawed pike, or whether he has got through the meshes.'

'Have you been on the moor already?'

'I have sent a report from Grimpen to Princetown as to the death of Selden. I think I can promise that none of you will be troubled in the matter. And I have also communicated with my faithful Cartwright, who would certainly have pined away at the door of my hut, as a dog does at his master's grave, if I had not set his mind at rest about my safety.'

'What is the next move?'

'To see Sir Henry. Ah, here he is!'

'Good-morning, Holmes,' said the baronet. 'You look like a general who is planning a battle with his chief of the staff.'

'That is the exact situation. Watson was asking for orders.'

'And so do I.'

'Very good. You are engaged, as I understand, to dine with our friends the Stapletons tonight.'

'I hope that you will come also. They are very hospitable people, and I am sure that they would be very glad to see you.'

'I fear that Watson and I must go to London.'

'To London?'

'Yes, I think that we should be more useful there at the present juncture.'

The baronet's face perceptibly lengthened.

'I hoped that you were going to see me through this business. The Hall and the moor are not very pleasant places when one is alone.'

'My dear fellow, you must trust me implicitly and do exactly what I tell you. You can tell your friends that we should have been happy to have come with you, but that urgent business required us to be in town. We hope very soon to return to Devonshire. Will you remember to give them that message?'

'If you insist upon it.'

'There is no alternative, I assure you.'

I saw by the baronet's clouded brow that he was deeply hurt by what he regarded as our desertion.

'When do you desire to go?' he asked coldly.

'Immediately after breakfast. We will drive in to Coombe Tracey, but Watson will leave his things as a pledge that he will come back to you. Watson, you will send a note to Stapleton to tell him that you regret that you cannot come.'

'I have a good mind to go to London with you,' said the baronet. 'Why should I stay here alone?'

'Because it is your post of duty. Because you gave me your word that you would do as you were told, and I tell you to stay.'

'All right, then, I'll stay.'

'One more direction! I wish you to drive to Merripit House. Send back your trap, however, and let them know that you intend to walk home.'

'To walk across the moor?'

'Yes.'

'But that is the very thing which you have so often cautioned me not to do.'

'This time you may do it with safety. If I had not every confidence in your nerve and courage I would not suggest it, but it is essential that you should do it.'

'Then I will do it.'

'And as you value your life do not go across the moor in any direction save along the straight path which leads from Merripit House to the Grimpen Road, and is your natural way home.'

'I will do just what you say.'

'Very good. I should be glad to get away as soon after breakfast as possible, so as to reach London in the afternoon.'

I was much astounded by this programme, though I remembered that Holmes had said to Stapleton on the night before that his visit would terminate next day. It had not crossed my mind however, that he would wish me to go with him, nor could I understand how we could both be absent at a moment which he himself declared to be critical. There was nothing for it, however, but implicit obedience; so we bade good-bye to our rueful friend, and a couple of hours afterwards we were at the station of Coombe Tracey and had dispatched the trap upon its return journey. A small boy was waiting upon the platform.

'Any orders, sir?'

'You will take this train to town, Cartwright. The moment you arrive you will send a wire to Sir Henry Baskerville, in my name, to say that if he finds the pocketbook which I have dropped he is to send it by registered post to Baker Street.'

'Yes, sir.'

'And ask at the station office if there is a message for me.'

The boy returned with a telegram, which Holmes handed to me. It ran:

"Wire received. Coming down with unsigned warrant. Arrive five-forty. Lestrade."

'That is in answer to mine of this morning. He is the best of the professionals, I think, and we may need his assistance. Now, Watson, I think that we cannot employ our time better than by calling upon your acquaintance, Mrs Laura Lyons.'

His plan of campaign was beginning to be evident. He would use the baronet in order to convince the Stapletons that we were really gone, while we should actually return at the instant when we were likely to be needed. That telegram from London, if mentioned by Sir Henry to the Stapletons, must remove the last suspicions from their minds. Already I seemed to see our nets drawing closer around that lean-jawed pike.

Mrs Laura Lyons was in her office, and Sherlock Holmes opened his interview with a frankness and directness which considerably amazed her.

'I am investigating the circumstances which attended the death of the late Sir Charles Baskerville,' said he. 'My friend here, Dr Watson, has informed me of what you have communicated, and also of what you have withheld in connection with that matter.'

'What have I withheld?' she asked defiantly.

'You have confessed that you asked Sir Charles to be at the gate at ten o'clock. We know that that was the place and hour of his death. You have withheld what the connection is between these events.'

'There is no connection.'

'In that case the coincidence must indeed be an extraordinary one. But I think that we shall succeed in establishing a connection, after all. I wish to be perfectly frank with you, Mrs Lyons. We regard this case as one of murder, and the evidence may implicate not only your friend Mr Stapleton but his wife as well.'

The lady sprang from her chair.

'His wife!' she cried.

'The fact is no longer a secret. The person who has passed for his sister is really his wife.'

Mrs Lyons had resumed her seat. Her hands were grasping the arms of her chair, and I saw that the pink nails had turned white with the pressure of her grip.

'His wife!' she said again. 'His wife! He is not a married man.'

Sherlock Holmes shrugged his shoulders.

'Prove it to me! Prove it to me! And if you can do so – !'

The fierce flash of her eyes said more than any words.

'I have come prepared to do so,' said Holmes, drawing several papers from his pocket. 'Here is a photograph of the couple taken in York four years ago. It is indorsed "Mr and Mrs Vandeleur," but you will have no difficulty in recognising him, and her also, if you know her by sight. Here are three written descriptions by trustworthy witnesses of Mr and Mrs

Vandeleur, who at that time kept St Oliver's private school. Read them and see if you can doubt the identity of these people.'

She glanced at them, and then looked up at us with the set, rigid face of a desperate woman.

'Mr Holmes,' she said, 'this man had offered me marriage on condition that I could get a divorce from my husband. He has lied to me, the villain, in every conceivable way. Not one word of truth has he ever told me. And why – why? I imagined that all was for my own sake. But now I see that I was never anything but a tool in his hands. Why should I preserve faith with him who never kept any with me? Why should I try to shield him from the consequences of his own wicked acts? Ask me what you like, and there is nothing which I shall hold back. One thing I swear to you, and that is that when I wrote the letter I never dreamed of any harm to the old gentleman, who had been my kindest friend.'

'I entirely believe you, madam,' said Sherlock Holmes. 'The recital of these events must be very painful to you, and perhaps it will make it easier if I tell you what occurred, and you can check me if I make any material mistake. The sending of this letter was suggested to you by Stapleton?'

'He dictated it.'

'I presume that the reason he gave was that you would receive help from Sir Charles for the legal expenses connected with your divorce?'

'Exactly.'

'And then after you had sent the letter he dissuaded you from keeping the appointment?'

'He told me that it would hurt his self-respect that any other man should find the money for such an object, and that though he was a poor man himself he would devote his last penny to removing the obstacles which divided us.'

'He appears to be a very consistent character. And then you heard nothing until you read the reports of the death in the paper?'

'No.'

'And he made you swear to say nothing about your appointment with Sir Charles?'

'He did. He said that the death was a very mysterious one, and that I should certainly be suspected if the facts came out. He frightened me into remaining silent.'

'Quite so. But you had your suspicions?'

She hesitated and looked down.

'I knew him,' she said. 'But if he had kept faith with me I should always have done so with him.'

'I think that on the whole you have had a fortunate escape,' said Sherlock Holmes. 'You have had him in your power and he knew it, and yet you are alive. You have been walking for some months very near to the edge of a precipice. We must wish you good-morning now, Mrs Lyons, and it is probable that you will very shortly hear from us again.'

'Our case becomes rounded off, and difficulty after difficulty thins away in front of us,' said Holmes as we stood waiting for the arrival of the express from town. 'I shall soon be in the position of being able to put into a single connected narrative one of the most singular and sensational crimes of modern times. Students of criminology will remember the analogous incidents in Godno, in Little Russia, in the year '66, and of course there are the Anderson murders in North Carolina, but this case possesses some features which are entirely its own. Even now we have no clear case against this very wily man. But I shall be very much surprised if it is not clear enough before we go to bed this night.'

The London express came roaring into the station, and a small, wiry bulldog of a man had sprung from a first-class carriage. We all three shook hands, and I saw at once from the reverential way in which Lestrade gazed at my companion that he had learned a good deal since the days when they had first worked together. I could well remember the scorn which the theories of the reasoner used then to excite in the practical man.

'Anything good?' he asked.

'The biggest thing for years,' said Holmes. 'We have two hours before we need think of starting. I think we might employ it in getting some dinner and then, Lestrade, we will take the London fog out of your throat by giving you a breath of the pure night air of Dartmoor. Never been there? Ah, well, I don't suppose you will forget your first visit.'

CHAPTER 14

THE HOUND OF THE BASKERVILLES

One of Sherlock Holmes's defects – if, indeed, one may call it a defect – was that he was exceedingly loath to communicate his full plans to any other person until the instant of their fulfilment. Partly it came no doubt from his own masterful nature, which loved to dominate and surprise those who were around him. Partly also from his professional caution, which urged him never to take any chances. The result, however, was very trying for those who were acting as his agents and assistants. I had often suffered under it, but never more so than during that long drive in the darkness. The great ordeal was in front of us; at last we were about to make our final effort, and yet Holmes had said nothing, and I could only surmise what his course of action would be. My nerves thrilled with anticipation when at last the cold wind upon our faces and the dark, void spaces on either side of the narrow road told me that we were back upon the moor once again. Every stride of the horses and every turn of the wheels was taking us nearer to our supreme adventure.

Our conversation was hampered by the presence of the driver of the hired wagonette, so that we were forced to talk of trivial matters when our nerves were tense with emotion and anticipation. It was a relief to me, after that unnatural restraint, when we at last passed Frankland's house and knew that we were drawing near to the Hall and to the scene of action. We did not drive up to the door but got down near the gate of the avenue. The wagonette was paid off and ordered to return to Coombe Tracey forthwith, while we started to walk to Merripit House.

'Are you armed, Lestrade?'

The little detective smiled. 'As long as I have my trousers I have a hip-pocket, and as long as I have my hip-pocket I have something in it.'

'Good! My friend and I are also ready for emergencies.'

'You're mighty close about this affair, Mr Holmes. What's the game now?'

'A waiting game.'

'My word, it does not seem a very cheerful place,' said

the detective with a shiver, glancing round him at the gloomy slopes of the hill and at the huge lake of fog which lay over the Grimpen Mire. 'I see the lights of a house ahead of us.'

'That is Merripit House and the end of our journey. I must request you to walk on tiptoe and not to talk above a whisper.'

We moved cautiously along the track as if we were bound for the house, but Holmes halted us when we were about two hundred yards from it.

'This will do,' said he. 'These rocks upon the right make an admirable screen.'

'We are to wait here?'

'Yes, we shall make our little ambush here. Get into this hollow, Lestrade. You have been inside the house, have you not, Watson? Can you tell the position of the rooms? What are those latticed windows at this end?'

'I think they are the kitchen windows.'

'And the one beyond, which shines so brightly?'

'That is certainly the dining-room.'

'The blinds are up. You know the lie of the land best. Creep forward quietly and see what they are doing – but for heaven's sake don't let them know that they are watched!'

I tiptoed down the path and stooped behind the low wall which surrounded the stunted orchard. Creeping in its shadow I reached a point whence I could look straight through the uncurtained window.

There were only two men in the room, Sir Henry and Stapleton. They sat with their profiles towards me on either side of the round table. Both of them were smoking cigars, and coffee and wine were in front of them. Stapleton was talking with animation, but the baronet looked pale and distrait. Perhaps the thought of that lonely walk across the ill-omened moor was weighing heavily upon his mind.

As I watched them Stapleton rose and left the room, while Sir Henry filled his glass again and leaned back in his chair, puffing at his cigar. I heard the creak of a door and the crisp sound of boots upon gravel. The steps passed along the path on the other side of the wall under which I crouched. Looking over, I saw the naturalist pause at the door of an out-house in the corner of the orchard. A key turned in a lock, and as he passed in there was a curious scuffling noise from within. He was only a minute or so inside, and then I heard the key turn once more and he passed me and re-entered the house. I saw him rejoin his guest, and I crept quietly back to where my companions were waiting to tell them what I had seen.

'You say, Watson, that the lady is not there?' Holmes asked when I had finished my report.

'No.'

'Where can she be, then, since there is no light in any other room except the kitchen?'

'I cannot think where she is.'

I have said that over the great Grimpen Mire there hung a dense, white fog. It was drifting slowly in our direction and banked itself up like a wall on that side of us, low but thick and well defined. The moon shone on it, and it looked like a great shimmering ice-field, with the heads of the distant tors as rocks borne upon its surface. Holmes's face was turned towards it, and he muttered impatiently as he watched its sluggish drift.

'It's moving towards us, Watson.'

'Is that serious?'

'Very serious, indeed – the one thing upon earth which could have disarranged my plans. He can't be very long, now. It is already ten o'clock. Our success and even his life may depend upon his coming out before the fog is over the path.'

The night was clear and fine above us. The stars shone cold and bright, while a half-moon bathed the whole scene in a soft, uncertain light. Before us lay the dark bulk of the house, its serrated roof and bristling chimneys hard outlined against the silver-spangled sky. Broad bars of golden light from the lower windows stretched across the orchard and the moor. One of them was suddenly shut off. The servants had left the kitchen. There only remained the lamp in the dining-room where the two men, the murderous host and the unconscious guest, still chatted over their cigars.

Every minute that white woolly plain which covered one-half of the moor was drifting closer and closer to the house. Already the first thin wisps of it were curling across the golden square of the lighted window. The farther wall of the orchard was already invisible, and the trees were standing out of a swirl of white vapour. As we watched it the fog-wreaths came crawling round both corners of the house and rolled slowly into one dense bank on which the upper floor and the roof floated like a strange ship upon a shadowy sea. Holmes struck his hand passionately upon the rock in front of us and stamped his feet in his impatience.

'If he isn't out in a quarter of an hour the path will be covered. In half an hour we won't be able to see our hands in front of us.'

'Shall we move farther back upon higher ground?'

'Yes, I think it would be as well.'

So as the fog-bank flowed onward we fell back before it until we were half a mile from the house, and still that dense white sea, with the moon silvering its upper edge, swept slowly and inexorably on.

'We are going too far,' said Holmes. 'We dare not take the chance of his being overtaken before he can reach us. At all costs we must hold our ground where we are.' He dropped on his knees and clapped his ear to the ground. 'Thank God, I think that I hear him coming.'

A sound of quick steps broke the silence of the moor. Crouching among the stones we stared intently at the silver-tipped bank in front of us. The steps grew louder, and through the fog, as through a curtain, there stepped the man whom we were awaiting. He looked round him in surprise as he emerged into the clear, starlit night. Then he came swiftly along the path, passed close to where we lay, and went on up the long slope behind us. As he walked he glanced continually over either shoulder, like a man who is ill at ease.

'Hist!' cried Holmes, and I heard the sharp click of a cocking pistol. 'Look out! It's coming!'

There was a thin, crisp, continuous patter from somewhere in the heart of that crawling bank. The cloud was within fifty yards of where we lay, and we glared at it, all three, uncertain what horror was about to break from the heart of it. I was at Holmes's elbow, and I glanced for an instant at his face. It was pale and exultant, his eyes shining brightly in the moonlight. But suddenly they started forward in a rigid, fixed stare, and his lips parted in amazement. At the same instant Lestrade gave a yell of terror and threw himself face downward upon the ground. I sprang to my feet, my inert hand grasping my pistol, my mind paralysed by the dreadful shape which had sprung out upon us from the shadows of the fog. A hound it was, an enormous coal-black hound, but not such a hound as mortal eyes have ever seen. Fire burst from its open mouth, its eyes glowed with a smouldering glare, its muzzle and hackles and dewlap were outlined in flickering flame. Never in the delirious dream of a disordered brain could anything more savage, more appalling, more hellish be conceived than that dark form and savage face which broke upon us out of the wall of fog.

With long bounds the huge black creature was leaping down the track, following hard upon the footsteps of our friend. So paralysed were we by the apparition that we allowed him to pass before we had recovered our nerve. Then Holmes and I both fired together, and the creature gave a hideous howl, which showed that one at least had hit him. He did not pause, however, but bounded onward. Far away on the path we saw Sir Henry looking back, his face white in the moonlight, his hands raised in horror, glaring helplessly at the frightful thing which was hunting him down. But that cry of pain from the hound had blown all our fears to the winds. If he was vulnerable he was mortal, and if we could wound him we could kill him. Never have I seen a man run as Holmes ran that night. I am reckoned fleet of foot, but he outpaced me as much as I outpaced the little professional. In front of us as we flew up the track we heard scream after scream from Sir Henry and the deep roar of the hound. I was in time to see the beast spring upon its victim, hurl him to the ground, and worry at his throat. But the next instant Holmes had emptied five barrels of his revolver into the creature's flank. With a last howl of agony and a vicious snap in the air, it rolled upon its back, four feet pawing furiously, and then fell limp upon its side. I stooped, panting, and pressed my pistol to the dreadful, shimmering head, but it was useless to press the trigger. The giant hound was dead.

Sir Henry lay insensible where he had fallen. We tore away his collar, and Holmes breathed a prayer of gratitude when we saw that there was no sign of a wound and that the rescue had been in time. Already our friend's eyelids shivered and he made a feeble effort to move. Lestrade thrust his brandy-flask between the baronet's teeth, and two frightened eyes were looking up at us.

'My God!' he whispered. 'What was it? What, in heaven's name, was it?'

'It's dead, whatever it is,' said Holmes. 'We've laid the family ghost once and forever.'

In mere size and strength it was a terrible creature which was lying stretched before us. It was not a pure bloodhound and it was not a pure mastiff; but it appeared to be a combination of the two – gaunt, savage, and as large as a small lioness. Even now in the stillness of death, the huge jaws seemed to be dripping with a bluish flame and the small, deep-set, cruel eyes were ringed with fire. I placed my hand upon the glowing muzzle, and as I held them up my own fingers smouldered and gleamed in the darkness.

'Phosphorus,' I said.

'A cunning preparation of it,' said Holmes, sniffing at the dead animal. 'There is no smell which might have interfered with his power of scent. We owe you a deep apology, Sir Henry, for having exposed you to this fright. I was prepared for a hound, but not for such a creature as this. And the fog gave us little time to receive him.'

'You have saved my life.'

'Having first endangered it. Are you strong enough to stand?'

'Give me another mouthful of that brandy and I shall be ready for anything. So! Now, if you will help me up. What do you propose to do?'

'To leave you here. You are not fit for further adventures tonight. If you will wait, one or other of us will go back with you to the Hall.'

He tried to stagger to his feet; but he was still ghastly pale and trembling in every limb. We helped him to a rock, where he sat shivering with his face buried in his hands.

'We must leave you now,' said Holmes. 'The rest of our work must be done, and every moment is of importance. We have our case, and now we only want our man.

'It's a thousand to one against our finding him at the house,' he continued as we retraced our steps swiftly down the path. 'Those shots must have told him that the game was up.'

'We were some distance off, and this fog may have deadened them.'

'He followed the hound to call him off – of that you may be certain. No, no, he's gone by this time! But we'll search the house and make sure.'

The front door was open, so we rushed in and hurried from room to room to the amazement of a doddering old manservant, who met us in the passage. There was no light save in the dining-room, but Holmes caught up the lamp and left no corner of the house unexplored. No sign could we see of the man whom we were chasing. On the upper floor, however, one of the bedroom doors was locked.

'There's someone in here,' cried Lestrade. 'I can hear a movement. Open this door!'

A faint moaning and rustling came from within. Holmes struck the door just over the lock with the flat of his foot and it flew open. Pistol in hand, we all three rushed into the room.

But there was no sign within it of that desperate and defiant villain whom we expected to see. Instead we were faced by an object so strange and so unexpected that we stood for a moment staring at it in amazement.

The room had been fashioned into a small museum, and the walls were lined by a number of glass-topped cases full of that collection of butterflies and moths the formation of which had been the relaxation of this complex and dangerous man. In the centre of this room there was an upright beam, which had been placed at some period as a support for the old worm-eaten baulk of timber which spanned the roof. To this post a figure was tied, so swathed and muffled in the sheets which had been used to secure it that one could not for the moment tell whether it was that of a man or a woman. One towel passed round the throat and was secured at the back of the pillar. Another covered the lower part of the face, and over it two dark eyes – eyes full of grief and shame and a dreadful questioning – stared back at us. In a minute we had torn off the gag, unswathed the bonds, and Mrs Stapleton sank upon the floor in front of us. As her beautiful head fell upon her chest I saw the clear red weal of a whip-lash across her neck.

'The brute!' cried Holmes. 'Here, Lestrade, your brandy-bottle! Put her in the chair! She has fainted from ill-usage and exhaustion.'

She opened her eyes again.

'Is he safe?' she asked. 'Has he escaped?'

'He cannot escape us, madam.' 'No, no, I did not mean my husband. Sir Henry? Is he safe?'

'Yes.'

'And the hound?'

'It is dead.'

She gave a long sigh of satisfaction.

'Thank God! Thank God! Oh, this villain! See how he has treated me!' She shot her arms out from her sleeves, and we saw with horror that they were all mottled with bruises. 'But this is nothing – nothing! It is my mind and soul that he has tortured and defiled. I could endure it all, ill-usage, solitude, a life of deception, everything, as long as I could still cling to the hope that I had his love, but now I know that in this also I have been his dupe and his tool.' She broke into passionate sobbing as she spoke.

'You bear him no good will, madam,' said Holmes. 'Tell us then where we shall find him. If you have ever aided him in evil, help us now and so atone.'

'There is but one place where he can have fled,' she answered. 'There is an old tin mine on an island in the heart of the mire. It was there that he kept his hound and there also he had made preparations so that he might have a refuge. That is where he would fly.'

The fog-bank lay like white wool against the window. Holmes held the lamp towards it.

'See,' said he. 'No one could find his way into the Grimpen Mire tonight.'

She laughed and clapped her hands. Her eyes and teeth gleamed with fierce merriment.

'He may find his way in, but never out,' she cried. 'How can he see the guiding wands tonight? We planted them together, he and I, to mark the pathway through the mire. Oh, if I could only have plucked them out today. Then indeed you would have had him at your mercy!'

It was evident to us that all pursuit was in vain until the fog had lifted. Meanwhile we left Lestrade in possession of the house while Holmes and I went back with the baronet to Baskerville Hall. The story of the Stapletons could no longer be withheld from him, but he took the blow bravely when he learned the truth about the woman whom he had loved. But the shock of the night's adventures had shattered his nerves, and before morning he lay delirious in a high fever under the care of Dr Mortimer. The two of them were destined to travel together round the world before Sir Henry had become once more the hale, hearty man that he had been before he became master of that ill-omened estate.

And now I come rapidly to the conclusion of this singular narrative, in which I have tried to make the reader share those dark fears and vague surmises which clouded our lives so long and ended in so tragic a manner. On the morning after the death of the hound the fog had lifted and we were guided by Mrs Stapleton to the point where they had found a pathway through the bog. It helped us to realise the horror of this woman's life when we saw the eagerness and joy with which she laid us on her husband's track. We left her standing upon the thin peninsula of firm, peaty soil which tapered out into the widespread bog. From the end of it a small wand planted here and there showed where the path zigzagged from tuft to tuft of rushes among those green-scummed pits and foul quagmires which barred the way to the stranger.

Rank reeds and lush, slimy water-plants sent an odour of decay and a heavy miasmatic vapour onto our faces, while a false step plunged us more than once thigh-deep into the dark, quivering mire, which shook for yards in soft undulations around our feet. Its tenacious grip plucked at our heels as we walked, and when we sank into it it was as if some malignant hand was tugging us down into those obscene depths, so grim and purposeful was the clutch in which it held us. Once only we saw a trace that someone had passed that perilous way before us. From amid a tuft of cotton grass which bore it up out of the slime some dark thing was projecting. Holmes sank to his waist as he stepped from the path to seize it, and had we not been there to drag him out he could never have set his foot upon firm land again. He held an old black boot in the air. 'Meyers, Toronto,' was printed on the leather inside.

'It is worth a mud bath,' said he. 'It is our friend Sir Henry's missing boot.'

'Thrown there by Stapleton in his flight.'

'Exactly. He retained it in his hand after using it to set the hound upon the track. He fled when he knew the game was up, still clutching it. And he hurled it away at this point of his flight. We know at least that he came so far in safety.'

But more than that we were never destined to know, though there was much which we might surmise. There was no chance of finding footsteps in the mire, for the rising mud oozed swiftly in upon them, but as we at last reached firmer ground beyond the morass we all looked eagerly for them. But no slightest sign of them ever met our eyes. If the earth told a true story, then Stapleton never reached that island of refuge towards which he struggled through the fog upon that last night. Somewhere in the heart of the great Grimpen Mire, down in the foul slime of the huge morass which had sucked him in, this cold and cruel-hearted man is forever buried.

Many traces we found of him in the bog-girt island where he had hid his savage ally. A huge driving-wheel and a shaft half-filled with rubbish showed the position of an abandoned mine. Beside it were the crumbling remains of the cottages of the miners, driven away no doubt by the foul reek of the surrounding swamp. In one of these a staple and chain with a quantity of gnawed bones showed where the animal had been confined. A skeleton with a tangle of brown hair adhering to it lay among the debris.

'A dog!' said Holmes. 'By Jove, a curly-haired spaniel. Poor Mortimer will never see his pet again. Well, I do not know that this place contains any secret which we have not already fathomed. He could hide his hound, but he could not hush its voice, and hence came those cries which even in daylight were not pleasant to hear. On an emergency he could keep the hound in the out-house at Merripit, but it was always a risk, and it was only on the supreme day, which he regarded as the end of all his efforts, that he dared do it. This paste in the tin is no doubt the luminous mixture with which the creature was daubed. It was suggested, of course, by the story of the family hell-hound, and by the desire to frighten old Sir Charles to death. No wonder the poor devil of a convict ran and screamed, even as our friend did, and as we ourselves might have done, when he saw such a creature bounding through the darkness of the moor upon his track. It was a cunning device, for, apart from the chance of driving your victim to his death, what peasant would venture to inquire too closely into such a creature should he get sight of it, as many have done, upon the moor? I said it in London, Watson, and I say it again now, that never yet have we helped to hunt down a more dangerous man than he who is lying yonder' – he swept his long arm towards the huge mottled expanse of green-splotched bog which stretched away until it merged into the russet slopes of the moor.

CHAPTER 15

A RETROSPECTION

It was the end of November, and Holmes and I sat, upon a raw and foggy night, on either side of a blazing fire in our sitting-room in Baker Street. Since the tragic upshot of our visit to Devonshire he had been engaged in two affairs of the utmost importance, in the first of which he had exposed the atrocious conduct of Colonel Upwood in connection with the famous card scandal of the Nonpareil Club, while in the second he had defended the unfortunate Mme. Montpensier from the charge of murder which hung over her in connection with the death of her step-daughter, Mlle. Carere, the young lady who, as it will be remembered, was found six months later alive and married in New York. My friend was in excellent spirits over the success which had attended a succession of difficult and important cases, so that I was able to induce him to discuss the details of the Baskerville mystery. I had waited patiently for the opportunity for I was aware that he would never permit cases to overlap, and that his clear and logical mind would not be drawn from its present work to dwell upon memories of the past. Sir Henry and Dr Mortimer were, however, in London, on their way to that long voyage which had been recommended for the restoration of his shattered nerves. They had called upon us that very afternoon, so that it was natural that the subject should come up for discussion.

'The whole course of events,' said Holmes, 'from the point of view of the man who called himself Stapleton was simple and direct, although to us, who had no means in the beginning of knowing the motives of his actions and could only learn part of the facts, it all appeared exceedingly complex. I have had the advantage of two conversations with Mrs Stapleton, and the case has now been so entirely cleared up that I am not aware that there is anything which has remained a secret to us.

You will find a few notes upon the matter under the heading B in my indexed list of cases.'

'Perhaps you would kindly give me a sketch of the course of events from memory.'

'Certainly, though I cannot guarantee that I carry all the facts in my mind. Intense mental concentration has a curious way of blotting out what has passed. The barrister who has his case at his fingers' ends and is able to argue with an expert upon his own subject finds that a week or two of the courts will drive it all out of his head once more. So each of my cases displaces the last, and Mlle. Carere has blurred my recollection of Baskerville Hall. Tomorrow some other little problem may be submitted to my notice which will in turn dispossess the fair French lady and the infamous Upwood. So far as the case of the hound goes, however, I will give you the course of events as nearly as I can, and you will suggest anything which I may have forgotten.

'My inquiries show beyond all question that the family portrait did not lie, and that this fellow was indeed a

Baskerville. He was a son of that Rodger Baskerville, the younger brother of Sir Charles, who fled with a sinister reputation to South America, where he was said to have died unmarried. He did, as a matter of fact, marry, and had one child, this fellow, whose real name is the same as his father's. He married Beryl Garcia, one of the beauties of Costa Rica, and, having purloined a considerable sum of public money, he changed his name to Vandeleur and fled to England, where he established a school in the east of Yorkshire. His reason for attempting this special line of business was that he had struck up an acquaintance with a consumptive tutor upon the voyage home, and that he had used this man's ability to make the undertaking a success. Fraser, the tutor, died however, and the school which had begun well sank from disrepute into infamy. The Vandeleurs found it convenient to change their name to Stapleton, and he brought the remains of his fortune, his schemes for the future, and his taste for entomology to the south of England. I learned at the British Museum that he was a recognised authority upon the subject, and that the name of Vandeleur has been permanently attached to a certain moth which he had, in his Yorkshire days, been the first to describe.

'We now come to that portion of his life which has proved to be of such intense interest to us. The fellow had evidently made inquiry and found that only two lives intervened between him and a valuable estate. When he went to Devonshire his plans were, I believe, exceedingly hazy, but that he meant mischief from the first is evident from the way in which he took his wife with him in the character of his sister. The idea of using her as a decoy was clearly already in his mind, though he may not have been certain how the

details of his plot were to be arranged. He meant in the end
to have the estate, and he was ready to use any tool or run
any risk for that end. His first act was to establish himself
as near to his ancestral home as he could, and his second
was to cultivate a friendship with Sir Charles Baskerville
and with the neighbours.

'The baronet himself told him about the family hound,
and so prepared the way for his own death. Stapleton, as I
will continue to call him, knew that the old man's heart was
weak and that a shock would kill him. So much he had
learned from Dr Mortimer. He had heard also that Sir Charles
was superstitious and had taken this grim legend very
seriously. His ingenious mind instantly suggested a way by
which the baronet could be done to death, and yet it would
be hardly possible to bring home the guilt to the real
murderer.

'Having conceived the idea he proceeded to carry it out with
considerable finesse. An ordinary schemer would have been
content to work with a savage hound. The use of artificial
means to make the creature diabolical was a flash of genius
upon his part. The dog he bought in London from Ross and
Mangles, the dealers in Fulham Road. It was the strongest and
most savage in their possession. He brought it down by the
North Devon line and walked a great distance over the moor
so as to get it home without exciting any remarks. He had
already on his insect hunts learned to penetrate the Grimpen
Mire, and so had found a safe hiding-place for the creature.
Here he kennelled it and waited his chance.

'But it was some time coming. The old gentleman could
not be decoyed outside of his grounds at night. Several times
Stapleton lurked about with his hound, but without avail. It

was during these fruitless quests that he, or rather his ally, was seen by peasants, and that the legend of the demon dog received a new confirmation. He had hoped that his wife might lure Sir Charles to his ruin, but here she proved unexpectedly independent. She would not endeavour to entangle the old gentleman in a sentimental attachment which might deliver him over to his enemy. Threats and even, I am sorry to say, blows refused to move her. She would have nothing to do with it, and for a time Stapleton was at a deadlock.

'He found a way out of his difficulties through the chance that Sir Charles, who had conceived a friendship for him, made him the minister of his charity in the case of this unfortunate woman, Mrs Laura Lyons. By representing himself as a single man he acquired complete influence over her, and he gave her to understand that in the event of her obtaining a divorce from her husband he would marry her. His plans were suddenly brought to a head by his knowledge that Sir Charles was about to leave the Hall on the advice of Dr Mortimer, with whose opinion he himself pretended to coincide. He must act at once, or his victim might get beyond his power. He therefore put pressure upon Mrs Lyons to write this letter, imploring the old man to give her an interview on the evening before his departure for London. He then, by a specious argument, prevented her from going, and so had the chance for which he had waited.

'Driving back in the evening from Coombe Tracey he was in time to get his hound, to treat it with his infernal paint, and to bring the beast round to the gate at which he had reason to expect that he would find the old gentleman waiting. The dog, incited by its master, sprang over the wicket-gate and pursued the unfortunate baronet, who fled screaming down the yew alley. In that gloomy tunnel it must indeed have been a dreadful sight to see that huge black creature, with its flaming jaws and blazing eyes, bounding after its victim. He fell dead at the end of the alley from heart disease and terror. The hound had kept upon the grassy border while the baronet had run down the path, so that no track but the man's was visible. On seeing him lying still the creature had probably approached to sniff at him, but finding him dead had turned away again. It was then that it left the print which was actually observed by Dr Mortimer. The hound was called off and hurried away to its lair in the Grimpen Mire, and a mystery was left which puzzled the authorities, alarmed the countryside, and finally brought the case within the scope of our observation.

'So much for the death of Sir Charles Baskerville. You perceive the devilish cunning of it, for really it would be almost impossible to make a case against the real murderer. His only accomplice was one who could never give him away, and the grotesque, inconceivable nature of the device only served to make it more effective. Both of the women concerned in the case, Mrs Stapleton and Mrs Laura Lyons, were left with a strong suspicion against Stapleton. Mrs Stapleton knew that he had designs upon the old man, and also of the existence of the hound. Mrs Lyons knew neither of these things, but had been impressed by the death occurring at the time of an uncancelled appointment which was only known to him. However, both of them were under his influence, and he had nothing to fear from them. The first half of his task was successfully accomplished but the more difficult still remained.

'It is possible that Stapleton did not know of the existence of an heir in Canada. In any case he would very soon learn it from his friend Dr Mortimer, and he was told by the latter all details about the arrival of Henry Baskerville. Stapleton's first idea was that this young stranger from Canada might possibly be done to death in London without coming down to Devonshire at all. He distrusted his wife ever since she had refused to help him in laying a trap for the old man, and he dared not leave her long out of his sight for fear he should lose his influence over her. It was for this reason that he took her to London with him. They lodged, I find, at the Mexborough Private Hotel, in Craven Street, which was actually one of those called upon by my agent in search of evidence. Here he kept his wife imprisoned in her room while he, disguised in a beard, followed Dr Mortimer to Baker Street and afterwards to the station and to the Northumberland Hotel. His wife had some inkling of his plans; but she had such a fear of her husband – a fear founded upon brutal ill-treatment – that she dare not write to warn the man whom she knew to be in danger. If the letter should fall into Stapleton's hands her own life would not be safe. Eventually, as we know, she adopted the expedient of cutting out the words which would form the message, and addressing the letter in a disguised hand. It reached the baronet, and gave him the first warning of his danger.

'It was very essential for Stapleton to get some article of Sir Henry's attire so that, in case he was driven to use the dog, he might always have the means of setting him upon his track. With characteristic promptness and audacity he set about this at once, and we cannot doubt that the boots or chamber-maid of the hotel was well bribed to help him in his design. By chance, however, the first boot which was procured for him was a new one and, therefore, useless for his purpose. He then had it returned and obtained another – a most instructive incident, since it proved conclusively to my mind that we were dealing with a real hound, as no other supposition could explain this anxiety to obtain an old boot and this indifference to a new one. The more outre and grotesque an incident is the more carefully it deserves to be examined, and the very point which appears to complicate a case is, when duly considered and scientifically handled, the one which is most likely to elucidate it.

'Then we had the visit from our friends next morning, shadowed always by Stapleton in the cab. From his knowledge of our rooms and of my appearance, as well as from his general conduct, I am inclined to think that Stapleton's career of crime has been by no means limited to this single Baskerville affair. It is suggestive that during the last three years there have been four considerable burglaries in the west country, for none of which was any criminal ever arrested. The last of these, at Folkestone Court, in May, was remarkable for the cold-blooded pistolling of the page, who surprised the masked and solitary burglar. I cannot doubt that Stapleton recruited his waning resources in this fashion, and that for years he has been a desperate and dangerous man.

'We had an example of his readiness of resource that morning when he got away from us so successfully, and also of his audacity in sending back my own name to me through the cabman. From that moment he understood that I had taken over the case in London, and that therefore there was no chance for him there. He returned to Dartmoor and awaited the arrival of the baronet.'

'One moment!' said I. 'You have, no doubt, described the sequence of events correctly, but there is one point which you have left unexplained. What became of the hound when its master was in London?'

'I have given some attention to this matter and it is undoubtedly of importance. There can be no question that Stapleton had a confidant, though it is unlikely that he ever placed himself in his power by sharing all his plans with him. There was an old manservant at Merripit House, whose name was Anthony. His connection with the Stapletons can be traced for several years, as far back as the school-mastering days, so that he must have been aware that his master and mistress were really husband and wife. This man has disappeared and has escaped from the country. It is suggestive that Anthony is not a common name in England, while Antonio is so in all Spanish or Spanish-American countries. The man, like Mrs Stapleton herself, spoke good English, but with a curious lisping accent. I have myself seen this old man cross the Grimpen Mire by the path which Stapleton had marked out. It is very probable, therefore, that in the absence of his master it was he who cared for the hound, though he may never have known the purpose for which the beast was used.

'The Stapletons then went down to Devonshire, whither they were soon followed by Sir Henry and you. One word now as to how I stood myself at that time. It may possibly recur to your memory that when I examined the paper upon which the printed words were fastened I made a close inspection for the water-mark. In doing so I held it within a few inches of my eyes, and was conscious of a faint smell of the scent known as white jessamine. There are seventy-five perfumes, which it is very necessary that a criminal expert should be able to distinguish from each other, and cases have more than once within my own experience depended upon their prompt recognition. The scent suggested the presence of a lady, and already my thoughts began to turn towards the Stapletons. Thus I had made certain of the hound, and had guessed at the criminal before ever we went to the west country.

'It was my game to watch Stapleton. It was evident, however, that I could not do this if I were with you, since he would be keenly on his guard. I deceived everybody, therefore, yourself included, and I came down secretly when I was supposed to be in London. My hardships were not so great as you imagined, though such trifling details must never interfere with the investigation of a case. I stayed for the most part at Coombe Tracey, and only used the hut upon the moor when it was necessary to be near the scene of action. Cartwright had come down with me, and in his disguise as a country boy he was of great assistance to me. I was dependent upon him for food and clean linen. When I was watching Stapleton, Cartwright was frequently watching you, so that I was able to keep my hand upon all the strings.

'I have already told you that your reports reached me rapidly, being forwarded instantly from Baker Street to Coombe Tracey. They were of great service to me, and especially that one incidentally truthful piece of biography of Stapleton's. I was able to establish the identity of the man and the woman and knew at last exactly how I stood. The case had been considerably complicated through the incident of the escaped convict and the relations between him and the Barrymores. This also you cleared up in a very effective way, though I had already come to the same conclusions from my own observations.

'By the time that you discovered me upon the moor I had a complete knowledge of the whole business, but I had not a case which could go to a jury. Even Stapleton's attempt upon Sir Henry that night which ended in the death of the unfortunate convict did not help us much in proving murder against our man. There seemed to be no alternative but to catch him red-handed, and to do so we had to use Sir Henry, alone and apparently unprotected, as a bait. We did so, and at the cost of a severe shock to our client we succeeded in completing our case and driving Stapleton to his destruction. That Sir Henry should have been exposed to this is, I must confess, a reproach to my management of the case, but we had no means of foreseeing the terrible and paralysing spectacle which the beast presented, nor could we predict the fog which enabled him to burst upon us at such short notice. We succeeded in our object at a cost which both the specialist and Dr Mortimer assure me will be a tempo-rary one. A long journey may enable our friend to recover not only from his shattered nerves but also from his wounded feelings. His love for the lady was deep and sincere, and to him the saddest part of all this black business was that he should have been deceived by her.

'It only remains to indicate the part which she had played throughout. There can be no doubt that Stapleton exercised an influence over her which may have been love or may have been fear, or very possibly both, since they are by no means incompatible emotions. It was, at least, absolutely effective. At his command she consented to pass as his sister, though he found the limits of his power over her when he endeavoured to make her the direct accessory to murder. She was ready to warn Sir Henry so far as she could without implicating her husband, and again and again she tried to do so. Stapleton himself seems to have been capable of jealousy, and when he saw the baronet paying court to the lady, even though it was part of his own plan, still he could not help interrupting with a passionate outburst which revealed the fiery soul which his self-contained manner so cleverly concealed. By encouraging the intimacy he made it certain that Sir Henry would frequently come to Merripit House and that he would sooner or later get the opportunity which he desired. On the day of the crisis, however, his wife turned suddenly against him. She had learned something of the death of the convict, and she knew that the hound was being kept in the outhouse on the evening that Sir Henry was coming to dinner. She taxed her husband with his intended crime, and a furious scene followed in which he showed her for the first time that she had a rival in his love. Her fidelity turned in an instant to bitter hatred, and he saw that she would betray him. He tied her up, therefore, that she might have no chance of warning Sir Henry, and he hoped, no doubt, that when the whole countryside put down the baronet's death to the curse of his family, as they certainly would do, he could win his wife back to accept an accomplished fact and to keep silent upon what she knew. In this I fancy that in any case he made a miscalculation, and that, if we had not been there, his doom would none the less have been sealed. A woman of Spanish blood does not condone such an injury so lightly. And now, my dear Watson, without referring to my notes, I cannot give you a more detailed account of this curious case. I do not know that anything essential has been left unexplained.'

'He could not hope to frighten Sir Henry to death as he had done the old uncle with his bogie hound.'

'The beast was savage and half-starved. If its appearance did not frighten its victim to death, at least it would paralyse the resistance which might be offered.'

'No doubt. There only remains one difficulty. If Stapleton came into the succession, how could he explain the fact that he, the heir, had been living unannounced under another name so close to the property? How could he claim it without causing suspicion and inquiry?'

'It is a formidable difficulty, and I fear that you ask too much when you expect me to solve it. The past and the present are within the field of my inquiry, but what a man may do in the future is a hard question to answer. Mrs Stapleton has heard her husband discuss the problem on several occasions. There were three possible courses. He might claim the property from South America, establish his identity before the British authorities there and so obtain the fortune without ever coming to England at all, or he might adopt an elaborate disguise during the short time that he need be in London; or, again, he might furnish an accomplice with the proofs and papers, putting him in as heir, and retaining a claim upon some proportion of his income. We cannot doubt from what we know of him that he would have found some way out of the difficulty. And now, my dear Watson, we have had some weeks of severe work, and for one evening, I think, we may turn our thoughts into more pleasant channels. I have a box for "Les Huguenots." Have you heard the De Reszkes? Might I trouble you then to be ready in half an hour, and we can stop at Marcini's for a little dinner on the way?'

The Valley
of Fear

CONTENTS

PART 1 – The Tragedy of Birlstone..........................219

Chapter 1 – The Warning...221

Chapter 2 – Sherlock Holmes Discourses................231

Chapter 3 – The Tragedy of Birlstone 240

Chapter 4 – Darkness...252

Chapter 5 – The People of the Drama 264

Chapter 6 – A Dawning Light 278

Chapter 7 – The Solution...294

PART 2 – The Scowrers..313

Chapter 1 – The Man..315

Chapter 2 – The Bodymaster....................................325

Chapter 3 – Lodge 341, Vermissa 344

Chapter 4 – The Valley of Fear................................362

Chapter 5 – The Darkest Hour 374

Chapter 6 – Danger...389

Chapter 7 – The Trapping of Birdy Edwards 400

Epilogue 412

PART 1

THE TRAGEDY OF BIRLSTONE

CHAPTER 1

THE WARNING

'I am inclined to think – ' said I.

'I should do so,' Sherlock Holmes remarked impatiently.

I believe that I am one of the most long-suffering of mortals; but I'll admit that I was annoyed at the sardonic interruption. 'Really, Holmes,' said I severely, 'you are a little trying at times.'

He was too much absorbed with his own thoughts to give any immediate answer to my remonstrance. He leaned upon his hand, with his untasted breakfast before him, and he stared at the slip of paper which he had just drawn from its envelope. Then he took the envelope itself, held it up to the light, and very carefully studied both the exterior and the flap.

'It is Porlock's writing,' said he thoughtfully. 'I can hardly doubt that it is Porlock's writing, though I have seen it only twice before. The Greek *e* with the peculiar top flourish is distinctive. But if it is Porlock, then it must be something of the very first importance.'

He was speaking to himself rather than to me; but my vexation disappeared in the interest which the words awakened.

'Who then is Porlock?' I asked.

'Porlock, Watson, is a *nom-de-plume*, a mere identification mark; but behind it lies a shifty and evasive personality. In a former letter he frankly informed me that the name was not his own, and defied me ever to trace him among the teeming millions of this great city. Porlock is important, not for himself, but for the great man with whom he is in touch. Picture to yourself the pilot fish with the shark, the jackal with the lion – anything that is insignificant in companionship with what is formidable: not only formidable, Watson, but sinister – in the highest degree sinister. That is where he comes within my purview. You have heard me speak of Professor Moriarty?'

'The famous scientific criminal, as famous among crooks as – '

'My blushes, Watson!' Holmes murmured in a deprecating voice.

'I was about to say, as he is unknown to the public.'

'A touch! A distinct touch!' cried Holmes. 'You are developing a certain unexpected vein of pawky humour, Watson, against which I must learn to guard myself. But in calling Moriarty a criminal you are uttering libel in the eyes of the law – and there lie the glory and the wonder of it! The greatest schemer of all time, the organiser of every devilry, the controlling brain of the underworld, a brain which might have made or marred the destiny of nations – that's the man! But so aloof is he from general suspicion, so immune from criticism, so admirable in his management and self-effacement, that for those very words that you have uttered he could hale you to a court and emerge with your year's pension as a solatium for his wounded character. Is he not the celebrated author of *The Dynamics of an Asteroid*, a book which ascends to such rarefied heights of pure mathematics that it is said that there was no man in the scientific press capable of criticising it? Is this a man to traduce? Foul-mouthed doctor and slandered professor – such would be your respective roles! That's genius, Watson. But if I am spared by lesser men, our day will surely come.'

'May I be there to see!' I exclaimed devoutly. 'But you were speaking of this man Porlock.'

'Ah, yes – the so-called Porlock is a link in the chain some little way from its great attachment. Porlock is not quite a sound link – between ourselves. He is the only flaw in that chain so far as I have been able to test it.'

'But no chain is stronger than its weakest link.'

'Exactly, my dear Watson! Hence the extreme importance of Porlock. Led on by some rudimentary aspirations towards right, and encouraged by the judicious stimulation of an occasional ten-pound note sent to him by devious methods, he has once or twice given me advance information which has been of value – that highest value which anticipates and prevents rather than avenges crime. I cannot doubt that, if we had the cipher, we should find that this communication is of the nature that I indicate.'

Again Holmes flattened out the paper upon his unused plate. I rose and, leaning over him, stared down at the curious inscription, which ran as follows:

534 C2 13 127 36 31 4 17 21 41 DOUGLAS 109 293 5 37 BIRLSTONE 26 BIRLSTONE 9 127 171

'What do you make of it, Holmes?'

'It is obviously an attempt to convey secret information.'

'But what is the use of a cipher message without the cipher?'

'In this instance, none at all.'

'Why do you say "in this instance"?'

'Because there are many ciphers which I would read as easily as I do the apocrypha of the agony column: such crude devices amuse the intelligence without fatiguing it. But this is different. It is clearly a reference to the words in a page of some book. Until I am told which page and which book I am powerless.'

'But why "Douglas" and "Birlstone"?'

'Clearly because those are words which were not contained in the page in question.'

'Then why has he not indicated the book?'

'Your native shrewdness, my dear Watson, that innate cunning which is the delight of your friends, would surely prevent you from enclosing cipher and message in the same envelope. Should it miscarry, you are undone. As it is, both have to go wrong before any harm comes from it. Our second post is now overdue, and I shall be surprised if it does not bring us either a further letter of explanation, or, as is more probable, the very volume to which these figures refer.'

Holmes's calculation was fulfilled within a very few minutes by the appearance of Billy, the page, with the very letter which we were expecting.

'The same writing,' remarked Holmes, as he opened the envelope, 'and actually signed,' he added in an exultant voice as he unfolded the epistle. 'Come, we are getting on, Watson.' His brow clouded, however, as he glanced over the contents.

'Dear me, this is very disappointing! I fear, Watson, that all our expectations come to nothing. I trust that the man Porlock will come to no harm.

'DEAR Mr HOLMES [he says]:

'I will go no further in this matter. It is too dangerous – he suspects me. I can see that he suspects me. He came to me quite unexpectedly after I had actually addressed this envelope with the intention of sending you the key to the cipher. I was able to cover it up. If he had seen it, it would have gone hard with me. But I read suspicion in his eyes. Please burn the cipher message, which can now be of no use to you.

'FRED PORLOCK'

Holmes sat for some little time twisting this letter between his fingers, and frowning, as he stared into the fire.

'After all,' he said at last, 'there may be nothing in it. It may be only his guilty conscience. Knowing himself to be a traitor, he may have read the accusation in the other's eyes.'

'The other being, I presume, Professor Moriarty.'

'No less! When any of that party talk about "He" you know whom they mean. There is one predominant "He" for all of them.'

'But what can he do?'

'Hum! That's a large question. When you have one of the first brains of Europe up against you, and all the powers of darkness at his back, there are infinite possibilities. Anyhow, friend Porlock is evidently scared out of his senses – kindly compare the writing in the note to that upon its envelope; which was done, he tells us, before this ill-omened visit. The one is clear and firm. The other hardly legible.'

'Why did he write at all? Why did he not simply drop it?'

'Because he feared I would make some inquiry after him in that case, and possibly bring trouble on him.'

'No doubt,' said I. 'Of course.' I had picked up the original cipher message and was bending my brows over it. 'It's pretty maddening to think that an important secret may lie here on this slip of paper, and that it is beyond human power to penetrate it.'

Sherlock Holmes had pushed away his untasted breakfast and lit the unsavoury pipe which was the companion of his deepest meditations. 'I wonder!' said he, leaning back and staring at the ceiling. 'Perhaps there are points which have escaped your Machiavellian intellect. Let us consider the problem in the light of pure reason. This man's reference is to a book. That is our point of departure.'

'A somewhat vague one.'

'Let us see then if we can narrow it down. As I focus my mind upon it, it seems rather less impenetrable. What indications have we as to this book?'

'None.'

'Well, well, it is surely not quite so bad as that. The cipher message begins with a large 534, does it not? We may take it as a working hypothesis that 534 is the particular page to which the cipher refers. So our book has already become a *large* book, which is surely something gained. What other indications have we as to the nature of this large book? The next sign is C2. What do you make of that, Watson?'

'Chapter the second, no doubt.'

'Hardly that, Watson. You will, I am sure, agree with me that if the page be given, the number of the chapter is immaterial. Also that if page 534 finds us only in the second chapter, the length of the first one must have been really intolerable.'

'Column!' I cried.

'Brilliant, Watson. You are scintillating this morning. If it is not column, then I am very much deceived. So now, you see, we begin to visualise a large book printed in double columns which are each of a considerable length, since one of the words is numbered in the document as the two hundred and ninety-third. Have we reached the limits of what reason can supply?'

'I fear that we have.'

'Surely you do yourself an injustice. One more coruscation, my dear Watson – yet another brain-wave! Had the volume been an unusual one, he would have sent it to me. Instead of that, he had intended, before his plans were nipped, to send me the clue in this envelope. He says so in his note. This would seem to indicate that the book is one which he thought I would have no difficulty in finding for myself. He had it – and he imagined that I would have it, too. In short, Watson, it is a very common book.'

'What you say certainly sounds plausible.'

'So we have contracted our field of search to a large book, printed in double columns and in common use.'

'The Bible!' I cried triumphantly.

'Good, Watson, good! But not, if I may say so, quite good enough! Even if I accepted the compliment for myself I could hardly name any volume which would be less likely to lie at the elbow of one of Moriarty's associates. Besides, the editions of Holy Writ are so numerous that he could hardly suppose that two copies would have the same pagination. This is clearly a book which is standardised. He knows for certain that his page 534 will exactly agree with my page 534.'

'But very few books would correspond with that.'

'Exactly. Therein lies our salvation. Our search is narrowed down to standardised books which anyone may be supposed to possess.'

'*Bradshaw*!'

'There are difficulties, Watson. The vocabulary of *Bradshaw* is nervous and terse, but limited. The selection of words would hardly lend itself to the sending of general messages. We will eliminate *Bradshaw*. The dictionary is, I fear, inadmissible for the same reason. What then is left?'

'An almanac!'

'Excellent, Watson! I am very much mistaken if you have not touched the spot. An almanac! Let us consider the claims of *Whitaker's Almanac*. It is in common use. It has the requisite number of pages. It is in double column. Though reserved in its earlier vocabulary, it becomes, if I remember right, quite garrulous towards the end.' He picked the volume from his desk. 'Here is page 534, column two, a substantial block of print dealing, I perceive, with the trade and resources of British India. Jot down the words, Watson! Number thirteen is "Mahratta". Not, I fear, a very auspicious beginning. Number one hundred and twenty-seven is "Government"; which at least makes sense, though somewhat irrelevant to ourselves and Professor Moriarty. Now let us try again. What does the Mahratta government do? Alas! The next word is "pig's-bristles". We are undone, my good Watson! It is finished!'

He had spoken in jesting vein, but the twitching of his bushy eyebrows bespoke his disappointment and irritation. I sat helpless and unhappy, staring into the fire. A long silence was broken by a sudden exclamation from Holmes, who dashed at a cupboard, from which he emerged with a second yellow-covered volume in his hand.

'We pay the price, Watson, for being too up-to-date!' he cried. 'We are before our time, and suffer the usual penalties. Being the seventh of January, we have very properly laid in the new almanac. It is more than likely that Porlock took his message from the old one. No doubt he would have told us so had his letter of explanation been written. Now let us see what page 534 has in store for us. Number thirteen is "There", which is much more promising. Number one hundred and twenty-seven is "is" – "There is" – Holmes's eyes were gleaming with excitement, and his thin, nervous fingers twitched as he counted the words – "danger". Ha! Ha! Capital! Put that down, Watson. "There is danger – may – come – very soon – one." Then we have the name "Douglas" – "rich – country – now – at – Birlstone – House – Birlstone – confidence – is – pressing". There, Watson! What do you think of pure reason and its fruit? If the green-grocer had such a thing as a laurel wreath, I should send Billy round for it.'

I was staring at the strange message which I had scrawled, as he deciphered it, upon a sheet of foolscap on my knee.

'What a queer, scrambling way of expressing his meaning!' said I.

'On the contrary, he has done quite remarkably well,' said Holmes. 'When you search a single column for words with which to express your meaning, you can hardly expect to get everything you want. You are bound to leave something to the intelligence of your correspondent. The purport is perfectly clear. Some devilry is intended against one Douglas, whoever he may be, residing as stated, a rich country gentleman. He is sure – "confidence" was as near as he could get to "confident" – that it is pressing. There is our result – and a very workmanlike little bit of analysis it was!'

Holmes had the impersonal joy of the true artist in his better work, even as he mourned darkly when it fell below the high level to which he aspired. He was still chuckling over his success when Billy swung open the door and Inspector MacDonald of Scotland Yard was ushered into the room.

Those were the early days at the end of the1880s, when Alec MacDonald was far from having attained the national fame which he has now achieved. He was a young but trusted member of the detective force, who had distinguished himself in several cases which had been entrusted to him. His tall, bony figure gave promise of exceptional physical strength, while his great cranium and deep-set, lustrous eyes spoke no less clearly of the keen intelligence which twinkled out from behind his bushy eyebrows. He was a silent, precise man with a dour nature and a hard Aberdonian accent.

Twice already in his career had Holmes helped him to attain success, his own sole reward being the intellectual joy of the problem. For this reason the affection and respect of the Scotchman for his amateur colleague were profound, and he showed them by the frankness with which he consulted Holmes in every difficulty. Mediocrity knows nothing higher than itself; but talent instantly recognises genius, and MacDonald had talent enough for his profession to enable him to perceive that there was no humiliation in seeking the assistance of one who already stood alone in Europe, both in his gifts and in his experience. Holmes was not prone to friendship, but he was tolerant of the big Scotchman, and smiled at the sight of him.

'You are an early bird, Mr Mac,' said he. 'I wish you luck with your worm. I fear this means that there is some mischief afoot.'

'If you said "hope" instead of "fear" it would be nearer the truth, I'm thinking, Mr Holmes,' the inspector answered, with a knowing grin. 'Well, maybe a wee nip would keep out the raw morning chill. No, I won't smoke, I thank you. I'll have to be pushing on my way; for the early hours of a case are the precious ones, as no man knows better than your own self. But – but – '

The inspector had stopped suddenly, and was staring with a look of absolute amazement at a paper upon the table. It was the sheet upon which I had scrawled the enigmatic message.

'Douglas!' he stammered. 'Birlstone! What's this, Mr Holmes? Man, it's witchcraft! Where in the name of all that is wonderful did you get those names?'

'It is a cipher that Dr Watson and I have had occasion to solve. But why – what's amiss with the names?'

The inspector looked from one to the other of us in dazed astonishment. 'Just this,' said he, 'that Mr Douglas of Birlstone Manor House was horribly murdered last night!'

CHAPTER 2

SHERLOCK HOLMES DISCOURSES

It was one of those dramatic moments for which my friend existed. It would be an overstatement to say that he was shocked or even excited by the amazing announcement. Without having a tinge of cruelty in his singular composition, he was undoubtedly callous from long overstimulation. Yet, if his emotions were dulled, his intellectual perceptions were exceedingly active. There was no trace then of the horror which I had myself felt at this curt declaration; but his face showed rather the quiet and interested composure of the chemist who sees the crystals falling into position from his oversaturated solution.

'Remarkable!' said he. 'Remarkable!'

'You don't seem surprised.'

'Interested, Mr Mac, but hardly surprised. Why should I be surprised? I receive an anonymous communication from a quarter which I know to be important, warning me that danger threatens a certain person. Within an hour I learn that this danger has actually materialised and that the person is dead. I am interested; but, as you observe, I am not surprised.'

In a few short sentences he explained to the inspector the facts about the letter and the cipher. MacDonald sat with his chin on his hands and his great sandy eyebrows bunched into a yellow tangle.

'I was going down to Birlstone this morning,' said he. 'I had come to ask you if you cared to come with me – you and your friend here. But from what you say we might perhaps be doing better work in London.'

'I rather think not,' said Holmes.

'Hang it all, Mr Holmes!' cried the inspector. 'The papers will be full of the Birlstone mystery in a day or two; but where's the mystery if there is a man in London who prophesied the crime before ever it occurred? We have only to lay our hands on that man, and the rest will follow.'

'No doubt, Mr Mac. But how do you propose to lay your hands on the so-called Porlock?'

MacDonald turned over the letter which Holmes had handed him. 'Posted in Camberwell – that doesn't help us much. Name, you say, is assumed. Not much to go on, certainly. Didn't you say that you have sent him money?'

'Twice.'

'And how?'

'In notes to Camberwell post office.'

'Did you ever trouble to see who called for them?'

'No.'

The inspector looked surprised and a little shocked. 'Why not?'

'Because I always keep faith. I had promised when he first wrote that I would not try to trace him.'

'You think there is someone behind him?'

'I *know* there is.'

'This professor that I've heard you mention?'

'Exactly!'

Inspector MacDonald smiled, and his eyelid quivered as he glanced towards me. 'I won't conceal from you, Mr Holmes, that we think in the CID that you have a wee bit of a bee in your bonnet over this professor. I made some enquiries myself about the matter. He seems to be a very respectable, learned and talented sort of man.'

'I'm glad you've got so far as to recognise the talent.'

'Man, you can't but recognise it! After I heard your view I made it my business to see him. I had a chat with him on eclipses. How the talk got that way I canna think; but he had out a reflector lantern and a globe, and made it all clear in a minute. He lent me a book; but I don't mind saying that it was a bit above my head, though I had a good Aberdeen upbringing. He'd have made a grand meenister with his thin face and grey hair and solemn-like way of talking. When he put his hand on my shoulder as we were parting, it was like a father's blessing before you go out into the cold, cruel world.'

Holmes chuckled and rubbed his hands. 'Great!' he said. 'Great! Tell me, Friend MacDonald, this pleasing and touching interview was, I suppose, in the professor's study?'

'That's so.'

'A fine room, is it not?'

'Very fine – very handsome indeed, Mr Holmes.'

'You sat in front of his writing desk?'

'Just so.'

'Sun in your eyes and his face in the shadow?'

'Well, it was evening; but I mind that the lamp was turned on my face.'

'It would be. Did you happen to observe a picture over the professor's head?'

'I don't miss much, Mr Holmes. Maybe I learned that from you. Yes, I saw the picture – a young woman with her head on her hands, peeping at you sideways.'

'That painting was by Jean Baptiste Greuze.'

The inspector endeavoured to look interested.

'Jean Baptiste Greuze', Holmes continued, joining his finger tips and leaning well back in his chair, 'was a French artist who flourished between the years 1750 and 1800. I allude, of course to his working career. Modern criticism has more than endorsed the high opinion formed of him by his contemporaries.'

The inspector's eyes grew abstracted. 'Hadn't we better – ' he said.

'We are doing so,' Holmes interrupted. 'All that I am saying has a very direct and vital bearing upon what you have called the Birlstone Mystery. In fact, it may in a sense be called the very centre of it.'

MacDonald smiled feebly, and looked appealingly to me. 'Your thoughts move a bit too quick for me, Mr Holmes. You leave out a link or two, and I can't get over the gap. What in the whole wide world can be the connection between this dead painting man and the affair at Birlstone?'

'All knowledge comes useful to the detective,' remarked Holmes. 'Even the trivial fact that in the year 1865 a picture by Greuze entitled *La Jeune Fille à l'Agneau* fetched one million two hundred thousand francs – more than forty thousand pounds – at the Portalis sale may start a train of reflection in your mind.'

It was clear that it did. The inspector looked honestly interested.

'I may remind you', Holmes continued, 'that the professor's salary can be ascertained in several trustworthy books of reference. It is seven hundred a year.'

'Then how could he buy – '

'Quite so! How could he?'

'Ay, that's remarkable,' said the inspector thoughtfully. 'Talk away, Mr Holmes. I'm just loving it. It's fine!'

Holmes smiled. He was always warmed by genuine admiration – the characteristic of the real artist. 'What about Birlstone?' he asked.

'We've time yet,' said the inspector, glancing at his watch. 'I've a cab at the door, and it won't take us twenty minutes to Victoria. But about this picture: I thought you told me once, Mr Holmes, that you had never met Professor Moriarty.'

'No, I never have.'

'Then how do you know about his rooms?'

'Ah, that's another matter. I have been three times in his rooms, twice waiting for him under different pretexts and leaving before he came. Once – well, I can hardly tell about the once to an official detective. It was on the last occasion that I took the liberty of running over his papers – with the most unexpected results.'

'You found something compromising?'

'Absolutely nothing. That was what amazed me. However, you have now seen the point of the picture. It shows him to be a very wealthy man. How did he acquire wealth? He is unmarried. His younger brother is a station master in the west of England. His chair is worth seven hundred a year. And he owns a Greuze.'

'Well?'

'Surely the inference is plain.'

'You mean that he has a great income and that he must earn it in an illegal fashion?'

'Exactly. Of course I have other reasons for thinking so – dozens of exiguous threads which lead vaguely up towards the centre of the web where the poisonous, motionless creature is lurking. I only mention the Greuze because it brings the matter within the range of your own observation.'

'Well, Mr Holmes, I admit that what you say is interesting: it's more than interesting – it's just wonderful. But let us have it a little clearer if you can. Is it forgery, coining, burglary – where does the money come from?'

'Have you ever read of Jonathan Wild?'

'Well, the name has a familiar sound. Someone in a novel, was he not? I don't take much stock of detectives in novels – chaps that do things and never let you see how they do them. That's just inspiration: not business.'

'Jonathan Wild wasn't a detective, and he wasn't in a novel. He was a master criminal, and he lived last century – 1750 or thereabouts.'

'Then he's no use to me. I'm a practical man.'

'Mr Mac, the most practical thing that you ever did in your life would be to shut yourself up for three months and read twelve hours a day at the annals of crime. Everything comes in circles – even Professor Moriarty. Jonathan Wild was the hidden force of the London criminals, to whom he sold his brains and his organisation on a fifteen per cent commission. The old wheel turns, and the same spoke comes up. It's all been done before, and will be again. I'll tell you one or two things about Moriarty which may interest you.'

'You'll interest me, right enough.'

'I happen to know who is the first link in his chain – a chain

with this Napoleon-gone-wrong at one end and a hundred broken
fighting men, pickpockets, blackmailers and card sharpers at the
other, with every sort of crime in between. His chief of staff is
Colonel Sebastian Moran, as aloof and guarded and inaccessible
to the law as himself. What do you think he pays him?'

'I'd like to hear.'

'Six thousand a year. That's paying for brains, you see – the
American business principle. I learned that detail quite by
chance. It's more than the Prime Minister gets. That gives you
an idea of Moriarty's gains and of the scale on which he works.
Another point: I made it my business to hunt down some of
Moriarty's cheques lately – just common innocent cheques that
he pays his household bills with. They were drawn on six
different banks. Does that make any impression on your mind?'

'Queer, certainly! But what do you gather from it?'

'That he wanted no gossip about his wealth. No single
man should know what he had. I have no doubt that he has
twenty banking accounts; the bulk of his fortune abroad in
the Deutsche Bank or the Crédit Lyonnais as likely as not.
Sometime when you have a year or two to spare I commend
to you the study of Professor Moriarty.'

Inspector MacDonald had grown steadily more impressed
as the conversation proceeded. He had lost himself in his
interest. Now his practical Scotch intelligence brought him
back with a snap to the matter in hand.

'He can keep, anyhow,' said he. 'You've got us side-tracked
with your interesting anecdotes, Mr Holmes. What really
counts is your remark that there is some connection between
the professor and the crime. That you get from the warning
received through the man Porlock. Can we for our present
practical needs get any further than that?'

'We may form some conception as to the motives of the crime. It is, as I gather from your original remarks, an inexplicable, or at least an unexplained, murder. Now, presuming that the source of the crime is as we suspect it to be, there might be two different motives. In the first place, I may tell you that Moriarty rules with a rod of iron over his people. His discipline is tremendous. There is only one punishment in his code. It is death. Now we might suppose that this murdered man – this Douglas whose approaching fate was known by one of the arch-criminal's subordinates – had in some way betrayed the chief. His punishment followed, and would be known to all – if only to put the fear of death into them.'

'Well, that is one suggestion, Mr Holmes.'

'The other is that it has been engineered by Moriarty in the ordinary course of business. Was there any robbery?'

'I have not heard.'

'If so, it would, of course, be against the first hypothesis and in favour of the second. Moriarty may have been engaged to engineer it on a promise of part spoils, or he may have been paid so much down to manage it. Either is possible. But whichever it may be, or if it is some third combination, it is down at Birlstone that we must seek the solution. I know our man too well to suppose that he has left anything up here which may lead us to him.'

'Then to Birlstone we must go!' cried MacDonald, jumping from his chair. 'My word! It's later than I thought. I can give you, gentlemen, five minutes for preparation, and that is all.'

'And ample for us both,' said Holmes, as he sprang up and hastened to change from his dressing gown to his coat. 'While we are on our way, Mr Mac, I will ask you to be good enough to tell me all about it.'

'All about it' proved to be disappointingly little, and yet there was enough to assure us that the case before us might well be worthy of the expert's closest attention. He brightened and rubbed his thin hands together as he listened to the meagre but remarkable details. A long series of sterile weeks lay behind us, and here at last there was a fitting object for those remarkable powers which, like all special gifts, become irksome to their owner when they are not in use. That razor brain blunted and rusted with inaction.

Sherlock Holmes's eyes glistened, his pale cheeks took a warmer hue, and his whole eager face shone with an inward light when the call for work reached him. Leaning forward in the cab, he listened intently to MacDonald's short sketch of the problem which awaited us in Sussex. The inspector was himself dependent, as he explained to us, upon a scribbled account forwarded to him by the milk train in the early hours of the morning. White Mason, the local officer, was a personal friend, and hence MacDonald had been notified much more promptly than is usual at Scotland Yard when provincials need their assistance. It is a very cold scent upon which the Metropolitan expert is generally asked to run.

'DEAR INSPECTOR MACDONALD' [said the letter which he read to us]:

'Official requisition for your services is in separate envelope. This is for your private eye. Wire me what train in the morning you can get for Birlstone, and I will meet it – or have it met if I am too occupied. This case is a snorter. Don't waste a moment in getting started. If you can bring Mr Holmes, please do so; for he will find something after his own heart. We would think the whole had been fixed up for theatrical effect if there wasn't a dead man in the middle of it. My word! It *is* a snorter.'

'Your friend seems to be no fool,' remarked Holmes.

'No, sir, White Mason is a very live man, if I am any judge.'

'Well, have you anything more?'

'Only that he will give us every detail when we meet.'

'Then how did you get at Mr Douglas and the fact that he had been horribly murdered?'

'That was in the enclosed official report. It didn't say "horrible": that's not a recognised official term. It gave the name John Douglas. It mentioned that his injuries had been in the head, from the discharge of a shotgun. It also mentioned the hour of the alarm, which was close on to midnight last night. It added that the case was undoubtedly one of murder, but that no arrest had been made, and that the case was one which presented some very perplexing and extraordinary features. That's absolutely all we have at present, Mr Holmes.'

'Then, with your permission, we will leave it at that, Mr Mac. The temptation to form premature theories upon insufficient data is the bane of our profession. I can see only two things for certain at present – a great brain in London, and a dead man in Sussex. It's the chain between that we are going to trace.'

CHAPTER 3

THE TRAGEDY OF BIRLSTONE

Now for a moment I will ask leave to remove my own insignificant personality and to describe events which occurred before we arrived upon the scene by the light of knowledge which came to us afterwards. Only in this way can I make the reader appreciate the people concerned and the strange setting in which their fate was cast.

The village of Birlstone is a small and very ancient cluster of half-timbered cottages on the northern border of the county of Sussex. For centuries it had remained unchanged; but within the last few years its picturesque appearance and situation have attracted a number of well-to-do residents, whose villas peep out from the woods around. These woods are locally supposed to be the extreme fringe of the great Weald forest, which thins away until it reaches the northern chalk downs. A number of small shops have come into being to meet the wants of the increased population; so there seems some prospect that Birlstone may soon grow from an ancient village into a modern town. It is the centre for a considerable area of country, since Tunbridge Wells, the nearest place of importance, is ten or twelve miles to the eastward, over the borders of Kent.

About half a mile from the town, standing in an old park famous for its huge beech trees, is the ancient Manor House of Birlstone. Part of this venerable building dates back to the time of the First Crusade, when Hugo de Capus built a fortalice in the centre of the estate, which had been granted to him by the Red King. This was destroyed by fire in 1543, and some of its smoke-blackened corner stones were used when, in Jacobean times, a brick country house rose upon the ruins of the feudal castle.

The Manor House, with its many gables and its small diamond-paned windows, was still much as the builder had left it in the early seventeenth century. Of the double moats which had guarded its more warlike predecessor, the outer had been allowed to dry up, and served the humble function of a kitchen garden. The inner one was still there, and lay forty feet in breadth, though now only a few feet in depth, round the whole house. A small stream fed it and continued beyond it, so that the sheet of water, though turbid, was never ditchlike or unhealthy. The ground floor windows were within a foot of the surface of the water.

The only approach to the house was over a drawbridge, the chains and windlass of which had long been rusted and broken. The latest tenants of the Manor House had, however, with characteristic energy, set this right, and the drawbridge was not only capable of being raised, but actually was raised every evening and lowered every morning. By thus renewing the custom of the old feudal days the Manor House was converted into an island during the night – a fact which had a very direct bearing upon the mystery which was soon to engage the attention of all England.

The house had been untenanted for some years and was threatening to moulder into a picturesque decay when the Douglases took possession of it. This family consisted of only two individuals – John Douglas and his wife. Douglas was a remarkable man, both in character and in person. In age he may have been about fifty, with a strong-jawed, rugged face, a grizzling moustache, peculiarly keen grey eyes, and a wiry, vigorous figure which had lost nothing of the strength and activity of youth. He was cheery and genial to all, but some-what offhand in his manners, giving the impression that he had seen life in social strata on some far lower horizon than the county society of Sussex.

Yet, though looked at with some curiosity and reserve by his more cultivated neighbours, he soon acquired a great popularity among the villagers, subscribing handsomely to all local objects, and attending their smoking concerts and other functions, where, having a remarkably rich tenor voice, he was always ready to oblige with an excellent song. He appeared to have plenty of money, which was said to have been gained in the California gold fields, and it was clear from his own talk and that of his wife that he had spent a part of his life in America.

The good impression which had been produced by his generosity and by his democratic manners was increased by a reputation gained for utter indifference to danger. Though a wretched rider, he turned out at every meet, and took the most amazing falls in his determination to hold his own with the best. When the vicarage caught fire he distinguished himself also by the fearlessness with which he re-entered the building to save property, after the local fire brigade had given it up as impossible. Thus it came about that John Douglas of the Manor House had within five years won himself quite a reputation in Birlstone.

His wife, too, was popular with those who had made her acquaintance; though, after the English fashion, the callers upon a stranger who settled in the county without introductions were few and far between. This mattered the less to her, as she was retiring by disposition, and very much absorbed, to all appearance, in her husband and her domestic duties. It was known that she was an English lady who had met Mr Douglas in London, he being at that time a widower. She was a beautiful woman, tall, dark and slender, some twenty years younger than her husband; a disparity which seemed in no wise to mar the contentment of their family life.

It was remarked sometimes, however, by those who knew them best, that the confidence between the two did not appear to be complete, since the wife was either very reticent about her husband's past life, or else, as seemed more likely, was imperfectly informed about it. It had also been noted and commented upon by a few observant people that there were signs sometimes of some nerve-strain upon the part of Mrs Douglas, and that she would display acute uneasiness if her absent husband should ever be particularly late in his return. On a quiet countryside, where all gossip is welcome, this weakness of the lady of the Manor House did not pass without remark, and it bulked larger upon people's memory when the events arose which gave it a very special significance.

There was yet another individual, whose residence under that roof was, it is true, only an intermittent one, but whose presence at the time of the strange happenings which will now be narrated brought his name prominently before the public. This was Cecil James Barker, of Hales Lodge, Hampstead.

Cecil Barker's tall, loose-jointed figure was a familiar one in the main street of Birlstone village; for he was a frequent and welcome visitor at the Manor House. He was the more noticed as being the only friend of the past unknown life of Mr Douglas who was ever seen in his new English surroundings. Barker was himself an undoubted Englishman; but by his remarks it was clear that he had first known Douglas in America and had there lived on intimate terms with him. He appeared to be a man of considerable wealth, and was reputed to be a bachelor.

In age he was rather younger than Douglas – forty-five at the most – a tall, straight, broad-chested fellow with a clean-shaven, prize-fighter face, thick, strong, black eyebrows and a pair of masterful black eyes which might, even without the aid of his very capable hands, clear a way for him through a hostile crowd. He neither rode nor shot, but spent his days in wandering round the old village with his pipe in his mouth, or in driving with his host, or in his absence with his hostess, over the beautiful countryside. 'An easy-going, free-handed gentleman,' said Ames, the butler. 'But, my word! I had rather not be the man that crossed him!' He was cordial and intimate with Douglas, and he was no less friendly with his wife – a friendship which more than once seemed to cause some irritation to the husband, so that even the servants were able to perceive his annoyance. Such was the third person who was one of the family when the catastrophe occurred.

As to the other denizens of the old building, it will suffice out of a large household to mention the prim, respectable and capable Ames, and Mrs Allen, a buxom and cheerful person, who relieved the lady of some of her household cares. The other six servants in the house bear no relation to the events of the night of January 6th.

It was at eleven forty-five that the first alarm reached the small local police station, in charge of Sergeant Wilson of the Sussex Constabulary. Cecil Barker, much excited, had rushed up to the door and pealed furiously upon the bell. A terrible tragedy had occurred at the Manor House, and John Douglas had been murdered. That was the breathless burden of his message. He had hurried back to the house, followed within a few minutes by the police sergeant, who arrived at the scene of the crime a little after twelve o'clock, after taking prompt steps to warn the county authorities that something serious was afoot.

On reaching the Manor House, the sergeant had found the drawbridge down, the windows lighted up, and the whole household in a state of wild confusion and alarm. The white-faced servants were huddling together in the hall, with the frightened butler wringing his hands in the doorway. Only Cecil Barker seemed to be master of himself and his emotions; he had opened the door which was nearest to the entrance and he had beckoned to the sergeant to follow him. At that moment there arrived Dr Wood, a brisk and capable general practitioner from the village. The three men entered the fatal room together, while the horror-stricken butler followed at their heels, closing the door behind him to shut out the terrible scene from the maid servants.

The dead man lay on his back, sprawling with outstretched limbs in the centre of the room. He was clad only in a pink dressing gown, which covered his night clothes. There were carpet slippers on his bare feet. The doctor knelt beside him and held down the hand lamp which had stood on the table. One glance at the victim was enough to show the healer that his presence could be dispensed with. The man had been horribly injured. Lying across his chest was a curious weapon, a shotgun with the barrel sawn off a foot in front of the triggers. It was clear that this had been fired at close range and that he had received the whole charge in the face, blowing his head almost to pieces. The triggers had been wired together, so as to make the simultaneous discharge more destructive.

The country policeman was unnerved and troubled by the tremendous responsibility which had come so suddenly upon him. 'We will touch nothing until my superiors arrive,' he said in a hushed voice, staring in horror at the dreadful head.

'Nothing has been touched up to now,' said Cecil Barker. 'I'll answer for that. You see it all exactly as I found it.'

'When was that?' The sergeant had drawn out his notebook.

'It was just half-past eleven. I had not begun to undress, and I was sitting by the fire in my bedroom when I heard the report. It was not very loud – it seemed to be muffled. I rushed down – I don't suppose it was thirty seconds before I was in the room.'

'Was the door open?'

'Yes, it was open. Poor Douglas was lying as you see him. His bedroom candle was burning on the table. It was I who lit the lamp some minutes afterward.'

'Did you see no one?'

'No. I heard Mrs Douglas coming down the stairs behind me, and I rushed out to prevent her from seeing this dreadful sight. Mrs Allen, the housekeeper, came and took her away. Ames had arrived, and we ran back into the room once more.'

'But surely I have heard that the drawbridge is kept up all night.'

'Yes, it was up until I lowered it.'

'Then how could any murderer have got away? It is out of the question! Mr Douglas must have shot himself.'

'That was our first idea. But see!' Barker drew aside the curtain, and showed that the long, diamond-paned window was open to its full extent. 'And look at this!' He held the lamp down and illuminated a smudge of blood like the mark of a boot-sole upon the wooden sill. 'Someone has stood there in getting out.'

'You mean that someone waded across the moat?'

'Exactly!'

'Then if you were in the room within half a minute of the crime, he must have been in the water at that very moment.'

'I have not a doubt of it. I wish to heaven that I had rushed to the window! But the curtain screened it, as you can see, and so it never occurred to me. Then I heard the step of Mrs Douglas, and I could not let her enter the room. It would have been too horrible.'

'Horrible enough!' said the doctor, looking at the shattered head and the terrible marks which surrounded it. 'I've never seen such injuries since the Birlstone railway smash.'

'But, I say,' remarked the police sergeant, whose slow, bucolic common sense was still pondering the open window. 'It's all very well your saying that a man escaped by wading this moat, but what I ask you is, how did he ever get into the house at all if the bridge was up?'

'Ah, that's the question,' said Barker.

'At what o'clock was it raised?'

'It was nearly six o'clock,' said Ames, the butler.

'I've heard', said the sergeant, 'that it was usually raised at sunset. That would be nearer half-past four than six at this time of year.'

'Mrs Douglas had visitors to tea,' said Ames. 'I couldn't raise it until they went. Then I wound it up myself.'

'Then it comes to this,' said the sergeant: 'If anyone came from outside – *if* they did – they must have got in across the bridge before six and been in hiding ever since, until Mr Douglas came into the room after eleven.'

'That is so! Mr Douglas went round the house every night the last thing before he turned in to see that the lights were right. That brought him in here. The man was waiting and shot him. Then he got away through the window and left his gun behind him. That's how I read it; for nothing else will fit the facts.'

The sergeant picked up a card which lay beside the dead man on the floor. The initials V.V. and under them the number

341 were rudely scrawled in ink upon it.

'What's this?' he asked, holding it up.

Barker looked at it with curiosity. 'I never noticed it before,' he said. 'The murderer must have left it behind him.'

'V.V. – 341. I can make no sense of that.'

The sergeant kept turning it over in his big fingers. 'What's V.V.? Somebody's initials, maybe. What have you got there, Dr Wood?'

It was a good-sized hammer which had been lying on the rug in front of the fireplace – a substantial, workmanlike hammer. Cecil Barker pointed to a box of brass-headed nails upon the mantelpiece.

'Mr Douglas was altering the pictures yesterday,' he said. 'I saw him myself, standing upon that chair and fixing the big picture above it. That accounts for the hammer.'

'We'd best put it back on the rug where we found it,' said the sergeant, scratching his puzzled head in his perplexity. 'It will want the best brains in the force to get to the bottom of this thing. It will be a London job before it is finished.' He raised the hand lamp and walked slowly round the room. 'Hullo!' he cried, excitedly, drawing the window curtain to one side. 'What o'clock were those curtains drawn?'

'When the lamps were lit,' said the butler. 'It would be shortly after four.'

'Someone had been hiding here, sure enough.' He held down the light, and the marks of muddy boots were very visible in the corner. 'I'm bound to say this bears out your theory, Mr Barker. It looks as if the man got into the house after four when the curtains were drawn, and before six when the bridge was raised. He slipped into this room, because it was the first that he saw. There was no other place where he could hide, so he popped in behind this curtain. That all seems clear enough. It is likely that his main idea was to burgle the house; but Mr Douglas chanced to come upon him, so he murdered him and escaped.'

'That's how I read it,' said Barker. 'But, I say, aren't we wasting precious time? Couldn't we start out and scout the country before the fellow gets away?'

The sergeant considered for a moment.

'There are no trains before six in the morning; so he can't get away by rail. If he goes by road with his legs all dripping, it's odds that someone will notice him. Anyhow, I can't leave here myself until I am relieved. But I think none of you should go until we see more clearly how we all stand.'

The doctor had taken the lamp and was narrowly scrutinising the body. 'What's this mark?' he asked. 'Could this have any connection with the crime?'

The dead man's right arm was thrust out from his dressing gown, and exposed as high as the elbow. About halfway up the forearm was a curious brown design, a triangle inside a circle, standing out in vivid relief upon the lard-coloured skin.

'It's not tattooed,' said the doctor, peering through his glasses. 'I never saw anything like it. The man has been branded at some time as they brand cattle. What is the meaning of this?'

'I don't profess to know the meaning of it,' said Cecil Barker; 'but I have seen the mark on Douglas many times this last ten years.'

'And so have I,' said the butler. 'Many a time when the master has rolled up his sleeves I have noticed that very mark. I've often wondered what it could be.'

'Then it has nothing to do with the crime, anyhow,' said the sergeant. 'But it's a rum thing all the same. Everything about this case is rum. Well, what is it now?'

The butler had given an exclamation of astonishment and was pointing at the dead man's outstretched hand.

'They've taken his wedding ring!' he gasped.

'What!'

'Yes, indeed. Master always wore his plain gold wedding ring on the little finger of his left hand. That ring with the rough nugget on it was above it, and the twisted snake ring on the third finger. There's the nugget and there's the snake, but the wedding ring is gone.'

'He's right,' said Barker.

'Do you tell me,' said the sergeant, 'that the wedding ring was *below* the other?'

'Always!'

'Then the murderer, or whoever it was, first took off this ring you call the nugget ring, then the wedding ring, and afterwards put the nugget ring back again.'

'That is so!'

The worthy country policeman shook his head. 'Seems to me the sooner we get London on to this case the better,' said he. 'White Mason is a smart man. No local job has ever been too much for White Mason. It won't be long now before he is here to help us. But I expect we'll have to look to London before we are through. Anyhow, I'm not ashamed to say that it is a deal too thick for the likes of me.'

CHAPTER 4

DARKNESS

At three in the morning the chief Sussex detective, obeying the urgent call from Sergeant Wilson of Birlstone, arrived from headquarters in a light dog-cart behind a breathless trotter. By the five-forty train in the morning he had sent his message to Scotland Yard, and he was at the Birlstone station at twelve o'clock to welcome us. White Mason was a quiet, comfortable-looking person in a loose tweed suit, with a clean-shaven, ruddy face, a stoutish body and powerful bandy legs adorned with gaiters, looking like a small farmer, a retired gamekeeper or anything upon earth except a very favourable specimen of the provincial criminal officer.

'A real downright snorter, Mr MacDonald!' he kept repeating. 'We'll have the pressmen down like flies when they understand it. I'm hoping we will get our work done before they get poking their noses into it and messing up all the trails. There has been nothing like this that I can remember. There are some bits that will come home to you, Mr Holmes, or I am mistaken. And you also, Dr Watson; for the medicos will have a word to say before we finish. Your room is at the Westville Arms. There's no other place; but I hear that it is clean and good. The man will carry your bags. This way, gentlemen, if you please.'

He was a very bustling and genial person, this Sussex detective. In ten minutes we had all found our quarters. In ten more we were seated in the parlour of the inn and being treated to a rapid sketch of those events which have been outlined in the previous chapter. MacDonald made an occasional note; while Holmes sat absorbed, with the expression of surprised and reverent admiration with which the botanist surveys the rare and precious bloom.

'Remarkable!' he said, when the story was unfolded. 'Most remarkable! I can hardly recall any case where the features have been more peculiar.'

'I thought you would say so, Mr Holmes,' said White Mason in great delight. 'We're well up with the times in Sussex. I've told you now how matters were, up to the time when I took over from Sergeant Wilson between three and four this morning. My word! I made the old mare go! But I need not have been in such a hurry, as it turned out; for there was nothing immediate that I could do. Sergeant Wilson had all the facts. I checked them and considered them and maybe added a few of my own.'

'What were they?' asked Holmes eagerly.

'Well, I first had the hammer examined. There was Dr Wood there to help me. We found no signs of violence upon it. I was hoping that if Mr Douglas defended himself with the hammer, he might have left his mark upon the murderer before he dropped it on the mat. But there was no stain.'

'That, of course, proves nothing at all,' remarked Inspector MacDonald. 'There has been many a hammer murder and no trace on the hammer.'

'Quite so. It doesn't prove it wasn't used. But there might have been stains, and that would have helped us. As a matter of fact there were none. Then I examined the gun. They were buckshot cartridges, and, as Sergeant Wilson pointed out, the triggers were wired together so that, if you pulled on the hinder one, both barrels were discharged. Whoever fixed that up had made up his mind that he was going to take no chances of missing his man. The sawn gun was not more than two foot long – one could carry it easily under one's coat. There was no complete maker's name; but the printed letters P-E-N were on the fluting between the barrels, and the rest of the name had been cut off by the saw.'

'A big P with a flourish above it, E and N smaller?' asked Holmes.

'Exactly.'

'Pennsylvania Small Arms Company – well-known American firm,' said Holmes.

White Mason gazed at my friend as the little village practitioner looks at the Harley Street specialist who by a word can solve the difficulties that perplex him.

'That is very helpful, Mr Holmes. No doubt you are right. Wonderful! Wonderful! Do you carry the names of all the gun makers in the world in your memory?'

Holmes dismissed the subject with a wave.

'No doubt it is an American shotgun,' White Mason continued. 'I seem to have read that a sawn-off shotgun is a weapon used in some parts of America. Apart from the name upon the barrel, the idea had occurred to me. There is some evidence then, that this man who entered the house and killed its master was an American.'

MacDonald shook his head. 'Man, you are surely travelling overfast,' said he. 'I have heard no evidence yet that any stranger was ever in the house at all.'

'The open window, the blood on the sill, the queer card, the marks of boots in the corner, the gun!'

'Nothing there that could not have been arranged. Mr Douglas was an American, or had lived long in America. So had Mr Barker. You don't need to import an American from outside in order to account for American doings.'

'Ames, the butler – '

'What about him? Is he reliable?'

'Ten years with Sir Charles Chandos – as solid as a rock. He has been with Douglas ever since he took the Manor House five years ago. He has never seen a gun of this sort in the house.'

'The gun was made to conceal. That's why the barrels were sawn. It would fit into any box. How could he swear there was no such gun in the house?'

'Well, anyhow, he had never seen one.'

MacDonald shook his obstinate Scotch head. 'I'm not convinced yet that there was ever anyone in the house,' said he. 'I'm asking you to conseedar' (his accent became more Aberdonian as he lost himself in his argument) 'I'm asking you to conseedar what it involves if you suppose that this gun was ever brought into the house, and that all these strange things were done by a person from outside. Oh, man, it's just inconceivable! It's clean against common sense! I put it to you, Mr Holmes, judging it by what we have heard.'

'Well, state your case, Mr Mac,' said Holmes in his most judicial style.

'The man is not a burglar, supposing that he ever existed. The ring business and the card point to premeditated murder for some private reason. Very good. Here is a man who slips into a house with the deliberate intention of committing murder. He knows, if he knows anything, that he will have a deeficulty in making his escape, as the house is surrounded with water. What weapon would he choose? You would say the most silent in the world. Then he could hope when the deed was done to slip quickly from the window, to wade the moat, and to get away at his leisure. That's understandable. But is it understandable that he should go out of his way to bring with him the most noisy weapon he could select, knowing well that it will fetch every human being in the house to the spot as quick as they can run, and that it is all odds that he will be seen before he can get across the moat? Is that credible, Mr Holmes?'

'Well, you put the case strongly,' my friend replied thoughtfully. 'It certainly needs a good deal of justification. May I ask, Mr White Mason, whether you examined the farther side of the moat at once to see if there were any signs of the man having climbed out from the water?'

'There were no signs, Mr Holmes. But it is a stone ledge, and one could hardly expect them.'

'No tracks or marks?'

'None.'

'Ha! Would there be any objection, Mr White Mason, to our going down to the house at once? There may possibly be some small point which might be suggestive.'

'I was going to propose it, Mr Holmes; but I thought it well to put you in touch with all the facts before we go. I suppose if anything should strike you – ' White Mason looked doubtfully at the amateur.

'I have worked with Mr Holmes before,' said Inspector MacDonald. 'He plays the game.'

'My own idea of the game, at any rate,' said Holmes, with a smile. 'I go into a case to help the ends of justice and the work of the police. If I have ever separated myself from the official force, it is because they have first separated themselves from me. I have no wish ever to score at their expense. At the same time, Mr White Mason, I claim the right to work in my own way and give my results at my own time – complete rather than in stages.'

'I am sure we are honoured by your presence and to show you all we know,' said White Mason cordially. 'Come along, Dr Watson, and when the time comes we'll all hope for a place in your book.'

We walked down the quaint village street with a row of pollarded elms on each side of it. Just beyond were two ancient stone pillars, weather-stained and lichen-blotched, bearing upon their summits a shapeless something which had once been the rampant lion of Capus of Birlstone. A short walk along the winding drive with such sward and oaks around it as one only sees in rural England, then a sudden turn, and the long, low Jacobean house of dingy, liver-coloured brick lay before us, with an old-fashioned garden of cut yews on each side of it. As we approached it, there was the wooden drawbridge and the beautiful broad moat as still and luminous as quicksilver in the cold winter sunshine.

Three centuries had flowed past the old Manor House, centuries of births and of homecomings, of country dances and of the meetings of fox hunters. Strange that now in its old age this dark business should have cast its shadow upon the venerable walls! And yet those strange peaked roofs and quaint overhung gables were a fitting covering to grim and terrible intrigue. As I looked at the deep-set windows and the long sweep of the dull-coloured, water-lapped front, I felt that no more fitting scene could be set for such a tragedy.

'That's the window,' said White Mason, 'that one on the immediate right of the drawbridge. It's open just as it was found last night.'

'It looks rather narrow for a man to pass.'

'Well, it wasn't a fat man, anyhow. We don't need your

deductions, Mr Holmes, to tell us that. But you or I could squeeze through all right.'

Holmes walked to the edge of the moat and looked across. Then he examined the stone ledge and the grass border beyond it.

'I've had a good look, Mr Holmes,' said White Mason. 'There is nothing there, no sign that anyone has landed – but why should he leave any sign?'

'Exactly. Why should he? Is the water always turbid?'

'Generally about this colour. The stream brings down the clay.'

'How deep is it?'

'About two feet at each side and three in the middle.'

'So we can put aside all idea of the man having been drowned in crossing.'

'No, a child could not be drowned in it.'

We walked across the drawbridge, and were admitted by a quaint, gnarled, dried-up person, who was the butler, Ames. The poor old fellow was white and quivering from the shock. The village sergeant, a tall, formal, melancholy man, still held his vigil in the room of Fate. The doctor had departed.

'Anything fresh, Sergeant Wilson?' asked White Mason.

'No, sir.'

'Then you can go home. You've had enough. We can send for you if we want you. The butler had better wait outside. Tell him to warn Mr Cecil Barker, Mrs Douglas and the housekeeper that we may want a word with them presently. Now, gentlemen, perhaps you will allow me to give you the views I have formed first, and then you will be able to arrive at your own.'

He impressed me, this country specialist. He had a solid

grip of fact and a cool, clear, common-sense brain, which should take him some way in his profession. Holmes listened to him intently, with no sign of that impatience which the official exponent too often produced.

'Is it suicide, or is it murder – that's our first question, gentlemen, is it not? If it were suicide, then we have to believe that this man began by taking off his wedding ring and concealing it; that he then came down here in his dressing gown, trampled mud into a corner behind the curtain in order to give the idea someone had waited for him, opened the window, put blood on the – '

'We can surely dismiss that,' said MacDonald.

'So I think. Suicide is out of the question. Then a murder has been done. What we have to determine is, whether it was done by someone outside or inside the house.'

'Well, let's hear the argument.'

'There are considerable difficulties both ways, and yet one or the other it must be. We will suppose first that some person or persons inside the house did the crime. They got this man down here at a time when everything was still and yet no one was asleep. They then did the deed with the queerest and noisiest weapon in the world so as to tell everyone what had happened – a weapon that was never seen in the house before. That does not seem a very likely start, does it?'

'No, it does not.'

'Well, then, everyone is agreed that after the alarm was given only a minute at the most had passed before the whole household – not Mr Cecil Barker alone, though he claims to have been the first, but Ames and all of them were on the spot. Do you tell me that in that time the guilty person managed to make footmarks in the corner, open the window, mark the sill with blood, take the wedding ring off the dead man's finger, and all the rest of it? It's impossible!'

'You put it very clearly,' said Holmes. 'I am inclined to agree with you.'

'Well, then, we are driven back to the theory that it was done by someone from outside. We are still faced with some big difficulties; but anyhow they have ceased to be impossibilities. The man got into the house between four-thirty and six; that is to say, between dusk and the time when the bridge was raised. There had been some visitors, and the door was open; so there was nothing to prevent him. He may have been a common burglar, or he may have had some private grudge against Mr Douglas. Since Mr Douglas has spent most of his life in America, and this shotgun seems to be an American weapon, it would seem that the private grudge is the more likely theory. He slipped into this room because it was the first he came to, and he hid behind the curtain. There he remained until past eleven at night. At that time Mr Douglas entered the room. It was a short interview, if there were any interview at all; for Mrs Douglas declares that her husband had not left her more than a few minutes when she heard the shot.'

'The candle shows that,' said Holmes.

'Exactly. The candle, which was a new one, is not burned more than half an inch. He must have placed it on the table before he was attacked; otherwise, of course, it would have fallen when he fell. This shows that he was not attacked the instant that he entered the room. When Mr Barker arrived the candle was lit and the lamp was out.'

'That's all clear enough.'

'Well, now, we can reconstruct things on those lines. Mr

Douglas enters the room. He puts down the candle. A man appears from behind the curtain. He is armed with this gun. He demands the wedding ring – Heaven only knows why, but so it must have been. Mr Douglas gave it up. Then either in cold blood or in the course of a struggle – Douglas may have gripped the hammer that was found upon the mat – he shot Douglas in this horrible way. He dropped his gun and also it would seem this queer card – V.V. 341, whatever that may mean – and he made his escape through the window and across the moat at the very moment when Cecil Barker was discovering the crime. How's that, Mr Holmes?'

'Very interesting, but just a little unconvincing.'

'Man, it would be absolute nonsense if it wasn't that anything else is even worse!' cried MacDonald. 'Somebody killed the man, and whoever it was I could clearly prove to you that he should have done it some other way. What does he mean by allowing his retreat to be cut off like that? What does he mean by using a shotgun when silence was his one chance of escape? Come, Mr Holmes, it's up to you to give us a lead, since you say Mr White Mason's theory is unconvincing.'

Holmes had sat intently observant during this long discussion, missing no word that was said, with his keen eyes darting to right and to left, and his forehead wrinkled with speculation.

'I should like a few more facts before I get so far as a theory, Mr Mac,' said he, kneeling down beside the body. 'Dear me! These injuries are really appalling. Can we have the butler in for a moment?... Ames, I understand that you have often seen this very unusual mark – a branded triangle inside a circle – upon Mr Douglas's forearm?'

'Frequently, sir.'

'You never heard any speculation as to what it meant?'

'No, sir.'

'It must have caused great pain when it was inflicted. It is undoubtedly a burn. Now, I observe, Ames, that there is a small piece of plaster at the angle of Mr Douglas's jaw. Did you observe that in life?'

'Yes, sir, he cut himself in shaving yesterday morning.'

'Did you ever know him to cut himself in shaving before?'

'Not for a very long time, sir.'

'Suggestive!' said Holmes. 'It may, of course, be a mere coincidence, or it may point to some nervousness which would indicate that he had reason to apprehend danger. Had you noticed anything unusual in his conduct, yesterday, Ames?'

'It struck me that he was a little restless and excited, sir.'

'Ha! The attack may not have been entirely unexpected. We do seem to make a little progress, do we not? Perhaps you would rather do the questioning, Mr Mac?'

'No, Mr Holmes, it's in better hands than mine.'

'Well, then, we will pass to this card – V.V. 341. It is rough cardboard. Have you any of the sort in the house?'

'I don't think so.'

Holmes walked across to the desk and dabbed a little ink from each bottle on to the blotting paper. 'It was not printed in this room,' he said; 'this is black ink and the other purplish. It was done by a thick pen, and these are fine. No, it was done elsewhere, I should say. Can you make anything of the inscription, Ames?'

'No, sir, nothing.'

'What do you think, Mr Mac?'

'It gives me the impression of a secret society of some sort; the same with his badge upon the forearm.'

'That's my idea, too,' said White Mason.

'Well, we can adopt it as a working hypothesis and then see how far our difficulties disappear. An agent from such a society makes his way into the house, waits for Mr Douglas, blows his head nearly off with this weapon, and escapes by wading the moat, after leaving a card beside the dead man, which will, when mentioned in the papers, tell other members of the society that vengeance has been done. That all hangs together. But why this gun, of all weapons?'

'Exactly.'

'And why the missing ring?'

'Quite so.'

'And why no arrest? It's past two now. I take it for granted that since dawn every constable within forty miles has been looking out for a wet stranger?'

'That is so, Mr Holmes.'

'Well, unless he has a burrow close by or a change of clothes ready, they can hardly miss him. And yet they *have* missed him up to now!' Holmes had gone to the window and was examining with his lens the blood mark on the sill. 'It is clearly the tread of a shoe. It is remarkably broad; a splay-foot, one would say. Curious, because, so far as one can trace any footmark in this mud-stained corner, one would say it was a more shapely sole. However, they are certainly very indistinct. What's this under the side table?'

'Mr Douglas's dumb-bells,' said Ames.

'Dumb-bell – there's only one. Where's the other?'

'I don't know, Mr Holmes. There may have been only one. I have not noticed them for months.'

'One dumb-bell – ' Holmes said seriously; but his remarks were interrupted by a sharp knock at the door.

A tall, sunburned, capable-looking, clean-shaven man looked in at us. I had no difficulty in guessing that it was the Cecil Barker of whom I had heard. His masterful eyes travelled quickly with a questioning glance from face to face.

'Sorry to interrupt your consultation,' said he, 'but you should hear the latest news.'

'An arrest?'

'No such luck. But they've found his bicycle. The fellow left his bicycle behind him. Come and have a look. It is within a hundred yards of the hall door.'

We found three or four grooms and idlers standing in the drive inspecting a bicycle which had been drawn out from a clump of evergreens in which it had been concealed. It was a well used Rudge-Whitworth, splashed as from a considerable journey. There was a saddlebag with spanner and oilcan, but no clue as to the owner.

'It would be a grand help to the police', said the inspector, 'if these things were numbered and registered. But we must be thankful for what we've got. If we can't find where he went to, at least we are likely to get where he came from. But what in the name of all that is wonderful made the fellow leave it behind? And how in the world has he got away without it? We don't seem to get a gleam of light in the case, Mr Holmes.'

'Don't we?' my friend answered thoughtfully. 'I wonder!'

CHAPTER 5

THE PEOPLE OF THE DRAMA

'Have you seen all you want of the study?' asked White Mason as we re-entered the house.

'For the time,' said the inspector, and Holmes nodded.

'Then perhaps you would now like to hear the evidence of some of the people in the house. We could use the dining room, Ames. Please come yourself first and tell us what you know.'

The butler's account was a simple and a clear one, and he gave a convincing impression of sincerity. He had been engaged five years before, when Douglas first came to Birlstone. He understood that Mr Douglas was a rich gentleman who had made his money in America. He had been a kind and considerate employer – not quite what Ames was used to, perhaps; but one can't have everything. He never saw any signs of apprehension in Mr Douglas: on the contrary, he was the most fearless man he had ever known. He ordered the drawbridge to be pulled up every night because it was the ancient custom of the old house, and he liked to keep the old ways up.

Mr Douglas seldom went to London or left the village; but on the day before the crime he had been shopping at Tunbridge Wells. He (Ames) had observed some restlessness and excitement on the part of Mr Douglas that day, for he had seemed impatient and irritable, which was unusual with him. He had not gone to bed that night, but was in the pantry at the back of the house, putting away the silver, when he heard the bell ring violently. He heard no shot, but it was hardly possible he would, as the pantry and kitchens were at the very back of the house and there were several closed doors and a long passage between. The housekeeper had come out of her room, attracted by the violent ringing of the bell. They had gone to the front of the house together.

As they reached the bottom of the stairs he had seen Mrs
Douglas coming down it. No, she was not hurrying; it did
not seem to him that she was particularly agitated. Just as
she reached the bottom of the stairs Mr Barker had rushed
out of the study. He had stopped Mrs Douglas and begged
her to go back.

'For God's sake, go back to your room!' he cried. 'Poor
Jack is dead! You can do nothing. For God's sake, go back!'

After some persuasion upon the stairs Mrs Douglas had
gone back. She did not scream. She made no outcry whatever.
Mrs Allen, the housekeeper, had taken her upstairs and stayed
with her in the bedroom. Ames and Mr Barker had then
returned to the study, where they had found everything exactly
as the police had seen it. The candle was not lit at that time;
but the lamp was burning. They had looked out of the window;
but the night was very dark and nothing could be seen or
heard. They had then rushed out into the hall, where Ames
had turned the windlass which lowered the drawbridge. Mr
Barker had then hurried off to get the police.

Such, in its essentials, was the evidence of the butler.

The account of Mrs Allen, the housekeeper, was, so far as
it went, a corroboration of that of her fellow servant. The
housekeeper's room was rather nearer to the front of the
house than the pantry in which Ames had been working. She
was preparing to go to bed when the loud ringing of the bell
had attracted her attention. She was a little hard of hearing.
Perhaps that was why she had not heard the shot; but in any
case the study was a long way off. She remembered hearing
some sound which she imagined to be the slamming of a
door. That was a good deal earlier – half an hour at least
before the ringing of the bell. When Mr Ames ran to the front

she went with him. She saw Mr Barker, very pale and excited, come out of the study. He intercepted Mrs Douglas, who was coming down the stairs. He entreated her to go back, and she answered him, but what she said could not be heard.

'Take her up! Stay with her!' he had said to Mrs Allen.

She had therefore taken her to the bedroom, and endeavoured to soothe her. She was greatly excited, trembling all over, but made no other attempt to go downstairs. She just sat in her dressing gown by her bedroom fire, with her head sunk in her hands. Mrs Allen stayed with her most of the night. As to the other servants, they had all gone to bed, and the alarm did not reach them until just before the police arrived. They slept at the extreme back of the house, and could not possibly have heard anything.

So far the housekeeper could add nothing on cross-examination save lamentations and expressions of amazement.

Cecil Barker succeeded Mrs Allen as a witness. As to the occurrences of the night before, he had very little to add to what he had already told the police. Personally, he was convinced that the murderer had escaped by the window. The bloodstain was conclusive, in his opinion, on that point. Besides, as the bridge was up, there was no other possible way of escaping. He could not explain what had become of the assassin or why he had not taken his bicycle, if it were indeed his. He could not possibly have been drowned in the moat, which was at no place more than three feet deep.

In his own mind he had a very definite theory about the murder. Douglas was a reticent man, and there were some chapters in his life of which he never spoke. He had emigrated to America when he was a very young man. He had prospered well, and Barker had first met him in California, where they had become partners in a successful mining claim at a place called Benito Canyon. They had done very well; but Douglas had suddenly sold out and started for England. He was a widower at that time. Barker had afterwards realised his money and come to live in London. Thus they had renewed their friendship.

Douglas had given him the impression that some danger was hanging over his head, and he had always looked upon his sudden departure from California, and also his renting a house in so quiet a place in England, as being connected with this peril. He imagined that some secret society, some implacable organisation, was on Douglas's track, which would never rest until it killed him. Some remarks of his had given him this idea; though he had never told him what the society was, nor how he had come to offend it. He could only suppose that the legend upon the placard had some reference to this secret society.

'How long were you with Douglas in California?' asked Inspector MacDonald.

'Five years altogether.'

'He was a bachelor, you say?'

'A widower.'

'Have you ever heard where his first wife came from?'

'No, I remember his saying that she was of German extraction, and I have seen her portrait. She was a very beautiful woman. She died of typhoid the year before I met him.'

'You don't associate his past with any particular part of America?'

'I have heard him talk of Chicago. He knew that city well and had worked there. I have heard him talk of the coal and iron districts. He had travelled a good deal in his time.'

'Was he a politician? Had this secret society to do with politics?'

'No, he cared nothing about politics.'

'You have no reason to think it was criminal?'

'On the contrary, I never met a straighter man in my life.'

'Was there anything curious about his life in California?'

'He liked best to stay and to work at our claim in the mountains. He would never go where other men were if he could help it. That's why I first thought that someone was after him. Then when he left so suddenly for Europe I made sure that it was so. I believe that he had a warning of some sort. Within a week of his leaving half a dozen men were enquiring for him.'

'What sort of men?'

'Well, they were a mighty hard-looking crowd. They came up to the claim and wanted to know where he was. I told them that he was gone to Europe and that I did not know where to find him. They meant him no good – it was easy to see that.'

'Were these men Americans – Californians?'

'Well, I don't know about Californians. They were Americans, all right. But they were not miners. I don't know what they were, and was very glad to see their backs.'

'That was six years ago?'

'Nearer seven.'

'And then you were together five years in California, so that this business dates back not less than eleven years at the least?'

'That is so.'

'It must be a very serious feud that would be kept up with such earnestness for as long as that. It would be no light thing that would give rise to it.'

'I think it shadowed his whole life. It was never quite out of his mind.'

'But if a man had a danger hanging over him, and knew what it was, don't you think he would turn to the police for protection?'

'Maybe it was some danger that he could not be protected against. There's one thing you should know. He always went about armed. His revolver was never out of his pocket. But, by bad luck, he was in his dressing gown and had left it in the bedroom last night. Once the bridge was up, I guess he thought he was safe.'

'I should like these dates a little clearer,' said MacDonald. 'It is quite six years since Douglas left California. You followed him the next year, did you not?'

'That is so.'

'And he had been married five years. You must have returned about the time of his marriage.'

'About a month before. I was his best man.'

'Did you know Mrs Douglas before her marriage?'

'No, I did not. I had been away from England for ten years.'

'But you have seen a good deal of her since.'

Barker looked sternly at the detective. 'I have seen a good deal of *him* since,' he answered. 'If I have seen her, it is because you cannot visit a man without knowing his wife. If you imagine there is any connection – '

'I imagine nothing, Mr Barker. I am bound to make every enquiry which can bear upon the case. But I mean no offence.'

'Some enquiries are offensive,' Barker answered angrily.

'It's only the facts that we want. It is in your interest and everyone's interest that they should be cleared up. Did Mr Douglas entirely approve of your friendship with his wife?'

Barker grew paler, and his great, strong hands were clasped convulsively together. 'You have no right to ask such questions!' he cried. 'What has this to do with the matter you are investigating?'

'I must repeat the question.'

'Well, I refuse to answer.'

'You can refuse to answer; but you must be aware that your refusal is in itself an answer, for you would not refuse if you had not something to conceal.'

Barker stood for a moment with his face set grimly and his strong black eyebrows drawn low in intense thought. Then he looked up with a smile. 'Well, I guess you gentlemen are only doing your clear duty after all, and I have no right to stand in the way of it. I'd only ask you not to worry Mrs Douglas over this matter; for she has enough upon her just now. I may tell you that poor Douglas had just one fault in the world, and that was his jealousy. He was fond of me – no man could be fonder of a friend. And he was devoted to his wife. He loved me to come here, and was forever sending for me. And yet if his wife and I talked together or there seemed any sympathy between us, a kind of wave of jealousy would pass over him, and he would be off the handle and saying the wildest things in a moment. More than once I've sworn off coming for that reason, and then he would write me such penitent, imploring letters that I just had to. But you can take it from me, gentlemen, if it was my last word, that no man ever had a more loving, faithful wife – and I can say also no friend could be more loyal than I!'

It was spoken with fervour and feeling, and yet Inspector MacDonald could not dismiss the subject.

'You are aware,' said he, 'that the dead man's wedding ring has been taken from his finger?'

'So it appears,' said Barker.

'What do you mean by "appears"? You know it as a fact.'

The man seemed confused and undecided. 'When I said "appears" I meant that it was conceivable that he had himself taken off the ring.'

'The mere fact that the ring should be absent, whoever may have removed it, would suggest to anyone's mind, would it not, that the marriage and the tragedy were connected?'

Barker shrugged his broad shoulders. 'I can't profess to say what it means,' he answered. 'But if you mean to hint that it could reflect in any way upon this lady's honour' – his eyes blazed for an instant, and then with an evident effort he got a grip upon his own emotions – 'well, you are on the wrong track, that's all.'

'I don't know that I've anything else to ask you at present,' said MacDonald, coldly.

'There was one small point,' remarked Sherlock Holmes. 'When you entered the room there was only a candle lighted on the table, was there not?'

'Yes, that was so.'

'By its light you saw that some terrible incident had occurred?'

'Exactly.'

'You at once rang for help?'

'Yes.'

'And it arrived very speedily?'

'Within a minute or so.'

'And yet when they arrived they found that the candle was

out and that the lamp had been lighted. That seems very remarkable.'

Again Barker showed some signs of indecision. 'I don't see that it was remarkable, Mr Holmes,' he answered after a pause. 'The candle threw a very bad light. My first thought was to get a better one. The lamp was on the table; so I lit it.'

'And blew out the candle?'

'Exactly.'

Holmes asked no further question, and Barker, with a deliberate look from one to the other of us, which had, as it seemed to me, something of defiance in it, turned and left the room.

Inspector MacDonald had sent up a note to the effect that he would wait upon Mrs Douglas in her room; but she had replied that she would meet us in the dining room. She entered now, a tall and beautiful woman of thirty, reserved and self-possessed to a remarkable degree, very different from the tragic and distracted figure I had pictured. It is true that her face was pale and drawn, like that of one who has endured a great shock; but her manner was composed, and the finely moulded hand which she rested upon the edge of the table was as steady as my own. Her sad, appealing eyes travelled from one to the other of us with a curiously inquisitive expression. That questioning gaze transformed itself suddenly into abrupt speech.

'Have you found anything out yet?' she asked.

Was it my imagination that there was an undertone of fear rather than of hope in the question?

'We have taken every possible step, Mrs Douglas,' said the inspector. 'You may rest assured that nothing will be neglected.'

'Spare no money,' she said in a dead, even tone. 'It is my desire that every possible effort should be made.'

'Perhaps you can tell us something which may throw some light upon the matter.'

'I fear not; but all I know is at your service.'

'We have heard from Mr Cecil Barker that you did not actually see – that you were never in the room where the tragedy occurred?'

'No, he turned me back upon the stairs. He begged me to return to my room.'

'Quite so. You had heard the shot, and you had at once come down.'

'I put on my dressing gown and then came down.'

'How long was it after hearing the shot that you were stopped on the stairs by Mr Barker?'

'It may have been a couple of minutes. It is so hard to reckon time at such a moment. He implored me not to go on. He assured me that I could do nothing. Then Mrs Allen, the housekeeper, led me upstairs again. It was all like some dreadful dream.'

'Can you give us any idea how long your husband had been downstairs before you heard the shot?'

'No, I cannot say. He went from his dressing room, and I did not hear him go. He did the rounds of the house every night, for he was nervous of fire. It is the only thing that I have ever known him nervous of.'

'That is just the point which I want to come to, Mrs Douglas. You have known your husband only in England, have you not?'

'Yes, we have been married five years.'

'Have you heard him speak of anything which occurred in America and might bring some danger upon him?'

Mrs Douglas thought earnestly before she answered. 'Yes,' she said at last, 'I have always felt that there was a danger hanging over him. He refused to discuss it with me. It was not from want of confidence in me – there was the most complete love and confidence between us – but it was out of his desire to keep all alarm away from me. He thought I should brood over it if I knew all, and so he was silent.'

'How did you know it, then?'

Mrs Douglas's face lit with a quick smile. 'Can a husband ever carry about a secret all his life and a woman who loves him have no suspicion of it? I knew it by his refusal to talk about some episodes in his American life. I knew it by certain precautions he took. I knew it by certain words he let fall. I knew it by the way he looked at unexpected strangers. I was perfectly certain that he had some powerful enemies, that he believed they were on his track, and that he was always on his guard against them. I was so sure of it that for years I have been terrified if ever he came home later than was expected.'

'Might I ask', asked Holmes, 'what the words were which attracted your attention?'

'The Valley of Fear,' the lady answered. 'That was an expression he has used when I questioned him. "I have been in the Valley of Fear. I am not out of it yet." – "Are we never to get out of the Valley of Fear?" I have asked him when I have seen him more serious than usual. "Sometimes I think that we never shall," he has answered.'

'Surely you asked him what he meant by the Valley of Fear?'

'I did; but his face would become very grave and he would shake his head. "It is bad enough that one of us should have been in its shadow," he said. "Please God it shall never fall upon you!" It was some real valley in which he had lived and in which something terrible had occurred to him, of that I am certain; but I can tell you no more.'

'And he never mentioned any names?'

'Yes, he was delirious with fever once when he had his hunting accident three years ago. Then I remember that there was a name that came continually to his lips. He spoke it with anger and a sort of horror. McGinty was the name – Bodymaster McGinty. I asked him when he recovered who Bodymaster McGinty was, and whose body he was master of. "Never of mine, thank God!" he answered with a laugh, and that was all I could get from him. But there is a connection between Bodymaster McGinty and the Valley of Fear.'

'There is one other point,' said Inspector MacDonald. 'You met Mr Douglas in a boarding house in London, did you not, and became engaged to him there? Was there any romance, anything secret or mysterious, about the wedding?'

'There was romance. There is always romance. There was nothing mysterious.'

'He had no rival?'

'No, I was quite free.'

'You have heard, no doubt, that his wedding ring has been taken. Does that suggest anything to you? Suppose that some enemy of his old life had tracked him down and committed this crime, what possible reason could he have for taking his wedding ring?'

For an instant I could have sworn that the faintest shadow of a smile flickered over the woman's lips.

'I really cannot tell,' she answered. 'It is certainly a most extraordinary thing.'

'Well, we will not detain you any longer, and we are sorry

to have put you to this trouble at such a time,' said the inspector. 'There are some other points, no doubt; but we can refer to you as they arise.'

She rose, and I was again conscious of that quick, questioning glance with which she had just surveyed us. 'What impression has my evidence made upon you?' The question might as well have been spoken. Then, with a bow, she swept from the room.

'She's a beautiful woman – a very beautiful woman,' said MacDonald thoughtfully, after the door had closed behind her. 'This man Barker has certainly been down here a good deal. He is a man who might be attractive to a woman. He admits that the dead man was jealous, and maybe he knew best himself what cause he had for jealousy. Then there's that wedding ring. You can't get past that. The man who tears a wedding ring off a dead man's – What do you say to it, Mr Holmes?'

My friend had sat with his head upon his hands, sunk in the deepest thought. Now he rose and rang the bell. 'Ames,' he said, when the butler entered, 'where is Mr Cecil Barker now?'

'I'll see, sir.'

He came back in a moment to say that Barker was in the garden.

'Can you remember, Ames, what Mr Barker had on his feet last night when you joined him in the study?'

'Yes, Mr Holmes. He had a pair of bedroom slippers. I brought him his boots when he went for the police.'

'Where are the slippers now?'

'They are still under the chair in the hall.'

'Very good, Ames. It is, of course, important for us to know which tracks may be Mr Barker's and which from outside.'

'Yes, sir. I may say that I noticed that the slippers were stained with blood – so indeed were my own.'

'That is natural enough, considering the condition of the room. Very good, Ames. We will ring if we want you.'

A few minutes later we were in the study. Holmes had brought with him the carpet slippers from the hall. As Ames had observed, the soles of both were dark with blood.

'Strange!' murmured Holmes, as he stood in the light of the window and examined them minutely. 'Very strange indeed!'

Stooping with one of his quick feline pounces, he placed the slipper upon the blood mark on the sill. It exactly corresponded. He smiled in silence at his colleagues.

The inspector was transfigured with excitement. His native accent rattled like a stick upon railings.

'Man,' he cried, 'there's not a doubt of it! Barker has just marked the window himself. It's a good deal broader than any bootmark. I mind that you said it was a splay-foot, and here's the explanation. But what's the game, Mr Holmes – what's the game?'

'Ay, what's the game?' my friend repeated thoughtfully.

White Mason chuckled and rubbed his fat hands together in his professional satisfaction. 'I said it was a snorter!' he cried. 'And a real snorter it is!'

CHAPTER 6

A DAWNING LIGHT

The three detectives had many matters of detail into which to enquire; so I returned alone to our modest quarters at the village inn. But before doing so I took a stroll in the curious old-world garden which flanked the house. Rows of very ancient yew trees cut into strange designs girded it round. Inside was a beautiful stretch of lawn with an old sundial in the middle, the whole effect so soothing and restful that it was welcome to my somewhat jangled nerves.

In that deeply peaceful atmosphere one could forget, or remember only as some fantastic nightmare, that darkened study with the sprawling, bloodstained figure on the floor. And yet, as I strolled round it and tried to steep my soul in its gentle balm, a strange incident occurred, which brought me back to the tragedy and left a sinister impression in my mind.

I have said that a decoration of yew trees circled the garden. At the end farthest from the house they thickened into a continuous hedge. On the other side of this hedge, concealed from the eyes of anyone approaching from the direction of the house, there was a stone seat. As I approached the spot I was aware of voices, some remark in the deep tones of a man, answered by a little ripple of feminine laughter.

An instant later I had come round the end of the hedge and my eyes lit upon Mrs Douglas and the man Barker before they were aware of my presence. Her appearance gave me a shock. In the dining-room she had been demure and discreet. Now all pretence of grief had passed away from her. Her eyes shone with the joy of living, and her face still quivered with amusement at some remark of her companion. He sat forward, his hands clasped and his forearms on his knees, with an answering smile upon his bold, handsome face. In an instant – but it was just one instant too late – they resumed their solemn masks as my figure came into view. A hurried

word or two passed between them, and then Barker rose and
came towards me.

'Excuse me, sir,' said he, 'but am I addressing Dr Watson?'

I bowed with a coldness which showed, I dare say, very
plainly the impression which had been produced upon my
mind.

'We thought that it was probably you, as your friendship
with Mr Sherlock Holmes is so well known. Would you mind
coming over and speaking to Mrs Douglas for one instant?'

I followed him with a dour face. Very clearly I could see
in my mind's eye that shattered figure on the floor. Here
within a few hours of the tragedy were his wife and his
nearest friend laughing together behind a bush in the garden
which had been his. I greeted the lady with reserve. I had
grieved with her grief in the dining room. Now I met her
appealing gaze with an unresponsive eye.

'I fear that you think me callous and hard-hearted,' said she.

I shrugged my shoulders. 'It is no business of mine,'
said I.

'Perhaps some day you will do me justice. If you only
realised – '

'There is no need why Dr Watson should realise,' said
Barker quickly. 'As he has himself said, it is no possible
business of his.'

'Exactly,' said I, 'and so I will beg leave to resume my
walk.'

'One moment, Dr Watson,' cried the woman in a pleading
voice. 'There is one question which you can answer with
more authority than anyone else in the world, and it may
make a very great difference to me. You know Mr Holmes
and his relations with the police better than anyone else can.

Supposing that a matter were brought confidentially to his knowledge, is it absolutely necessary that he should pass it on to the detectives?'

'Yes, that's it,' said Barker eagerly. 'Is he on his own or is he entirely in with them?'

'I really don't know that I should be justified in discussing such a point.'

'I beg – I implore that you will, Dr Watson! I assure you that you will be helping us – helping me greatly if you will guide us on that point.'

There was such a ring of sincerity in the woman's voice that for the instant I forgot all about her levity and was moved only to do her will.

'Mr Holmes is an independent investigator,' I said. 'He is his own master, and would act as his own judgement directed. At the same time, he would naturally feel loyalty towards the officials who were working on the same case, and he would not conceal from them anything which would help them in bringing a criminal to justice. Beyond this I can say nothing, and I would refer you to Mr Holmes himself if you wanted fuller information.'

So saying I raised my hat and went upon my way, leaving them still seated behind that concealing hedge. I looked back as I rounded the far end of it, and saw that they were still talking very earnestly together, and, as they were gazing after me, it was clear that it was our interview that was the subject of their debate.

'I wish none of their confidences,' said Holmes, when I reported to him what had occurred. He had spent the whole afternoon at the Manor House in consultation with his two colleagues, and returned about five with a ravenous appetite for a high tea which I had ordered for him. 'No confidences, Watson; for they are mighty awkward if it comes to an arrest for conspiracy and murder.'

'You think it will come to that?'

He was in his most cheerful and debonair humour. 'My dear Watson, when I have exterminated that fourth egg I shall be ready to put you in touch with the whole situation. I don't say that we have fathomed it – far from it – but when we have traced the missing dumb-bell – '

'The dumb-bell!'

'Dear me, Watson, is it possible that you have not penetrated the fact that the case hangs upon the missing dumb-bell? Well, well, you need not be downcast; for between ourselves I don't think that either Inspector Mac or the excellent local practitioner has grasped the overwhelming importance of this incident. One dumb-bell, Watson! Consider an athlete with one dumb-bell! Picture to yourself the unilateral development, the imminent danger of a spinal curvature. Shocking, Watson, shocking!'

He sat with his mouth full of toast and his eyes sparkling with mischief, watching my intellectual entanglement. The mere sight of his excellent appetite was an assurance of success; for I had very clear recollections of days and nights without a thought of food, when his baffled mind had chafed before some problem while his thin, eager features became more attenuated with the asceticism of complete mental concentration. Finally he lit his pipe, and sitting in the ingle-nook of the old village inn, he talked slowly and at random about his case, rather as one who thinks aloud than as one who makes a considered statement.

'A lie, Watson – a great, big, thumping, obtrusive, uncompromising lie – that's what meets us on the threshold! There

is our starting point. The whole story told by Barker is a lie.
But Barker's story is corroborated by Mrs Douglas. Therefore
she is lying also. They are both lying, and in a conspiracy.
So now we have the clear problem. Why are they lying, and
what is the truth which they are trying so hard to conceal?
Let us try, Watson, you and I, if we can get behind the lie
and reconstruct the truth.

'How do I know that they are lying? Because it is a clumsy
fabrication which simply could not be true. Consider!
According to the story given to us, the assassin had less than
a minute after the murder had been committed to take that
ring, which was under another ring, from the dead man's
finger, to replace the other ring – a thing which he would
surely never have done – and to put that singular card beside
his victim. I say that this was obviously impossible.

'You may argue – but I have too much respect for your
judgement, Watson, to think that you will do so – that the
ring may have been taken before the man was killed. The
fact that the candle had been lit only a short time shows that
there had been no lengthy interview. Was Douglas, from what
we hear of his fearless character, a man who would be likely
to give up his wedding ring at such short notice, or could we
conceive of his giving it up at all? No, no, Watson, the assassin
was alone with the dead man for some time with the lamp
lit. Of that I have no doubt at all.

'But the gunshot was apparently the cause of death.
Therefore the shot must have been fired some time earlier
than we are told. But there could be no mistake about such
a matter as that. We are in the presence, therefore, of a deliberate conspiracy upon the part of the two people who heard
the gunshot – of the man Barker and of the woman Douglas.

When on the top of this I am able to show that the blood mark on the windowsill was deliberately placed there by Barker, in order to give a false clue to the police, you will admit that the case grows dark against him.

'Now we have to ask ourselves at what hour the murder actually did occur. Up to half-past ten the servants were moving about the house; so it was certainly not before that time. At a quarter to eleven they had all gone to their rooms with the exception of Ames, who was in the pantry. I have been trying some experiments after you left us this afternoon, and I find that no noise which MacDonald can make in the study can penetrate to me in the pantry when the doors are all shut.

'It is otherwise, however, from the housekeeper's room. It is not so far down the corridor, and from it I could vaguely hear a voice when it was very loudly raised. The sound from a shotgun is to some extent muffled when the discharge is at very close range, as it undoubtedly was in this instance. It would not be very loud, and yet in the silence of the night it should have easily penetrated to Mrs Allen's room. She is, as she has told us, somewhat deaf; but none the less she mentioned in her evidence that she did hear something like a door slamming half an hour before the alarm was given. Half an hour before the alarm was given would be a quarter to eleven. I have no doubt that what she heard was the report of the gun, and that this was the real instant of the murder.

'If this is so, we have now to determine what Barker and Mrs Douglas, presuming that they are not the actual murderers, could have been doing from quarter to eleven, when the sound of the shot brought them down, until quarter past eleven, when they rang the bell and summoned the servants. What were they doing, and why did they not instantly give the alarm? That is the question which faces us, and when it has been answered we shall surely have gone some way to solve our problem.'

'I am convinced myself', said I, 'that there is an understanding between those two people. She must be a heartless creature to sit laughing at some jest within a few hours of her husband's murder.'

'Exactly. She does not shine as a wife even in her own account of what occurred. I am not a whole-souled admirer of womankind, as you are aware, Watson, but my experience of life has taught me that there are few wives, having any regard for their husbands, who would let any man's spoken word stand between them and that husband's dead body. Should I ever marry, Watson, I should hope to inspire my wife with some feeling which would prevent her from being walked off by a housekeeper when my corpse was lying within a few yards of her. It was badly stage-managed; for even the rawest investigators must be struck by the absence of the usual feminine ululation. If there had been nothing else, this incident alone would have suggested a prearranged conspiracy to my mind.'

'You think then, definitely, that Barker and Mrs Douglas are guilty of the murder?'

'There is an appalling directness about your questions, Watson,' said Holmes, shaking his pipe at me. 'They come at me like bullets. If you put it that Mrs Douglas and Barker know the truth about the murder, and are conspiring to conceal it, then I can give you a whole-souled answer. I am sure they do. But your more deadly proposition is not so clear. Let us for a moment consider the difficulties which stand in the way.

'We will suppose that this couple are united by the bonds of a guilty love, and that they have determined to get rid of the man who stands between them. It is a large supposition; for discreet enquiry among servants and others has failed to corroborate it in any way. On the contrary, there is a good deal of evidence that the Douglases were very attached to each other.'

'That, I am sure, cannot be true,' said I, thinking of the beautiful smiling face in the garden.

'Well at least they gave that impression. However, we will suppose that they are an extraordinarily astute couple, who deceive everyone upon this point, and conspire to murder the husband. He happens to be a man over whose head some danger hangs – '

'We have only their word for that.'

Holmes looked thoughtful. 'I see, Watson. You are sketching out a theory by which everything they say from the beginning is false. According to your idea, there was never any hidden menace, or secret society, or Valley of Fear, or Boss MacSomebody, or anything else. Well, that is a good sweeping generalisation. Let us see what that brings us to. They invent this theory to account for the crime. They then play up to the idea by leaving this bicycle in the park as proof of the existence of some outsider. The stain on the windowsill conveys the same idea. So does the card on the body, which might have been prepared in the house. That all fits into your hypothesis, Watson. But now we come on the nasty, angular, uncompromising bits which won't slip into their places. Why a cut-off shotgun of all weapons – and an American one at that? How could they be so sure that the sound of it would not bring someone on to them? It's a mere chance as it is that Mrs Allen did not start out to enquire for the slamming door. Why did your guilty couple do all this, Watson?'

'I confess that I can't explain it.'

'Then again, if a woman and her lover conspire to murder a husband, are they going to advertise their guilt by ostentatiously removing his wedding ring after his death? Does that strike you as very probable, Watson?'

'No, it does not.'

'And once again, if the thought of leaving a bicycle concealed outside had occurred to you, would it really have seemed worth doing when the dullest detective would naturally say this is an obvious blind, as the bicycle is the first thing which the fugitive needed in order to make his escape.'

'I can conceive of no explanation.'

'And yet there should be no combination of events for which the wit of man cannot conceive an explanation. Simply as a mental exercise, without any assertion that it is true, let me indicate a possible line of thought. It is, I admit, mere imagination; but how often is imagination the mother of truth?

'We will suppose that there was a guilty secret, a really shameful secret in the life of this man Douglas. This leads to his murder by someone who is, we will suppose, an avenger, someone from outside. This avenger, for some reason which I confess I am still at a loss to explain, took the dead man's wedding ring. The vendetta might conceivably date back to the man's first marriage, and the ring be taken for some such reason.

'Before this avenger got away, Barker and the wife had reached the room. The assassin convinced them that any attempt to arrest him would lead to the publication of some hideous scandal. They were converted to this idea, and preferred to let him go. For this purpose they probably lowered the bridge, which can be done quite noiselessly, and then raised it again. He made his escape, and for some reason thought that he could do so more safely on foot than on the bicycle. He therefore left his machine where it would not be discovered until he had got safely away. So far we are within the bounds of possibility, are we not?'

'Well, it is possible, no doubt,' said I, with some reserve.

'We have to remember, Watson, that whatever occurred is certainly something very extraordinary. Well, now, to continue our supposititious case, the couple – not necessarily a guilty couple – realise after the murderer is gone that they have placed themselves in a position in which it may be difficult for them to prove that they did not themselves either do the deed or connive at it. They rapidly and rather clumsily met the situation. The mark was put by Barker's bloodstained slipper upon the windowsill to suggest how the fugitive got away. They obviously were the two who must have heard the sound of the gun; so they gave the alarm exactly as they would have done, but a good half hour after the event.'

'And how do you propose to prove all this?'

'Well, if there were an outsider, he may be traced and taken. That would be the most effective of all proofs. But if not – well, the resources of science are far from being exhausted. I think that an evening alone in that study would help me much.'

'An evening alone!'

'I propose to go up there presently. I have arranged it with the estimable Ames, who is by no means wholehearted about Barker. I shall sit in that room and see if its atmosphere brings me inspiration. I'm a believer in the *genius loci*. You smile, friend Watson. Well, we shall see. By the way, you have that big umbrella of yours, have you not?'

'It is here.'

'Well, I'll borrow that if I may.'

'Certainly – but what a wretched weapon! If there is danger – '

'Nothing serious, my dear Watson, or I should certainly ask for your assistance. But I'll take the umbrella. At present I am only awaiting the return of our colleagues from Tunbridge Wells, where they are at present engaged in trying for a likely owner to the bicycle.'

It was nightfall before Inspector MacDonald and White Mason came back from their expedition, and they arrived exultant, reporting a great advance in our investigation.

'Man, I'll admeet that I had my doubts if there was ever an outsider,' said MacDonald, 'but that's all past now. We've had the bicycle identified, and we have a description of our man; so that's a long step on our journey.'

'It sounds to me like the beginning of the end,' said Holmes. 'I'm sure I congratulate you both with all my heart.'

'Well, I started from the fact that Mr Douglas had seemed disturbed since the day before, when he had been at Tunbridge Wells. It was at Tunbridge Wells then that he had become conscious of some danger. It was clear, therefore, that if a man had come over with a bicycle it was from Tunbridge Wells that he might be expected to have come. We took the bicycle over with us and showed it at the hotels. It was identified at once by the manager of the Eagle Commercial as belonging to a man named Hargrave, who had taken a room there two days before. This bicycle and a small valise were his whole belongings. He had registered his name as coming from London, but had given no address. The valise was London made, and the contents were British; but the man himself was undoubtedly an American.'

'Well, well,' said Holmes gleefully, 'you have indeed done some solid work while I have been sitting spinning theories with my friend! It's a lesson in being practical, Mr Mac.'

'Ay, it's just that, Mr Holmes,' said the inspector with satisfaction.

'But this may all fit in with your theories,' I remarked.

'That may or may not be. But let us hear the end, Mr Mac. Was there nothing to identify this man?'

'So little that it was evident that he had carefully guarded himself against identification. There were no papers or letters, and no marking upon the clothes. A cycle map of the county lay on his bedroom table. He had left the hotel after breakfast yesterday morning on his bicycle, and no more was heard of him until our enquiries.'

'That's what puzzles me, Mr Holmes,' said White Mason. 'If the fellow did not want the hue and cry raised over him, one would imagine that he would have returned and remained at the hotel as an inoffensive tourist. As it is, he must know that he will be reported to the police by the hotel manager and that his disappearance will be connected with the murder.'

'So one would imagine. Still, he has been justified of his wisdom up to date, at any rate, since he has not been taken. But his description – what of that?'

MacDonald referred to his notebook. 'Here we have it so far as they could give it. They don't seem to have taken any very particular stock of him; but still the porter, the clerk,

and the chambermaid are all agreed that this about covers
the points. He was a man about five foot nine in height, fifty
or so years of age, his hair slightly grizzled, a greyish moustache, a curved nose, and a face which all of them described
as fierce and forbidding.'

'Well, bar the expression, that might almost be a description of Douglas himself,' said Holmes. 'He is just over fifty,
with grizzled hair and moustache, and about the same height.
Did you get anything else?'

'He was dressed in a heavy grey suit with a reefer jacket,
and he wore a short yellow overcoat and a soft cap.'

'What about the shotgun?'

'It is less than two feet long. It could very well have fitted
into his valise. He could have carried it inside his overcoat
without difficulty.'

'And how do you consider that all this bears upon the
general case?'

'Well, Mr Holmes,' said MacDonald, 'when we have got
our man – and you may be sure that I had his description
on the wires within five minutes of hearing it – we shall
be better able to judge. But, even as it stands, we have
surely gone a long way. We know that an American calling
himself Hargrave came to Tunbridge Wells two days ago
with bicycle and valise. In the latter was a sawn-off shotgun;
so he came with the deliberate purpose of crime. Yesterday
morning he set off for this place on his bicycle, with his
gun concealed in his overcoat. No one saw him arrive, so
far as we can learn; but he need not pass through the village
to reach the park gates, and there are many cyclists upon
the road. Presumably he at once concealed his cycle among
the laurels where it was found, and possibly lurked there

himself, with his eye on the house, waiting for Mr Douglas to come out. The shotgun is a strange weapon to use inside a house; but he had intended to use it outside, and there it has very obvious advantages, as it would be impossible to miss with it, and the sound of shots is so common in an English sporting neighbourhood that no particular notice would be taken.'

'That is all very clear,' said Holmes.

'Well, Mr Douglas did not appear. What was he to do next? He left his bicycle and approached the house in the twilight. He found the bridge down and no one about. He took his chance, intending, no doubt, to make some excuse if he met anyone. He met no one. He slipped into the first room that he saw, and concealed himself behind the curtain. Thence he could see the drawbridge go up, and he knew that his only escape was through the moat. He waited until quarter-past eleven, when Mr Douglas upon his usual nightly rounds came into the room. He shot him and escaped, as arranged. He was aware that the bicycle would be described by the hotel people and be a clue against him; so he left it there and made his way by some other means to London or to some safe hiding place which he had already arranged. How is that, Mr Holmes?'

'Well, Mr Mac, it is very good and very clear so far as it goes. That is your end of the story. My end is that the crime was committed half an hour earlier than reported; that Mrs Douglas and Barker are both in a conspiracy to conceal something; that they aided the murderer's escape – or at least that they reached the room before he escaped – and that they fabricated evidence of his escape through the window, whereas in all probability they had themselves let him go by lowering the bridge. That's my reading of the first half.'

The two detectives shook their heads.

'Well, Mr Holmes, if this is true, we only tumble out of one mystery into another,' said the London inspector.

'And in some ways a worse one,' added White Mason. 'The lady has never been in America in all her life. What possible connection could she have with an American assassin which would cause her to shelter him?'

'I freely admit the difficulties,' said Holmes. 'I propose to make a little investigation of my own tonight, and it is just possible that it may contribute something to the common cause.'

'Can we help you, Mr Holmes?'

'No, no! Darkness and Dr Watson's umbrella – my wants are simple. And Ames, the faithful Ames, no doubt he will stretch a point for me. All my lines of thought lead me back invariably to the one basic question – why should an athletic man develop his frame upon so unnatural an instrument as a single dumb-bell?'

It was late that night when Holmes returned from his solitary excursion. We slept in a double-bedded room, which was the best that the little country inn could do for us. I was already asleep when I was partly awakened by his entrance.

'Well, Holmes,' I murmured, 'have you found anything out?'

He stood beside me in silence, his candle in his hand. Then the tall, lean figure inclined towards me. 'I say, Watson,' he whispered, 'would you be afraid to sleep in the same room with a lunatic, a man with softening of the brain, an idiot whose mind has lost its grip?'

'Not in the least,' I answered in astonishment.

'Ah, that's lucky,' he said, and not another word would he utter that night.

CHAPTER 7

THE SOLUTION

Next morning, after breakfast, we found Inspector MacDonald and White Mason seated in close consultation in the small parlour of the local police sergeant. On the table in front of them were piled a number of letters and telegrams, which they were carefully sorting and docketing. Three had been placed on one side.

'Still on the track of the elusive bicyclist?' Holmes asked cheerfully. 'What is the latest news of the ruffian?'

MacDonald pointed ruefully to his heap of correspondence.

'He is at present reported from Leicester, Nottingham, Southampton, Derby, East Ham, Richmond, and fourteen other places. In three of them – East Ham, Leicester, and Liverpool – there is a clear case against him, and he has actually been arrested. The country seems to be full of the fugitives with yellow coats.'

'Dear me!' said Holmes sympathetically. 'Now, Mr Mac and you, Mr White Mason, I wish to give you a very earnest piece of advice. When I went into this case with you I bargained, as you will no doubt remember, that I should not present you with half-proved theories, but that I should retain and work out my own ideas until I had satisfied myself that they were correct. For this reason I am not at the present moment telling you all that is in my mind. On the other hand, I said that I would play the game fairly by you, and I do not think it is a fair game to allow you for one unnecessary moment to waste your energies upon a profitless task. Therefore I am here to advise you this morning, and my advice to you is summed up in three words – abandon the case.'

MacDonald and White Mason stared in amazement at their celebrated colleague.

'You consider it hopeless!' cried the inspector.

'I consider *your* case to be hopeless. I do not consider that it is hopeless to arrive at the truth.'

'But this cyclist. He is not an invention. We have his description, his valise, his bicycle. The fellow must be somewhere. Why should we not get him?'

'Yes, yes, no doubt he is somewhere, and no doubt we shall get him; but I would not have you waste your energies in East Ham or Liverpool. I am sure that we can find some shorter cut to a result.'

'You are holding something back. It's hardly fair of you, Mr Holmes.' The inspector was annoyed.

'You know my methods of work, Mr Mac. But I will hold it back for the shortest time possible. I only wish to verify my details in one way, which can very readily be done, and then I make my bow and return to London, leaving my results entirely at your service. I owe you too much to act otherwise; for in all my experience I cannot recall any more singular and interesting study.'

'This is clean beyond me, Mr Holmes. We saw you when we returned from Tunbridge Wells last night, and you were in general agreement with our results. What has happened since then to give you a completely new idea of the case?'

'Well, since you ask me, I spent, as I told you that I would, some hours last night at the Manor House.'

'Well, what happened?'

'Ah, I can only give you a very general answer to that for the moment. By the way, I have been reading a short but clear and interesting account of the old building, purchasable at the modest sum of one penny from the local tobacconist.'

Here Holmes drew a small tract, embellished with a rude engraving of the ancient Manor House, from his waistcoat pocket.

'It immensely adds to the zest of an investigation, my dear Mr Mac, when one is in conscious sympathy with the historical atmosphere of one's surroundings. Don't look so impatient; for I assure you that even so bald an account as this raises some sort of picture of the past in one's mind. Permit me to give you a sample. "Erected in the fifth year of the reign of James I, and standing upon the site of a much older building, the Manor House of Birlstone presents one of the finest surviving examples of the moated Jacobean residence – "'

'You are making fools of us, Mr Holmes!'

'Tut, tut, Mr Mac! – The first sign of temper I have detected in you. Well, I won't read it verbatim, since you feel so strongly upon the subject. But when I tell you that there is some account of the taking of the place by a parliamentary colonel in 1644, of the concealment of Charles for several days in the course of the Civil War, and finally of a visit there by the second George, you will admit that there are various associations of interest connected with this ancient house.'

'I don't doubt it, Mr Holmes; but that is no business of ours.'

'Is it not? Is it not? Breadth of view, my dear Mr Mac, is one of the essentials of our profession. The interplay of ideas and the oblique uses of knowledge are often of extraordinary interest. You will excuse these remarks from one who, though a mere connoisseur of crime, is still rather older and perhaps more experienced than yourself.'

'I'm the first to admit that,' said the detective heartily. 'You get to your point, I admit; but you have such a deuced round-the-corner way of doing it.'

'Well, well, I'll drop past history and get down to present-day facts. I called last night, as I have already said, at the Manor House. I did not see either Barker or Mrs Douglas. I saw no necessity to disturb them; but I was pleased to hear that the lady was not visibly pining and that she had partaken of an excellent dinner. My visit was specially made to the good Mr Ames, with whom I exchanged some amiabilities, which culminated in his allowing me, without reference to anyone else, to sit alone for a time in the study.'

'What! With that?' I ejaculated.

'No, no, everything is now in order. You gave permission for that, Mr Mac, as I am informed. The room was in its normal state, and in it I passed an instructive quarter of an hour.'

'What were you doing?'

'Well, not to make a mystery of so simple a matter, I was looking for the missing dumb-bell. It has always bulked rather large in my estimate of the case. I ended by finding it.'

'Where?'

'Ah, there we come to the edge of the unexplored. Let me go a little further, a very little further, and I will promise that you shall share everything that I know.'

'Well, we're bound to take you on your own terms,' said

the inspector; 'but when it comes to telling us to abandon the case – why in the name of goodness should we abandon the case?'

'For the simple reason, my dear Mr Mac, that you have not got the first idea what it is that you are investigating.'

'We are investigating the murder of Mr John Douglas of Birlstone Manor.'

'Yes, yes, so you are. But don't trouble to trace the mysterious gentleman upon the bicycle. I assure you that it won't help you.'

'Then what do you suggest that we do?'

'I will tell you exactly what to do, if you will do it.'

'Well, I'm bound to say I've always found you had reason behind all your queer ways. I'll do what you advise.'

'And you, Mr White Mason?'

The country detective looked helplessly from one to the other. Holmes and his methods were new to him. 'Well, if it is good enough for the inspector, it is good enough for me,' he said at last.

'Capital!' said Holmes. 'Well, then, I should recommend a nice, cheery country walk for both of you. They tell me that the views from Birlstone Ridge over the Weald are very remarkable. No doubt lunch could be got at some suitable hostelry; though my ignorance of the country prevents me from recommending one. In the evening, tired but happy – '

'Man, this is getting past a joke!' cried MacDonald, rising angrily from his chair.

'Well, well, spend the day as you like,' said Holmes, patting him cheerfully upon the shoulder. 'Do what you like and go where you will, but meet me here before dusk without fail – without fail, Mr Mac.'

'That sounds more like sanity.'

'All of it was excellent advice; but I don't insist, so long as you are here when I need you. But now, before we part, I want you to write a note to Mr Barker.'

'Well?'

'I'll dictate it, if you like. Ready?

'Dear Sir:

'It has struck me that it is our duty to drain the moat, in the hope that we may find some – '

'It's impossible,' said the inspector. 'I've made enquiry.'

'Tut, tut! My dear sir, please do what I ask you.'

'Well, go on.'

' – in the hope that we may find something which may bear upon our investigation. I have made arrangements, and the workmen will be at work early tomorrow morning diverting the stream – '

'Impossible!'

' – diverting the stream; so I thought it best to explain matters beforehand.

'Now sign that, and send it by hand about four o'clock. At that hour we shall meet again in this room. Until then we may each do what we like; for I can assure you that this enquiry has come to a definite pause.'

Evening was drawing in when we reassembled. Holmes was very serious in his manner, myself curious, and the detectives obviously critical and annoyed.

'Well, gentlemen,' said my friend gravely, 'I am asking you now to put everything to the test with me, and you will judge for yourselves whether the observations I have made justify the conclusions to which I have come. It is a chill evening, and I do not know how long our expedition may last; so I beg that you will wear your warmest coats. It is of the first importance that we should be in our places before it grows dark; so with your permission we shall get started at once.'

We passed along the outer bounds of the Manor House park until we came to a place where there was a gap in the rails which fenced it. Through this we slipped, and then in the gathering gloom we followed Holmes until we had reached a shrubbery which lies nearly opposite to the main door and the drawbridge. The latter had not been raised. Holmes crouched down behind the screen of laurels, and we all three followed his example.

'Well, what are we to do now?' asked MacDonald with some gruffness.

'Possess our souls in patience and make as little noise as possible,' Holmes answered.

'What are we here for at all? I really think that you might treat us with more frankness.'

Holmes laughed. 'Watson insists that I am the dramatist in real life,' said he. 'Some touch of the artist wells up within me, and calls insistently for a well-staged perfor-mance. Surely our profession, Mr Mac, would be a drab and sordid one if we did not sometimes set the scene so as to glorify our results. The blunt accusation, the brutal tap upon the shoulder – what can one make of such a *dénoue-ment*? But the quick inference, the subtle trap, the clever forecast of coming events, the triumphant vindication of bold theories – are these not the pride and the justification of our life's work? At the present moment you thrill with the glamour of the situation and the anticipation of the hunt. Where would be that thrill if I had been as definite as a timetable? I only ask a little patience, Mr Mac, and all will be clear to you.'

'Well, I hope the pride and justification and the rest of it will come before we all get our death of cold,' said the London detective with comic resignation.

We all had good reason to join in the aspiration; for our vigil was a long and bitter one. Slowly the shadows darkened over the long, sombre face of the old house. A cold, damp reek from the moat chilled us to the bones and set our teeth chattering. There was a single lamp over the gateway and a steady globe of light in the fatal study. Everything else was dark and still.

'How long is this to last?' asked the inspector finally. 'And what is it we are watching for?'

'I have no more notion than you how long it is to last,' Holmes answered with some asperity. 'If criminals would always schedule their movements like railway trains, it would certainly be more convenient for all of us. As to what it is we – well, *that's* what we are watching for!'

As he spoke the bright, yellow light in the study was obscured by somebody passing to and fro before it. The laurels among which we lay were immediately opposite the window and not more than a hundred feet from it. Presently it was thrown open with a whining of hinges, and we could dimly see the dark outline of a man's head and shoulders looking out into the gloom. For some minutes he peered forth in furtive, stealthy fashion, as one who wishes to be assured that he is unobserved. Then he leaned forward, and in the intense silence we were aware of the soft lapping of agitated water. He seemed to be stirring up the moat with something which he held in his hand. Then suddenly he hauled something in as a fisherman lands a fish – some large, round object which obscured the light as it was dragged through the open casement.

'Now!' cried Holmes. 'Now!'

We were all upon our feet, staggering after him with our stiffened limbs, while he ran swiftly across the bridge and rang violently at the bell. There was the rasping of bolts from the other side, and the amazed Ames stood in the entrance. Holmes brushed him aside without a word and, followed by all of us, rushed into the room which had been occupied by the man whom we had been watching.

The oil lamp on the table represented the glow which we had seen from outside. It was now in the hand of Cecil Barker, who held it towards us as we entered. Its light shone upon his strong, resolute, clean-shaven face and his menacing eyes.

'What the devil is the meaning of all this?' he cried. 'What are you after, anyhow?'

Holmes took a swift glance round, and then pounced upon a sodden bundle tied together with cord which lay where it had been thrust under the writing table.

'This is what we are after, Mr Barker – this bundle, weighted with a dumb-bell, which you have just raised from the bottom of the moat.'

Barker stared at Holmes with amazement in his face. 'How in thunder came you to know anything about it?' he asked.

'Simply that I put it there.'

'You put it there! You!'

'Perhaps I should have said "replaced it there", said Holmes. 'You will remember, Inspector MacDonald, that I was somewhat struck by the absence of a dumb-bell. I drew your attention to it; but with the pressure of other events you had hardly the time to give it the consideration which would have enabled you to draw deductions from it. When water is near and a weight is missing it is not a very far-fetched supposition that something has been sunk in the water. The idea was at least worth testing; so with the help of Ames, who admitted me to the room, and the crook of Dr Watson's umbrella, I was able last night to fish up and inspect this bundle.

'It was of the first importance, however, that we should be able to prove who placed it there. This we accomplished by the very obvious device of announcing that the moat would be dried tomorrow, which had, of course, the effect that whoever had hidden the bundle would most certainly withdraw it the moment that darkness enabled him to do so. We have no less than four witnesses as to who it was who took advantage of the opportunity, and so, Mr Barker, I think the word lies now with you.'

Sherlock Holmes put the sopping bundle upon the table beside the lamp and undid the cord which bound it. From within he extracted a dumb-bell, which he tossed down to its fellow in the corner. Next he drew forth a pair of boots. 'American, as you perceive,' he remarked, pointing to the toes. Then he laid upon the table a long, deadly, sheathed knife. Finally he unravelled a bundle of clothing, comprising a complete set of underclothes, socks, a grey tweed suit, and a short yellow overcoat.

'The clothes are commonplace,' remarked Holmes, 'save only the overcoat, which is full of suggestive touches.' He held it tenderly towards the light. 'Here, as you perceive, is the inner pocket prolonged into the lining in such fashion as to give ample space for the truncated fowling piece. The

tailor's tab is on the neck – "Neal, Outfitter, Vermissa, USA".
I have spent an instructive afternoon in the rector's library,
and have enlarged my knowledge by adding the fact that
Vermissa is a flourishing little town at the head of one of the
best known coal and iron valleys in the United States. I have
some recollection, Mr Barker, that you associated the coal
districts with Mr Douglas's first wife, and it would surely not
be too far-fetched an inference that the V.V. upon the card
by the dead body might stand for Vermissa Valley, or that
this very valley which sends forth emissaries of murder may
be that Valley of Fear of which we have heard. So much is
fairly clear. And now, Mr Barker, I seem to be standing rather
in the way of your explanation.'

It was a sight to see Cecil Barker's expressive face during
this exposition of the great detective. Anger, amazement,
consternation, and indecision swept over it in turn. Finally
he took refuge in a somewhat acrid irony.

'You know such a lot, Mr Holmes, perhaps you had better
tell us some more,' he sneered.

'I have no doubt that I could tell you a great deal more,
Mr Barker; but it would come with a better grace from you.'

'Oh, you think so, do you? Well, all I can say is that if
there's any secret here it is not my secret, and I am not the
man to give it away.'

'Well, if you take that line, Mr Barker,' said the inspector
quietly, 'we must just keep you in sight until we have the
warrant and can hold you.'

'You can do what you damn please about that,' said Barker
defiantly.

The proceedings seemed to have come to a definite end
so far as he was concerned; for one had only to look at that

granite face to realise that no *peine forte et dure* would ever force him to plead against his will. The deadlock was broken, however, by a woman's voice. Mrs Douglas had been standing listening at the half opened door, and now she entered the room.

'You have done enough for now, Cecil,' said she. 'Whatever comes of it in the future, you have done enough.'

'Enough and more than enough,' remarked Sherlock Holmes gravely. 'I have every sympathy with you, madam, and should strongly urge you to have some confidence in the common sense of our jurisdiction and to take the police voluntarily into your complete confidence. It may be that I am myself at fault for not following up the hint which you conveyed to me through my friend, Dr Watson; but, at that time I had every reason to believe that you were directly concerned in the crime. Now I am assured that this is not so. At the same time, there is much that is unexplained, and I should strongly recommend that you ask *Mr Douglas* to tell us his own story.'

Mrs Douglas gave a cry of astonishment at Holmes's words. The detectives and I must have echoed it, when we were aware of a man who seemed to have emerged from the wall, who advanced now from the gloom of the corner in which he had appeared. Mrs Douglas turned, and in an instant her arms were round him. Barker had seized his outstretched hand.

'It's best this way, Jack,' his wife repeated; 'I am sure that it is best.'

'Indeed, yes, Mr Douglas,' said Sherlock Holmes, 'I am sure that you will find it best.'

The man stood blinking at us with the dazed look of one

who comes from the dark into the light. It was a remarkable face, bold grey eyes, a strong, short-clipped, grizzled moustache, a square, projecting chin, and a humorous mouth. He took a good look at us all, and then to my amazement he advanced to me and handed me a bundle of paper.

'I've heard of you,' said he in a voice which was not quite English and not quite American, but was altogether mellow and pleasing. 'You are the historian of this bunch. Well, Dr Watson, you've never had such a story as that pass through your hands before, and I'll lay my last dollar on that. Tell it your own way; but there are the facts, and you can't miss the public so long as you have those. I've been cooped up two days, and I've spent the daylight hours – as much daylight as I could get in that rat trap – in putting the thing into words. You're welcome to them – you and your public. There's the story of the Valley of Fear.'

'That's the past, Mr Douglas,' said Sherlock Holmes quietly. 'What we desire now is to hear your story of the present.'

'You'll have it, sir,' said Douglas. 'May I smoke as I talk? Well, thank you, Mr Holmes. You're a smoker yourself, if I remember right, and you'll guess what it is to be sitting for two days with tobacco in your pocket and afraid that the smell will give you away.' He leaned against the mantelpiece and sucked at the cigar which Holmes had handed him. 'I've heard of you, Mr Holmes. I never guessed that I should meet you. But before you are through with that,' he nodded at my papers, 'you will say I've brought you something fresh.'

Inspector MacDonald had been staring at the newcomer with the greatest amazement. 'Well, this fairly beats me!' he cried at last. 'If you are Mr John Douglas of Birlstone Manor, then whose death have we been investigating for these two days, and where in the world have you sprung from now? You seemed to me to come out of the floor like a jack-in-a-box.'

'Ah, Mr Mac,' said Holmes, shaking a reproving forefinger, 'you would not read that excellent local compilation which described the concealment of King Charles. People did not hide in those days without excellent hiding places, and the hiding place that has once been used may be again. I had persuaded myself that we should find Mr Douglas under this roof.'

'And how long have you been playing this trick upon us, Mr Holmes?' said the inspector angrily. 'How long have you allowed us to waste ourselves upon a search that you knew to be an absurd one?'

'Not one instant, my dear Mr Mac. Only last night did I form my views of the case. As they could not be put to the proof until this evening, I invited you and your colleague to take a holiday for the day. Pray what more could I do? When I found the suit of clothes in the moat, it at once became apparent to me that the body we had found could not have been the body of Mr John Douglas at all, but must be that of the bicyclist from Tunbridge Wells. No other conclusion was possible. Therefore I had to determine where Mr John Douglas himself could be, and the balance of probability was that with the connivance of his wife and his friend he was concealed in a house which had such conveniences for a fugitive, and awaiting quieter times when he could make his final escape.'

'Well, you figured it out about right,' said Douglas approvingly. 'I thought I'd dodge your British law; for I was not

sure how I stood under it, and also I saw my chance to throw
these hounds once for all off my track. Mind you, from first
to last I have done nothing to be ashamed of, and nothing
that I would not do again; but you'll judge that for yourselves
when I tell you my story. Never mind warning me, Inspector:
I'm ready to stand pat upon the truth.

'I'm not going to begin at the beginning. That's all there,'
he indicated my bundle of papers, 'and a mighty queer yarn
you'll find it. It all comes down to this: That there are some
men that have good cause to hate me and would give their last
dollar to know that they had got me. So long as I am alive
and they are alive, there is no safety in this world for me. They
hunted me from Chicago to California, then they chased me
out of America; but when I married and settled down in this
quiet spot I thought my last years were going to be peaceable.

'I never explained to my wife how things were. Why should
I pull her into it? She would never have a quiet moment
again; but would always be imagining trouble. I fancy she
knew something, for I may have dropped a word here or a
word there; but until yesterday, after you gentlemen had seen
her, she never knew the rights of the matter. She told you all
she knew, and so did Barker here; for on the night when this
thing happened there was mighty little time for explanations.
She knows everything now, and I would have been a wiser
man if I had told her sooner. But it was a hard question, dear,'
he took her hand for an instant in his own, 'and I acted for
the best.

'Well, gentlemen, the day before these happenings I was
over in Tunbridge Wells, and I got a glimpse of a man in the
street. It was only a glimpse; but I have a quick eye for these
things, and I never doubted who it was. It was the worst

enemy I had among them all – one who has been after me like a hungry wolf after a caribou all these years. I knew there was trouble coming, and I came home and made ready for it. I guessed I'd fight through it all right on my own, my luck was a proverb in the States about 1876. I never doubted that it would be with me still.

'I was on my guard all that next day, and never went out into the park. It's as well, or he'd have had the drop on me with that buckshot gun of his before ever I could draw on him. After the bridge was up – my mind was always more restful when that bridge was up in the evenings – I put the thing clear out of my head. I never dreamed of his getting into the house and waiting for me. But when I made my round in my dressing gown, as was my habit, I had no sooner entered the study than I scented danger. I guess when a man has had dangers in his life – and I've had more than most in my time – there is a kind of sixth sense that waves the red flag. I saw the signal clear enough, and yet I couldn't tell you why. Next instant I spotted a boot under the window curtain, and then I saw why plain enough.

'I'd just the one candle that was in my hand; but there was a good light from the hall lamp through the open door. I put down the candle and jumped for a hammer that I'd left on the mantel. At the same moment he sprang at me. I saw the glint of a knife, and I lashed at him with the hammer. I got him somewhere; for the knife tinkled down on the floor. He dodged round the table as quick as an eel, and a moment later he'd got his gun from under his coat. I heard him cock it; but I had got hold of it before he could fire. I had it by the barrel, and we wrestled for it all ends up for a minute or more. It was death to the man that lost his grip.

'He never lost his grip; but he got it butt downward for a moment too long. Maybe it was I that pulled the trigger. Maybe we just jolted it off between us. Anyhow, he got both barrels in the face, and there I was, staring down at all that was left of Ted Baldwin. I'd recognised him in the township, and again when he sprang for me; but his own mother wouldn't recognise him as I saw him then. I'm used to rough work; but I fairly turned sick at the sight of him.

'I was hanging on the side of the table when Barker came hurrying down. I heard my wife coming, and I ran to the door and stopped her. It was no sight for a woman. I promised I'd come to her soon. I said a word or two to Barker – he took it all in at a glance – and we waited for the rest to come along. But there was no sign of them. Then we understood that they could hear nothing, and that all that had happened was known only to ourselves.

'It was at that instant that the idea came to me. I was fairly dazzled by the brilliance of it. The man's sleeve had slipped up and there was the branded mark of the lodge upon his forearm. See here!'

The man whom we had known as Douglas turned up his own coat and cuff to show a brown triangle within a circle exactly like that which we had seen upon the dead man.

'It was the sight of that which started me on it. I seemed to see it all clear at a glance. There were his height and hair and figure, about the same as my own. No one could swear to his face, poor devil! I brought down this suit of clothes, and in a quarter of an hour Barker and I had put my dressing gown on him and he lay as you found him. We tied all his things into a bundle, and I weighted them with the only weight I could find and put them through the window. The card he had meant to lay upon my body was lying beside his own.

'My rings were put on his finger; but when it came to the wedding ring,' he held out his muscular hand, 'you can see for yourselves that I had struck the limit. I have not moved it since the day I was married, and it would have taken a file to get it off. I don't know, anyhow, that I should have cared to part with it; but if I had wanted to I couldn't. So we just had to leave that detail to take care of itself. On the other hand, I brought a bit of plaster down and put it where I am wearing one myself at this instant. You slipped up there, Mr Holmes, clever as you are; for if you had chanced to take off that plaster you would have found no cut underneath it.

'Well, that was the situation. If I could lie low for a while and then get away where I could be joined by my "widow" we should have a chance at last of living in peace for the rest of our lives. These devils would give me no rest so long as I was above ground; but if they saw in the papers that Baldwin had got his man, there would be an end of all my troubles. I hadn't much time to make it all clear to Barker and to my wife; but they understood enough to be able to help me. I knew all about this hiding place, so did Ames; but it never entered his head to connect it with the matter. I retired into it, and it was up to Barker to do the rest.

'I guess you can fill in for yourselves what he did. He opened the window and made the mark on the sill to give an idea of how the murderer escaped. It was a tall order, that; but as the bridge was up there was no other way. Then, when everything was fixed, he rang the bell for all he was worth. What happened afterward you know. And so, gentlemen, you can do what you please; but I've told you the truth and the whole truth, so help me God! What I ask you now is how do I stand by the English law?'

There was a silence which was broken by Sherlock Holmes.

'The English law is in the main a just law. You will get no worse than your deserts from that, Mr Douglas. But I would ask you how did this man know that you lived here, or how to get into your house, or where to hide to get you?'

'I know nothing of this.'

Holmes's face was very white and grave. 'The story is not over yet, I fear,' said he. 'You may find worse dangers than the English law, or even than your enemies from America. I see trouble before you, Mr Douglas. You'll take my advice and still be on your guard.'

And now, my long-suffering readers, I will ask you to come away with me for a time, far from the Sussex Manor House of Birlstone, and far also from the year of grace in which we made our eventful journey which ended with the strange story of the man who had been known as John Douglas. I wish you to journey back some twenty years in time, and westward some thousands of miles in space, that I may lay before you a singular and terrible narrative – so singular and so terrible that you may find it hard to believe that even as I tell it, even so did it occur.

Do not think that I intrude one story before another is finished. As you read on you will find that this is not so. And when I have detailed those distant events and you have solved this mystery of the past, we shall meet once more in those rooms on Baker Street, where this, like so many other wonderful happenings, will find its end.

PART 2

THE SCOWRERS

CHAPTER 1

THE MAN

It was the fourth of February in the year 1875. It had been a severe winter, and the snow lay deep in the gorges of the Gilmerton Mountains. The steam ploughs had, however, kept the railroad open, and the evening train which connects the long line of coal-mining and iron-working settlements was slowly groaning its way up the steep gradients which lead from Stagville on the plain to Vermissa, the central township which lies at the head of Vermissa Valley. From this point the track sweeps downward to Bartons Crossing, Helmdale, and the purely agricultural county of Merton. It was a single track railroad; but at every siding – and they were numerous – long lines of trucks piled with coal and iron ore told of the hidden wealth which had brought a rude population and a bustling life to this most desolate corner of the United States of America.

For desolate it was! Little could the first pioneer who had traversed it have ever imagined that the fairest prairies and the most lush water pastures were valueless compared to this gloomy land of black crag and tangled forest. Above the dark and often scarcely penetrable woods upon their flanks, the high, bare crowns of the mountains, white snow, and jagged rock towered upon each flank, leaving a long, winding, tortuous valley in the centre. Up this the little train was slowly crawling.

The oil lamps had just been lit in the leading passenger car, a long, bare carriage in which some twenty or thirty people were seated. The greater number of these were workmen returning from their day's toil in the lower part of the valley. At least a dozen, by their grimed faces and the safety lanterns which they carried, proclaimed themselves miners. These sat smoking in a group and conversed in low voices, glancing occasionally at two men on the opposite side of the car, whose uniforms and badges showed them to be policemen.

Several women of the labouring class and one or two travellers who might have been small local storekeepers made up the rest of the company, with the exception of one young man in a corner by himself. It is with this man that we are concerned. Take a good look at him; for he is worth it.

He is a fresh-complexioned, middle-sized young man, not far, one would guess, from his thirtieth year. He has large, shrewd, humorous grey eyes which twinkle enquiringly from time to time as he looks round through his spectacles at the people about him. It is easy to see that he is of a sociable and possibly simple disposition, anxious to be friendly to all men. Anyone could pick him at once as gregarious in his habits and communicative in his nature, with a quick wit and a ready smile. And yet the man who studied him more closely might discern a certain firmness of jaw and grim tightness about the lips which would warn him that there were depths beyond, and that this pleasant, brown-haired young Irishman might conceivably leave his mark for good or evil upon any society to which he was introduced.

Having made one or two tentative remarks to the nearest miner, and receiving only short, gruff replies, the traveller resigned himself to uncongenial silence, staring moodily out of the window at the fading landscape.

It was not a cheering prospect. Through the growing gloom there pulsed the red glow of the furnaces on the sides of the hills. Great heaps of slag and dumps of cinders loomed up on each side, with the high shafts of the collieries towering above them. Huddled groups of mean, wooden houses, the windows of which were beginning to outline themselves in light, were scattered here and there along the line, and the frequent halting places were crowded with their swarthy inhabitants.

The iron and coal valleys of the Vermissa district were no resorts for the leisured or the cultured. Everywhere there were stern signs of the crudest battle of life, the rude work to be done, and the rude, strong workers who did it.

The young traveller gazed out into this dismal country with a face of mingled repulsion and interest, which showed that the scene was new to him. At intervals he drew from his pocket a bulky letter to which he referred, and on the margins of which he scribbled some notes. Once from the back of his waist he produced something which one would hardly have expected to find in the possession of so mild-mannered a man. It was a navy revolver of the largest size. As he turned it slantwise to the light, the glint upon the rims of the copper shells within the drum showed that it was fully loaded. He quickly restored it to his secret pocket, but not before it had been observed by a working man who had seated himself upon the adjoining bench.

'Hullo, mate!' said he. 'You seem heeled and ready.'

The young man smiled with an air of embarrassment.

'Yes,' said he, 'we need them sometimes in the place I come from.'

'And where may that be?'

'I'm last from Chicago.'

'A stranger in these parts?'

'Yes.'

'You may find you need it here,' said the workman.

'Ah! Is that so?' The young man seemed interested.

'Have you heard nothing of doings hereabouts?'

'Nothing out of the way.'

'Why, I thought the country was full of it. You'll hear quick enough. What made you come here?'

'I heard there was always work for a willing man.'

'Are you a member of the union?'

'Sure.'

'Then you'll get your job, I guess. Have you any friends?'

'Not yet; but I have the means of making them.'

'How's that, then?'

'I am one of the Eminent Order of Freemen. There's no town without a lodge, and where there is a lodge I'll find my friends.'

The remark had a singular effect upon his companion. He glanced round suspiciously at the others in the car. The miners were still whispering among themselves. The two police officers were dozing. He came across, seated himself close to the young traveller, and held out his hand.

'Put it there,' he said.

A hand-grip passed between the two.

'I see you speak the truth,' said the workman. 'But it's well to make certain.' He raised his right hand to his right eyebrow. The traveller at once raised his left hand to his left eyebrow.

'Dark nights are unpleasant,' said the workman.

'Yes, for strangers to travel,' the other answered.

'That's good enough. I'm Brother Scanlan, Lodge 341, Vermissa Valley. Glad to see you in these parts.'

'Thank you. I'm Brother John McMurdo, Lodge 29, Chicago. Bodymaster J.H. Scott. But I am in luck to meet a brother so early.'

'Well, there are plenty of us about. You won't find the order more flourishing anywhere in the States than right here in Vermissa Valley. But we could do with some lads like you.

I can't understand a spry man of the union finding no work to do in Chicago.'

'I found plenty of work to do,' said McMurdo.

'Then why did you leave?'

McMurdo nodded towards the policemen and smiled. 'I guess those chaps would be glad to know,' he said.

Scanlan groaned sympathetically. 'In trouble?' he asked in a whisper.

'Deep.'

'A penitentiary job?'

'And the rest.'

'Not a killing!'

'It's early days to talk of such things,' said McMurdo with the air of a man who had been surprised into saying more than he intended. 'I've my own good reasons for leaving Chicago, and let that be enough for you. Who are you that you should take it on yourself to ask such things?' His grey eyes gleamed with sudden and dangerous anger from behind his glasses.

'All right, mate, no offence meant. The boys will think none the worse of you, whatever you may have done. Where are you bound for now?'

'Vermissa.'

'That's the third halt down the line. Where are you staying?'

McMurdo took out an envelope and held it close to the murky oil lamp. 'Here is the address – Jacob Shafter, Sheridan Street. It's a boarding house that was recommended by a man I knew in Chicago.'

'Well, I don't know it; but Vermissa is out of my beat. I live at Hobson's Patch, and that's here where we are drawing up. But, say, there's one bit of advice I'll give you before we part: if you're in trouble in Vermissa, go straight to the Union House and see Boss McGinty. He is the Bodymaster of Vermissa Lodge, and nothing can happen in these parts unless Black Jack McGinty wants it. So long, mate! Maybe we'll meet in lodge one of these evenings. But mind my words: if you are in trouble, go to Boss McGinty.'

Scanlan descended, and McMurdo was left once again to his thoughts. Night had now fallen, and the flames of the frequent furnaces were roaring and leaping in the darkness. Against their lurid background dark figures were bending and straining, twisting and turning, with the motion of winch or of windlass, to the rhythm of an eternal clank and roar.

'I guess hell must look something like that,' said a voice.

McMurdo turned and saw that one of the policemen had shifted in his seat and was staring out into the fiery waste.

'For that matter,' said the other policeman, 'I allow that hell must *be* something like that. If there are worse devils down yonder than some we could name, it's more than I'd expect. I guess you are new to this part, young man?'

'Well, what if I am?' McMurdo answered in a surly voice.

'Just this, mister, that I should advise you to be careful in choosing your friends. I don't think I'd begin with Mike Scanlan or his gang if I were you.'

'What the hell is it to you who are my friends?' roared McMurdo in a voice which brought every head in the carriage round to witness the altercation. 'Did I ask you for your advice, or did you think me such a sucker that I couldn't move without it? You speak when you are spoken to, and by the Lord you'd have to wait a long time if it was me!' He thrust out his face and grinned at the patrolmen like a snarling dog.

The two policemen, heavy, good-natured men, were taken

aback by the extraordinary vehemence with which their friendly advances had been rejected.

'No offence, stranger,' said one. 'It was a warning for your own good, seeing that you are, by your own showing, new to the place.'

'I'm new to the place; but I'm not new to you and your kind!' cried McMurdo in cold fury. 'I guess you're the same in all places, shoving your advice in when nobody asks for it.'

'Maybe we'll see more of you before very long,' said one of the patrolmen with a grin. 'You're a real hand-picked one, if I am a judge.'

'I was thinking the same,' remarked the other. 'I guess we may meet again.'

'I'm not afraid of you, and don't you think it!' cried McMurdo. 'My name's Jack McMurdo – see? If you want me, you'll find me at Jacob Shafter's on Sheridan Street, Vermissa; so I'm not hiding from you, am I? Day or night I dare to look the like of you in the face – don't make any mistake about that!'

There was a murmur of sympathy and admiration from the miners at the dauntless demeanour of the newcomer, while the two policemen shrugged their shoulders and renewed a conversation between themselves.

A few minutes later the train ran into the ill-lit station, and there was a general clearing; for Vermissa was by far the largest town on the line. McMurdo picked up his leather gripsack and was about to start off into the darkness, when one of the miners accosted him.

'By Gar, mate! You know how to speak to the cops,' he said in a voice of awe. 'It was grand to hear you. Let me carry your grip and show you the road. I'm passing Shafter's on the way to my own shack.'

There was a chorus of friendly 'Good-nights' from the other miners as they passed from the platform. Before ever he had set foot in it, McMurdo the turbulent had become a character in Vermissa.

The country had been a place of terror; but the town was in its way even more depressing. Down that long valley there was at least a certain gloomy grandeur in the huge fires and the clouds of drifting smoke, while the strength and industry of man found fitting monuments in the hills which he had spilled by the side of his monstrous excavations. But the town showed a dead level of mean ugliness and squalor. The broad street was churned up by the traffic into a horrible rutted paste of muddy snow. The sidewalks were narrow and uneven. The numerous gas-lamps served only to show more clearly a long line of wooden houses, each with its veranda facing the street, unkempt and dirty.

As they approached the centre of the town the scene was brightened by a row of well-lit stores, and even more by a cluster of saloons and gaming houses, in which the miners spent their hard-earned but generous wages.

'That's the Union House,' said the guide, pointing to one saloon which rose almost to the dignity of being a hotel. 'Jack McGinty is the boss there.'

'What sort of a man is he?' McMurdo asked.

'What! Have you never heard of the boss?'

'How could I have heard of him when you know that I am a stranger in these parts?'

'Well, I thought his name was known clear across the country. It's been in the papers often enough.'

'What for?'

'Well,' the miner lowered his voice, – 'over the affairs.'

'What affairs?'

'Good Lord, mister! You are queer, if I must say it without offense. There's only one set of affairs that you'll hear of in these parts, and that's the affairs of the Scowrers.'

'Why, I seem to have read of the Scowrers in Chicago. A gang of murderers, are they not?'

'Hush, on your life!' cried the miner, standing still in alarm, and gazing in amazement at his companion. 'Man, you won't live long in these parts if you speak in the open street like that. Many a man has had the life beaten out of him for less.'

'Well, I know nothing about them. It's only what I have read.'

'And I'm not saying that you have not read the truth.' The man looked nervously round him as he spoke, peering into the shadows as if he feared to see some lurking danger. 'If killing is murder, then God knows there is murder and to spare. But don't you dare to breathe the name of Jack McGinty in connection with it, stranger; for every whisper goes back to him, and he is not one that is likely to let it pass. Now, that's the house you're after, that one standing back from the street. You'll find old Jacob Shafter that runs it as honest a man as lives in this township.'

'I thank you,' said McMurdo, and shaking hands with his new acquaintance he plodded, gripsack in hand, up the path which led to the dwelling house, at the door of which he gave a resounding knock.

It was opened at once by someone very different from what he had expected. It was a woman, young and singularly beautiful. She was of the German type, blonde and fair-haired, with the piquant contrast of a pair of beautiful dark eyes with which she surveyed the stranger with surprise and a pleasing embarrassment which brought a wave of colour over her pale face. Framed in the bright light of the open doorway, it seemed to McMurdo that he had never seen a more beautiful picture; the more attractive for its contrast with the sordid and gloomy surroundings. A lovely violet growing upon one of those black slag-heaps of the mines would not have seemed more surprising. So entranced was he that he stood staring without a word, and it was she who broke the silence.

'I thought it was father,' said she with a pleasing little touch of a German accent. 'Did you come to see him? He is down town. I expect him back every minute.'

McMurdo continued to gaze at her in open admiration until her eyes dropped in confusion before this masterful visitor.

'No, miss,' he said at last, 'I'm in no hurry to see him. But your house was recommended to me for board. I thought it might suit me – and now I know it will.'

'You are quick to make up your mind,' said she with a smile.

'Anyone but a blind man could do as much,' the other answered.

She laughed at the compliment. 'Come right in, sir,' she said. 'I'm Miss Ettie Shafter, Mr Shafter's daughter. My mother's dead, and I run the house. You can sit down by the stove in the front room until father comes along. Ah, here he is! So you can fix things with him right away.'

A heavy, elderly man came plodding up the path. In a few words McMurdo explained his business. A man of the name of Murphy had given him the address in Chicago. He in turn had had it from someone else. Old Shafter was quite ready. The stranger made no bones about terms, agreed at once to every condition, and was apparently fairly flush of money. For seven dollars a week paid in advance he was to have board and lodging.

So it was that McMurdo, the self-confessed fugitive from justice, took up his abode under the roof of the Shafters, the first step which was to lead to so long and dark a train of events, ending in a far distant land.

CHAPTER 2

THE BODYMASTER

McMurdo was a man who made his mark quickly. Wherever he was the folk around soon knew it. Within a week he had become infinitely the most important person at Shafter's. There were ten or a dozen boarders there; but they were honest foremen or commonplace clerks from the stores, of a very different calibre from the young Irishman. Of an evening when they gathered together his joke was always the readiest, his conversation the brightest, and his song the best. He was a born boon companion, with a magnetism which drew good humour from all around him.

And yet he showed again and again, as he had shown in the railway carriage, a capacity for sudden, fierce anger, which compelled the respect and even the fear of those who met him. For the law, too, and all who were connected with it, he exhibited a bitter contempt which delighted some and alarmed others of his fellow boarders.

From the first he made it evident, by his open admiration, that the daughter of the house had won his heart from the instant that he had set eyes upon her beauty and her grace. He was no backward suitor. On the second day he told her that he loved her, and from then onward he repeated the same story with an absolute disregard of what she might say to discourage him.

'Someone else?' he would cry. 'Well, the worse luck for someone else! Let him look out for himself! Am I to lose my life's chance and all my heart's desire for someone else? You can keep on saying no, Ettie: the day will come when you will say yes, and I'm young enough to wait.'

He was a dangerous suitor, with his glib Irish tongue, and his pretty, coaxing ways. There was about him also that glamour of experience and of mystery which attracts a woman's interest, and finally her love. He could talk of the sweet valleys of County Monaghan from which he came, of the lovely, distant island, the low hills and green meadows which seemed the more beautiful when imagination viewed them from this place of grime and snow.

Then he was versed in the life of the cities of the North, of Detroit and the lumber camps of Michigan, and finally of Chicago, where he had worked in a planing mill. And afterwards came the hint of romance, the feeling that strange things had happened to him in that great city, so strange and so intimate that they might not be spoken of. He spoke wistfully of a sudden leaving, a breaking of old ties, a flight into a strange world, ending in this dreary valley, and Ettie listened, her dark eyes gleaming with pity and with sympathy – those two qualities which may turn so rapidly and so naturally to love.

McMurdo had obtained a temporary job as bookkeeper for he was a well-educated man. This kept him out most of the day, and he had not found occasion yet to report himself to the head of the lodge of the Eminent Order of Freemen. He was reminded of his omission, however, by a visit one evening from Mike Scanlan, the fellow member whom he had met in the train. Scanlan, the small, sharp-faced, nervous, black-eyed man, seemed glad to see him once more. After a glass or two of whisky he broached the object of his visit.

'Say, McMurdo,' said he, 'I remembered your address, so I made bold to call. I'm surprised that you've not reported to the bodymaster. Why haven't you seen Boss McGinty yet?'

'Well, I had to find a job. I have been busy.'

'You must find time for him if you have none for anything else. Good Lord, man! you're a fool not to have been down to the Union House and registered your name the first morning after you came here! If you run against him – well, you *mustn't*, that's all!'

McMurdo showed mild surprise. 'I've been a member of the lodge for over two years, Scanlan, but I never heard that duties were so pressing as all that.'

'Maybe not in Chicago.'

'Well, it's the same society here.'

'Is it?' Scanlan looked at him long and fixedly. There was something sinister in his eyes.

'Isn't it?'

'You'll tell me that in a month's time. I hear you had a talk with the patrolmen after I left the train.'

'How did you know that?'

'Oh, it got about – things do get about for good and for bad in this district.'

'Well, yes. I told the hounds what I thought of them.'

'By the Lord, you'll be a man after McGinty's heart!'

'What, does he hate the police too?'

Scanlan burst out laughing. 'You go and see him, my lad,' said he as he took his leave. 'It's not the police but you that he'll hate if you don't! Now, take a friend's advice and go at once!'

It chanced that on the same evening McMurdo had another more pressing interview which urged him in the same direction. It may have been that his attentions to Ettie had been more evident than before, or that they had gradually obtruded themselves into the slow mind of his good German host; but, whatever the cause, the boarding-house keeper beckoned the young man into his private room and started on the subject without any circumlocution.

'It seems to me, mister,' said he, 'that you are gettin' set on my Ettie. Ain't that so, or am I wrong?'

'Yes, that is so,' the young man answered.

'Vell, I vant to tell you right now that it ain't no manner of use. There's someone slipped in afore you.'

'She told me so.'

'Vell, you can lay that she told you truth. But did she tell you who it vas?'

'No, I asked her; but she wouldn't tell.'

'I dare say not, the leetle baggage! Perhaps she did not vish to frighten you avay.'

'Frighten!' McMurdo was on fire in a moment.

'Ah, yes, my friend! You need not be ashamed to be frightened of him. It is Teddy Baldwin.'

'And who the devil is he?'

'He is a boss of Scowrers.'

'Scowrers! I've heard of them before. It's Scowrers here and Scowrers there, and always in a whisper! What are you all afraid of? Who *are* the Scowrers?'

The boarding-house keeper instinctively sank his voice, as everyone did who talked about that terrible society. 'The Scowrers', said he, 'are the Eminent Order of Freemen!'

The young man stared. 'Why, I am a member of that order myself.'

'You! I vould never have had you in my house if I had known it – not if you vere to pay me a hundred dollar a veek.'

'What's wrong with the order? It's for charity and good fellowship. The rules say so.'

'Maybe in some places. Not here!'

'What is it here?'

'It's a murder society, that's vat it is.'

McMurdo laughed incredulously. 'How can you prove that?' he asked.

'Prove it! Are there not fifty murders to prove it? Vat about Milman and Van Shorst, and the Nicholson family, and old Mr Hyam, and little Billy James, and the others? Prove it! Is there a man or a voman in this valley vat does not know it?'

'See here!' said McMurdo earnestly. 'I want you to take back what you've said, or else make it good. One or the other you must do before I quit this room. Put yourself in my place. Here am I, a stranger in the town. I belong to a society that I know only as an innocent one. You'll find it through the length and breadth of the States, but always as an innocent one. Now, when I am counting upon joining it here, you tell me that it is the same as a murder society called the Scowrers. I guess you owe me either an apology or else an explanation, Mr Shafter.'

'I can but tell you vat the whole world knows, mister. The bosses of the one are the bosses of the other. If you offend the one, it is the other vat vill strike you. We have proved it too often.'

'That's just gossip – I want proof!' said McMurdo.

'If you live here long you vill get your proof. But I forget that you are yourself one of them. You vill soon be as bad as the rest. But you vill find other lodgings, mister. I cannot have you here. Is it not bad enough that one of these people come courting my Ettie, and that I dare not turn him down, but that I should have another for my boarder? Yes, indeed, you shall not sleep here after tonight!'

McMurdo found himself under sentence of banishment both from his comfortable quarters and from the girl whom he loved. He found her alone in the sitting-room that same evening, and he poured his troubles into her ear.

'Sure, your father is after giving me notice,' he said. 'It's little I would care if it was just my room, but indeed, Ettie, though it's only a week that I've known you, you are the very breath of life to me, and I can't live without you!'

'Oh, hush, Mr McMurdo, don't speak so!' said the girl. 'I have told you, have I not, that you are too late? There is another, and if I have not promised to marry him at once, at least I can promise no one else.'

'Suppose I had been first, Ettie, would I have had a chance?'

The girl sank her face into her hands. 'I wish to heaven that you had been first!' she sobbed.

McMurdo was down on his knees before her in an instant. 'For God's sake, Ettie, let it stand at that!' he cried. 'Will you ruin your life and my own for the sake of this promise? Follow your heart, acushla! 'Tis a safer guide than any promise before you knew what it was that you were saying.'

He had seized Ettie's white hand between his own strong brown ones.

'Say that you will be mine, and we will face it out together!'

'Not here?'

'Yes, here.'

'No, no, Jack!' His arms were round her now. 'It could not be here. Could you take me away?'

A struggle passed for a moment over McMurdo's face; but it ended by setting like granite. 'No, here,' he said. 'I'll hold you against the world, Ettie, right here where we are!'

'Why should we not leave together?'

'No, Ettie, I can't leave here.'

'But why?'

'I'd never hold my head up again if I felt that I had been driven out. Besides, what is there to be afraid of? Are we not free folks in a free country? If you love me, and I you, who will dare to come between?'

'You don't know, Jack. You've been here too short a time. You don't know this Baldwin. You don't know McGinty and his Scowrers.'

'No, I don't know them, and I don't fear them, and I don't believe in them!' said McMurdo. 'I've lived among rough men, my darling, and instead of fearing them it has always ended that they have feared me – always, Ettie. It's mad on the face of it! If these men, as your father says, have done crime after crime in the valley, and if everyone knows them by name, how comes it that none are brought to justice? You answer me that, Ettie!'

'Because no witness dares to appear against them. He would not live a month if he did. Also because they have always their own men to swear that the accused one was far from the scene of the crime. But surely, Jack, you must have read all this. I had understood that every paper in the United States was writing about it.'

'Well, I have read something, it is true; but I had thought it was a story. Maybe these men have some reason in what they do. Maybe they are wronged and have no other way to help themselves.'

'Oh, Jack, don't let me hear you speak so! That is how he speaks – the other one!'

'Baldwin – he speaks like that, does he?'

'And that is why I loathe him so. Oh, Jack, now I can tell you the truth. I loathe him with all my heart; but I fear him also. I fear him for myself; but above all I fear him for father. I know that some great sorrow would come upon us if I dared to say what I really felt. That is why I have put him off with half-promises. It was in real truth our only hope. But if you would fly with me, Jack, we could take father with us and live forever far from the power of these wicked men.'

Again there was the struggle upon McMurdo's face, and again it set like granite. 'No harm shall come to you, Ettie – nor to your father either. As to wicked men, I expect you may find that I am as bad as the worst of them before we're through.'

'No, no, Jack! I would trust you anywhere.'

McMurdo laughed bitterly. 'Good Lord! How little you know of me! Your innocent soul, my darling, could not even guess what is passing in mine. But, hullo, who's the visitor?'

The door had opened suddenly, and a young fellow came swaggering in with the air of one who is the master. He was a handsome, dashing young man of about the same age and build as McMurdo himself. Under his broad-brimmed black felt hat, which he had not troubled to remove, a handsome face with fierce, domineering eyes and a curved hawk-bill of a nose looked savagely at the pair who sat by the stove.

Ettie had jumped to her feet full of confusion and alarm. 'I'm glad to see you, Mr Baldwin,' said she. 'You're earlier than I had thought. Come and sit down.'

Baldwin stood with his hands on his hips looking at McMurdo. 'Who is this?' he asked curtly.

'It's a friend of mine, Mr Baldwin, a new boarder here. Mr McMurdo, may I introduce you to Mr Baldwin?'

The young men nodded in surly fashion to each other.

'Maybe Miss Ettie has told you how it is with us?' said Baldwin.

'I didn't understand that there was any relation between you.'

'Didn't you? Well, you can understand it now. You can take it from me that this young lady is mine, and you'll find it a very fine evening for a walk.'

'Thank you, I am in no humour for a walk.'

'Aren't you?' The man's savage eyes were blazing with anger. 'Maybe you are in a humour for a fight, Mr Boarder!'

'That I am!' cried McMurdo, springing to his feet. 'You never said a more welcome word.'

'For God's sake, Jack! Oh, for God's sake!' cried poor, distracted Ettie. 'Oh, Jack, Jack, he will hurt you!'

'Oh, it's Jack, is it?' said Baldwin with an oath. 'You've come to that already, have you?'

'Oh, Ted, be reasonable – be kind! For my sake, Ted, if ever you loved me, be big-hearted and forgiving!'

'I think, Ettie, that if you were to leave us alone we could get this thing settled,' said McMurdo quietly. 'Or maybe, Mr Baldwin, you will take a turn down the street with me. It's a fine evening, and there's some open ground beyond the next block.'

'I'll get even with you without needing to dirty my hands,' said his enemy. 'You'll wish you had never set foot in this house before I am through with you!'

'No time like the present,' cried McMurdo.

'I'll choose my own time, mister. You can leave the time to me. See here!' He suddenly rolled up his sleeve and showed upon his forearm a peculiar sign which appeared to have been branded there. It was a circle with a triangle within it. 'D'you know what that means?'

'I neither know nor care!'

'Well, you will know, I'll promise you that. You won't be much older, either. Perhaps Miss Ettie can tell you something about it. As to you, Ettie, you'll come back to me on your knees – d'ye hear, girl? – on your knees – and then I'll tell you what your punishment may be. You've sowed – and by the Lord, I'll see that you reap!' He glanced at them both in fury. Then he turned upon his heel, and an instant later the outer door had banged behind him.

For a few moments McMurdo and the girl stood in silence. Then she threw her arms around him.

'Oh, Jack, how brave you were! But it is no use, you must fly! Tonight – Jack – tonight! It's your only hope. He will have your life. I read it in his horrible eyes. What chance have you against a dozen of them, with Boss McGinty and all the power of the lodge behind them?'

McMurdo disengaged her hands, kissed her, and gently pushed her back into a chair. 'There, acushla, there! Don't be disturbed or fear for me. I'm a Freeman myself. I'm after telling your father about it. Maybe I am no better than the others; so don't make a saint of me. Perhaps you hate me too, now that I've told you as much?'

'Hate you, Jack? While life lasts I could never do that! I've heard that there is no harm in being a Freeman anywhere but here; so why should I think the worse of you for that?

But if you are a Freeman, Jack, why should you not go down and make a friend of Boss McGinty? Oh, hurry, Jack, hurry! Get your word in first, or the hounds will be on your trail.'

'I was thinking the same thing,' said McMurdo. 'I'll go right now and fix it. You can tell your father that I'll sleep here tonight and find some other quarters in the morning.'

The bar of McGinty's saloon was crowded as usual, for it was the favourite loafing place of all the rougher elements of the town. The man was popular, for he had a rough, jovial disposition which formed a mask, covering a great deal which lay behind it. But apart from this popularity, the fear in which he was held throughout the township, and indeed down the whole thirty miles of the valley and past the mountains on each side of it, was enough in itself to fill his bar; for none could afford to neglect his goodwill.

Besides those secret powers which it was universally believed that he exercised in so pitiless a fashion, he was a high public official, a municipal councillor and a commissioner of roads, elected to the office through the votes of the ruffians who in turn expected to receive favours at his hands. Assessments and taxes were enormous; the public works were notoriously neglected, the accounts were slurred over by bribed auditors, and the decent citizen was terrorised into paying public blackmail, and holding his tongue lest some worse thing befall him.

Thus it was that, year by year, Boss McGinty's diamond pins became more obtrusive, his gold chains more weighty across a more gorgeous vest, and his saloon stretched farther and farther, until it threatened to absorb one whole side of the Market Square.

McMurdo pushed open the swinging door of the saloon and made his way amid the crowd of men within, through an atmosphere blurred with tobacco smoke and heavy with the smell of spirits. The place was brilliantly lighted, and the huge, heavily gilt mirrors upon every wall reflected and multiplied the garish illumination. There were several bartenders in their shirt sleeves, hard at work mixing drinks for the loungers who fringed the broad, brass-trimmed counter.

At the far end, with his body resting upon the bar and a cigar stuck at an acute angle from the corner of his mouth, stood a tall, strong, heavily built man who could be none other than the famous McGinty himself. He was a black-maned giant, bearded to the cheek-bones and with a shock of raven hair which fell to his collar. His complexion was as swarthy as that of an Italian, and his eyes were of a strange dead black, which, combined with a slight squint, gave them a particularly sinister appearance.

All else in the man – his noble proportions, his fine features and his frank bearing – fitted in with that jovial, man-to-man manner which he affected. Here, one would say, is a bluff, honest fellow, whose heart would be sound however rude his outspoken words might seem. It was only when those dead, dark eyes, deep and remorseless, were turned upon a man that he shrank within himself, feeling that he was face to face with an infinite possibility of latent evil, with a strength and courage and cunning behind it which made it a thousand times more deadly.

Having had a good look at his man, McMurdo elbowed his way forward with his usual careless audacity, and pushed himself through the little group of courtiers who were fawning upon the powerful boss, laughing uproariously at the smallest of his jokes. The young stranger's bold grey eyes looked back fearlessly through their glasses at the deadly black ones which turned sharply upon him.

'Well, young man, I can't call your face to mind.'

'I'm new here, Mr McGinty.'

'You are not so new that you can't give a gentleman his proper title.'

'He's Councillor McGinty, young man,' said a voice from the group.

'I'm sorry, councillor. I'm strange to the ways of the place. But I was advised to see you.'

'Well, you see me. This is all there is. What d'you think of me?'

'Well, it's early days. If your heart is as big as your body, and your soul as fine as your face, then I'd ask for nothing better,' said McMurdo.

'By Gar! You've got an Irish tongue in your head anyhow,' cried the saloon-keeper, not quite certain whether to humour this audacious visitor or to stand upon his dignity.

'So you are good enough to pass my appearance?'

'Sure,' said McMurdo.

'And you were told to see me?'

'I was.'

'And who told you?'

'Brother Scanlan of Lodge 341, Vermissa. I drink your health, councillor, and to our better acquaintance.' He raised a glass with which he had been served to his lips and elevated his little finger as he drank it.

McGinty, who had been watching him narrowly, raised his thick black eyebrows. 'Oh, it's like that, is it?' said he. 'I'll have to look a bit closer into this, Mister – '

'McMurdo.'

'A bit closer, Mr McMurdo; for we don't take folk on trust

in these parts, nor believe all we're told neither. Come in here for a moment, behind the bar.'

There was a small room there, lined with barrels. McGinty carefully closed the door, and then seated himself on one of them, biting thoughtfully on his cigar and surveying his companion with those disquieting eyes. For a couple of minutes he sat in complete silence. McMurdo bore the inspection cheerfully, one hand in his coat pocket, the other twisting his brown moustache. Suddenly McGinty stooped and produced a wicked-looking revolver.

'See here, my joker,' said he, 'if I thought you were playing any game on us, it would be short work for you.'

'This is a strange welcome', McMurdo answered with some dignity, 'for the bodymaster of a lodge of Freemen to give to a stranger brother.'

'Ay, but it's just that same that you have to prove,' said McGinty, 'and God help you if you fail! Where were you made?'

'Lodge 29, Chicago.'

'When?'

'June 24, 1872.'

'What bodymaster?'

'James H. Scott.'

'Who is your district ruler?'

'Bartholomew Wilson.'

'Hum! You seem glib enough in your tests. What are you doing here?'

'Working, the same as you – but a poorer job.'

'You have your back answer quick enough.'

'Yes, I was always quick of speech.'

'Are you quick of action?'

'I have had that name among those that knew me best.'

'Well, we may try you sooner than you think. Have you heard anything of the lodge in these parts?'

'I've heard that it takes a man to be a brother.'

'True for you, Mr McMurdo. Why did you leave Chicago?'

'I'm damned if I tell you that!'

McGinty opened his eyes. He was not used to being answered in such fashion, and it amused him. 'Why won't you tell me?'

'Because no brother may tell another a lie.'

'Then the truth is too bad to tell?'

'You can put it that way if you like.'

'See here, mister, you can't expect me, as bodymaster, to pass into the lodge a man for whose past he can't answer.'

McMurdo looked puzzled. Then he took a worn newspaper cutting from an inner pocket.

'You wouldn't squeal on a fellow?' said he.

'I'll wipe my hand across your face if you say such words to me!' cried McGinty hotly.

'You are right, councillor,' said McMurdo meekly. 'I should apologise. I spoke without thought. Well, I know that I am safe in your hands. Look at that clipping.'

McGinty glanced his eyes over the account of the shooting of one Jonas Pinto, in the Lake Saloon, Market Street, Chicago, in the New Year week of 1874.

'Your work?' he asked, as he handed back the paper.

McMurdo nodded.

'Why did you shoot him?'

'I was helping Uncle Sam to make dollars. Maybe mine were not as good gold as his, but they looked as well and were cheaper to make. This man Pinto helped me to shove the queer – '

'To do what?'

'Well, it means to pass the dollars out into circulation. Then he said he would split. Maybe he did split. I didn't wait to see. I just killed him and lighted out for the coal country.'

'Why the coal country?'

''Cause I'd read in the papers that they weren't too particular in those parts.'

McGinty laughed. 'You were first a coiner and then a murderer, and you came to these parts because you thought you'd be welcome.'

'That's about the size of it,' McMurdo answered.

'Well, I guess you'll go far. Say, can you make those dollars yet?'

McMurdo took half a dozen from his pocket. 'Those never passed the Philadelphia mint,' said he.

'You don't say!' McGinty held them to the light in his enormous hand, which was hairy as a gorilla's. 'I can see no difference. Gar! You'll be a mighty useful brother, I'm thinking! We can do with a bad man or two among us, friend McMurdo: for there are times when we have to take our own part. We'd soon be against the wall if we didn't shove back at those that were pushing us.'

'Well, I guess I'll do my share of shoving with the rest of the boys.'

'You seem to have a good nerve. You didn't squirm when I shoved this gun at you.'

'It was not me that was in danger.'

'Who then?'

'It was you, councillor.' McMurdo drew a cocked pistol from the side pocket of his peajacket. 'I was covering you all the time. I guess my shot would have been as quick as yours.'

'By Gar!' McGinty flushed an angry red and then burst into a roar of laughter. 'Say, we've had no such holy terror come to hand this many a year. I reckon the lodge will learn to be proud of you.... Well, what the hell do you want? And can't I speak alone with a gentleman for five minutes but you must butt in on us?'

The bartender stood abashed. 'I'm sorry, councillor, but it's Ted Baldwin. He says he must see you this very minute.'

The message was unnecessary; for the set, cruel face of the man himself was looking over the servant's shoulder. He pushed the bartender out and closed the door on him.

'So,' said he with a furious glance at McMurdo, 'you got here first, did you? I've a word to say to you, councillor, about this man.'

'Then say it here and now before my face,' cried McMurdo.

'I'll say it at my own time, in my own way.'

'Tut! Tut!' said McGinty, getting off his barrel. 'This will never do. We have a new brother here, Baldwin, and it's not for us to greet him in such fashion. Hold out your hand, man, and make it up!'

'Never!' cried Baldwin in a fury.

'I've offered to fight him if he thinks I have wronged him,' said McMurdo. 'I'll fight him with fists, or, if that won't satisfy him, I'll fight him any other way he chooses. Now, I'll leave it to you, councillor, to judge between us as a bodymaster should.'

'What is it, then?'

'A young lady. She's free to choose for herself.'

'Is she?' cried Baldwin.

'As between two brothers of the lodge I should say that she was,' said the Boss.

'Oh, that's your ruling, is it?'

'Yes, it is, Ted Baldwin,' said McGinty, with a wicked stare. 'Is it you that would dispute it?'

'You would throw over one that has stood by you this five years in favour of a man that you never saw before in your life? You're not bodymaster for life, Jack McGinty, and by God, when next it comes to a vote – '

The councillor sprang at him like a tiger. His hand closed round the other's neck, and he hurled him back across one of the barrels. In his mad fury he would have squeezed the life out of him if McMurdo had not interfered.

'Easy, councillor! For heaven's sake, go easy!' he cried, as he dragged him back.

McGinty released his hold, and Baldwin, cowed and shaken, gasping for breath and shivering in every limb, as one who has looked over the very edge of death, sat up on the barrel over which he had been hurled.

'You've been asking for it this many a day, Ted Baldwin – now you've got it!' cried McGinty, his huge chest rising and falling. 'Maybe you think if I was voted down from bodymaster you would find yourself in my shoes. It's for the lodge to say that. But so long as I am the chief I'll have no man lift his voice against me or my rulings.'

'I have nothing against you,' mumbled Baldwin, feeling his throat.

'Well, then,' cried the other, relapsing in a moment into a bluff joviality, 'we are all good friends again and there's an end of the matter.'

He took a bottle of champagne down from the shelf and twisted out the cork.

'See now,' he continued, as he filled three high glasses. 'Let us drink the quarrelling toast of the lodge. After that, as you know, there can be no bad blood between us. Now then, the left hand on the apple of my throat. I say to you, Ted Baldwin, what is the offence, sir?'

'The clouds are heavy,' answered Baldwin.

'But they will forever brighten.'

'And this I swear!'

The men drank their glasses, and the same ceremony was performed between Baldwin and McMurdo.

'There!' cried McGinty, rubbing his hands. 'That's the end of the black blood. You come under lodge discipline if it goes further, and that's a heavy hand in these parts, as Brother Baldwin knows – and as you will damn soon find out, Brother McMurdo, if you ask for trouble!'

'Faith, I'd be slow to do that,' said McMurdo. He held out his hand to Baldwin. 'I'm quick to quarrel and quick to forgive. It's my hot Irish blood, they tell me. But it's over for me, and I bear no grudge.'

Baldwin had to take the proffered hand, for the baleful eye of the terrible Boss was upon him. But his sullen face showed how little the words of the other had moved him.

McGinty clapped them both on the shoulders. 'Tut! These girls! These girls!' he cried. 'To think that the same petticoats should come between two of my boys! It's the devil's own luck! Well, it's the colleen inside of them that must settle the question; for it's outside the jurisdiction of a bodymaster – and the Lord be praised for that! We have enough on us, without the women as well. You'll have to be affiliated to Lodge 341, Brother McMurdo. We have our own ways and methods, different from Chicago. Saturday night is our meeting, and if you come then, we'll make you free forever of the Vermissa Valley.'

CHAPTER 3

LODGE 341, VERMISSA

On the day following the evening which had contained so many exciting events, McMurdo moved his lodgings from old Jacob Shafter's and took up his quarters at the Widow MacNamara's on the extreme outskirts of the town. Scanlan, his original acquaintance aboard the train, had occasion shortly afterwards to move into Vermissa, and the two lodged together. There was no other boarder, and the hostess was an easy-going old Irishwoman who left them to themselves, so that they had a freedom for speech and action welcome to men who had secrets in common.

Shafter had relented to the extent of letting McMurdo come to his meals there when he liked, so that his intercourse with Ettie was by no means broken. On the contrary, it drew closer and more intimate as the weeks went by.

In his bedroom at his new abode McMurdo felt it safe to take out the coining moulds, and under many a pledge of secrecy a number of brothers from the lodge were allowed to come in and see them, each carrying away in his pocket some examples of the false money, so cunningly struck that there was never the slightest difficulty or danger in passing it. Why, with such a wonderful art at his command, McMurdo should condescend to work at all was a perpetual mystery to his companions; though he made it clear to anyone who asked him that if he lived without any visible means it would very quickly bring the police upon his track.

One policeman was indeed after him already; but the incident, as luck would have it, did the adventurer a great deal more good than harm. After the first introduction there were few evenings when he did not find his way to McGinty's saloon, there to make closer acquaintance with 'the boys', which was the jovial title by which the dangerous gang who infested the place were known to one another. His dashing manner and fearlessness of speech made him a favourite with them all, while the rapid and scientific way in which he polished off his antagonist in an 'all in' bar-room scrap earned the respect of that rough community. Another incident, however, raised him even higher in their estimation.

Just at the crowded hour one night, the door opened and a man entered with the quiet blue uniform and peaked cap of the mine police. This was a special body raised by the railways and colliery owners to supplement the efforts of the ordinary civil police, who were perfectly helpless in the face of the organised ruffianism which terrorised the district. There was a hush as he entered, and many a curious glance was cast at him; but the relations between policemen and criminals are peculiar in some parts of the States, and McGinty himself, standing behind his counter, showed no surprise when the policeman enrolled himself among his customers.

'A straight whisky; for the night is bitter,' said the police officer. 'I don't think we have met before, councillor?'

'You'll be the new captain?' said McGinty.

'That's so. We're looking to you, councillor, and to the other leading citizens, to help us in upholding law and order in this township. Captain Marvin is my name.'

'We'd do better without you, Captain Marvin,' said McGinty coldly, 'for we have our own police of the township, and no need for any imported goods. What are you but the paid tool of the capitalists, hired by them to club or shoot your poorer fellow citizen?'

'Well, well, we won't argue about that,' said the police officer good-humouredly. 'I expect we all do our duty same as we see it; but we can't all see it the same.' He had drunk off his glass and had turned to go, when his eyes fell upon the face of Jack McMurdo, who was scowling at his elbow. 'Hullo! Hullo!' he cried, looking him up and down. 'Here's an old acquaintance!'

McMurdo shrank away from him. 'I was never a friend to you nor any other cursed copper in my life,' said he.

'An acquaintance isn't always a friend,' said the police captain, grinning. 'You're Jack McMurdo of Chicago, right enough, and don't you deny it!'

McMurdo shrugged his shoulders. 'I'm not denying it,' said he. 'D'ye think I'm ashamed of my own name?'

'You've got good cause to be, anyhow.'

'What the devil d'you mean by that?' he roared with his fists clenched.

'No, no, Jack, bluster won't do with me. I was an officer in Chicago before ever I came to this darned coal bunker, and I know a Chicago crook when I see one.'

McMurdo's face fell. 'Don't tell me that you're Marvin of the Chicago Central!' he cried.

'Just the same old Teddy Marvin, at your service. We haven't forgotten the shooting of Jonas Pinto up there.'

'I never shot him.'

'Did you not? That's good impartial evidence, ain't it? Well, his death came in uncommon handy for you, or they would have had you for shoving the queer. Well, we can let that be bygones; for, between you and me – and perhaps I'm going further than my duty in saying it – they could get no clear case against you, and Chicago's open to you tomorrow.'

'I'm very well where I am.'

'Well, I've given you the pointer, and you're a sulky dog not to thank me for it.'

'Well, I suppose you mean well, and I do thank you,' said McMurdo in no very gracious manner.

'It's mum with me so long as I see you living on the straight,' said the captain. 'But, by the Lord! if you get off after this, it's another story! So good-night to you – and good-night, councillor.'

He left the bar-room; but not before he had created a local hero. McMurdo's deeds in far Chicago had been whispered before. He had put off all questions with a smile, as one who did not wish to have greatness thrust upon him. But now the thing was officially confirmed. The bar loafers crowded round him and shook him heartily by the hand. He was free of the community from that time on. He could drink hard and show little trace of it; but that evening, had his mate Scanlan not been at hand to lead him home, the feted hero would surely have spent his night under the bar.

On a Saturday night McMurdo was introduced to the lodge. He had thought to pass in without ceremony as being an initiate of Chicago; but there were particular rites in Vermissa of which they were proud, and these had to be undergone by every postulant. The assembly met in a large room reserved for such purposes at the Union House. Some sixty members assembled at Vermissa; but that by no means represented the full strength of the organisation, for there were several other lodges in the valley, and others across the mountains on each side, who exchanged members when any serious business was afoot, so that a crime might be done by men who were strangers to the locality. Altogether there were not less than five hundred scattered over the coal district.

In the bare assembly room the men were gathered round a long table. At the side was a second one laden with bottles and glasses, on which some members of the company were already turning their eyes. McGinty sat at the head with a flat black velvet cap upon his shock of tangled black hair, and a coloured purple stole round his neck, so that he seemed to be a priest presiding over some diabolical ritual. To right and left of him were the higher lodge officials, the cruel, handsome face of Ted Baldwin among them. Each of these wore some scarf or medallion as emblem of his office.

They were, for the most part, men of mature age; but the rest of the company consisted of young fellows from eighteen to twenty-five, the ready and capable agents who carried out the commands of their seniors. Among the older men were many whose features showed the tigerish, lawless souls within; but looking at the rank and file it was difficult to believe that these eager and open-faced young fellows were in very truth a dangerous gang of murderers, whose minds had suffered such complete moral perversion that they took a horrible pride in their proficiency at the business, and looked with deepest respect at the man who had the reputation of making what they called 'a clean job'.

To their contorted natures it had become a spirited and chivalrous thing to volunteer for service against some man who had never injured them, and whom in many cases they had never seen in their lives. The crime committed, they quarrelled as to who had actually struck the fatal blow, and amused one another and the company by describing the cries and contortions of the murdered man.

At first they had shown some secrecy in their arrangements; but at the time which this narrative describes their proceedings were extraordinarily open, for the repeated failure of the law had proved to them that, on the one hand, no one would dare to witness against them, and on the other they had an unlimited number of stanch witnesses upon whom they could call, and a well-filled treasure chest from which they could draw the funds to engage the best legal talent in the state. In ten long years of outrage there had been no single conviction, and the only danger that ever threatened the Scowrers lay in the victim himself – who, however outnumbered and taken by surprise, might and occasionally did leave his mark upon his assailants.

McMurdo had been warned that some ordeal lay before him; but no one would tell him in what it consisted. He was led now into an outer room by two solemn brothers. Through the plank partition he could hear the murmur of many voices from the assembly within. Once or twice he caught the sound of his own name, and he knew that they were discussing his candidacy. Then there entered an inner guard with a green and gold sash across his chest.

'The bodymaster orders that he shall be trussed, blinded and entered,' said he.

The three of them removed his coat, turned up the sleeve of his right arm, and finally passed a rope round above the elbows and made it fast. They next placed a thick black cap right over his head and the upper part of his face, so that he could see nothing. He was then led into the assembly hall.

It was pitch dark and very oppressive under his hood. He heard the rustle and murmur of the people round him, and then the voice of McGinty sounded dull and distant through the covering of his ears.

'John McMurdo,' said the voice, 'are you already a member of the Ancient Order of Freemen?'

He bowed in assent.

'Is your lodge No. 29, Chicago?'

He bowed again.

'Dark nights are unpleasant,' said the voice.

'Yes, for strangers to travel,' he answered.

'The clouds are heavy.'

'Yes, a storm is approaching.'

'Are the brethren satisfied?' asked the bodymaster.

There was a general murmur of assent.

'We know, Brother, by your sign and by your countersign that you are indeed one of us,' said McGinty. 'We would have you know, however, that in this county and in other counties of these parts we have certain rites, and also certain duties of our own which call for good men. Are you ready to be tested?'

'I am.'

'Are you of stout heart?'

'I am.'

'Take a stride forward to prove it.'

As the words were said he felt two hard points in front of his eyes, pressing upon them so that it appeared as if he could not move forward without a danger of losing them. None the less, he nerved himself to step resolutely out, and as he did so the pressure melted away. There was a low murmur of applause.

'He is of stout heart,' said the voice. 'Can you bear pain?'

'As well as another,' he answered.

'Test him!'

It was all he could do to keep himself from screaming out, for an agonising pain shot through his forearm. He nearly fainted at the sudden shock of it; but he bit his lip and clenched his hands to hide his agony.

'I can take more than that,' said he.

This time there was loud applause. A finer first appearance had never been made in the lodge. Hands clapped him on the back, and the hood was plucked from his head. He stood blinking and smiling amid the congratulations of the brothers.

'One last word, Brother McMurdo,' said McGinty. 'You have already sworn the oath of secrecy and fidelity, and you are aware that the punishment for any breach of it is instant and inevitable death?'

'I am,' said McMurdo.

'And you accept the rule of the bodymaster for the time being under all circumstances?'

'I do.'

'Then in the name of Lodge 341, Vermissa, I welcome you to its privileges and debates. You will put the liquor on the table, Brother Scanlan, and we will drink to our worthy brother.'

McMurdo's coat had been brought to him; but before putting it on he examined his right arm, which still smarted heavily. There on the flesh of the forearm was a circle with a triangle within it, deep and red, as the branding iron had left it. One or two of his neighbours pulled up their sleeves and showed their own lodge marks.

'We've all had it,' said one, 'but not all as brave as you over it.'

'Tut! It was nothing,' said he; but it burned and ached all the same.

When the drinks which followed the ceremony of initiation had all been disposed of, the business of the lodge proceeded. McMurdo, accustomed only to the prosaic performances of

Chicago, listened with open ears and more surprise than he ventured to show to what followed.

'The first business on the agenda paper', said McGinty, 'is to read the following letter from Division Master Windle of Merton County Lodge 249. He says:

'DEAR SIR:

'There is a job to be done on Andrew Rae of Rae & Sturmash, coal owners near this place. You will remember that your lodge owes us a return, having had the service of two brethren in the matter of the patrolman last fall. You will send two good men, they will be taken charge of by Treasurer Higgins of this lodge, whose address you know. He will show them when to act and where. Yours in freedom,

'J.W. WINDLE, D.M.A.O.F.

'Windle has never refused us when we have had occasion to ask for the loan of a man or two, and it is not for us to refuse him.' McGinty paused and looked round the room with his dull, malevolent eyes. 'Who will volunteer for the job?'

Several young fellows held up their hands. The bodymaster looked at them with an approving smile.

'You'll do, Tiger Cormac. If you handle it as well as you did the last, you won't be wrong. And you, Wilson.'

'I've no pistol,' said the volunteer, a mere boy in his teens.

'It's your first, is it not? Well, you have to be blooded some time. It will be a great start for you. As to the pistol, you'll find it waiting for you, or I'm mistaken. If you report yourselves on Monday, it will be time enough. You'll get a great welcome when you return.'

'Any reward this time?' asked Cormac, a thick-set, dark-faced, brutal-looking young man, whose ferocity had earned him the nickname of 'Tiger'.

'Never mind the reward. You just do it for the honour of the thing. Maybe when it is done there will be a few odd dollars at the bottom of the box.'

'What has the man done?' asked young Wilson.

'Sure, it's not for the likes of you to ask what the man has done. He has been judged over there. That's no business of ours. All we have to do is to carry it out for them, same as they would for us. Speaking of that, two brothers from the Merton lodge are coming over to us next week to do some business in this quarter.'

'Who are they?' asked someone.

'Faith, it is wiser not to ask. If you know nothing, you can testify nothing, and no trouble can come of it. But they are men who will make a clean job when they are about it.'

'And time, too!' cried Ted Baldwin. 'Folk are gettin' out of hand in these parts. It was only last week that three of our men were turned off by Foreman Blaker. It's been owing him a long time, and he'll get it full and proper.'

'Get what?' McMurdo whispered to his neighbour.

'The business end of a buckshot cartridge!' cried the man with a loud laugh. 'What think you of our ways, Brother?'

McMurdo's criminal soul seemed to have already absorbed the spirit of the vile association of which he was now a member. 'I like it well,' said he. ''Tis a proper place for a lad of mettle.'

Several of those who sat around heard his words and applauded them.

'What's that?' cried the black-maned bodymaster from the end of the table.

''Tis our new brother, sir, who finds our ways to his taste.'

McMurdo rose to his feet for an instant. 'I would say, eminent bodymaster, that if a man should be wanted I should take it as an honour to be chosen to help the lodge.'

There was great applause at this. It was felt that a new sun was pushing its rim above the horizon. To some of the elders it seemed that the progress was a little too rapid.

'I would move,' said the secretary, Harraway, a vulture-faced old greybeard who sat near the chairman, 'that Brother McMurdo should wait until it is the good pleasure of the lodge to employ him.'

'Sure, that was what I meant; I'm in your hands,' said McMurdo.

'Your time will come, Brother,' said the chairman. 'We have marked you down as a willing man, and we believe that you will do good work in these parts. There is a small matter tonight in which you may take a hand if it so please you.'

'I will wait for something that is worth while.'

'You can come tonight, anyhow, and it will help you to know what we stand for in this community. I will make the announcement later. Meanwhile,' he glanced at his agenda paper, 'I have one or two more points to bring before the meeting. First of all, I will ask the treasurer as to our bank balance. There is the pension to Jim Carnaway's widow. He was struck down doing the work of the lodge, and it is for us to see that she is not the loser.'

'Jim was shot last month when they tried to kill Chester Wilcox of Marley Creek,' McMurdo's neighbour informed him.

'The funds are good at the moment,' said the treasurer, with the bankbook in front of him. 'The firms have been generous of late. Max Linder & Co. paid five hundred to be left alone.

Walker Brothers sent in a hundred; but I took it on myself to
return it and ask for five. If I do not hear by Wednesday, their
winding gear may get out of order. We had to burn their breaker
last year before they became reasonable. Then the West Section
Coaling Company has paid its annual contribution. We have
enough on hand to meet any obligations.'

'What about Archie Swindon?' asked a brother.

'He has sold out and left the district. The old devil left a
note for us to say that he had rather be a free crossing sweeper
in New York than a large mine owner under the power of a
ring of blackmailers. By Gar! It was as well that he made a
break for it before the note reached us! I guess he won't show
his face in this valley again.'

An elderly, clean-shaven man with a kindly face and a
good brow rose from the end of the table which faced the
chairman. 'Mr Treasurer,' he asked, 'may I ask who has
bought the property of this man that we have driven out of
the district?'

'Yes, Brother Morris. It has been bought by the State &
Merton County Railroad Company.'

'And who bought the mines of Todman and of Lee that
came into the market in the same way last year?'

'The same company, Brother Morris.'

'And who bought the ironworks of Manson and of Shuman
and of Van Deher and of Atwood, which have all been given
up of late?'

'They were all bought by the West Gilmerton General
Mining Company.'

'I don't see, Brother Morris,' said the chairman, 'that it
matters to us who buys them, since they can't carry them out
of the district.'

'With all respect to you, eminent bodymaster, I think it may matter very much to us. This process has been going on now for ten long years. We are gradually driving all the small men out of trade. What is the result? We find in their places great companies like the Railroad or the General Iron, who have their directors in New York or Philadelphia, and care nothing for our threats. We can take it out of their local bosses; but it only means that others will be sent in their stead. And we are making it dangerous for ourselves. The small men could not harm us. They had not the money nor the power. So long as we did not squeeze them too dry, they would stay on under our power. But if these big companies find that we stand between them and their profits, they will spare no pains and no expense to hunt us down and bring us to court.'

There was a hush at these ominous words, and every face darkened as gloomy looks were exchanged. So omnipotent and unchallenged had they been that the very thought that there was possible retribution in the background had been banished from their minds. And yet the idea struck a chill to the most reckless of them.

'It is my advice', the speaker continued, 'that we go easier upon the small men. On the day that they have all been driven out the power of this society will have been broken.'

Unwelcome truths are not popular. There were angry cries as the speaker resumed his seat. McGinty rose with gloom upon his brow.

'Brother Morris,' said he, 'you were always a croaker. So long as the members of this lodge stand together there is no power in the United States that can touch them. Sure, have we not tried it often enough in the lawcourts? I expect the big companies will find it easier to pay than to fight, same as the little companies do. And now, Brethren,' McGinty took off his black velvet cap and his stole as he spoke, 'this lodge has finished its business for the evening, save for one small matter which may be mentioned when we are parting. The time has now come for fraternal refreshment and for harmony.'

Strange indeed is human nature. Here were these men, to whom murder was familiar, who again and again had struck down the father of the family, some man against whom they had no personal feeling, without one thought of compunction or of compassion for his weeping wife or helpless children, and yet the tender or pathetic in music could move them to tears. McMurdo had a fine tenor voice, and if he had failed to gain the good will of the lodge before, it could no longer have been withheld after he had thrilled them with 'I'm Sitting on the Stile, Mary' and 'On the Banks of Allan Water'.

In his very first night the new recruit had made himself one of the most popular of the brethren, marked already for advancement and high office. There were other qualities needed, however, besides those of good fellowship, to make a worthy Freeman, and of these he was given an example before the evening was over. The whisky bottle had passed round many times, and the men were flushed and ripe for mischief when their bodymaster rose once more to address them.

'Boys,' said he, 'there's one man in this town that wants trimming up, and it's for you to see that he gets it. I'm speaking of James Stanger of the *Herald*. You've seen how he's been opening his mouth against us again?'

There was a murmur of assent, with many a muttered oath. McGinty took a slip of paper from his waistcoat pocket. '"Law and Order!" That's how he heads it.

'Reign of terror in the coal and iron district. Twelve years have now elapsed since the first assassinations which proved the existence of a criminal organisation in our midst. From that day these outrages have never ceased, until now they have reached a pitch which makes us the opprobrium of the civilised world. Is it for such results as this that our great country welcomes to its bosom the alien who flies from the despotisms of Europe? Is it that they shall themselves become tyrants over the very men who have given them shelter, and that a state of terrorism and lawlessness should be established under the very shadow of the sacred folds of the starry Flag of Freedom which would raise horror in our minds if we read of it as existing under the most effete monarchy of the East? The men are known. The organisation is patent and public. How long are we to endure it? Can we forever live –

'Sure, I've read enough of the slush!' cried the chairman, tossing the paper down upon the table. 'That's what he says of us. The question I'm asking you is what shall we say to him?'

'Kill him!' cried a dozen fierce voices.

'I protest against that,' said Brother Morris, the man of the good brow and shaven face. 'I tell you, Brethren, that our hand is too heavy in this valley, and that there will come a point where in self-defence every man will unite to crush us out. James Stanger is an old man. He is respected in the township and the district. His paper stands for all that is solid in the valley. If that man is struck down, there will be a stir through this state that will only end with our destruction.'

'And how would they bring about our destruction, Mr Standback?' cried McGinty. 'Is it by the police? Sure, half of them are in our pay and half of them afraid of us. Or is it by the law courts and the judge? Haven't we tried that before now, and what ever came of it?'

'There is a Judge Lynch that might try the case,' said Brother Morris.

A general shout of anger greeted the suggestion.

'I have but to raise my finger,' cried McGinty, 'and I could put two hundred men into this town that would clear it out from end to end.' Then suddenly raising his voice and bending his huge black brows into a terrible frown, 'See here, Brother Morris, I have my eye on you, and have had for some time! You've no heart yourself, and you try to take the heart out of others. It will be an ill day for you, Brother Morris, when your own name comes on our agenda paper, and I'm thinking that it's just there that I ought to place it.'

Morris had turned deadly pale, and his knees seemed to give way under him as he fell back into his chair. He raised his glass in his trembling hand and drank before he could answer. 'I apologise, eminent bodymaster, to you and to every brother in this lodge if I have said more than I should. I am a faithful member – you all know that – and it is my fear lest evil come to the lodge which makes me speak in anxious words. But I have greater trust in your judgement than in my own, eminent bodymaster, and I promise you that I will not offend again.'

The bodymaster's scowl relaxed as he listened to the humble words. 'Very good, Brother Morris. It's myself that would be sorry if it were needful to give you a lesson. But so long as I am in this chair we shall be a united lodge in word and in deed. And now, boys,' he continued, looking round at the company, 'I'll say this much, that if Stanger got his full deserts there would be more trouble than we need ask for. These editors hang together, and every journal in the state would be crying out for police and troops. But I guess you can give him a pretty severe warning. Will you fix it, Brother Baldwin?'

'Sure!' said the young man eagerly.

'How many will you take?'

'Half a dozen, and two to guard the door. You'll come, Gower, and you, Mansel, and you, Scanlan, and the two Willabys.'

'I promised the new brother he should go,' said the chairman.

Ted Baldwin looked at McMurdo with eyes which showed that he had not forgotten nor forgiven. 'Well, he can come if he wants,' he said in a surly voice. 'That's enough. The sooner we get to work the better.'

The company broke up with shouts and yells and snatches of drunken song. The bar was still crowded with revellers, and many of the brethren remained there. The little band who had been told off for duty passed out into the street, proceeding in twos and threes along the sidewalk so as not to provoke attention. It was a bitterly cold night, with a half-moon shining brilliantly in a frosty, star-spangled sky. The men stopped and gathered in a yard which faced a high building. The words 'Vermissa Herald' were printed in gold lettering between the brightly lit windows. From within came the clanking of the printing press.

'Here, you,' said Baldwin to McMurdo, 'you can stand below at the door and see that the road is kept open for us. Arthur Willaby can stay with you. You others come with me. Have no fears, boys; for we have a dozen witnesses that we are in the Union Bar at this very moment.'

It was nearly midnight, and the street was deserted save

for one or two revellers upon their way home. The party crossed the road, and, pushing open the door of the newspaper office, Baldwin and his men rushed in and up the stairs which faced them. McMurdo and another remained below. From the room above came a shout, a cry for help, and then the sound of trampling feet and of falling chairs. An instant later a grey-haired man rushed out on the landing.

He was seized before he could get farther, and his spectacles came tinkling down to McMurdo's feet. There was a thud and a groan. He was on his face, and half a dozen sticks were clattering together as they fell upon him. He writhed, and his long, thin limbs quivered under the blows. The others ceased at last; but Baldwin, his cruel face set in an infernal smile, was hacking at the man's head, which he vainly endeavoured to defend with his arms. His white hair was dabbled with patches of blood. Baldwin was still stooping over his victim, putting in a short, vicious blow whenever he could see a part exposed, when McMurdo dashed up the stairs and pushed him back.

'You'll kill the man,' said he. 'Drop it!'

Baldwin looked at him in amazement. 'Curse you!' he cried. 'Who are you to interfere – you that are new to the lodge? Stand back!' He raised his stick; but McMurdo had whipped his pistol out of his pocket.

'Stand back yourself!' he cried. 'I'll blow your face in if you lay a hand on me. As to the lodge, wasn't it the order of the bodymaster that the man was not to be killed – and what are you doing but killing him?'

'It's truth he says,' remarked one of the men.

'By Gar! You'd best hurry yourselves!' cried the man below. 'The windows are all lighting up, and you'll have the whole town here inside of five minutes.'

There was indeed the sound of shouting in the street, and a little group of compositors and pressmen was forming in the hall below and nerving itself to action. Leaving the limp and motionless body of the editor at the head of the stairs, the criminals rushed down and made their way swiftly along the street. Having reached the Union House, some of them mixed with the crowd in McGinty's saloon, whispering across the bar to the Boss that the job had been well carried through. Others, and among them McMurdo, broke away into side streets, and so by devious paths to their own homes.

CHAPTER 4

THE VALLEY OF FEAR

When McMurdo awoke next morning he had good reason to remember his initiation into the lodge. His head ached with the effect of the drink, and his arm, where he had been branded, was hot and swollen. Having his own peculiar source of income, he was irregular in his attendance at his work; so he had a late breakfast, and remained at home for the morning writing a long letter to a friend. Afterwards he read the *Daily Herald*. In a special column put in at the last moment he read: 'Outrage at the *Herald* office – Editor seriously injured.' It was a short account of the facts with which he was himself more familiar than the writer could have been. It ended with the statement:

The matter is now in the hands of the police; but it can hardly be hoped that their exertions will be attended by any better results than in the past. Some of the men were recognised, and there is hope that a conviction may be obtained. The source of the outrage was, it need hardly be said, that infamous society which has held this community in bondage for so long a period, and against which the *Herald* has taken so uncompromising a stand. Mr Stanger's many friends will rejoice to hear that, though he has been cruelly and brutally beaten, and though he has sustained severe injuries about the head, there is no immediate danger to his life.

Below it stated that a guard of police, armed with Winchester rifles, had been requisitioned for the defence of the office.

McMurdo had laid down the paper, and was lighting his pipe with a hand which was shaky from the excesses of the previous evening, when there was a knock outside, and his landlady brought to him a note which had just been handed in by a lad. It was unsigned, and ran thus:

I should wish to speak to you, but would rather not do so in your house. You will find me beside the flagstaff upon Miller Hill. If you will come there now, I have something which it is important for you to hear and for me to say.

McMurdo read the note twice with the utmost surprise; for he could not imagine what it meant or who was the author of it. Had it been in a feminine hand, he might have imagined that it was the beginning of one of those adventures which had been familiar enough in his past life. But it was the writing of a man, and of a well-educated one, too. Finally, after some hesitation, he determined to see the matter through.

Miller Hill is an ill-kept public park in the very centre of the town. In summer it is a favourite resort of the people, but in winter it is desolate enough. From the top of it one has a view not only of the whole straggling, grimy town, but of the winding valley beneath, with its scattered mines and factories blackening the snow on each side of it, and of the wooded and white-capped ranges flanking it.

McMurdo strolled up the winding path hedged in with evergreens until he reached the deserted restaurant which forms the centre of summer gaiety. Beside it was a bare flagstaff, and underneath it a man, his hat drawn down and the collar of his overcoat turned up. When he turned his face McMurdo saw that it was Brother Morris, he who had incurred the anger of the bodymaster the night before. The lodge sign was given and exchanged as they met.

'I wanted to have a word with you, Mr McMurdo,' said the older man, speaking with a hesitation which showed that he was on delicate ground. 'It was kind of you to come.'

'Why did you not put your name to the note?'

'One has to be cautious, mister. One never knows in times like these how a thing may come back to one. One never knows either who to trust or who not to trust.'

'Surely one may trust brothers of the lodge.'

'No, no, not always,' cried Morris with vehemence. 'Whatever we say, even what we think, seems to go back to that man McGinty.'

'Look here!' said McMurdo sternly. 'It was only last night, as you know well, that I swore good faith to our bodymaster. Would you be asking me to break my oath?'

'If that is the view you take,' said Morris sadly, 'I can only say that I am sorry I gave you the trouble to come and meet me. Things have come to a bad pass when two free citizens cannot speak their thoughts to each other.'

McMurdo, who had been watching his companion very narrowly, relaxed somewhat in his bearing. 'Sure I spoke for myself only,' said he. 'I am a newcomer, as you know, and I am strange to it all. It is not for me to open my mouth, Mr Morris, and if you think well to say anything to me I am here to hear it.'

'And to take it back to Boss McGinty!' said Morris bitterly.

'Indeed, then, you do me injustice there,' cried McMurdo. 'For myself I am loyal to the lodge, and so I tell you straight; but I would be a poor creature if I were to repeat to any other what you might say to me in confidence. It will go no further than me; though I warn you that you may get neither help nor sympathy.'

'I have given up looking for either the one or the other,' said Morris. 'I may be putting my very life in your hands by what I say; but, bad as you are – and it seemed to me last night that you were shaping to be as bad as the worst – still you are new to it, and your conscience cannot yet be as hardened as theirs. That was why I thought to speak with you.'

'Well, what have you to say?'

'If you give me away, may a curse be on you!'

'Sure, I said I would not.'

'I would ask you, then, when you joined the Freeman's society in Chicago and swore vows of charity and fidelity, did ever it cross your mind that you might find it would lead you to crime?'

'If you call it crime,' McMurdo answered.

'Call it crime!' cried Morris, his voice vibrating with passion. 'You have seen little of it if you can call it anything else. Was it crime last night when a man old enough to be your father was beaten till the blood dripped from his white hairs? Was that crime – or what else would you call it?'

'There are some would say it was war,' said McMurdo, 'a war of two classes with all in, so that each struck as best it could.'

'Well, did you think of such a thing when you joined the Freeman's society at Chicago?'

'No, I'm bound to say I did not.'

'Nor did I when I joined it at Philadelphia. It was just a benefit club and a meeting place for one's fellows. Then I heard of this place – curse the hour that the name first fell upon my ears! – and I came to better myself! My God! To better myself! My wife and three children came with me. I started a dry-goods store on Market Square, and I prospered well. The word had gone round that I was a Freeman, and I was forced to join the local lodge, same as you did last night. I've the badge of shame on my forearm and something worse branded on my heart. I found that I was under the orders of a black villain and caught in a meshwork of crime. What could I do? Every word I said to make things better was taken as treason, same as it was last night. I can't get away; for all I have in the world is in my store. If I leave the society, I know well that it means murder to me, and God knows what to my wife and children. Oh, man, it is awful – awful!' He put his hands to his face, and his body shook with convulsive sobs.

McMurdo shrugged his shoulders. 'You were too soft for the job,' said he. 'You are the wrong sort for such work.'

'I had a conscience and a religion; but they made me a criminal among them. I was chosen for a job. If I backed down I knew well what would come to me. Maybe I'm a coward. Maybe it's the thought of my poor little woman and the children that makes me one. Anyhow I went. I guess it will haunt me forever.

'It was a lonely house, twenty miles from here, over the range yonder. I was told off for the door, same as you were last night. They could not trust me with the job. The others went in. When they came out their hands were crimson to the wrists. As we turned away a child was screaming out of the house behind us. It was a boy of five who had seen his father murdered. I nearly fainted with the horror of it, and yet I had to keep a bold and smiling face; for well I knew that if I did not it would be out of my house that they would come next with their bloody hands and it would be my little Fred that would be screaming for his father.

'But I was a criminal then, part sharer in a murder, lost forever in this world, and lost also in the next. I am a good Catholic; but the priest would have no word with me when he heard I was a Scowrer, and I am excommunicated from my faith. That's how it stands with me. And I see you going down the same road, and I ask you what the end is to be. Are you ready to be a cold-blooded murderer also, or can we do anything to stop it?'

'What would you do?' asked McMurdo abruptly. 'You would not inform?'

'God forbid!' cried Morris. 'Sure, the very thought would cost me my life.'

'That's well,' said McMurdo. 'I'm thinking that you are a weak man and that you make too much of the matter.'

'Too much! Wait till you have lived here longer. Look down the valley! See the cloud of a hundred chimneys that overshadows it! I tell you that the cloud of murder hangs thicker and lower than that over the heads of the people. It is the Valley of Fear, the Valley of Death. The terror is in the hearts of the people from the dusk to the dawn. Wait, young man, and you will learn for yourself.'

'Well, I'll let you know what I think when I have seen more,' said McMurdo carelessly. 'What is very clear is that you are not the man for the place, and that the sooner you sell out – if you only get a dime a dollar for what the business is worth – the better it will be for you. What you have said is safe with me; but, by Gar, if I thought you were an informer – '

'No, no!' cried Morris piteously.

'Well, let it rest at that. I'll bear what you have said in mind, and maybe some day I'll come back to it. I expect you meant kindly by speaking to me like this. Now I'll be getting home.'

'One word before you go,' said Morris. 'We may have been seen together. They may want to know what we have spoken about.'

'Ah! That's well thought of.'

'I offer you a clerkship in my store.'

'And I refuse it. That's our business. Well, so long, Brother Morris, and may you find things go better with you in the future.'

That same afternoon, as McMurdo sat smoking, lost in thought beside the stove of his sitting-room, the door swung open and its framework was filled with the huge figure of Boss McGinty. He passed the sign, and then seating himself opposite to the young man he looked at him steadily for some time, a look which was as steadily returned.

'I'm not much of a visitor, Brother McMurdo,' he said at last. 'I guess I am too busy over the folk that visit me. But I thought I'd stretch a point and drop down to see you in your own house.'

'I'm proud to see you here, councillor,' McMurdo answered heartily, bringing his whisky bottle out of the cupboard. 'It's an honour that I had not expected.'

'How's the arm?' asked the Boss.

McMurdo made a wry face. 'Well, I'm not forgetting it,' he said, 'but it's worth it.'

'Yes, it's worth it,' the other answered, 'to those that are loyal and go through with it and are a help to the lodge. What were you speaking to Brother Morris about on Miller Hill this morning?'

The question came so suddenly that it was well that he had his answer prepared. He burst into a hearty laugh. 'Morris didn't know I could earn a living here at home. He shan't know either; for he has got too much conscience for the likes of me. But he's a good-hearted old chap. It was his idea that I was at a loose end, and that he would do me a good turn by offering me a clerkship in a drygoods store.'

'Oh, that was it?'

'Yes, that was it.'

'And you refused it?'

'Sure. Couldn't I earn ten times as much in my own bedroom with four hours' work?'

'That's so. But I wouldn't get about too much with Morris.'

'Why not?'

'Well, I guess because I tell you not. That's enough for most folk in these parts.'

'It may be enough for most folk; but it ain't enough for me, councillor,' said McMurdo boldly. 'If you are a judge of men, you'll know that.'

The swarthy giant glared at him, and his hairy paw closed for an instant round the glass as though he would hurl it at the head of his companion. Then he laughed in his loud, boisterous, insincere fashion.

'You're a queer card, for sure,' said he. 'Well, if you want reasons, I'll give them. Did Morris say nothing to you against the lodge?'

'No.'

'Nor against me?'

'No.'

'Well, that's because he daren't trust you. But in his heart he is not a loyal brother. We know that well. So we watch him and we wait for the time to admonish him. I'm thinking that the time is drawing near. There's no room for scabby sheep in our pen. But if you keep company with a disloyal man, we might think that you were disloyal, too. See?'

'There's no chance of my keeping company with him; for I dislike the man,' McMurdo answered. 'As to being disloyal, if it was any man but you he would not use the word to me twice.'

'Well, that's enough,' said McGinty, draining off his glass. 'I came down to give you a word in season, and you've had it.'

'I'd like to know,' said McMurdo, 'how you ever came to learn that I had spoken with Morris at all?'

McGinty laughed. 'It's my business to know what goes on in this township,' said he. 'I guess you'd best reckon on my hearing all that passes. Well, time's up, and I'll just say – '

But his leave-taking was cut short in a very unexpected fashion. With a sudden crash the door flew open, and three frowning, intent faces glared in at them from under the peaks of police caps. McMurdo sprang to his feet and half drew his revolver; but his arm stopped midway as he became conscious that two Winchester rifles were levelled at his head. A man in uniform advanced into the room, a six-shooter in his hand.

It was Captain Marvin, once of Chicago, and now of the Mine Constabulary. He shook his head with a half-smile at McMurdo.

'I thought you'd be getting into trouble, Mr Crooked McMurdo of Chicago,' said he. 'Can't keep out of it, can you? Take your hat and come along with us.'

'I guess you'll pay for this, Captain Marvin,' said McGinty. 'Who are you, I'd like to know, to break into a house in this fashion and molest honest, law-abiding men?'

'You're standing out in this deal, Councillor McGinty,' said the police captain. 'We are not out after you, but after this man McMurdo. It is for you to help, not to hinder us in our duty.'

'He is a friend of mine, and I'll answer for his conduct,' said the Boss.

'By all accounts, Mr McGinty, you may have to answer for your own conduct some of these days,' the captain answered. 'This man McMurdo was a crook before ever he came here, and he's a crook still. Cover him, Patrolman, while I disarm him.'

'There's my pistol,' said McMurdo coolly. 'Maybe, Captain Marvin, if you and I were alone and face to face you would not take me so easily.'

'Where's your warrant?' asked McGinty. 'By Gar! A man might as well live in Russia as in Vermissa while folk like you are running the police. It's a capitalist outrage, and you'll hear more of it, I reckon.'

'You do what you think is your duty the best way you can, councillor. We'll look after ours.'

'What am I accused of?' asked McMurdo.

'Of being concerned in the beating of old Editor Stanger at the *Herald* office. It wasn't your fault that it isn't a murder charge.'

'Well, if that's all you have against him,' cried McGinty with a laugh, 'you can save yourself a deal of trouble by dropping it right now. This man was with me in my saloon playing poker up to midnight, and I can bring a dozen to prove it.'

'That's your affair, and I guess you can settle it in court tomorrow. Meanwhile, come on, McMurdo, and come quietly if you don't want a gun across your head. You stand wide, Mr McGinty; for I warn you I will stand no resistance when I am on duty!'

So determined was the appearance of the captain that both McMurdo and his boss were forced to accept the situation. The latter managed to have a few whispered words with the prisoner before they parted.

'What about – ' he jerked his thumb upward to signify the coining plant.

'All right,' whispered McMurdo, who had devised a safe hiding place under the floor.

'I'll bid you goodbye,' said the Boss, shaking hands. 'I'll see Reilly the lawyer and take the defence upon myself. Take my word for it that they won't be able to hold you.'

'I wouldn't bet on that. Guard the prisoner, you two, and shoot him if he tries any games. I'll search the house before I leave.'

He did so, but apparently found no trace of the concealed plant. When he had descended, he and his men escorted McMurdo to headquarters. Darkness had fallen, and a keen blizzard was blowing so that the streets were nearly deserted; but a few loiterers followed the group, and emboldened by invisibility shouted imprecations at the prisoner.

'Lynch the cursed Scowrer!' they cried. 'Lynch him!' They laughed and jeered as he was pushed into the police station.

After a short, formal examination from the inspector in charge he was put into the common cell. Here he found Baldwin and three other criminals of the night before, all arrested that afternoon and waiting their trial next morning.

But even within this inner fortress of the law the long arm of the Freemen was able to extend. Late at night there came a jailer with a straw bundle for their bedding, out of which he extracted two bottles of whisky, some glasses and a pack of cards. They spent a hilarious night, without an anxious thought as to the ordeal of the morning.

Nor had they cause, as the result was to show. The magistrate could not possibly, on the evidence, have held them for a higher court. On the one hand the compositors and pressmen were forced to admit that the light was uncertain, that they were themselves much perturbed, and that it was difficult for them to swear to the identity of the assailants; although they believed that the accused were among them. Cross-examined by the clever attorney who had been engaged by McGinty, they were even more nebulous in their evidence.

The injured man had already deposed that he was so taken by surprise by the suddenness of the attack that he could state nothing beyond the fact that the first man who struck him wore a moustache. He added that he knew them to be Scowrers, since no one else in the community could possibly have any enmity to him, and he had long been threatened on account of his outspoken editorials. On the other hand, it was clearly shown by the united and unfaltering evidence of six citizens, including that high municipal official, Councillor McGinty, that the men had been at a card party at the Union House until an hour very much later than the commission of the outrage.

Needless to say that they were discharged with something

very near to an apology from the bench for the inconvenience to which they had been put, together with an implied censure of Captain Marvin and the police for their officious zeal.

The verdict was greeted with loud applause by a court in which McMurdo saw many familiar faces. Brothers of the lodge smiled and waved. But there were others who sat with compressed lips and brooding eyes as the men filed out of the dock. One of them, a little, dark-bearded, resolute fellow, put the thoughts of himself and comrades into words as the ex-prisoners passed him.

'You damned murderers!' he said. 'We'll fix you yet!'

CHAPTER 5

THE DARKEST HOUR

If anything had been needed to give an impetus to Jack McMurdo's popularity among his fellows it would have been his arrest and acquittal. That a man on the very night of joining the lodge should have done something which brought him before the magistrate was a new record in the annals of the society. Already he had earned the reputation of a good boon companion, a cheery reveller, and withal a man of high temper, who would not take an insult even from the all-powerful Boss himself. But in addition to this he impressed his comrades with the idea that among them all there was not one whose brain was so ready to devise a bloodthirsty scheme, or whose hand would be more capable of carrying it out. 'He'll be the boy for the clean job,' said the oldsters to one another, and waited their time until they could set him to his work.

McGinty had instruments enough already; but he recognised that this was a supremely able one. He felt like a man holding a fierce bloodhound in leash. There were curs to do the smaller work; but some day he would slip this creature upon its prey. A few members of the lodge, Ted Baldwin among them, resented the rapid rise of the stranger and hated him for it; but they kept clear of him, for he was as ready to fight as to laugh.

But if he gained favour with his fellows, there was another quarter, one which had become even more vital to him, in which he lost it. Ettie Shafter's father would have nothing more to do with him, nor would he allow him to enter the house. Ettie herself was too deeply in love to give him up altogether, and yet her own good sense warned her of what would come from a marriage with a man who was regarded as a criminal.

One morning after a sleepless night she determined to see him, possibly for the last time, and make one strong endeavour to draw him from those evil influences which were sucking him down. She went to his house, as he had often begged her to do, and made her way into the room which he used as his sitting-room. He was seated at a table, with his back turned and a letter in front of him. A sudden spirit of girlish mischief came over her – she was still only nineteen. He had not heard her when she pushed open the door. Now she tiptoed forward and laid her hand lightly upon his bended shoulders.

If she had expected to startle him, she certainly succeeded; but only in turn to be startled herself. With a tiger spring he turned on her, and his right hand was feeling for her throat. At the same instant with the other hand he crumpled up the paper that lay before him. For an instant he stood glaring. Then astonishment and joy took the place of the ferocity which had convulsed his features – a ferocity which had sent her shrinking back in horror as from something which had never before intruded into her gentle life.

'It's you!' said he, mopping his brow. 'And to think that you should come to me, heart of my heart, and I should find nothing better to do than to want to strangle you! Come then, darling,' and he held out his arms, 'let me make it up to you.'

But she had not recovered from that sudden glimpse of guilty fear which she had read in the man's face. All her woman's instinct told her that it was not the mere fright of a man who is startled. Guilt – that was it – guilt and fear!

'What's come over you, Jack?' she cried. 'Why were you so scared of me? Oh, Jack, if your conscience was at ease, you would not have looked at me like that!'

'Sure, I was thinking of other things, and when you came tripping so lightly on those fairy feet of yours – '

'No, no, it was more than that, Jack.' Then a sudden suspicion seized her. 'Let me see that letter you were writing.'

'Ah, Ettie, I couldn't do that.'

Her suspicions became certainties. 'It's to another woman,' she cried. 'I know it! Why else should you hold it from me? Was it to your wife that you were writing? How am I to know that you are not a married man – you, a stranger, that nobody knows?'

'I am not married, Ettie. See now, I swear it! You're the only one woman on earth to me. By the cross of Christ I swear it!'

He was so white with passionate earnestness that she could not but believe him.

'Well, then,' she cried, 'why will you not show me the letter?'

'I'll tell you, acushla,' said he. 'I'm under oath not to show it, and just as I wouldn't break my word to you so I would keep it to those who hold my promise. It's the business of the lodge, and even to you it's secret. And if I was scared when a hand fell on me, can't you understand it when it might have been the hand of a detective?'

She felt that he was telling the truth. He gathered her into his arms and kissed away her fears and doubts.

'Sit here by me, then. It's a queer throne for such a queen; but it's the best your poor lover can find. He'll do better for you some of these days, I'm thinking. Now your mind is easy once again, is it not?'

'How can it ever be at ease, Jack, when I know that you are a criminal among criminals, when I never know the day that I may hear you are in court for murder? "McMurdo the Scowrer", that's what one of our boarders called you yesterday. It went through my heart like a knife.'

'Sure, hard words break no bones.'

'But they were true.'

'Well, dear, it's not so bad as you think. We are but poor men that are trying in our own way to get our rights.'

Ettie threw her arms round her lover's neck. 'Give it up, Jack! For my sake, for God's sake, give it up! It was to ask you that I came here today. Oh, Jack, see – I beg it of you on my bended knees! Kneeling here before you I implore you to give it up!'

He raised her and soothed her with her head against his breast.

'Sure, my darlin', you don't know what it is you are asking. How could I give it up when it would be to break my oath and to desert my comrades? If you could see how things stand with me you could never ask it of me. Besides, if I wanted to, how could I do it? You don't suppose that the lodge would let a man go free with all its secrets?'

'I've thought of that, Jack. I've planned it all. Father has saved some money. He is weary of this place where the fear of these people darkens our lives. He is ready to go. We would fly together to Philadelphia or New York, where we would be safe from them.'

McMurdo laughed. 'The lodge has a long arm. Do you think it could not stretch from here to Philadelphia or New York?'

'Well, then, to the West, or to England, or to Germany, where father came from – anywhere to get away from this Valley of Fear!'

McMurdo thought of old Brother Morris. 'Sure, it is the second time I have heard the valley so named,' said he. 'The shadow does indeed seem to lie heavy on some of you.'

'It darkens every moment of our lives. Do you suppose that Ted Baldwin has ever forgiven us? If it were not that he fears you, what do you suppose our chances would be? If you saw the look in those dark, hungry eyes of his when they fall on me!'

'By Gar! I'd teach him better manners if I caught him at it! But see here, little girl. I can't leave here. I can't – take that from me once and for all. But if you will leave me to find my own way, I will try to prepare a way of getting honourably out of it.'

'There is no honour in such a matter.'

'Well, well, it's just how you look at it. But if you'll give me six months, I'll work it so that I can leave without being ashamed to look others in the face.'

The girl laughed with joy. 'Six months!' she cried. 'Is it a promise?'

'Well, it may be seven or eight. But within a year at the furthest we will leave the valley behind us.'

It was the most that Ettie could obtain, and yet it was something. There was this distant light to illuminate the gloom of the immediate future. She returned to her father's house more light-hearted than she had ever been since Jack McMurdo had come into her life.

It might be thought that as a member, all the doings of the society would be told to him; but he was soon to discover that the organisation was wider and more complex than the simple lodge. Even Boss McGinty was ignorant as to many things; for there was an official named the County Delegate, living at Hobson's Patch farther down the line, who had power over several different lodges which he wielded in a sudden and arbitrary way. Only once did McMurdo see him, a sly, little grey-haired rat of a man, with a slinking gait and a sidelong glance which was charged with malice. Evans Pott was his name, and even the great Boss of Vermissa felt towards him something of the repulsion and fear which the huge Danton may have felt for the puny but dangerous Robespierre.

One day Scanlan, who was McMurdo's fellow boarder, received a note from McGinty enclosing one from Evans Pott, which informed him that he was sending over two good men, Lawler and Andrews, who had instructions to act in the neighbourhood; though it was best for the cause that no particulars as to their objects should be given. Would the bodymaster see to it that suitable arrangements be made for their lodgings and comfort until the time for action should arrive? McGinty added that it was impossible for anyone to remain secret at the Union House, and that, therefore, he would be obliged if McMurdo and Scanlan would put the strangers up for a few days in their boarding house.

The same evening the two men arrived, each carrying his gripsack. Lawler was an elderly man, shrewd, silent and self-contained, clad in an old black frock coat, which with his soft felt hat and ragged, grizzled beard gave him a general resemblance to an itinerant preacher. His companion Andrews was little more than a boy, frank-faced and cheerful, with the breezy manner of one who is out for a holiday and means to enjoy every minute of it. Both men were total abstainers, and behaved in all ways as exemplary members of the society, with the one simple exception that they were assassins who had often proved themselves to be most capable instruments for this association of murder. Lawler had already carried out fourteen commissions of the kind, and Andrews three.

They were, as McMurdo found, quite ready to converse about their deeds in the past, which they recounted with the half-bashful pride of men who had done good and unselfish service for the community. They were reticent, however, as to the immediate job in hand.

'They chose us because neither I nor the boy here drink,' Lawler explained. 'They can count on us saying no more than we should. You must not take it amiss, but it is the orders of the County Delegate that we obey.'

'Sure, we are all in it together,' said Scanlan, McMurdo's mate, as the four sat together at supper.

'That's true enough, and we'll talk till the cows come home of the killing of Charlie Williams or of Simon Bird, or any other job in the past. But till the work is done we say nothing.'

'There are half a dozen about here that I have a word to say to,' said McMurdo, with an oath. 'I suppose it isn't Jack Knox of Ironhill that you are after. I'd go some way to see him get his deserts.'

'No, it's not him yet.'

'Or Herman Strauss?'

'No, nor him either.'

'Well, if you won't tell us we can't make you; but I'd be glad to know.'

Lawler smiled and shook his head. He was not to be drawn.

In spite of the reticence of their guests, Scanlan and McMurdo were quite determined to be present at what they called 'the fun'. When, therefore, at an early hour one morning McMurdo heard them creeping down the stairs he awakened Scanlan, and the two hurried on their clothes. When they were dressed they found that the others had stolen out, leaving the door open behind them. It was not yet dawn, and by the light of the lamps they could see the two men some distance down the street. They followed them warily, treading noiselessly in the deep snow.

The boarding house was near the edge of the town, and soon they were at the crossroads which is beyond its boundary. Here three men were waiting, with whom Lawler and Andrews held a short, eager conversation. Then they all moved on together. It was clearly some notable job which needed numbers. At this point there are several trails which lead to various mines. The strangers took that which led to the Crow Hill, a huge business which was in strong hands which had been able, thanks to their energetic and fearless New England manager, Josiah H. Dunn, to keep some order and discipline during the long reign of terror.

Day was breaking now, and a line of workmen were slowly making their way, singly and in groups, along the blackened path.

McMurdo and Scanlan strolled on with the others, keeping in sight of the men whom they followed. A thick mist lay over them, and from the heart of it there came the sudden scream of a steam whistle. It was the ten-minute signal before the cages descended and the day's labour began.

When they reached the open space round the mine shaft there were a hundred miners waiting, stamping their feet and blowing on their fingers; for it was bitterly cold. The strangers stood in a little group under the shadow of the engine house. Scanlan and McMurdo climbed a heap of slag from which the whole scene lay before them. They saw the mine engineer, a great bearded Scotchman named Menzies, come out of the engine house and blow his whistle for the cages to be lowered.

At the same instant a tall, loose-framed young man with a clean-shaven, earnest face advanced eagerly towards the pit head. As he came forward his eyes fell upon the group, silent and motionless, under the engine house. The men had drawn down their hats and turned up their collars to screen their faces. For a moment the presentiment of Death laid its cold hand upon the manager's heart. At the next he had shaken it off and saw only his duty towards intrusive strangers.

'Who are you?' he asked as he advanced. 'What are you loitering there for?'

There was no answer; but the lad Andrews stepped forward and shot him in the stomach. The hundred waiting miners stood as motionless and helpless as if they were paralysed. The manager clapped his two hands to the wound and doubled himself up. Then he staggered away; but another of the assassins fired, and he went down sidewise, kicking and clawing among a heap of clinkers. Menzies, the Scotchman, gave a roar of rage at the sight and rushed with an iron spanner at the murderers, but was met by two balls in the face which dropped him dead at their very feet.

There was a surge forward of some of the miners, and an inarticulate cry of pity and of anger; but a couple of the strangers emptied their six-shooters over the heads of the crowd, and they broke and scattered, some of them rushing wildly back to their homes in Vermissa.

When a few of the bravest had rallied, and there was a return to the mine, the murderous gang had vanished in the mists of morning, without a single witness being able to swear to the identity of these men who in front of a hundred spectators had wrought this double crime.

Scanlan and McMurdo made their way back; Scanlan somewhat subdued, for it was the first murder job that he had seen with his own eyes, and it appeared less funny than he had been led to believe. The horrible screams of the dead manager's wife pursued them as they hurried to the town. McMurdo was absorbed and silent, but he showed no sympathy for the weakening of his companion.

'Sure, it is like a war,' he repeated. 'What is it but a war between us and them, and we hit back where we best can.'

There was high revel in the lodge room at the Union House that night, not only over the killing of the manager and engineer of the Crow Hill mine, which would bring this organisation into line with the other blackmailed and terror-stricken companies of the district, but also over a distant triumph which had been wrought by the hands of the lodge itself.

It would appear that when the County Delegate had sent over

five good men to strike a blow in Vermissa, he had demanded that in return three Vermissa men should be secretly selected and sent across to kill William Hales of Stake Royal, one of the best-known and most popular mine owners in the Gilmerton district, a man who was believed not to have an enemy in the world; for he was in all ways a model employer. He had insisted, however, upon efficiency in the work, and had, therefore, paid off certain drunken and idle employees who were members of the all-powerful society. Coffin notices hung outside his door had not weakened his resolution, and so in a free, civilised country he found himself condemned to death.

The execution had now been duly carried out. Ted Baldwin, who sprawled now in the seat of honour beside the body-master, had been chief of the party. His flushed face and glazed, bloodshot eyes told of sleeplessness and drink. He and his two comrades had spent the night before among the mountains. They were unkempt and weather-stained. But no heroes, returning from a forlorn hope, could have had a warmer welcome from their comrades.

The story was told and retold amid cries of delight and shouts of laughter. They had waited for their man as he drove home at nightfall, taking their station at the top of a steep hill, where his horse must be at a walk. He was so furred to keep out the cold that he could not lay his hand on his pistol. They had pulled him out and shot him again and again. He had screamed for mercy. The screams were repeated for the amusement of the lodge.

'Let's hear again how he squealed,' they cried.

None of them knew the man; but there is eternal drama in a killing, and they had shown the Scowrers of Gilmerton that the Vermissa men were to be relied upon.

There had been one *contretemps*; for a man and his wife had driven up while they were still emptying their revolvers into the silent body. It had been suggested that they should shoot them both; but they were harmless folk who were not connected with the mines, so they were sternly bidden to drive on and keep silent, lest a worse thing befall them. And so the blood-mottled figure had been left as a warning to all such hard-hearted employers, and the three noble avengers had hurried off into the mountains where unbroken nature comes down to the very edge of the furnaces and the slag heaps. Here they were, safe and sound, their work well done, and the plaudits of their companions in their ears.

It had been a great day for the Scowrers. The shadow had fallen even darker over the valley. But as the wise general chooses the moment of victory in which to redouble his efforts, so that his foes may have no time to steady themselves after disaster, so Boss McGinty, looking out upon the scene of his operations with his brooding and malicious eyes, had devised a new attack upon those who opposed him. That very night, as the half-drunken company broke up, he touched McMurdo on the arm and led him aside into that inner room where they had their first interview.

'See here, my lad,' said he, 'I've got a job that's worthy of you at last. You'll have the doing of it in your own hands.'

'Proud I am to hear it,' McMurdo answered.

'You can take two men with you – Manders and Reilly. They have been warned for service. We'll never be right in this district until Chester Wilcox has been settled, and you'll have the thanks of every lodge in the coal fields if you can down him.'

'I'll do my best, anyhow. Who is he, and where shall I find him?'

McGinty took his eternal half-chewed, half-smoked cigar from the corner of his mouth, and proceeded to draw a rough diagram on a page torn from his notebook.

'He's the chief foreman of the Iron Dike Company. He's a hard citizen, an old colour sergeant of the war, all scars and grizzle. We've had two tries at him; but had no luck, and Jim Carnaway lost his life over it. Now it's for you to take it over. That's the house – all alone at the Iron Dike crossroad, same as you see here on the map – without another within earshot. It's no good by day. He's armed and shoots quick and straight, with no questions asked. But at night – well, there he is with his wife, three children and a hired help. You can't pick or choose. It's all or none. If you could get a bag of blasting powder at the front door with a slow match to it – '

'What's the man done?'

'Didn't I tell you he shot Jim Carnaway?'

'Why did he shoot him?'

'What in thunder has that to do with you? Carnaway was about his house at night, and he shot him. That's enough for me and you. You've got to settle the thing right.'

'There's these two women and the children. Do they go up too?'

'They have to – else how can we get him?'

'It seems hard on them; for they've done nothing.'

'What sort of fool's talk is this? Do you back out?'

'Easy, councillor, easy! What have I ever said or done that you should think I would be after standing back from an order of the bodymaster of my own lodge? If it's right or if it's wrong, it's for you to decide.'

'You'll do it, then?'

'Of course I will do it.'

'When?'

'Well, you had best give me a night or two that I may see the house and make my plans. Then – '

'Very good,' said McGinty, shaking him by the hand. 'I leave it with you. It will be a great day when you bring us the news. It's just the last stroke that will bring them all to their knees.'

McMurdo thought long and deeply over the commission which had been so suddenly placed in his hands. The isolated house in which Chester Wilcox lived was about five miles off in an adjacent valley. That very night he started off all alone to prepare for the attempt. It was daylight before he returned from his reconnaissance. Next day he interviewed his two subordinates, Manders and Reilly, reckless youngsters who were as elated as if it were a deer-hunt.

Two nights later they met outside the town, all three armed, and one of them carrying a sack stuffed with the powder which was used in the quarries. It was two in the morning before they came to the lonely house. The night was a windy one, with broken clouds drifting swiftly across the face of a three-quarter moon. They had been warned to be on their guard against bloodhounds; so they moved forward cautiously, with their pistols cocked in their hands. But there was no sound save the howling of the wind, and no movement but the swaying branches above them.

McMurdo listened at the door of the lonely house; but all was still within. Then he leaned the powder bag against it, ripped a hole in it with his knife, and attached the fuse. When it was well alight he and his two companions took to their heels, and were some distance off, safe and snug in a sheltering ditch, before the shattering roar of the explosion, with the low, deep rumble of the collapsing building, told them that their work was done. No cleaner job had ever been carried out in the bloodstained annals of the society.

But alas that work so well organised and boldly carried out should all have gone for nothing! Warned by the fate of the various victims, and knowing that he was marked down for destruction, Chester Wilcox had moved himself and his family only the day before to some safer and less-known quarters, where a guard of police should watch over them. It was an empty house which had been torn down by the gunpowder, and the grim old colour sergeant of the war was still teaching discipline to the miners of Iron Dike.

'Leave him to me,' said McMurdo. 'He's my man, and I'll get him sure if I have to wait a year for him.'

A vote of thanks and confidence was passed in full lodge, and so for the time the matter ended. When a few weeks later it was reported in the papers that Wilcox had been shot at from an ambuscade, it was an open secret that McMurdo was still at work upon his unfinished job.

Such were the methods of the Society of Freemen, and such were the deeds of the Scowrers by which they spread their rule of fear over the great and rich district which was for so long a period haunted by their terrible presence. Why should these pages be stained by further crimes? Have I not said enough to show the men and their methods?

These deeds are written in history, and there are records wherein one may read the details of them. There one may learn of the shooting of Policemen Hunt and Evans because they had ventured to arrest two members of the society – a double outrage planned at the Vermissa lodge and carried out in cold blood upon two helpless and disarmed men. There also one may read of the shooting of Mrs Larbey when she was nursing her husband, who had been beaten almost to death by orders of Boss McGinty. The killing of the elder Jenkins, shortly followed by that of his brother, the mutilation of James Murdoch, the blowing up of the Staphouse family and the murder of the Stendals all followed hard upon one another in the same terrible winter.

Darkly the shadow lay upon the Valley of Fear. The spring had come with running brooks and blossoming trees. There was hope for all Nature bound so long in an iron grip; but nowhere was there any hope for the men and women who lived under the yoke of the terror. Never had the cloud above them been so dark and hopeless as in the early summer of the year 1875.

CHAPTER 6

DANGER

It was the height of the reign of terror. McMurdo, who had already been appointed Inner Deacon, with every prospect of someday succeeding McGinty as bodymaster, was now so necessary to the councils of his comrades that nothing was done without his help and advice. The more popular he became, however, with the Freemen, the blacker were the scowls which greeted him as he passed along the streets of Vermissa. In spite of their terror the citizens were taking heart to band themselves together against their oppressors. Rumours had reached the lodge of secret gatherings in the *Herald* office and of distribution of firearms among the law-abiding people. But McGinty and his men were undisturbed by such reports. They were numerous, resolute, and well armed. Their opponents were scattered and powerless. It would all end, as it had done in the past, in aimless talk and possibly in impotent arrests. So said McGinty, McMurdo, and all the bolder spirits.

It was a Saturday evening in May. Saturday was always the lodge night, and McMurdo was leaving his house to attend it when Morris, the weaker brother of the order, came to see him. His brow was creased with care, and his kindly face was drawn and haggard.

'Can I speak with you freely, Mr McMurdo?'

'Sure.'

'I can't forget that I spoke my heart to you once, and that you kept it to yourself, even though the Boss himself came to ask you about it.'

'What else could I do if you trusted me? It wasn't that I agreed with what you said.'

'I know that well. But you are the one that I can speak to and be safe. I've a secret here,' he put his hand to his breast, 'and it is just burning the life out of me. I wish it had come to any one of you but me. If I tell it, it will mean murder, for sure. If I don't, it may bring the end of us all. God help me, but I am near out of my wits over it!'

McMurdo looked at the man earnestly. He was trembling in every limb. He poured some whisky into a glass and handed it to him. 'That's the physic for the likes of you,' said he. 'Now let me hear of it.'

Morris drank, and his white face took a tinge of colour. 'I can tell it to you all in one sentence,' said he. 'There's a detective on our trail.'

McMurdo stared at him in astonishment. 'Why, man, you're crazy,' he said. 'Isn't the place full of police and detectives and what harm did they ever do us?'

'No, no, it's no man of the district. As you say, we know them, and it is little that they can do. But you've heard of Pinkerton's?'

'I've read of some folk of that name.'

'Well, you can take it from me you've no show when they are on your trail. It's not a take-it-or-miss-it government concern. It's a dead earnest business proposition that's out for results and keeps out till by hook or crook it gets them. If a Pinkerton man is deep in this business, we are all destroyed.'

'We must kill him.'

'Ah, it's the first thought that came to you! So it will be up at the lodge. Didn't I say to you that it would end in murder?'

'Sure, what is murder? Isn't it common enough in these parts?'

'It is, indeed; but it's not for me to point out the man that is to be murdered. I'd never rest easy again. And yet it's our own necks that may be at stake. In God's name what shall I do?' He rocked to and fro in his agony of indecision.

But his words had moved McMurdo deeply. It was easy to see that he shared the other's opinion as to the danger, and the need for meeting it. He gripped Morris's shoulder and shook him in his earnestness.

'See here, man,' he cried, and he almost screeched the words in his excitement, 'you won't gain anything by sitting keening like an old wife at a wake. Let's have the facts. Who is the fellow? Where is he? How did you hear of him? Why did you come to me?'

'I came to you for you are the one man that would advise me. I told you that I had a store in the East before I came here. I left good friends behind me, and one of them is in the telegraph service. Here's a letter that I had from him yesterday. It's this part from the top of the page. You can read it yourself.'

This was what McMurdo read:

How are the Scowrers getting on in your parts? We read plenty of them in the papers. Between you and me I expect to hear news from you before long. Five big corporations and the two railroads have taken the thing up in dead earnest. They mean it, and you can bet they'll get there! They are right deep down into it. Pinkerton has taken hold under their orders, and his best man, Birdy Edwards, is operating. The thing has got to be stopped right now.

'Now read the postscript.'

Of course, what I give you is what I learned in business; so it goes no further. It's a queer cipher that you handle by the yard every day and can get no meaning from.

McMurdo sat in silence for some time, with the letter in his listless hands. The mist had lifted for a moment, and there was the abyss before him.

'Does anyone else know of this?' he asked.

'I have told no one else.'

'But this man – your friend – has he any other person that he would be likely to write to?'

'Well, I dare say he knows one or two more.'

'Of the lodge?'

'It's likely enough.'

'I was asking because it is likely that he may have given some description of this fellow Birdy Edwards – then we could get on his trail.'

'Well, it's possible. But I should not think he knew him. He is just telling me the news that came to him by way of business. How would he know this Pinkerton man?'

McMurdo gave a violent start.

'By Gar!' he cried. 'I've got him. What a fool I was not to know it. Lord! But we're in luck! We will fix him before he can do any harm. See here, Morris, will you leave this thing in my hands?'

'Sure, if you will only take it off mine.'

'I'll do that. You can stand right back and let me run it. Even your name need not be mentioned. I'll take it all on myself, as if it were to me that this letter has come. Will that content you?'

'It's just what I would ask.'

'Then leave it at that and keep your head shut. Now I'll get down to the lodge, and we'll soon make old man Pinkerton sorry for himself.'

'You wouldn't kill this man?'

'The less you know, friend Morris, the easier your conscience will be, and the better you will sleep. Ask no questions, and let these things settle themselves. I have hold of it now.'

Morris shook his head sadly as he left. 'I feel that his blood is on my hands,' he groaned.

'Self-protection is no murder, anyhow,' said McMurdo, smiling grimly. 'It's him or us. I guess this man would destroy us all if we left him long in the valley. Why, Brother Morris, we'll have to elect you bodymaster yet; for you've surely saved the lodge.'

And yet it was clear from his actions that he thought more seriously of this new intrusion than his words would show.

It may have been his guilty conscience, it may have been the reputation of the Pinkerton organisation, it may have been the knowledge that great, rich corporations had set themselves the task of clearing out the Scowrers; but, whatever his reason, his actions were those of a man who is preparing for the worst. Every paper which would incriminate him was destroyed before he left the house. After that he gave a long sigh of satisfaction; for it seemed to him that he was safe. And yet the danger must still have pressed somewhat upon him; for on his way to the lodge he stopped at old man Shafter's. The house was forbidden him; but when he tapped at the window Ettie came out to him. The dancing Irish devilry had gone from her lover's eyes. She read his danger in his earnest face.

'Something has happened!' she cried. 'Oh, Jack, you are in danger!'

'Sure, it is not very bad, my sweetheart. And yet it may be wise that we make a move before it is worse.'

'Make a move?'

'I promised you once that I would go some day. I think the time is coming. I had news tonight, bad news, and I see trouble coming.'

'The police?'

'Well, a Pinkerton. But, sure, you wouldn't know what that is, acushla, nor what it may mean to the likes of me. I'm too deep in this thing, and I may have to get out of it quick. You said you would come with me if I went.'

'Oh, Jack, it would be the saving of you!'

'I'm an honest man in some things, Ettie. I wouldn't hurt a hair of your bonny head for all that the world can give, nor ever pull you down one inch from the golden throne above the clouds where I always see you. Would you trust me?'

She put her hand in his without a word. 'Well, then, listen to what I say, and do as I order you, for indeed it's the only way for us. Things are going to happen in this valley. I feel it in my bones. There may be many of us that will have to look out for ourselves. I'm one, anyhow. If I go, by day or night, it's you that must come with me!'

'I'd come after you, Jack.'

'No, no, you shall come *with* me. If this valley is closed to me and I can never come back, how can I leave you behind, and me perhaps in hiding from the police with never a chance of a message? It's with me you must come. I know a good woman in the place I come from, and it's there I'd leave you till we can get married. Will you come?'

'Yes, Jack, I will come.'

'God bless you for your trust in me! It's a fiend·out of hell that I should be if I abused it. Now, mark you, Ettie, it will be just a word to you, and when it reaches you, you will drop everything and come right down to the waiting room at the depot and stay there till I come for you.'

'Day or night, I'll come at the word, Jack.'

Somewhat eased in mind, now that his own preparations for escape had been begun, McMurdo went on to the lodge. It had already assembled, and only by complicated signs and counter-signs could he pass through the outer guard and inner guard who close-tiled it. A buzz of pleasure and welcome greeted him as he entered. The long room was crowded, and through the haze of tobacco smoke he saw the tangled black mane of the bodymaster, the cruel, unfriendly features of Baldwin, the vulture face of Harraway, the secretary, and a dozen more who were among the leaders of the lodge. He rejoiced that they should all be there to take counsel over his news.

'Indeed, it's glad we are to see you, Brother!' cried the chairman. 'There's business here that wants a Solomon in judgement to set it right.'

'It's Lander and Egan,' explained his neighbour as he took his seat. 'They both claim the head money given by the lodge for the shooting of old man Crabbe over at Stylestown, and who's to say which fired the bullet?'

McMurdo rose in his place and raised his hand. The expression of his face froze the attention of the audience. There was a dead hush of expectation.

'Eminent bodymaster,' he said, in a solemn voice, 'I claim urgency!'

'Brother McMurdo claims urgency,' said McGinty. 'It's a claim that by the rules of this lodge takes precedence. Now Brother, we attend you.'

McMurdo took the letter from his pocket.

'Eminent Bodymaster and Brethren,' he said, 'I am the bearer of ill news this day; but it is better that it should be known and discussed, than that a blow should fall upon us without warning which would destroy us all. I have information that the most powerful and richest organisations in this state have bound themselves together for our destruction, and that at this very moment there is a Pinkerton detective, one Birdy Edwards, at work in the valley collecting the evidence which may put a rope round the necks of many of us, and send every man in this room into a felon's cell. That is the situation for the discussion of which I have made a claim of urgency.'

There was a dead silence in the room. It was broken by the chairman.

'What is your evidence for this, Brother McMurdo?' he

asked.

'It is in this letter which has come into my hands,' said McMurdo. He read the passage aloud. 'It is a matter of honour with me that I can give no further particulars about the letter, nor put it into your hands; but I assure you that there is nothing else in it which can affect the interests of the lodge. I put the case before you as it has reached me.'

'Let me say, Mr Chairman,' said one of the older brethren, 'that I have heard of Birdy Edwards, and that he has the name of being the best man in the Pinkerton service.'

'Does anyone know him by sight?' asked McGinty.

'Yes,' said McMurdo, 'I do.'

There was a murmur of astonishment through the hall.

'I believe we hold him in the hollow of our hands,' he continued with an exulting smile upon his face. 'If we act quickly and wisely, we can cut this thing short. If I have your confidence and your help, it is little that we have to fear.'

'What have we to fear, anyhow? What can he know of our affairs?'

'You might say so if all were as staunch as you, councillor. But this man has all the millions of the capitalists at his back. Do you think there is no weaker brother among all our lodges that could not be bought? He will get at our secrets – maybe has got them already. There's only one sure cure.'

'That he never leaves the valley,' said Baldwin.

McMurdo nodded. 'Good for you, Brother Baldwin,' he said. 'You and I have had our differences, but you have said the true word tonight.'

'Where is he, then? Where shall we know him?'

'Eminent bodymaster,' said McMurdo, earnestly, 'I would put it to you that this is too vital a thing for us to discuss in open lodge. God forbid that I should throw a doubt on anyone here; but if so much as a word of gossip got to the ears of this man, there would be an end of any chance of our getting him. I would ask the lodge to choose a trusty committee, Mr Chairman – yourself, if I might suggest it, and Brother Baldwin here, and five more. Then I can talk freely of what I know and of what I advise should be done.'

The proposition was at once adopted, and the committee chosen. Besides the chairman and Baldwin there were the vulture-faced secretary, Harraway, Tiger Cormac, the brutal young assassin, Carter, the treasurer and the brothers Willaby, fearless and desperate men who would stick at nothing.

The usual revelry of the lodge was short and subdued: for there was a cloud upon the men's spirits, and many there for the first time began to see the cloud of avenging Law drifting up in that serene sky under which they had dwelt so long. The horrors they had dealt out to others had been so much a part of their settled lives that the thought of retribution had become a remote one, and so seemed the more startling now that it came so closely upon them. They broke up early and left their leaders to their council.

'Now, McMurdo!' said McGinty when they were alone. The seven men sat frozen in their seats.

'I said just now that I knew Birdy Edwards,' McMurdo explained. 'I need not tell you that he is not here under that name. He's a brave man, but not a crazy one. He passes under the name of Steve Wilson, and he is lodging at Hobson's Patch.'

'How do you know this?'

'Because I fell into talk with him. I thought little of it at the time, nor would have given it a second thought but for this letter; but now I'm sure it's the man. I met him on the cars when I went down the line on Wednesday – a hard case if ever there was one. He said he was a reporter. I believed it for the moment. Wanted to know all he could about the Scowrers and what he called "the outrages" for a New York paper. Asked me every kind of question so as to get something. You bet I was giving nothing away. "I'd pay for it and pay well," said he, "if I could get some stuff that would suit my editor." I said what I thought would please him best, and he handed me a twenty-dollar bill for my information. "There's ten times that for you," said he, "if you can find me all that I want."'

'What did you tell him, then?'

'Any stuff I could make up.'

'How do you know he wasn't a newspaper man?'

'I'll tell you. He got out at Hobson's Patch, and so did I. I chanced into the telegraph bureau, and he was leaving it. "See here," said the operator after he'd gone out, "I guess we should charge double rates for this." – "I guess you should," said I. He had filled the form with stuff that might have been Chinese, for all we could make of it. "He fires a sheet of this off every day," said the clerk. "Yes," said I; "it's special news for his paper, and he's scared that the others should tap it." That was what the operator thought and what I thought at the time; but I think differently now.'

'By Gar! I believe you are right,' said McGinty. 'But what do you allow that we should do about it?'

'Why not go right down now and fix him?' someone suggested.

'Ay, the sooner the better.'

'I'd start this next minute if I knew where we could find him,' said McMurdo. 'He's in Hobson's Patch; but I don't know the house. I've got a plan, though, if you'll only take my advice.'

'Well, what is it?'

'I'll go to the Patch tomorrow morning. I'll find him through the operator. He can locate him, I guess. Well, then I'll tell him that I'm a Freeman myself. I'll offer him all the secrets of the lodge for a price. You bet he'll tumble to it. I'll tell him the papers are at my house, and that it's as much as my life would be worth to let him come while folk were about. He'll see that that's horse sense. Let him come at ten o'clock at night, and he shall see everything. That will fetch him sure.'

'Well?'

'You can plan the rest for yourselves. Widow MacNamara's is a lonely house. She's as true as steel and as deaf as a post. There's only Scanlan and me in the house. If I get his promise – and I'll let you know if I do – I'd have the whole seven of you come to me by nine o'clock. We'll get him in. If ever he gets out alive – well, he can talk of Birdy Edwards's luck for the rest of his days!'

'There's going to be a vacancy at Pinkerton's or I'm mistaken. Leave it at that, McMurdo. At nine tomorrow we'll be with you. You once get the door shut behind him, and you can leave the rest with us.'

CHAPTER 7

THE TRAPPING OF BIRDY EDWARDS

As McMurdo had said, the house in which he lived was a lonely one and very well suited for such a crime as they had planned. It was on the extreme fringe of the town and stood well back from the road. In any other case the conspirators would have simply called out their man, as they had many a time before, and emptied their pistols into his body; but in this instance it was very necessary to find out how much he knew, how he knew it, and what had been passed on to his employers.

It was possible that they were already too late and that the work had been done. If that was indeed so, they could at least have their revenge upon the man who had done it. But they were hopeful that nothing of great importance had yet come to the detective's knowledge, as otherwise, they argued, he would not have troubled to write down and forward such trivial information as McMurdo claimed to have given him. However, all this they would learn from his own lips. Once in their power, they would find a way to make him speak. It was not the first time that they had handled an unwilling witness.

McMurdo went to Hobson's Patch as agreed. The police seemed to take particular interest in him that morning, and Captain Marvin – he who had claimed the old acquaintance with him at Chicago – actually addressed him as he waited at the station. McMurdo turned away and refused to speak with him. He was back from his mission in the afternoon, and saw McGinty at the Union House.

'He is coming,' he said.

'Good!' said McGinty. The giant was in his shirt sleeves, with chains and seals gleaming athwart his ample waistcoat and a diamond twinkling through the fringe of his bristling beard. Drink and politics had made the Boss a very rich as well as powerful man. The more terrible, therefore, seemed that glimpse of the prison or the gallows which had risen before him the night before.

'Do you reckon he knows much?' he asked anxiously.

McMurdo shook his head gloomily. 'He's been here some

time – six weeks at the least. I guess he didn't come into these parts to look at the prospect. If he has been working among us all that time with the railroad money at his back, I should expect that he has got results, and that he has passed them on.'

'There's not a weak man in the lodge,' cried McGinty. 'True as steel, every man of them. And yet, by the Lord! there is that skunk Morris. What about him? If any man gives us away, it would be he. I've a mind to send a couple of the boys round before evening to give him a beating up and see what they can get from him.'

'Well, there would be no harm in that,' McMurdo answered. 'I won't deny that I have a liking for Morris and would be sorry to see him come to harm. He has spoken to me once or twice over lodge matters, and though he may not see them the same as you or I, he never seemed the sort that squeals. But still it is not for me to stand between him and you.'

'I'll fix the old devil!' said McGinty with an oath. 'I've had my eye on him this year past.'

'Well, you know best about that,' McMurdo answered. 'But whatever you do must be tomorrow; for we must lie low until the Pinkerton affair is settled up. We can't afford to set the police buzzing, today of all days.'

'True for you,' said McGinty. 'And we'll learn from Birdy Edwards himself where he got his news if we have to cut his heart out first. Did he seem to scent a trap?'

McMurdo laughed. 'I guess I took him on his weak point,' he said. 'If he could get on a good trail of the Scowrers, he's ready to follow it into hell. I took his money,' McMurdo grinned as he produced a wad of dollar notes, 'and as much more when he has seen all my papers.'

'What papers?'

'Well, there are no papers. But I filled him up about constitutions and books of rules and forms of membership. He expects to get right down to the end of everything before he leaves.'

'Faith, he's right there,' said McGinty grimly. 'Didn't he ask you why you didn't bring him the papers?'

'As if I would carry such things, and me a suspected man, and Captain Marvin after speaking to me this very day at the depot!'

'Ay, I heard of that,' said McGinty. 'I guess the heavy end of this business is coming on to you. We could put him down an old shaft when we've done with him; but however we work it we can't get past the man living at Hobson's Patch and you being there today.'

McMurdo shrugged his shoulders. 'If we handle it right, they can never prove the killing,' said he. 'No one can see him come to the house after dark, and I'll lay to it that no one will see him go. Now see here, councillor, I'll show you my plan and I'll ask you to fit the others into it. You will all come in good time. Very well. He comes at ten. He is to tap three times, and me to open the door for him. Then I'll get behind him and shut it. He's our man then.'

'That's all easy and plain.'

'Yes; but the next step wants considering. He's a hard proposition. He's heavily armed. I've fooled him proper, and yet he is likely to be on his guard. Suppose I show him right into a room with seven men in it where he expected to find me alone. There is going to be shooting, and somebody is going to be hurt.'

'That's so.'

'And the noise is going to bring every damned copper in

the township on top of it.'

'I guess you are right.'

'This is how I should work it. You will all be in the big room – same as you saw when you had a chat with me. I'll open the door for him, show him into the parlour beside the door, and leave him there while I get the papers. That will give me the chance of telling you how things are shaping. Then I will go back to him with some faked papers. As he is reading them I will jump for him and get my grip on his pistol arm. You'll hear me call and in you will rush. The quicker the better; for he is as strong a man as I, and I may have more than I can manage. But I allow that I can hold him till you come.'

'It's a good plan,' said McGinty. 'The lodge will owe you a debt for this. I guess when I move out of the chair I can put a name to the man that's coming after me.'

'Sure, councillor, I am little more than a recruit,' said McMurdo; but his face showed what he thought of the great man's compliment.

When he had returned home he made his own preparations for the grim evening in front of him. First he cleaned, oiled, and loaded his Smith & Wesson revolver. Then he surveyed the room in which the detective was to be trapped. It was a large apartment, with a long deal table in the centre, and the big stove at one side. At each of the other sides were windows. There were no shutters on these: only light curtains which drew across. McMurdo examined these attentively. No doubt it must have struck him that the apartment was very exposed for so secret a meeting. Yet its distance from the road made it of less consequence. Finally he discussed the matter with his fellow lodger. Scanlan, though a Scowrer, was an inoffensive little man who was too weak to stand against the opinion of his comrades, but was secretly horrified by the deeds of blood at which he had sometimes been forced to assist. McMurdo told him shortly what was intended.

'And if I were you, Mike Scanlan, I would take a night off and keep clear of it. There will be bloody work here before morning.'

'Well, indeed then, Mac,' Scanlan answered. 'It's not the will but the nerve that is wanting in me. When I saw Manager Dunn go down at the colliery yonder it was just more than I could stand. I'm not made for it, same as you or McGinty. If the lodge will think none the worse of me, I'll just do as you advise and leave you to yourselves for the evening.'

The men came in good time as arranged. They were outwardly respectable citizens, well clad and cleanly; but a judge of faces would have read little hope for Birdy Edwards in those hard mouths and remorseless eyes. There was not a man in the room whose hands had not been reddened a dozen times before. They were as hardened to human murder as a butcher to sheep.

Foremost, of course, both in appearance and in guilt, was the formidable Boss. Harraway, the secretary, was a lean, bitter man with a long, scraggy neck and nervous, jerky limbs, a man of incorruptible fidelity where the finances of the order were concerned, and with no notion of justice or honesty to anyone beyond. The treasurer, Carter, was a middle-aged man, with an impassive, rather sulky expression, and a yellow parchment skin. He was a capable organiser, and the actual details of nearly every outrage had sprung from his plotting brain. The two Willabys were men of action, tall, lithe young fellows with determined faces, while their companion, Tiger Cormac, a heavy, dark youth, was feared even by his own comrades for the ferocity of his disposition. These were the men who assembled that night under the roof of McMurdo for the killing of the Pinkerton detective.

Their host had placed whisky upon the table, and they had hastened to prime themselves for the work before them. Baldwin and Cormac were already half-drunk, and the liquor had brought out all their ferocity. Cormac placed his hands on the stove for an instant – it had been lighted, for the nights were still cold.

'That will do,' said he, with an oath.

'Ay,' said Baldwin, catching his meaning. 'If he is strapped to that, we will have the truth out of him.'

'We'll have the truth out of him, never fear,' said McMurdo. He had nerves of steel, this man; for though the whole weight of the affair was on him his manner was as cool and uncon-cerned as ever. The others marked it and applauded.

'You are the one to handle him,' said the Boss approvingly. 'Not a warning will he get till your hand is on his throat. It's a pity there are no shutters to your windows.'

McMurdo went from one to the other and drew the curtains tighter. 'Sure no one can spy upon us now. It's close upon the hour.'

'Maybe he won't come. Maybe he'll get a sniff of danger,' said the secretary.

'He'll come, never fear,' McMurdo answered. 'He is as eager to come as you can be to see him. Hark to that!'

They all sat like wax figures, some with their glasses arrested halfway to their lips. Three loud knocks had sounded at the door.

'Hush!' McMurdo raised his hand in caution. An exulting glance went round the circle, and hands were laid upon their weapons.

'Not a sound, for your lives!' McMurdo whispered, as he went from the room, closing the door carefully behind him.

With strained ears the murderers waited. They counted the steps of their comrade down the passage. Then they heard him open the outer door. There were a few words as of greeting. Then they were aware of a strange step inside and of an unfamiliar voice. An instant later came the slam of the door and the turning of the key in the lock. Their prey was safe within the trap. Tiger Cormac laughed horribly, and Boss McGinty clapped his great hand across his mouth.

'Be quiet, you fool!' he whispered. 'You'll be the undoing of us yet!'

There was a mutter of conversation from the next room. It seemed interminable. Then the door opened, and McMurdo appeared, his finger upon his lip.

He came to the end of the table and looked round at them. A subtle change had come over him. His manner was as of one who has great work to do. His face had set into granite firmness. His eyes shone with a fierce excitement behind his spectacles. He had become a visible leader of men. They stared at him with eager interest; but he said nothing. Still with the same singular gaze he looked from man to man.

'Well!' cried Boss McGinty at last. 'Is he here? Is Birdy Edwards here?'

'Yes,' McMurdo answered slowly. 'Birdy Edwards is here. I am Birdy Edwards!'

There were ten seconds after that brief speech during which the room might have been empty, so profound was the silence. The hissing of a kettle upon the stove rose sharp and strident to the ear. Seven white faces, all turned upward to this man who dominated them, were set motionless with utter terror. Then, with a sudden shivering of glass, a bristle of glistening rifle barrels broke through each window, while the curtains were torn from their hangings.

At the sight Boss McGinty gave the roar of a wounded bear and plunged for the half-opened door. A levelled revolver met him there with the stern blue eyes of Captain Marvin of the Mine Police gleaming behind the sights. The Boss recoiled and fell back into his chair.

'You're safer there, councillor,' said the man whom they had known as McMurdo. 'And you, Baldwin, if you don't take your hand off your pistol, you'll cheat the hangman yet. Pull it out, or by the Lord that made me – there, that will do. There are forty armed men round this house, and you can figure it out for yourself what chance you have. Take their pistols, Marvin!'

There was no possible resistance under the menace of those rifles. The men were disarmed. Sulky, sheepish, and amazed, they still sat round the table.

'I'd like to say a word to you before we separate,' said the man who had trapped them. 'I guess we may not meet again until you see me on the stand in the courthouse. I'll give you something to think over between now and then. You know me now for what I am. At last I can put my cards on the table. I am Birdy Edwards of Pinkerton's. I was chosen to break up your gang. I had a hard and dangerous game to play. Not a soul, not one soul, not my nearest and dearest, knew that I was playing it. Only Captain Marvin here and my employers knew that. But it's over tonight, thank God, and I am the winner!'

The seven pale, rigid faces looked up at him. There was

unappeasable hatred in their eyes. He read the relentless threat.

'Maybe you think that the game is not over yet. Well, I take my chance of that. Anyhow, some of you will take no further hand, and there are sixty more besides yourselves that will see a jail this night. I'll tell you this, that when I was put upon this job I never believed there was such a society as yours. I thought it was paper talk, and that I would prove it so. They told me it was to do with the Freemen; so I went to Chicago and was made one. Then I was surer than ever that it was just paper talk; for I found no harm in the society, but a deal of good.

'Still, I had to carry out my job, and I came to the coal valleys. When I reached this place I learned that I was wrong and that it wasn't a dime novel after all. So I stayed to look after it. I never killed a man in Chicago. I never minted a dollar in my life. Those I gave you were as good as any others; but I never spent money better. But I knew the way into your good wishes and so I pretended to you that the law was after me. It all worked just as I thought.

'So I joined your infernal lodge, and I took my share in your councils. Maybe they will say that I was as bad as you. They can say what they like, so long as I get you. But what is the truth? The night I joined you beat up old man Stanger. I could not warn him, for there was no time; but I held your hand, Baldwin, when you would have killed him. If ever I have suggested things, so as to keep my place among you, they were things which I knew I could prevent. I could not save Dunn and Menzies, for I did not know enough; but I will see that their murderers are hanged. I gave Chester Wilcox warning, so that when I blew his house in he and his folk were in hiding. There was many a crime that I could not stop;

but if you look back and think how often your man came home the other road, or was down in town when you went for him, or stayed indoors when you thought he would come out, you'll see my work.'

'You blasted traitor!' hissed McGinty through his closed teeth.

'Ay, John McGinty, you may call me that if it eases your smart. You and your like have been the enemy of God and man in these parts. It took a man to get between you and the poor devils of men and women that you held under your grip. There was just one way of doing it, and I did it. You call me a traitor; but I guess there's many a thousand will call me a deliverer that went down into hell to save them. I've had three months of it. I wouldn't have three such months again if they let me loose in the treasury at Washington for it. I had to stay till I had it all, every man and every secret right here in this hand. I'd have waited a little longer if it hadn't come to my knowledge that my secret was coming out. A letter had come into the town that would have set you wise to it all. Then I had to act and act quickly.

'I've nothing more to say to you, except that when my time comes I'll die the easier when I think of the work I have done in this valley. Now, Marvin, I'll keep you no more. Take them in and get it over.'

There is little more to tell. Scanlan had been given a sealed note to be left at the address of Miss Ettie Shafter, a mission which he had accepted with a wink and a knowing smile. In the early hours of the morning a beautiful woman and a much muffled man boarded a special train which had been sent by the railroad company, and made a swift, unbroken journey out of the land of danger. It was the last time that ever either Ettie or her lover set foot in the Valley of Fear. Ten days later they were married in Chicago, with old Jacob Shafter as witness of the wedding.

The trial of the Scowrers was held far from the place where their adherents might have terrified the guardians of the law. In vain they struggled. In vain the money of the lodge – money squeezed by blackmail out of the whole countryside – was spent like water in the attempt to save them. That cold, clear, unimpassioned statement from one who knew every detail of their lives, their organisation, and their crimes was unshaken by all the wiles of their defenders. At last after so many years they were broken and scattered. The cloud was lifted forever from the valley.

McGinty met his fate upon the scaffold, cringing and whining when the last hour came. Eight of his chief followers shared his fate. Fifty-odd had various degrees of imprisonment. The work of Birdy Edwards was complete.

And yet, as he had guessed, the game was not over yet. There was another hand to be played, and yet another and another. Ted Baldwin, for one, had escaped the scaffold; so had the Willabys; so had several others of the fiercest spirits of the gang. For ten years they were out of the world, and then came a day when they were free once more – a day which Edwards, who knew his men, was very sure would be an end of his life of peace. They had sworn an oath on all that they thought holy to have his blood as a vengeance for their comrades. And well they strove to keep their vow!

From Chicago he was chased, after two attempts so near success that it was sure that the third would get him. From Chicago he went under a changed name to California, and it was there that the light went for a time out of his life when

Ettie Edwards died. Once again he was nearly killed, and once again under the name of Douglas he worked in a lonely canyon, where with an English partner named Barker he amassed a fortune. At last there came a warning to him that the bloodhounds were on his track once more, and he cleared – only just in time – for England. And thence came the John Douglas who for a second time married a worthy mate, and lived for five years as a Sussex county gentleman, a life which ended with the strange happenings of which we have heard.

EPILOGUE

The police trial had passed, in which the case of John Douglas was referred to a higher court. So had the Quarter Sessions, at which he was acquitted as having acted in self-defence.

'Get him out of England at any cost,' wrote Holmes to the wife. 'There are forces here which may be more dangerous than those he has escaped. There is no safety for your husband in England.'

Two months had gone by, and the case had to some extent passed from our minds. Then one morning there came an enigmatic note slipped into our letter box. 'Dear me, Mr Holmes. Dear me!' said this singular epistle. There was neither superscription nor signature. I laughed at the quaint message; but Holmes showed unwonted seriousness.

'Devilry, Watson!' he remarked, and sat long with a clouded brow.

Late last night Mrs Hudson, our landlady, brought up a message that a gentleman wished to see Mr Holmes, and that the matter was of the utmost importance. Close at the heels of his messenger came Cecil Barker, our friend of the moated Manor House. His face was drawn and haggard.

'I've had bad news – terrible news, Mr Holmes,' said he.

'I feared as much,' said Holmes.

'You have not had a cable, have you?'

'I have had a note from someone who has.'

'It's poor Douglas. They tell me his name is Edwards; but he will always be Jack Douglas of Benito Canyon to me. I told you that they started together for South Africa in the *Palmyra* three weeks ago.'

'Exactly.'

'The ship reached Cape Town last night. I received this cable from Mrs Douglas this morning: "Jack has been lost overboard in gale off St. Helena. No one knows how accident occurred. IVY DOUGLAS."'

'Ha! It came like that, did it?' said Holmes thoughtfully. 'Well, I've no doubt it was well stage-managed.'

'You mean that you think there was no accident?'

'None in the world.'

'He was murdered?'

'Surely!'

'So I think also. These infernal Scowrers, this cursed vindictive nest of criminals – '

'No, no, my good sir,' said Holmes. 'There is a master hand here. It is no case of sawn-off shotguns and clumsy six-shooters. You can tell an old master by the sweep of his brush. I can tell a Moriarty when I see one. This crime is from London, not from America.'

'But for what motive?'

'Because it is done by a man who cannot afford to fail,

one whose whole unique position depends upon the fact that all he does must succeed. A great brain and a huge organisation have been turned to the extinction of one man. It is crushing the nut with the trip-hammer – an absurd extravagance of energy – but the nut is very effectually crushed all the same.'

'How came this man to have anything to do with it?'

'I can only say that the first word that ever came to us of the business was from one of his lieutenants. These Americans were well advised. Having an English job to do, they took into partnership, as any foreign criminal could do, this great consultant in crime. From that moment their man was doomed. At first he would content himself by using his machinery in order to find their victim. Then he would indicate how the matter might be treated. Finally, when he read in the reports of the failure of this agent, he would step in himself with a master touch. You heard me warn this man at Birlstone Manor House that the coming danger was greater than the past. Was I right?'

Barker beat his head with his clenched fist in his impotent anger. 'Do not tell me that we have to sit down under this? Do you say that no one can ever get level with this king devil?'

'No, I don't say that,' said Holmes, and his eyes seemed to be looking far into the future. 'I don't say that he can't be beat. But you must give me time – you must give me time!'

We all sat in silence for some minutes while those fateful eyes still strained to pierce the veil.